THE CUSTODIAN

THE CUSTODIAN

NICK GUTHRIE

NO EXIT PRESS

First published in the UK in 2026 by Bedford Square Publishers Ltd,
London, UK

noexit.co.uk
@noexitpress

A CIP catalogue record for this book is available from the British Library.

ISBN
978-1-83501-584-1 (Paperback)
978-1-83501-585-8 (eBook)

2 4 6 8 10 9 7 5 3 1

Typeset in 11 on 13pt Adobe Garamond Pro
by Avocet Typeset, Bideford, Devon, EX39 2BP
Printed and bound in Great Britain by
CPI Group (UK) Ltd, Croydon CR0 4YY

FSC
www.fsc.org
MIX
Paper | Supporting responsible forestry
FSC® C013604

The manufacturer's authorised representative in the EU for product safety is Easy Access System Europe, Mustamäe tee 50, 10621 Tallinn, Estonia
gpsr.requests@easproject.com

For Debbie

Prologue

Nineteen Years Earlier

It was a routine call for Russell Shaw – which meant someone would quite possibly end up dead. As it turned out, though, this death was anything but routine.

'Ambulance 22?' the dispatcher called as Russ pulled out of Harbour Road. 'We've got a category one for you.' Russ and his partner, Ginnie Lloyd, were heading back from a false alarm at the docks. A dog-walker had called in a serious fall from a crane which had turned out to be a group of dockers larking about. 'Suspected myocardial infarction at 12 West Street. Eighty-six-year-old male. Are you free to take it?'

Russ looked across at Ginnie and rolled his eyes. He had the football commentary playing on a small battery-operated radio he'd wedged onto the dashboard, the volume turned down while he took the call. 'Sure,' he replied into the handset. 'We're not far from West Street.'

Despite the roll of the eyes, he didn't begrudge the call. It's what they were here for, and Russ had never regretted giving up a career in the Army to be doing something so much more worthwhile with his life than defending a few square miles of desert sand.

Ginnie switched on the blues and twos, even though they were only a few streets away, and soon they pulled up, double-parked in a cramped street lined with cars, just back from the seafront. It had only taken them a minute to get there, but the incident had occurred some unspecified time before. An elderly man, no doubt with a long and complicated medical history: the prospects weren't great.

The game was still nil-nil after twenty minutes as they reached for their doors to get out.

'The radio, Russ.'

He saw a brief flash of frustration in Ginnie's dark eyes, heard it in her tone. He was being sloppy, unprofessional. She hated when she was put on shift with him.

He reached out to turn the radio off and Ginnie smiled, and he realised he was being paranoid again. Overthinking. Over-interpreting. It was just another long evening in January, and they were both tired.

He blinked, looked up, and she was banging on the door of one of the terraced houses already. Had he experienced a few seconds' absence again? He was getting worse – to the extent that Ginnie had noticed and was trying to persuade him to see a doctor. He knew she was right. He needed to focus. Concentrate. No more lapses.

A grey-haired man opened the door, and for a moment Russ thought it was another false alarm. As Russ approached, he nodded at the man, noting that he was younger than he had first appeared, although his age was hard to pin down – anywhere from fifty to seventy. He stood like an old man, with a hunched frame and round shoulders, but his eyes were sharp, fixing you to the spot.

Russ looked away.

'We're responding to a 999 call,' Ginnie said, apparently oblivious to the man's piercing gaze. 'Did you—'

'Yes, yes, in the front room, won't you?' the man said, his voice calm, efficient. He stepped back, ushering them in. 'It's Ron. He…' Now his voice faltered and he looked down at the ground.

'Is he still breathing?' Ginnie asked, brutal but kindly.

'He is, but…'

Ginnie turned sideways so she could slip past the man. It was a squeeze to get through, even with her tiny frame, and Russ was grateful he was skinny, too, as he followed her into a narrow hallway and then a small living room, cluttered with furniture that wouldn't have been out of place in a 1970s sitcom. An old man half-sat, half-reclined in a wing-back armchair, a tartan blanket pulled over his lap. His mouth was open, a glistening trail of drool spilling from one side.

Immediately, Ginnie was crouching before him, a finger pressed to his neck for a pulse. 'He's still with us,' she said. 'Weak pulse, but steady.'

Russ turned to the man who'd opened the door and tried to give him a reassuring smile. He wasn't usually so ineffectual, but tonight… He'd picked up body parts from the desert, he'd sat in the back of Army ambulances holding wounds closed even as the fallen had died beneath his hands. But this old couple – or at least he presumed that was their relationship… That pathetic old shell of a man slumped in his chair… and the man with the sharp eyes and the steady voice who stood by even as his world was stripped away before him…

The man caught his look and Russ realised he reminded him of his grandfather. Eyes that saw right through him.

He looked away again. When he looked back, he saw just an old man, nothing like his grandfather. His mind was playing tricks again, making him see things in odd, disturbing ways.

'I *said*, get the chair, would you?'

He'd missed what Ginnie said the first time, clearly. The evacuation chair… they'd never be able to get the patient out of this cramped house on a stretcher.

They manoeuvred the old man out of the front door in a folding wheelchair, his partner following them out into the chill night air, cocooned in a long winter coat and gloves.

Russ helped Ginnie get the chair into the back, then ease their frail patient onto the gurney, where Ginnie hooked him up to the ECG while Russ fitted an oxygen mask.

'Shall I…?' Russ was about to volunteer to stay in the back with the patient, but he stopped, stung by the look on the face of their patient's partner: he clearly didn't want Russ to be in the back, responsible for life or death care. Was it really so obvious that Russ was struggling tonight?

He saw that flash of irritation cross Ginnie's face again, then she put a hand on his arm, and said, 'It's okay, Russ. You drive. I'll take this.'

He hated the understanding even more than the irritation. She saw the weakness in him, and she clearly understood why someone might not want Russ to be responsible for caring for the patient en route to the hospital. And so she gave him the easy out. They both knew she couldn't turn a blind eye to his state of mind for much longer.

'You know I'm far better with the wrinklies, and you can listen to the game.' She even made it seem trivial, as if she was merely letting him listen to some dumb football match rather than covering for another of his wobbles.

Considering he'd been so damaged by his time in the Gulf, why had he ever chosen a career that constantly threw him into the thick of crisis? He'd been okay for the longest time, but he was letting things slip again…

He looked away, glanced back, forced a smile. Ginnie was the closest thing he had to a friend, he supposed.

He sat in the driver's seat and pressed his hands to his temples. His head was bad tonight. Too much noise. Too many voices. He tried to focus on the commentary, the route back across town to the hospital imprinted on his brain so he could get there on autopilot if he needed to.

England had gone a goal up, half-time approaching.

Just before the entrance to Whitesands General Hospital he had to stop. The clamour of voices inside his skull was almost too much to bear, and his head was spinning. He pressed hard against his temples again, as if he might be able to squeeze out all the noise in his head. He thought of the old boy in the back: his chances of making it were slim, to say the least – and made worse by Russ's problems. He couldn't go on like this. He would see his GP tomorrow.

The ambulance turned into the hospital entrance on the stroke of half-time. Russ eased past the visitors' car park and into the ambulance bay, lining up to reverse into the slot nearest the entrance.

The night was cold, frost hanging in the air. Ginnie had been quiet in the back, which was unlike her, but good. If there had been any kind of crisis he'd have known about it, so that must mean the old boy was hanging on.

He banged lightly on the side of the ambulance as he walked around, wondering why Ginnie wasn't already swinging the back doors open.

He reached for the latch, released it, and pulled the doors open.

He hadn't seen so much blood since Basra. Dark red that was almost black in the dim light of the interior. Pooling on the floor, smeared and sprayed up the walls, spattered across the ceiling.

1

Present Day

'I received this in the mail this afternoon.' Matthew Sturridge indicated a padded brown envelope on the kitchen table, then paused. 'You're an inspector, you say? Well, that will have to do, I suppose. I requested someone senior, someone with gravitas, you know?'

Sturridge was white-haired, his face delineated by tucks and folds and pouches, as if it had been painted by an artist trying too hard to make it three-dimensional. He wore a tweed jacket and tie that was clearly his informal wear for around the house, and for once DI Bolam didn't feel overdressed in his dark blue three-piece pinstripe.

Bolam wasn't sure he'd ever been described as having gravitas before, but he didn't argue. He was intrigued more than anything. This genteel house with everything lined up precisely in its place, the sound of multiple clocks ticking and the almondy smell of wood polish. This diffident character before him, now sipping milky tea from a delicate blue and white china cup. Normally it would take much more to get Bolam on the scene and two uniforms on the door, and he suspected the pulling of strings, perhaps the verbal equivalent of a Masonic handshake when Sturridge had made the call. But, gravitas or not, Bolam was the best he was going to get: a faltering senior detective, struggling just to cope with life, let alone a new job he wasn't convinced he should ever have taken.

When Sturridge had indicated the envelope he had pointed without touching, and now Bolam reached across.

'I'd suggest latex gloves, if I were you,' Sturridge told him.

Bolam paused, studying the envelope more closely. It was a C5 manila Jiffy bag. A label bearing the printed address but no name was positioned symmetrically in the centre of the envelope, and there was no postage. It had clearly been hand-delivered.

Bolam found a new pair of gloves in a jacket pocket and unwrapped them and put them on before reaching for the envelope again. The flap was already unsealed from where Sturridge had opened it before realising what it contained. Bolam lifted the flap and pushed the sides of the envelope inwards so he could peer inside.

Now he reached for an evidence bag and carefully tipped the contents of the envelope into it.

There was only a single item. A finger, severed at the base. Slim, the nail short but carefully shaped and painted red, a dress ring set with a smooth, oval stone.

'An opal,' Sturridge helpfully informed him. 'A gem considered unlucky by some.'

Including the owner, Bolam would hazard.

'Who is it?' Bolam asked. 'Who's missing?' This must either be a threat or the opening gambit of a ransom demand.

'That's the thing, Inspector. I don't know. I'm unaware of anyone missing, and I'm afraid at my stage in life there is no longer anyone close to me – certainly no one who may have been abducted.'

'You think they sent it to the wrong address?'

'What else could explain it?'

Bolam sat in one corner of the open-plan Serious Crimes office with two members of his team. He wanted their input before escalating things.

'We have a severed finger,' Bolam said, indicating the image showing on a computer monitor, 'but we know of no one missing a finger. And we have Matthew Sturridge, the gentlest retired schoolteacher you could imagine, who seems perplexed more than anything that the finger ended up being posted through his letterbox. What else do we have?'

'The preliminary pathology report says it's a little finger severed at the metacarpophalangeal joint,' said DC Billie Grayson. Billie was copper-haired, slim, but with the kind of square frame that suggested she could take care of herself. Half an hour ago Bolam had told her she would be acting as exhibits officer on this one. 'That's the base knuckle, where the finger joins the hand. We should have a full report in the morning. Samples have been sent for DNA, but we won't get anything back for a few days unless you want to put a prioritisation on it, sir.'

'Prints?'

'Not on the system,' said DS Aisha Nawaz, 'so she doesn't have a criminal record.'

'She?' prompted Bolam.

Aisha shrugged. 'Slim finger, dress ring, cared-for nails with varnish—'

'And that's conclusive?' Aisha was a solid detective, promoted early in her career, but she had a tendency to make easy assumptions – so much so that Bolam wanted to challenge any assumptions she made, even when they were almost certainly correct.

Moving on, Bolam asked, 'What do we have on misspers?'

'We're working through all the active missing person cases,' said Billie, 'and we've put feelers out to the national Missing Persons Unit. There's no fingerprint match at FINDS, so it's not a missing person for whom we have a set of prints on record. We don't have much to go on at all, other than the victim liked painted nails. We can exclude on age, ethnicity, body type – we're not looking for anyone clinically obese here – and when we have the labs back we can exclude on blood type and sex, but still…'

'There was a ring,' said Bolam. 'An opal. That can't be common.'

'It's with forensics,' said Aisha. 'We might be able to trace where it was made, where it might have been bought. And we can assume this was a person who liked jewellery. No one wears only a ring on the little finger, so she almost certainly wore more rings on other fingers, which might stick in someone's memory.' Aisha didn't wear jewellery, or any other hint of ostentation that might punctuate her grey trouser suit and blouse.

'Pursue the ring, would you, Aisha? If it's distinctive it might lead somewhere.'

'From what Mr Sturridge tells us, the delivery must have been made between four and five this afternoon,' said Billie. 'He lives on a quiet residential street, so there are no traffic cameras, and no commercial CCTV closer than the off-licence around the corner, and that's on a busy street, so lots of traffic. A neighbour three doors down has a Ring doorbell camera, but other than a legitimate Amazon delivery at four-thirty, the camera didn't pick up any activity in the street during our period of interest.'

'So whoever gave Sturridge the finger was either lucky or knew to avoid that doorcam,' said Aisha. Billie laughed at her choice of phrase, and Bolam let it pass.

Bolam straightened his tie and jacket, then swept a hand across the even, dark stubble on his head. 'Okay, it's going to be a late one,' he said. 'I'll pull in the rest of the team to look at this. We need to treat this as an active missing person case, where life is at serious risk. We need to identify the victim, we need to gather whatever information we can about the delivery of the envelope, and we need to establish motive. Is this abduction for ransom, some kind of attempt to intimidate, or something else entirely? I'll assume the lead on Sturridge, as he seems comfortable with me and we want to keep him on board. Is he somehow involved, perhaps as the target? Does he know who's missing and isn't saying because he fears for their safety? Might there be another reason why the finger was delivered to him? Is it some gruesome mistake, a wrong address…?'

Or was there another possibility they hadn't even considered?

As Bolam stood up to leave, Billie Grayson's desk phone rang. She exchanged a few words, then caught his eye, moving the phone away from her face. 'Boss,' she said. 'It's the Missing Persons Unit. They have something for us.'

2

The house three down from Sturridge's had security lights that came on when Bolam passed. Was it deliberate that whoever had delivered the envelope had avoided that house's security camera, or pure chance?

Bolam crossed the road and stood under a tree to shelter from the steady rain. A light shone from behind curtains in Sturridge's living room, another above the front door.

He had no real reason to come this way, so late. Sturridge's house was in the older part of Whitesands, just off the town centre and a couple of streets back from the bay. It was only a small detour on Bolam's way home from the station, but it was still a deviation, and he had no intention of pressing Sturridge more tonight. He'd been the last to leave, finally immersed in the investigation, his mind buzzing with possibilities and contradictions. He always used to get this way when he was on a case, and he knew it made him virtually impossible to live with. Fran had often joked about that, but it had been a joke with a serious edge, a warning that he was drifting.

He reached under his grey trench coat to straighten his jacket.

He looked at the other houses, each of them its own world, its occupants with their own preoccupations and dramas. He'd put uniformed officers on door-to-door this evening, but that had turned up nothing. No one frantic with worry over a missing daughter or wife. No one who appeared to be hiding anything, and no one who had seen the delivery. Just normal people, oblivious to the fact that another equally normal person in their midst had been the recipient of a particularly macabre package that afternoon. Billie Grayson had tracked down the delivery driver who'd been recorded on the neighbour's door camera, but he'd seen nobody in the street when he'd been there at 4.30.

Bolam was struggling to get this case straight in his head, and it helped him to think, putting himself back on the scene and imagining the lives of these people, the life of Matthew Sturridge. Back at the station it was easy to forget that they were dealing with actual people, each with their own lives and concerns. Easy to forget that an occurrence like this was a once in a lifetime thing for most, not something that was just part of the job.

The door opened, light spilling out and illuminating the rain like falling shards of glass.

'Come in from the rain, man,' said Sturridge, beckoning. 'You'll catch your death.'

'Very kind,' said Bolam. 'Are you sure? It's late and I'm soaked through.' But it was only a matter of saying the right thing, because even as he spoke these words Bolam was stepping into the house, shrugging off his coat, and squeezing past the taller man.

They sat at the kitchen table, Sturridge still in his tweed jacket and tie, the only thing out of place a few strands of white hair that had drifted down across his forehead. There was nothing about him that suggested he might be hiding something. Bolam was very aware of the dampness of his suit and that his coat, draped over the back of a chair, was dripping onto the floor. The retired teacher had made cocoa, thick and sweet. It was a taste of Bolam's childhood and it was almost as if they'd stepped back in time, which, in turn, made the inspector feel uncomfortable, on edge.

'I always worry about the penguins,' Bolam said, pausing to sip at his cocoa.

Sturridge studied him closely, before finally saying, 'Penguins? You have me at a loss, Inspector.'

'Penguins.' Another sip. 'Thick feathers. South Pole. Walk like they're constipated.'

'I know what a penguin is, Inspector.'

'They mate for life.'

'And that worries you?'

'What happens when one dies young? Does its mate pine for the rest of its life? And conversely, what if a pair lives longer than the average penguin does? Do they get bored with each other? Do all the minor irritations of penguin life add up until all the old penguin has left is regret?'

'You worry too much, Inspector.'

'Perhaps,' said Bolam. The sweetness of the cocoa was making him queasy now, but it was warming him through, at least. 'It's not the first time, is it, Mr Sturridge? That you've been involved in a missing persons investigation.'

'Ah.' And in that moment, that quiver of the lip and instant glazing of the eyes, Bolam had his answer. The penguin would never grow bored or irritated, and it would never stop pining for its lost love.

'Your wife, Mr Sturridge. Why didn't you mention Jayne?'

'It was almost thirty years ago, Inspector. It hardly seems relevant.'

'We don't know what's relevant at this stage. It's all about building up the big picture. Seeing which pieces fit, and which don't.'

Sturridge gave Bolam a sharp look. 'You don't think…?'

'Was your wife ever located, Mr Sturridge?' Bolam knew the official answer – Jayne Sturridge was still filed as a missing person – but sometimes things don't make the official record. Rumours. Stray sightings reported by a friend of a friend, maybe months or even years after the event.

A shake of the head. 'I didn't mention my wife because I didn't want to lead you astray,' Sturridge said. 'It seemed so improbable, and I couldn't quite bring myself to believe that the horror should revisit me in this way.' He paused, looked away, and then back at Bolam, and said again, 'You don't think…?'

'We'll get the preliminary pathology report tomorrow,' Bolam told him, 'and I hope that will help us with the identification. Can you tell us about the opal ring? Was it hers?'

Sturridge shrugged. 'I… It was twenty-nine years ago, and jewellery, well… Some men may notice these things, but I'm afraid I'm not one of them.'

Bolam would have noticed such things, even at his most distracted, but he didn't press. He knew men who would forget what their wife was wearing if they looked away for a moment, and maybe the ring was just a cheap dress item, hardly ever worn.

'Tomorrow, you say? You will let me know?'

'Of course.'

As if they'd somehow forget to tell Sturridge that his wife, missing for nearly thirty years, had finally – if only partially – shown up.

'We have a positive identification with a reasonable degree of confidence,' Bolam said, standing by the big screen once again, running through the case for eight members of the Serious Crimes Unit. They'd all come in early today, pausing only at the coffee machine before gathering in the team's main office.

Bolam had been up since the early hours, reading case files, googling old news reports and letting what he knew of the case settle and resettle in his mind. Then he'd run a cordless trimmer over the near-black stubble coating his head and chin, showered, put on a fresh suit, and arrived at the office ahead of anyone else.

'We should get DNA confirmation by the end of the week. And this is no longer a missing persons investigation. We're looking at murder. The finger belongs to Jayne Sturridge, reported missing twenty-nine years ago, and according to Raj Khatri in Pathology it was severed post-mortem and has been preserved in a frozen state until about forty-eight hours ago.'

'A cold case, then?' Aisha Nawaz again. Macabre humour was part and parcel of the job, and Bolam left it for a few seconds before moving on.

He pressed the *Forward* button on the remote and the cover page of Jayne Sturridge's case file appeared on the screen. Some text and a photo of her raising a champagne flute towards the camera, a blonde woman with a high-collared blouse and her hair cut in a pageboy style.

'You'll see she's wearing rings on index, ring and little fingers of the hand holding the glass. The image quality's poor, but I'm pretty sure none of the items is our opal ring, although as you said yesterday, Aisha, she clearly liked her jewellery so maybe she switched them around.'

Accompanying the photo was some basic summary text: description, address, date of birth.

'You know what doesn't fit?' said Aisha. 'The ring.'

For a moment Bolam thought she was making another bad joke, but then she went on. 'The opal. It's usually seen as a bad luck stone, unless it happens to be your birthstone.'

'Explain.'

'Opals are the birthstone for October, but Jayne Sturridge was born in March.'

'So maybe she wasn't superstitious,' Bolam said. 'Maybe she just liked opals. Or are you suggesting that we've somehow misidentified the finger? That would take either a major error in the lab, or someone actively interfering with the investigation.'

'I'm not saying anything,' Aisha said, instantly defensive. 'Just making an observation.'

Bolam moved on to give a quick precis of the case from twenty-nine years ago: woman reported missing, no history of mental health issues, no ransom demands or threats, no subsequent sightings, no body. The case file never said anything explicitly, but it was clear enough from the phrasing of reports that it was assumed she had left home as the result of a domestic disagreement, with no evidence of any crime having been committed.

'So what we have is a little finger severed at the metacarpophalangeal joint,' he concluded, 'plus an opal ring, and the victim is the wife of the recipient, missing for almost thirty years.'

Later, Bolam paused by Aisha Nawaz's desk where she was hammering away at her keyboard. She sat as if she'd drawn back into herself, a tortoise retreating into its shell. She was quite clearly ignoring his looming presence.

'I'm sorry,' Bolam said. 'I didn't mean to be dismissive.' And he knew he *had* been dismissive, or at least come across that way. Always pushing back against her for leaping to conclusions. Normally, he prided himself on being good with the people around him – it was a skill he'd worked hard to acquire – but lately he'd been struggling.

Aisha continued to type for a couple of seconds more, long enough to show she was cross with him. Then she stopped, met his look, shrugged. 'It happens all the time,' she said. Her words could be taken as an accusation, but her tone was more resigned. 'I used to be a real high-flyer, you know. Fast-tracked. Folks paid attention to me then.'

Bolam had worked out as much from reading her file when he had come to the Whitesands Serious Crimes Unit a few weeks ago. He'd expected more from her, but somehow her spark seemed to have been extinguished.

'The old "I could have been a contender", you know?' She gave a soft laugh. 'Everyone assumed it was because I ticked so many of the boxes, though. Asian. Female. Gay. But when I didn't live up to the hype I was sidelined like a failed experiment. Made to feel as if I'd somehow betrayed the top brass's faith in me.'

Bolam nodded. Aisha wasn't the first officer he'd seen who'd suffered for reasons entirely separate from their actual abilities.

'And now that I don't get that special treatment I'm just another copper who doesn't fit in, for exactly the same reasons: not white, not male, not straight.'

Bolam suspected there was a lot of truth in her interpretation, but also knew how easy it must be to use that as an excuse, too. He chose not to say anything now, though.

'All I ever wanted was to be a decent copper.'

'You are,' Bolam told her. 'Now follow up on that ring.'

3

It was a mistake to come home to Whitesands, he was sure, but where else did he have?

Russell Shaw got off the train at the station in town, one stop short of the track's end at the docks. Everything he owned he was either wearing or was in the canvas bag slung over his shoulder, and even that was only half full. Just a few clothes, a book, and some personal documents in a Jiffy bag.

The day was sunny, warm for late April. He should feel something, he knew – the awakenings of spring, a sense of liberation, of new beginnings – but the drugs dulled his perception. If anything, he felt the opposite, a sensation of weight descending, of dread.

At least the drugs kept him functioning, though.

He left the station, and within minutes was in the town centre, his senses being assaulted from all quarters. People crowded the pavement, cars and vans queued at the traffic lights. The sunlight was harsh, the shadows deep; the smells of traffic fumes and fast food and dog shit intense.

At any moment he expected someone to recognise him, but no: each look that met his quickly slipped away. He suspected he seemed a bit mad, his gaze jumping from face to face like this. Confrontational. Challenging. Nobody wanted to make eye contact.

He hadn't seen this many people in nineteen years.

He swallowed, and nearly ended up choking. His throat was drier than it had ever been in the Gulf.

You are not the man you were.

For most, the mantra circling round and round in Russ's brain would have been a chastisement, a diminishment, but for him it was something positive to which he clung. He was *not* the person he had been. He was a new man, starting afresh. And he knew that to do so he must finally confront the places and memories from his past that haunted his every minute, waking or asleep.

You are not the man you were.

Years of avoiding such confrontation, and then years of therapy to bring him to this point, and finally he was ready.

He was back. Back in the town where a life that had already been battered and torn had finally been ripped to shreds.

And, he realised, he had no idea what came next.

He paused on the pavement by the traffic lights. The Co-Op Home Store had become a Poundland, but otherwise it was how he remembered: the bank to his left, the Boots opposite, the greengrocer's to his right.

He heard a voice at his shoulder, the words loud but indistinct. He turned and opened his mouth to speak, but the woman just stared, then looked away, still talking. It took him a moment to understand that she was not addressing him, but was talking into a tiny microphone protruding from an earpiece – talking on her hands-free mobile phone.

Some things in this world were very different. He was only in his mid-fifties, but all of a sudden he felt transplanted from his own time to one that was entirely alien.

He shuffled sideways, one hand reaching out until he made reassuring contact with the wall of the bank. He leaned a shoulder against the brickwork, trying to look casual. Voices all around him now. People jostling each other, jockeying for position as they waited for the crossing lights to change to green.

He felt that he might explode at any moment.

He swallowed. Breathed deep and held it, before letting the air slowly release. Again. His heart thumped.

The green crossing man appeared, started bleeping, and the throng moved as one. All apart from Russ, standing with a shoulder pressed so hard against the bank wall he thought surely it would bruise.

He found the scrap of paper in his pocket. Nurse Ward had

told him to find the address on Google Maps on his phone, but he didn't need to – not that he even had a phone. He knew this town's geography inside out. He was the last to cross, just as the green man finished flashing and turned red. A white van nudged forward, the driver gesturing. Russ ducked his head down and mounted the pavement. The Boots store to his left, he followed the street towards East Bay Drive, the road that followed the long curve of the bay.

At the end, he crossed the street and came to stand leaning against the metal railings, above the greensward separating the road from the promenade. The North Sea was a deep brown-grey, under uniform white clouds. At least that was as it had always been: Whitesands, grey sea. A solitary container ship edged along the horizon.

He breathed deep and held it, then let the air slowly escape through gritted teeth. After the claustrophobic onslaught of the town, at least the beach and the sea gave him hints of that sense of freedom he craved.

He felt pathetic to be so intimidated by the world, so scared and on edge. He was not the man he had been.

He followed the curve of the road, the bay to his right. Commercial properties gave way to houses – grand Victorian villas commanding views over the bay. Nestled among these was a squat red-brick building that might once have been a small school. Russ checked the address again, then crossed.

He entered a lobby, displays of leaflets in Perspex racks fixed to one wall, a line of wooden chairs below them. A woman studied him curiously from behind a clear screen.

'I was told to come here,' Russ said. 'They said you'd have somewhere for me to stay.'

Now the woman looked puzzled. 'This is the office of the town council,' she said, uncertainly. She glanced away then, off to one side to where a door opened into an office.

Was she summoning help with that look? Was she scared of him, grateful for that flimsy barrier between them? Russ looked away.

'I don't know who told you to come here,' she went on. Not scared: sympathetic, trying to be kind. Talking to him as if he were a child, or simple. 'The town council isn't responsible for housing. Or shelters,' she added, looking him up and down.

'I… They said to come here.' He waved the scrap of paper with the address at her. 'They wrote it down.'

'There's a hostel by the quay,' the woman said. 'It's called Fresh Start. They'll take you in. Or… perhaps you should go to the hospital? They can help… *assess* your needs.'

Russ backed away. She thought he was homeless. Mad.

And the worst of it was, he realised, she was right.

The Martello tower occupied a small hill towards the northern end of Whitesands Bay. A squat barrel-like fortress built in Napoleonic times to defend against French invasion, the tower had been abandoned and bricked up in Russ's day, but now had been gentrified, the top level glassed in, and entry gained via a high bridge from the surrounding embankment. A big wooden hoarding advertised apartments for sale.

Russ didn't care about access to the tower itself. What mattered to him was the rough strip of land between the tower and the foreshore, where a couple of World War Two gun emplacements remained, overgrown by brambles and nettles. Now, he sat on the concrete parapet of one of the emplacements, looking out over the North Sea.

It was sunset, which he reckoned meant it must be mid-evening at least, which in turn meant he hadn't eaten for eight hours or more. He'd even looked in a couple of bins along the promenade, but this early in the year people didn't come to the beach with picnics and chips, and there was nothing remotely edible.

He tried to stop thinking about it, despite the groaning in his belly. To have come to this… a new low.

He took the scrap of paper out of his pocket again, stared at it. Nurse Ward had written the address for him – he must have made a mistake, the wrong number or street name or something.

'I've been assured they'll look after you, Russ,' Ward had said. 'They'll find you a place. They'll connect you with the local mental health team and they'll take care of you.'

Russ had thought he was ready. He'd been prepared for this day – trained in the ways of the modern world, taken on day trips into Cambridge to the shops, the post office, the bank, learning to use buses and the train. But out in the real world on his own was an entirely different proposition.

The mildness of the spring day had departed with the setting sun. Russ pulled another shirt and a jersey from his bag and pulled them on, even though it made him feel like the Michelin Man. His spare jeans, too, over the top of the ones he was wearing.

He still felt cold to the marrow.

He climbed down from the emplacement. These old buildings had been boarded up for years, but long ago the barriers had been broken and pulled aside, and it was easy to squeeze inside. The ground was uneven, piled up with rubble and litter, old cans and bottles and god knows what else. The damp air smelled of piss and worse. He couldn't sleep in here…

He backed out, and took a long, deep breath of fresh air.

He'd slept in the open desert; he'd slept in a bivouac dug out of the snow high in the Cairngorms on a training exercise. He could do this. Get through the night, and then work out what the hell he was going to do in the morning.

He didn't last the night, though. They didn't let him.

4

'We could hand this over to a specialist team now, you know.'

DCI McBride's office was one floor above Serious Crimes, smaller than most, with a pair of narrow sash windows looking out over the main road. Bolam was still to decide whether this was a deliberate show of modesty on his superior's part, or simply a consequence of the station occupying a nineteenth-century building that had never been designed to house a modern police force.

McBride himself was balding, with round, jovial features that belied a steely and distant nature. Right now he was doing his best to do *understanding*, but it came across as something he'd been forced to learn on a management course.

'I didn't know we had a cold case unit,' Bolam said, standing in the doorway because he'd only intended this to be a brief update on the case.

'We don't, but we do have officers who have relevant experience. A murder case from three decades ago might not be the best resource allocation for Serious Crimes. Yours is a new team, Bolam. I had to fight to get the resources to build such a unit in what our colleagues at Martlesham regard as a poky little port town on the Suffolk coast. That's a decision that could easily be reversed if your team doesn't prove its worth.'

Bolam was also aware that McBride had fought for Bolam's role to have a degree of autonomy, and remain more hands-on than a detective inspector would normally expect to be. He appreciated this – he'd go mad stuck behind a desk all day – and knew he shouldn't push.

'It's a case that only came to light this week,' Bolam said. In truth, he wasn't sure himself why he was so reluctant to let this one go. He hated the cliché of the detective's hunch, or gut feelings, but there was something *missing* from all this... 'At least give me long enough to go and visit Sturridge to tell him we've confirmed the identity.'

'You've bonded?'

'I'd hardly say that. But I'm the one who's dealt with him, and he's old and a bit more vulnerable than he first appears, I think.'

McBride nodded. 'Okay,' he said. 'But once you've done that...'

Bolam made to leave, but McBride raised a hand to stop him. 'Are you okay, Inspector? Settling in all right, and all that?'

Bolam nodded. 'I have a good team,' he said.

'Good. Everyone would have understood if you'd backed out from this post,' the DCI said. 'Coastal Suffolk is very different to the hustle and bustle of Newcastle, and... well, all the rest. Nobody would have judged you.' For a moment McBride's concern seemed genuine, not textbook.

'Thank you, sir. I'm coping fine.' Everything was so much more complicated when people tried to be sympathetic.

He'd never meant to come here... To this job, this town. It had all been a ghastly misunderstanding, compounded by tragedy, but although he'd stumbled into this role, he was here now, and he was determined to make a go of things.

'The job's my life, sir,' he said. 'It's who I am.' He stopped short of adding, *So would you please just let me get on with it?*

Bolam spent the rest of the morning keeping track of his team's progress and chasing fruitless leads of his own. Names from a missing persons file that hadn't been looked at in more than a quarter of a century. Friends and relatives who had been interviewed about the state of the Sturridges' marriage, Jayne's day-to-day activities, the state of her mind. He tried to contact some of them, but her parents were both dead now and her sister lived in Canada, where he left a message on voicemail asking her to call him back. Jayne's brother *did* answer the phone, but he worked night shifts and seemed more bothered at having his sleep disturbed than the fact that he was finally being informed of the fate of his long-missing sister. Families were the strangest things, Bolam thought. Perhaps it was his job, but the one thing he had learned was to never try to anticipate how relatives would react in any given circumstance.

By the end of the morning, Bolam's eyes were aching from staring at computer screens and old handwritten notes. This wasn't a side of the job that appealed to him, and he caught his mind wandering several times. He wanted more than anything to talk with Fran, aware of the irony that when the opportunity had been there he had always struggled to do so. It was too late now. Maybe that was why he felt a connection with Matthew Sturridge, and also why he was struggling now: he understood loss all too well.

He made himself focus on the historical case files, even though he hated the sense of growing frustration as he struggled to get anything from the old notes and records. Where he came into his own was when he was face-to-face with people, talking to them, getting inside their heads. He'd never found people easy, which was the reason why he'd worked so hard to understand them.

The only real person involved in this investigation was Matthew Sturridge, and at lunchtime Bolam found himself standing outside that now-familiar front door. He'd been putting this off – not least because he knew that for DCI McBride it marked a cut-off point, after which the case should be put in the hands of someone with the time and aptitude for raking over a decades-old cold case. He knew he should have come here as soon as they got the full report back from Pathology. He straightened his tie and rang the bell.

As soon as Sturridge opened the door and saw Bolam's expression, it was clear he had made the mental leap and knew exactly why the inspector was here. He had clearly been expecting this.

'I'm sorry, Mr Sturridge,' Bolam told him. 'But we've confirmed the identity. The amputated finger belonged to your wife.'

'But… how? Has she been alive all this time?'

Bolam shook his head. 'The finger was removed post-mortem and preserved.' He didn't say how. 'Your wife passed away a long time ago, presumably around the time of her disappearance twenty-nine years ago. Further testing will verify this. My condolences, Mr Sturridge… perhaps we should go in and sit down?'

A short time later Sturridge sat at the kitchen table while Bolam filled the kettle and put it on to boil.

'Why?' A single word that encompassed so much. Why would someone preserve his wife's finger for so long, and why send it to him now? Why kill her in the first place?

Some people, when they received tragic news, went into complete meltdown, crying and screaming and lashing out. Sturridge was at the opposite end of the spectrum, but the fact that he sat here at his kitchen table looking puzzled more than anything did not, in Bolam's experience, mean that he felt any less intensely than a screamer and rager. He'd suffered twenty-nine years of limbo, and now was faced with adjusting to a new status that embraced both the certainty of his wife's fate and a whole new set of unknowns about how and why.

'Do you have photographs? Old home videos? Diaries?' asked Bolam. 'Anything that might help us build up a picture of Jayne's life in the weeks or months before this happened.' It was notable that the house was devoid of photographs or other mementoes of Jayne Sturridge. It had been a long time, but Bolam would still have expected there to be *something*, but it was as if Sturridge had filed her away.

Bolam poured hot water, stirring and pressing the teabags with a spoon before removing them and adding milk. Sturridge was the kind of man who would have a particular sequence for making tea, and Bolam wondered if he had got it right.

'Photographs?' he prompted, when he brought the blue and white china cups over to the table and sat down in what was now his usual chair by the door to the utility room.

'Oh yes, of course.' Sturridge stood, straightened his clothes, and then left the room.

The kitchen spoke of an ordered life. No dirty dishes from the night before. Everything in its place. No crumbs on the floor or cobwebs in the corners of ceiling and wall. Had there been anyone else in Sturridge's life since Jayne?

Sturridge reappeared with two photo albums, clear plastic covering spiral-bound card pages that would be slightly tacky to hold the photographs in place.

Three pages into the first album he opened, Bolam was oddly taken aback to find the now-familiar picture of Jayne with the champagne flute. It seemed incongruous to come across an image they had all seen so many times in Jayne's case file here in a more normal, everyday context.

Sturridge watched closely as Bolam turned the pages. This exercise was, in truth, just as much about studying the man's reactions as it was about Jayne herself. Bolam found it hard to escape the conclusion that, from the start, Sturridge had been evasive, always holding something back.

'This one?' asked Bolam, nodding towards a picture of Jayne sitting at a café table in a street, somewhere sunny. She wore big sunglasses and a wide-brimmed straw hat, and had a drink with two straws on the table before her.

'Barcelona,' Sturridge answered. 'Our third wedding anniversary. We returned there five years in a row. My wife liked the familiar.'

'This?' Jayne standing at a viewpoint over a wide bend in a river.

'The Dordogne. We considered buying a holiday home there, for a time. Another of my wife's favourite places.'

Bolam noted the emerging theme of Jayne's favourites, Jayne's preferred ways of doing things. She seemed to be a creature of habit, and Matthew Sturridge's preference for order and tidiness had probably been a good match for her. But there was more to it than that: every time he spoke of Jayne's preferences there was a hesitation and a tensing in his jaw, a subtle visual subtext to the story of a life dictated by his wife. A tightly contained resentment, perhaps: he had lived his life in her shadow when they had been together, and ever since losing her his life had been framed by that loss.

And the way he referred to Jayne as 'my wife' rather than by her name… There was a distancing there.

Bolam became aware of Sturridge staring at him.

'You've stopped turning the pages,' the man said. 'Have you seen something?'

Bolam looked down at the photos: Jayne on a beach, wrapped up against the cold; Jayne cutting a birthday cake. His eyes had glazed over. He had stopped looking, was a million miles away.

'I'm thinking about the penguins again,' Bolam said.

Sturridge kept staring, but said nothing this time.

'Emperor penguins migrate to their breeding grounds once a year,' Bolam told him. 'They can walk a hundred miles across the most hostile terrain on this planet, taking a different route each time because every year the ice has shifted and reshaped itself, but they always get there. They always remember their breeding grounds. Every last detail.'

Still Sturridge stared.

'And that's the thing, isn't it, Mr Sturridge? They remember. Just as *you* would remember whether Jayne wore rings, as she very clearly did from these photographs. Two rings on one hand, three on the other. You'd remember that, wouldn't you? Just like the penguins. You'd remember that she wore rings, but more, you'd remember the individual rings themselves. You'd run every small detail over and over in your mind so you could keep her alive in your memories. Just as you've clearly looked at these photographs a million times, even though you don't keep any visual reminders of Jayne around the house. You'd remember.'

'What are you saying, Inspector?'

'We considered the possibility that the envelope was delivered to you as some kind of ransom demand, but clearly that's not the case now that we know whose finger it was. We considered that it might be some kind of threat, an attempt to intimidate. But again, how would that work, now that we know the victim's identity? My preferred theory before we knew the victim was your wife was that it was some kind of almighty cock-up, delivered to the wrong address, but we never managed to work out who it *should* have been sent to. And then there was another possibility.'

'Inspector?'

'That you knew far more than you were letting on, Mr Sturridge. I've been paying close attention to you and you haven't shown real surprise or shock at any stage of this investigation. Not when the finger arrived. Not when I told you it belonged to your wife. Not when I showed up at your door and you were clearly expecting me, and knew why I had come. Not even when it's become pretty damned clear that I've started to view you more with suspicion than sympathy. Not even now, when I've spelled all that out for you. You just sit there nodding and waiting for me to go on.'

'I am a calm man, Inspector.'

'Oh yes, you certainly are that. I described you to colleagues as gentle and reserved, but now I see I was wrong. Not reserved, but *controlled*. In fact, I'd go so far as to say *cold*.'

Sturridge's genteel manner was a veneer, and now, for the first time, there was a genuine reaction, a slight narrowing of the eyes.

'Is there anything you'd like to tell me, Mr Sturridge?'

'Tell you?'

'Do you know where your wife has been all this time?'

This time there was no reaction on Sturridge's features. The cold veneer Bolam had mistaken for gentleness had descended, once again.

For now, Bolam found himself unable to ignore the strong possibility that Sturridge knew far more than he had been letting on. Indeed, that he may even have been responsible for his wife's death and had harboured his secret all this time.

Twenty-nine years of guilt. Twenty-nine years of a life frozen in that moment when something tragic had happened – an eruption of anger from a man who had always played second fiddle to his wife, perhaps? Because he clearly had: every anecdote attached to an old photograph had been framed in terms of 'my wife liked this' or 'my wife preferred to do things that way'. And now that he had spotted that bottled-up resentment, it underscored everything Sturridge said about his wife.

Would they find the rest of Jayne Sturridge in a chest freezer in the utility room? Or had her husband disposed of her all those years ago, only retaining the finger as some kind of twisted memento?

And now, all these years on, had something made him snap again? Some perverse need to finally step out of his wife's shadow and be noticed? No longer able to live with those years of guilt and a secret carefully maintained across the decades, yet still unable to confess directly, that finger might be a bizarre kind of admission. A clue that would quite literally point to Sturridge's guilt.

The psychologists would have a field day with this one if Sturridge did, indeed, turn out to be responsible.

Bolam hesitated. This was a huge call to make, with no physical evidence and only his assessment of the man's responses to questioning so far, but a line had been crossed: they'd initially viewed Sturridge as a victim, but at the very least he had now demonstrated himself to be someone who had been an evasive and potentially misleading witness, or even a person suspected of playing some part in his wife's disappearance. Any subsequent questioning would have to be on a more formal basis.

'Matthew Sturridge,' he said, 'there's no easy way to do this, but I think you need to accompany me to the station, where you'll be interviewed under caution...'

5

'What's wrong, boss?'

'Wrong?' Bolam looked at Billie Grayson and she raised her sharply defined eyebrows at him. He wasn't quite comfortable that his DC could read him so easily. He'd been drifting again. He couldn't even pretend he'd been focused on the case: he'd just been… drifting.

He sat on the edge of a table in the small kitchen area next to the briefing room, a double espresso in a too-big mug at his side. Grayson was at the kettle making tea. Aisha Nawaz stood by the window gazing out, her mental equivalent of being outside with the smokers, even though she'd given up several weeks ago.

'There's something about him that I find hard to read,' he said. 'I really believed he was a gentle old soul at first, but underneath there's a coldness. A sense of distance from everyone around him.'

'He's a broken man putting up a front,' Grayson said. 'He's lived with this for nearly three decades. He deliberately gave himself away in the hope he'd find closure, but now he doesn't know whether to feel relieved or terrified and so he's put the barriers up.'

That was one of the narratives they'd constructed when it turned out that Sturridge wasn't exactly forthcoming in interview. But still Bolam felt he was missing something: if Sturridge had done this in order to expose his own guilt, then you'd expect the confession to come tumbling out once he'd been brought in for questioning, but no, not a thing. Perhaps they were wrong about Sturridge… Had he somehow misread the old man's renewed grieving for Jayne as resentment, and even hostility, towards her? And even if that resentment had been there, it might be understandable: Jayne's disappearance had defined her husband's life for the last three decades. Bolam knew well that grief was a complex, and often contradictory, thing.

'We've overlooked something,' Bolam said.

Back in his office, he flicked through the photo albums again. They'd been released from forensics after a closer examination had revealed no more than Sturridge's fingerprints all over them.

Bolam was hoping that something would leap out at him, but all he got from the exercise was a sense of a life tragically snatched away. He found his mind drifting again, thinking of Fran. He was painfully familiar with loss, and he understood the complexities of a relationship that defied any easy labelling. Was he trying too hard to find a simple and straightforward understanding of the Sturridges' relationship?

He thought of what DCI McBride had said, that everyone would have understood if Bolam had backed out of this job. Perhaps if McBride had said that sooner, Bolam would never have come here.

Sometime later, he took a phone call, a woman with a mixed-up mid-Atlantic accent.

'Inspector Bolam? It's Melissa Walton. Jayne Sturridge's sister. You left a voicemail for me.'

'Ah, Ms Walton. I'm afraid I have—'

'I know. I've already spoken with my brother. I know about Jayne.'

'My condolences, nonetheless. It's never easy to deal with such news.' Especially by transatlantic telephone call.

'No. Well. Anyway. You said you wanted to talk with me. I don't know what I can do, but fire away.'

'I spoke to your brother.'

'Robbie's not an easy person. He doesn't find it easy to talk about things that matter. Particularly Jayne.'

'And Matthew?'

'Robbie never liked Matthew.'

Bolam wondered what it was that made Robbie dislike Sturridge, but he didn't say that out loud.

'Your sister,' he said instead. 'There was a ring.'

'Jayne loved her rings. They held a lot of sentimental value for her.'

'I know,' Bolam said. 'I have photos of her here on my desk. Three rings on one hand, two on the other.'

'So what do you want to know about the rings?' asked Melissa.

'We have a ring that we believe belonged to your sister. It's quite distinctive. A large opal, pearl-coloured with a sheen of pink to it, set in white gold. Worn on the little finger of the left hand.'

'No.'

'What do you mean, no?'

'That's not Jayne's. She never had a ring like that.'

'Perhaps it was new. Perhaps she liked to swap her jewellery around and wore different rings sometimes?'

'No.' Again, that simple answer, before Melissa went on. 'Jayne's rings were important to her. One was two gold strands twisted that I gave her on her twenty-first. Another was a rather ugly silver ring with a chunky flower design that Robbie gave her.'

The two rings worn on her right hand in the photos. Now that Bolam looked more closely he saw that this was one of the things that had been tugging away at his subconscious: yes, she wore rings, but always the same ones.

'And on her left hand, her wedding ring on the usual finger. She wore her engagement ring on the forefinger because it had been too big when Matthew gave it to her and they hadn't been able to afford to have it resized, and then later she'd gotten used to wearing it on that finger.'

'And on her little finger?' The one where they'd found the opal ring.

'A silver band with a little gold heart. She wore that for the baby they lost. She never took it off. She just wouldn't.'

Aisha Nawaz was at her desk when Bolam got off the phone with Melissa Walton. She saw his expression straight away, and came to stand in his office doorway, listening as he updated her.

'There are going to be more, aren't there?' she said.

'What do you mean?'

'The ring,' she said. 'If it wasn't Jayne's then who did it belong to? Another victim...?'

*

Bolam sat across the interview room table from Sturridge, saying nothing. Normally, he would leave the interviewing at this stage to a specialist like Aisha Nawaz, preferring to hang back and observe on the video feed, but there was something about Sturridge that drew him in. DCI McBride's glib comment was perceptive: he and Sturridge had bonded.

Sturridge had called on the services of a solicitor, a neat, white-haired man who looked as if he'd come out of retirement especially for this interview. Sharing similar deeply lined features and fastidious manners, the two might have been brothers, or a double act past their prime.

'Raymond Cowper,' the solicitor said, leaning across the table to shake Bolam's hand, then swaying away unsteadily when the inspector made no move to reciprocate. 'I hope we can get this nonsense over with as expediently as possible, just as we did twenty-nine years ago when one of your predecessors made the same rush to judgement. My client is a highly respected member of the community, and not in the halest of health. For the record, I'd like to reiterate that he is not under arrest but is here on a voluntary basis to assist with enquiries.'

Again, Bolam remained silent. The solicitor's take on this was interesting, because there was nothing in the case notes to indicate Sturridge had been interviewed in any capacity other than concerned husband of the missing person twenty-nine years ago.

Finally, he spoke. 'Was it guilt, Matthew? That drove you to exposing yourself like this? You've got away with this for almost thirty years, but somewhere inside you know that your wife deserves justice. You couldn't just confess, so you pointed the way.'

Sturridge and his solicitor exchanged looks. 'Really, Inspector,' Cowper said. 'Unless you have anything substantial and you intend to press charges, and if all you have to go on is supposition and innuendo, then I think we're in a position to conclude this swiftly.'

'Oh, rest assured, Mr Cowper. My colleagues are in conversation with the Crown Prosecution Service as we speak. But do you know what, Matthew? I worry that there's more to this. That this isn't driven by guilt but by a sense of your own injustice: that you haven't achieved any kind of recognition.'

'Recognition?' It was the first time Sturridge had spoken, and his tone was more curious than defensive, or concerned. Again, his manner struck Bolam as peculiar.

Aisha Nawaz had made the mental – and emotional – leap far quicker than Bolam had. Now he thought again about the finger in the padded envelope, the ring that was not Jayne Sturridge's. When he had spoken to Jayne's sister, he had considered the possibility that the lab had misidentified the finger. A pathology error? Interference with the evidence of some sort?

But no, they'd been over it all again. The finger was certainly Jayne Sturridge's. But the ring was not.

That meant there was a distinct possibility that they were looking at two victims, at least. And given how long Jayne Sturridge's murder had gone unsolved…

'You haven't left your mark on the world, have you, Matthew?' An old man, perhaps not long for this world, who has had no children, apart from the lost baby, and who has left no legacy. 'You lived in your wife's shadow when she was alive, and when she was gone your life was defined forever more by that loss. When you're gone, too, who will remember you? Who will remember what you've done?'

Sturridge simply sat there, that slightly vacant look on his face, waiting for Bolam to continue.

'How many more are there?' Bolam asked. 'We have a team at your house right now. What will we find there? We already have the finger of your wife, and a ring that wasn't hers – did that belong to another victim? What else will we find? How many more trophies did you keep?'

6

'Do you really think Matthew Sturridge is a serial killer?' asked Aisha Nawaz, an interesting question, given that she was the one who had first raised the possibility.

A small group sat and stood in a cluster in the open-plan Serious Crimes office. Projected onto the screen was a montage of photos: Matthew Sturridge, Jayne Sturridge, the opal ring, and a scan of a handwritten list of names and dates and other notes.

'We must wait to see the outcome of the search of his home,' Bolam cautioned. 'This is only one possible scenario, albeit one that Mr Sturridge has done nothing to dismiss. But at the very least, we'd be foolish not to consider the likelihood that there are at least two victims: Jayne Sturridge, and whoever that ring belongs to. And if the finger is some bizarre kind of confession, then if that's come about simply through accumulated guilt, why would he go to such lengths to make it into a puzzle, or performance? So if we pursue that line of speculation, then there's a good chance it's some kind of ego thing, to show us how clever he is. "Look at what I've got away with all these years, aren't I smart?" An old man near the end of his life who wants to be sure he's left his mark before his time is up. That's the kind of behaviour we see in compulsive killers, not someone who's committed a single domestic crime of passion and lived with the guilt for the rest of his life. As is the collection and retention of trophies.'

'And if he's compelled to kill, driven at least in part by ego, then over a thirty-year period there won't just be two, will there?' Aisha rushed to complete Bolam's line of reasoning. 'What if this is a sign that he's escalating in some way, or losing the self-restraint that's kept him free all this time?'

'Unless you were just testing him,' said Billie Grayson, sitting at her desk to one side of the gathering. 'We know he hasn't been straight with us, so maybe you were just seeing if you could shock the truth out of him by confronting him with something way off the scale.'

'As I say, this is only one possible scenario,' Bolam said. 'We need to ask the question, but it's the evidence that will decide things for us.' In truth, he didn't know what he thought, but he didn't mind that: it was too early to be settling on conclusions.

When he'd levelled the accusation at Sturridge he had still been struggling to accept it as the most likely explanation, but he was convinced this was way more than a straightforward domestic.

But he was also aware that the kind of compulsive, long-term killer they had just been speculating about was an incredibly rare phenomenon. Had they jumped in too soon? It wasn't like Bolam to push so hard to tidy up a case, and he was beginning to question himself now.

He was struggling with this new role, this new life, and he was unaccustomed to feeling so out of his depth. Again, he considered the possibility that DCI McBride had been right to suggest he shouldn't have come here.

They were staring at him, waiting.

'Okay, folks,' he said, clapping his hands. 'We have work to do. Unless we make a formal arrest, Sturridge can walk out of here at any point and all we have is a detached finger and a mystery ring, but nothing to tell us what actually happened. And, bumbling old duffer that Raymond Cowper appears on the surface, he's a savvy solicitor and he knows we have nothing on Sturridge that will stick. Aisha, carry on with the ring. See if there's any way at all we can trace its provenance, particularly if we can link it to a crime or a missper. Billie and Tommo: historical case files. I know, we're looking for proverbial needles, but all we need to do is find one old case that corresponds with this one – unsolved murders, particularly if trophies have been removed; missing persons, anything that fits.'

'And you, boss?' asked Grayson.

'I'm going to catch up with Pathology, and then I'll head over to

Sturridge's house to see how Cath Marshall and the search team are getting on.'

Even as he returned to his desk his phone was ringing, the Public Access Officer on the front desk calling to let him know Sturridge's solicitor was waiting for him at reception.

Bolam ran a hand over hair that was shaved too short to need smoothing, straightened his jacket and tie, and headed down. 'Mr Cowper,' he said.

Cowper made a show of easing himself to his feet, leaning on a gnarly old walking stick so that he tipped slightly forward towards Bolam, almost but not quite invading his personal space.

'Inspector,' he said. 'I expect I'll be seeing quite a lot of you in the future, in one capacity or another. Whitesands is a small town, you know.'

Bolam knew this was a thinly veiled way of pointing out that he was the newcomer and the old solicitor was well-connected.

'As I said,' Cowper went on, 'I hope we can deal with this business as expediently as possible. Matthew is an old man, and frail, and I have concerns about his mental and emotional state. We would both like to assist with your investigation in any way we can, but my duty is to protect the interests of my client – and, I should add, friend – and I will protect him as fiercely as is necessary. I've advised Matthew to remain here while you complete your search of his home, but rest assured that I will be scrutinising every action you take.'

Bolam nodded. The solicitor's words were a fine balance between friendly cooperation and threat. He had been right not to dismiss Raymond Cowper as the bumbling old duffer he might first appear to be.

'Your concerns are noted, Mr Cowper,' he said carefully. 'We appreciate your client's cooperation, and I do hope he will follow your advice and stay here while we clarify his account of events. If you would like a medical assessment for Mr Sturridge before we continue to interview him, that can be arranged. But the situation as it stands is that we have a finger of the long-missing wife of your client confirming that she was murdered, and we have a ring belonging to a yet-to-be-identified third party, both found in the possession of, and reported by, your client. Who has, I might add, been economical, at best, with what he chooses to tell us. We have perfectly legitimate reasons to be interviewing him under caution, and the outcome of the search of his property will play a large part in determining how we proceed.'

'Of course, of course,' said Cowper. 'I'm not questioning the legitimacy of your approach, but rather highlighting my concerns about the impact on a fragile and vulnerable individual.'

Cowper gestured around the station's reception area. 'This world,' he said. 'It's been such a significant part of my life. Don't you think we punish and reward the wrong people? The victims… Like Matthew Sturridge: his only fault is that he loved too much, and for too long. And yet even now he is the one who pays the price. Reopening the loss of Jayne is…' For a moment the old solicitor faltered, and Bolam reminded himself that Cowper was representing a friend here.

'I would never claim that getting to the truth is a painless process,' Bolam told him. 'But that is what this is about: the truth. For people like your client.'

He watched as Cowper left the building, aware that the old man had played him. He'd asserted his authority by summoning him down here, made it clear that the investigation would not get away with putting a foot wrong, and made sure Bolam understood that he was a man of local influence – all dressed up in the insistence that he and his client only wanted to help.

And also, he'd succeeded in reminding Bolam that at the end of all this Sturridge might be an entirely innocent victim.

Bolam's office was little more than a glass-walled booth sectioned off from one corner of his team's open-plan area. He'd been here three months, but he was yet to personalise the space. No photos, no books; nothing that might make this office his own in any way.

He didn't even have a photo of Fran on his desk, because he still couldn't bear to create bridges between old life and new. Ironically, she would have known what to do, the best way for him to handle his loss. He wanted to talk to her, more than anything. She'd understood the workings of his mind more clearly than anyone ever had.

His previous office had been very different to this one, no complications about whether to personalise or not. The station back in his home town in the Northeast had been modern, purpose-built, the offices so stark – breezeblock walls, metal-framed windows, suspended ceiling tiles – that everyone had felt compelled to add homely touches. Bolam had kept photographs on his desk and wall, and an eclectic selection of books on the shelves; he'd been known behind his back as the Gardener, due to the lush greenery he'd crammed into every corner.

Things changed, though, and he had no desire to breathe life into this new space.

He opened up Microsoft Teams, found Raj Khatri's listing under Contacts, and made the call. A young man with a hairnet over his thick beard, a topknot turban, and a white lab coat buttoned up to the neck appeared onscreen. The backdrop was his office over in the hospital's pathology lab, so Bolam had not interrupted a post-mortem.

Bolam had set his own Teams backdrop to be blurred out, self-conscious of how anonymous his office was, but that only served to emphasise his small frame and narrow features, and the way his blue eyes had something intensely piercing about them, even on a small video thumbnail view.

'Inspector Bolam.' The pathologist looked away from the camera – checking case notes on another screen, Bolam guessed. 'Jayne Sturridge, right?'

Bolam nodded. 'Does a finger count as a post-mortem?' he asked.

Raj smiled. 'Well, technically, yes,' he said. 'We know the finger was amputated post-mortem, and therefore we know its owner is dead, so any examination is post-mortem… But the finger, as such, doesn't meet the criteria for, shall we say, full cadaver status.'

They'd already skirted around this in a previous conversation, and Bolam wasn't quite sure why he was dwelling on the question. Perhaps it was simply that he liked to get things ordered in his mind.

'Anything more you can tell me?' Bolam said. They had the preliminary report, covering the basics.

Raj shrugged. 'Sorry,' he said, 'but there's just not a lot we can get from the forensics on a severed finger. We've confirmed ID by comparison of fingerprints with those taken from possessions when she went missing, and I'm confident that DNA analysis will support that when the results come through. State of preservation, bearing in mind the finger was stored at sub-zero temperatures, supports a time of death perhaps twenty to fifty years ago, which we'll be able to narrow down when we get more test results in. Initial toxicity screening has identified nothing suspicious, although it'll be some time before we get a full report: there's no suggestion of illegal drugs, though, and nothing to indicate sedation or intoxication. The victim was apparently in good health at the time of death.'

'All that, just from a finger.'

'Indeed. One thing I can tell you. I know you're working on the theory that the ring did not belong to this finger, and we can confirm that. The opal ring is simply too small to pass over the proximal interphalangeal knuckle.'

'You're saying the ring must have been put on from the severed end of the finger, after amputation?'

Raj nodded. 'Your killer dressed his victim after death,' he said. 'After a fashion.' Then he went on. 'I can also confirm that the victim *did* habitually wear a ring on this finger – just not the opal ring we have in evidence. You can tell from the tanning marks, and there's indentation and skin smoothing that suggests long-term wearing of a ring with a narrower band than the ring we have. Does that help?'

'It provides confirmation,' Bolam said. They already knew from the photographs and Melissa Walton's statement that Jayne had worn a silver band with a small gold heart on that finger.

What had become of that ring, he wondered? She'd worn it in memory of a stillborn baby, never parted with it. It was the kind of memento Matthew Sturridge might have removed, as it would hold special significance for him too. Perhaps it would be found at the house, which would at least circumstantially support the theory that Sturridge had been involved in his wife's death.

He thanked the pathologist and ended the call. He'd talk to Aisha Nawaz next. She was already looking into the provenance of the mystery opal ring, so he could see if she could find out anything about the missing ring too.

Maybe the clue was not in the ring their victim was wearing, but in the one that had been *removed*.

7

Russell Shaw was awoken by the sound of voices. He reached instinctively for his combat helmet but, of course, it wasn't there.

He rose to a sitting position, the steam of his breath caught in the light from a nearby street. He was cold, despite the layers of clothing. Shivering, as he hugged his knees to his chest.

A dog barked, far too close.

Who took their dog for a walk at this kind of hour? It must be well after midnight.

A shout, and the dog started to bark frantically. It wasn't a walk: it was a hunt.

Russ stood, peering around in the darkness, and almost immediately a figure burst through the undergrowth, a bearded man, the whites of his eyes as mad and staring as Russ's ever were.

For a moment Russ thought the man had come for him, but then he took in his appearance – the ripped coat, the thick layers of clothing, the general air of grubbiness evident even in this low light. A rough sleeper, just like Russ.

Someone shouted nearby and the man melted away into the undergrowth.

Russ peered all around again, his brain racing to catch up, to work out what was going on. He saw the beams of torchlights swinging across the bushes. Heard someone call out, 'Over here! They've got a tent. It's a sodding *camp*site.'

Russ had seen the small tent when he picked his spot in the evening. He'd spoken briefly to the young Kurdish couple sleeping there – homeless, perhaps in the country illegally. In their broken English they'd told him this was a popular spot for the homeless to seek shelter. He hadn't known that, but it made sense that others would be drawn here for the same reasons Russ had been: away from the main part of town, shelter offered by the ruined defences.

He saw blue lights now; a police car pulled up by the bridge to the Martello tower. This was some kind of raid: drug-users liked the old gun emplacements too, or it might simply be an effort to move out the rough sleepers.

Another shout, a flash of light right in his eyes. Russ put an arm up to shield his face, then turned and ran.

As soon as he rounded a tree, another light picked him out. Voices, all around him. Dogs barking.

It felt like walls closing in from every direction. A blanket of pressure descending, smothering him, so that now he couldn't tell if the voices were real or in his head.

He stopped. He'd reached the promenade now, the emplacements behind him, a metal rail a short distance before him, guarding the two-metre drop to the beach. He pressed hands to his temples.

Silence, briefly, and then a shout again, a beam of light sweeping down from the embankment behind him.

He ran, limbs flailing so that he felt like a cartoon version of himself, every movement exaggerated.

He reached the railing, grabbed the top bar, and swung himself over.

The drop was greater than he'd judged, the landing on seaweed-festooned rocks uneven and jarring. He was lucky not to have broken any bones, and only to be winded by the impact.

He squatted, doubled up by the vacuum in his lungs, struggling to breathe again.

Finally, he managed to inhale, in deep, ragged gasps.

He stood, and he ran, skidding and stumbling over the rocks until he found the firm sand of the newly exposed beach, and now could run full-sprint.

Run until he could run no more and he tumbled to the ground, the breath burning in his lungs once again.

When he could breathe again, he walked up the beach, across the shifting, dry sand to a set of concrete steps that led up to the promenade which, in turn, was lined with a row of beach huts. He considered checking the locks to see if one of the huts might be open, but decided against that option. The police were out tonight and if they found him in a beach hut he would have no excuse.

He couldn't afford to do anything that might expose him to trouble.

He found a concrete storm shelter, nestled on the grassy bank between the promenade and East Bay Drive. Three walls shielded him from the town side, if not from the piercingly cold sea breeze that came in the open front. He stretched out on the wooden slats of the bench and tried to stop shivering through power of will alone.

It was a long night, and he was still wide awake when the sky took on a wash of pastel tones in the long blue hour before dawn.

He got up and walked, not knowing where he was heading.

He wished he'd never come back to this awful place, although he knew that even that was a stupid thought. If he hadn't come back to Whitesands, he'd always have wondered how he would have coped if he *had*, and he would never escape the feeling he had shied away from confronting the past.

To have come back and found it something of an anticlimax was, perhaps, the best of all outcomes. To have encountered no accusing voices, no recognition on the streets. To see the familiar and the new, and to realise that this place, and its community, had moved on.

He did not know what would come next, where he would go. He had even less in the world now than when he had arrived in this town, for he'd left his canvas holdall somewhere in the ruins of the old gun emplacement. All he had were the multiple layers of clothes he had put on to insulate himself against the cold of the night.

He slipped into a space behind the beach huts and pulled the second pair of jeans off, and then the extra shirt and jumper. He bundled them into a ball, but had nothing to carry them in. He would find a bag somewhere; if he felt bold enough, he would go back to the embankment by the Martello tower and see if he could find his bag.

One thing he knew: he couldn't handle another night in the open. He was not the hardened soldier he'd once been. Too much of the night spooked him, took him close to a mental precipice he did not dare approach. And the cold – not so much the physical cold, but the sense of utter desolation it brought…

He recalled the look on the face of the woman in the council office. She'd said there was a shelter for people like him somewhere near the quay.

It was still early in the day. He didn't know how places like that operated, but he suspected they wouldn't welcome newcomers so early. They would probably only take people in towards the end of the day.

So he walked, not knowing where he was going, or when he would stop. Just walked. And it was all he could do to stop himself from breaking into a run, as if he might somehow escape from all this if he merely ran fast enough.

8

The video doorbell overlooking the street three doors down from Matthew Sturridge's house would have seen a lot of action today. Two unmarked vans were parked by the kerb, a man in plain clothes stood at the foot of the steps to the retired teacher's front door, and others would have been coming and going all morning. Bolam didn't recognise the man on the door, so he guessed he was part of the forensics unit rather than a police officer.

Bolam flashed his ID and the man nodded, then called inside.

Cath Marshall emerged from the front door, treading on the heel of a pale blue over-shoe bootee with one foot to pull it off the other, then reversing the procedure, before stooping to bag them up in case she'd carried any trace evidence out on her feet. The crime scene manager was a tall woman, square in face and frame, but her most striking feature was blonde eyelashes longer than those of a baby deer. She'd been off on sick leave when Bolam had started here and so, while Bolam had sat in on a couple of meetings where she'd presented, he hadn't worked with her yet.

There was no police tape across the gateway, no marked cars in the street, so they were clearly trying to be discreet here – perhaps the influence of the solicitor, Cowper, coming to bear – but it must still be obvious to neighbours what was going on. Particularly so, now that Cath stood in full view in her white crime-scene over-suit.

'Inspector Bolam,' Cath said. 'I hope you don't mind.' She waved back towards the house.

The place wasn't officially a crime scene, as yet, because there was no evidence that a crime had actually been committed here, but even so, they were all following protocol to avoid contamination.

There was no need for Bolam to go inside, other than to jog his own somewhat arcane thought processes – which was why he'd come here in the first place – so they stood in the street to talk.

Cath drew on a vape, breathing out apple-scented clouds that hung in the air around them and made Bolam feel vaguely queasy.

'Tell me who Matthew Sturridge is,' Bolam said.

For a moment Cath paused, eyeing him suspiciously, then she barked a short laugh and said, 'DCI McBride warned me about you.'

Bolam wasn't sure how to take that, other than at face value: people often didn't know what to make of him. His mind worked differently to other people's.

'Sturridge?' he prompted.

'Matthew Sturridge. Taught at the local high school for forty-five years. Went to church at Christmas and Easter, member of—'

'No, not the Wikipedia version. What did you see of him in there? What did you read?'

Another pause. 'Tidy,' Cath eventually said. 'The kind of tidy that makes other people uncomfortable. Organised and methodical. The accumulated artefacts of a quiet and lonely existence – the tidiness disguises just how much he didn't throw away. I wouldn't go quite so far as to label him a hoarder, but away from the more public rooms, the place was rammed. The house fits the life he led: taught at high school for forty-five years, went to church when duty required, involved in worthy community activities, but at arm's length.'

'Serial killer?' pressed Bolam.

'If that turns out to be the case,' she said, 'there's lots about this house that fits: not so much antisocial as *a*-social; controlling; guarded.'

'How many people are like that, though?'

'Far more than there are serial killers, Inspector.'

'An impassioned, spur-of-the moment killer, then?'

'You're asking me to speculate.'

Silence.

'There's not much passion in that house, Inspector.'

Bolam nodded. The pieces just wouldn't fit together. It was as if the more they learned of Sturridge, the easier it became to construct just about any narrative that explained what they knew.

'Most crucially, though, Inspector... No more severed fingers in the freezer, and no indication that it was ever *his* freezer where the finger had been stored. No body buried in the garden, and we've been using ground-penetrating radar to survey the ground for historical disturbances or bones. The dog team didn't find anything, either, and those mutts can find trace evidence dating back years.'

'Another ring?' Bolam asked. 'Perhaps hidden. A silver band with a small gold heart.'

Cath was shaking her head already. 'As I say, the man kept everything, so the house was full of stuff and, of course, there are lots of places you could hide a ring. But I'm guessing you think it's some kind of trophy, in which case it'd be kept somewhere accessible rather than dumped with all the other junk, or sealed into the brickwork, or buried in the garden... In which case I think we'd have found it.'

The ring mattered. He was sure of that. It had mattered to Jayne Sturridge, and to Matthew. Its absence must tell them something.

'There were no forensics on the envelope, the finger, or the opal ring, other than your suspect's on the envelope,' Cath said. 'And his could easily be explained by the fact that he opened the package when it was delivered.'

'If anyone other than Sturridge had handled it, they'd leave some kind of evidence, wouldn't they? There's usually something. Trace DNA, a partial finger mark. *Something.*'

'We've swabbed for DNA, but it'll be a few days before we see any results from that,' said Cath. 'There's nothing to suggest we'll get anything, though.'

'In which case,' said Bolam, 'why would a retired school teacher send himself his own wife's finger twenty-nine years after she died?'

'I just deal with the evidence,' said Cath. 'You're the poor sod who has to explain it...'

DI Kenneth Bulmer had been retired for twenty-five years. He was in his mid-eighties, but he looked even older, a shrivelled husk of a man who hunched in his chair with a permanent curvature of the spine, leaning on a stick that Bolam guessed he rarely ever actually used for walking. He had a permanent tremor in the hand he raised slowly from the head of the cane, and when Bolam shook that hand he feared that if he gripped too tightly the bones would simply crumble to dust.

Bolam's hopes that the man might be a reliable witness to events from almost three decades before were almost as shrunken as the man himself.

'I'm guessing this isn't a social call,' Bulmer said. 'What with the formal introductions and the way you waved your ID under my nose, eh?'

He laughed, and Bolam guessed he didn't care if it was social or not – Bolam's visit was a change to routine, which was probably the best thing that had happened to the old copper in months.

Bolam sat opposite him, their two armchairs occupying a bay window two storeys above East Bay Drive. Their position commanded a dramatic view over the bay, although Bolam suspected the old man's cloudy eyes struggled to see much beyond the length of his arms.

The place smelled of disinfectant and air freshener, and Bolam wondered if this care home ever fell silent, with the steady background jabber from TVs and radios, and from carers talking in laboured, slow sentences.

'Jayne Sturridge,' Bolam said. 'Missing person, twenty-nine years ago. What can you tell me about her?'

'Just wait here while I go fetch my case notes,' Bulmer said, and for an instant Bolam expected him to leap to his feet and rush from the room. Then he saw that the man was joking, and now laughing. The old boy was a lot sharper than his physical appearance would suggest. Perhaps his recollections might be useful after all.

'Jayne Sturridge?' Bolam prompted. Bulmer was staring out of the window. 'Thirty-four-year-old female, reported missing twenty-nine years ago. No history of mental health issues, no subsequent sightings or body, no evidence of any crime having been committed. You're down in the file as the senior investigating officer, Inspector Bulmer.'

Bulmer had been nodding as Bolam spoke, but it wasn't clear if that was a sign of his engagement or simply a repetitive movement he would make anyway.

'They fought,' the old man finally said. 'Her and her husband, the teacher. Everyone knew she ran away, had too much of him in the end. Why the interest now, after all these years?' Bulmer had clearly worked out something had happened.

'She's dead,' Bolam told him. 'Every indication is that she died twenty-nine years ago.' There was no need for detail.

Bulmer was still nodding, his whole upper body rocking back and forward in his chair.

'Are you saying we got it wrong? We should have found her.'

It was hard to tell if the last was a question or a statement.

'She was murdered, we believe. And concealed.' And most of her still *was* concealed… 'You searched her house?' The notes from the original investigation were patchy, at best.

'We did. There was nothing. No body. No suggestion that any crime had been committed.'

'And the husband?' He wanted to bring it back to what Bulmer had said about Sturridge and his wife fighting. 'Matthew Sturridge.'

'He was an odd one,' Bulmer said. 'Helpful. Soft-spoken. *Gentle.*' He said that as if it was some kind of criticism.

'But they fought?'

'He controlled her,' Bulmer said. 'He controlled everything in that house.'

'I had rather the opposite impression,' Bolam said. He recalled how Sturridge had emphasised that they did things, went to places, because that was what Jayne had wanted. He gave every indication of being a man who would have done anything to please his wife, even if he always ended up resenting it.

Bulmer's head-rocking shifted slightly, shaking from side to side now. 'He ruled over her,' he said. 'Suspicious of everything she did. That's what everyone said, although you'd never know it to talk to him. He was… what is it? Mitty. Walter Mitty. A fantasist. Question him hard enough and all the lies break down, but there wasn't any harm in him in the end. Just a pathetic man, building a world around himself he could control. So eventually she had enough and she upped and ran away. Or so we thought.'

'Might he have killed her? What do you mean, you questioned him "hard enough"?'

Bulmer looked suddenly defensive, and for a moment Bolam thought he was going to clam up. Then he said, 'We weren't soft in my day. You know what I mean? *Inspector*. We took him in and we questioned him, man to man. See if he'd break, you know?'

Bolam knew. He'd come across enough old-school coppers like Bulmer to understand *exactly* what he meant. No wonder Sturridge's solicitor had been so protective of him this time.

'He seemed genuine,' Bulmer went on. 'Just a bit pathetic. I almost felt guilty at the end.' A pause, then, 'You think he killed her?'

'We're investigating a number of possibilities,' Bolam said. 'That's why I came to see you. In case you had anything to add.'

Bulmer waggled his head. 'I'll give it some thought,' he said. 'And if I think of anything…'

Bolam stood. 'Thank you,' he said. '*Inspector*.' He took a couple of steps, then paused, waiting for the old man to notice. 'And I'm glad,' he added.

'Glad? Eh?'

'Glad you at least felt *almost* guilty.'

He still didn't know if Sturridge was a cold, psychopathic murderer, or simply an innocent man who'd been living with grief and uncertainty for close to thirty years, but the one thing he had learned from this interview was that the old teacher was not a man who would have a confession bullied out of him.

Back in Serious Crimes, they gathered around the projector screen once again.

'We've completed the search of his home, and there's nothing to stop Sturridge walking free, and we still haven't got far beyond what we already knew,' Bolam said to his team. 'Little finger severed at the metacarpophalangeal joint, our victim is the wife of the recipient, missing and presumed dead for thirty years, wearing an opal ring that does not appear to have ever belonged to her. Do we have any more?'

'We've been looking for old cases,' said Billie Grayson. 'Starting twenty-nine years ago, testing the hypothesis that if Sturridge *is* a multiple killer then the one that triggered it all was probably the most spontaneous – his wife.'

'Any cases with jewellery missing? Any reference to an opal ring?'

Billie nodded. 'Oh yes, boss. Violent death and stolen jewellery go hand in hand.'

For a moment Bolam had thought she had something, but no. 'Of course,' he said. 'But we're not interested in violent jewellery theft, per se, are we? Is there anything that might fit the pattern of trophy collection? Any deaths associated with body parts missing?'

'A couple of local things in the past thirty or so years,' Billie said. 'There was a particularly violent punishment killing twenty years ago where both hands were amputated with a machete. No one was ever prosecuted for that, but the investigating team clearly believed that it was something to do with drugs gangs operating through the port. And there was a double killing in the back of an ambulance nineteen years ago. One finger was cut off in that attack and never found, but it was thought that was a defensive injury and the finger disposed of somewhere. The killer in that case was arrested at the scene and given a long-term hospital order in a secure facility. If we widen the net to neighbouring forces, or down as far as London, there are more. I've compiled a list with notes.'

Bolam nodded. 'Keep digging,' he said. 'Those first two, in particular, but also abductions and violent assaults that might have been failed murder attempts. We still don't know what we're dealing with here.'

And that was what bothered him most of all. More than twenty-four hours into a major investigation and they still didn't know if they were looking at some bizarre kind of domestic cold case or something much bigger.

'Aisha, what have you got?'

'Not much,' she said. 'I interviewed Matthew Sturridge again this afternoon. Mostly just rephrasing things we'd already asked him, trying to dig a little deeper, but his solicitor is controlling things closely, won't let him give more than the most basic answers. He might as well be giving us "no comment" to everything.'

Bolam sighed. 'I can see why he'd do that. Earlier today I spoke to the SIO from twenty-nine years ago. A proper old-school thug. Our side got heavy with Sturridge when Jayne went missing, and he has the same solicitor now, Raymond Cowper. They don't forget that kind of thing. Mr Cowper took me aside after our first interview with his client to make sure we're playing everything by the book. I did get one useful thing from the old SIO, though: he was adamant that Matthew Sturridge is an irredeemable liar, living in a world of fantasy. I don't know how he reached that conclusion, but it's something we should bear in mind when we're considering what Sturridge has told us. Even if he's an innocent bystander in all this, we shouldn't assume he's a reliable witness.'

He stood, stretched, then straightened his suit. 'Thanks, Aisha. Did you find anything on the opal ring?'

'Nothing. No unique identifiers on it. I don't think it was expensive, or particularly special.'

'Probably got it from a charity shop,' DC Wayne Thompson chipped in. 'Is there anything to convince us there's another victim and that the ring isn't just a bit of frippery bought by a fetishist to dress the finger when he wanted to get off on it? Everyone knows Sturridge has always been a bit weird.'

'Everyone?'

Tommo shrugged, suddenly defensive. 'He's a teacher. Half the town knows him.'

Bolam finally made the connection. Unlike the rest of the team, Tommo had grown up locally. Despite his prematurely balding head and grey fringes, Tommo was only forty. 'You went to the high school?' Bolam asked. 'Did Sturridge teach you?'

Tommo nodded.

'And you've only just thought to mention this?'

Another shrug. 'He probably taught half the town,' Tommo said. He had the tone of a schoolboy caught out.

'So what was he like?' Now wasn't the time to chastise the officer for failing to make the most obvious connections.

'Weird but harmless,' said Tommo. 'That's what I'd have said until all this. Soft-spoken, didn't like to mix with people, always wore a suit…' He stopped, eyeing Bolam, realising that everything he'd said applied to his new DI too. Including the weird but harmless, perhaps.

'Did people like him?'

'He always looked out for people,' Tommo said. 'He had a sensitivity towards kids at risk, as we'd call them now. They were the only people he ever got involved with. He probably turned a few lives around.'

'He was a nice guy.'

'More that he was capable of niceness, if that makes sense. Like he always tried to do good, but it didn't come naturally.'

Bolam wondered if that was the mark of Sturridge's true nature, or of a man trying to cope with a world that had stolen his wife from him without explanation. Was the attempt to force niceness a case of making amends for his actions, or trying to make peace with a world that had done him wrong?

'So what is he?' Bolam said. 'A serial killer – or at least a double killer – who has successfully pulled the wool over our eyes for close to three decades? A one-off wife-killer who's lived with guilt for all this time? An innocent victim who never quite fit with the world? Or something else…'

'We haven't got enough, have we?' said Billie. 'He's going to walk out of here.'

'We've set him free.' Again, Bolam stood in the doorway to DCI McBride's office, with every intention that this should be a brief discussion.

McBride peered up at him, his rounded cheerful features doing little to hide his frustration. 'Perhaps you should never have hauled him in here in the first place,' he said. 'You know as well as I do that every move in this game has to be considered and sure-footed. We can't afford to give the defence easy wins.'

Bolam said nothing. He'd rushed in with Sturridge. Perhaps making a point, perhaps simply thinking he had an easy win in what would be a major case; perhaps trying to impress his new team by making a bold move.

'I got it wrong,' he finally said. He could make all the excuses he liked, but he knew that none held water. He'd allowed himself to get carried away. The irony was that they might even be proved right in the long run, but the solicitor, Cowper, had been allowed to draw his lines in the sand, and any further action in pursuit of Sturridge would be fraught with difficulties.

'I spoke with Raymond Cowper,' McBride said. 'I managed to smooth things over.'

Bolam recalled how Cowper had summoned him down to the station reception, the way the old solicitor had proved himself to be the master of the friendly warning. McBride might well believe that he'd smoothed things over, but it had almost certainly been on Cowper's terms, and passing this warning on to Bolam was a part of that.

'We all get things wrong occasionally,' McBride said now. 'Don't beat yourself up.' He was trying to be nice, even though it didn't really suit him.

'But we can't afford to get it wrong, can we?' said Bolam. 'The consequences are far too great.'

'No, but we learn. Even at my age, we learn. And we have to remind ourselves why we're in this: to make a difference.'

'I interviewed one of my predecessors today,' Bolam said. 'A DI Bulmer. It's people like him that got me into this job.'

'An inspiration?'

Bolam grunted a short laugh. 'Not exactly. I was eighteen, a student. Wrong place, wrong time, and all that. I was picked up in an assault investigation in Newcastle and the investigating officer took a dislike to me because I was different – an oddball with an answer for everything. He tried his best to bully a false confession out of me even though I was clearly not their man.'

McBride stayed silent for a few seconds, clearly trying to work out where to go from here. Finally, he said, 'So you joined up because you thought you could make things better?'

Bolam was shaking his head already. 'No, nothing so noble. I joined up because I was puzzled. Why do people like that cop, or DI Bulmer, or any of the other bad apples, join up? Why do they want to right wrongs when they're so wrong themselves in the first place? People are such complicated sets of contradictions like that: good people who do bad, bad people who are still capable of doing good. They confuse me, and they fascinate me, and doing this job is the best way I've found to try to work them out.'

He stopped, surprised at himself. He'd never really thought of it in those terms before, but he knew he'd always struggled to understand the people around him, to put himself into their heads, their perspectives on the world. So what he'd done was study them closely, and that's exactly why that incident had made him want to join the force. The job was his way of trying to understand people – by unravelling the triggers and motivations of the broken and contradictory ones, the bad who are capable of doing good and the good who sometimes do bad.

'Do you think you came back too soon?' McBride said.

The words conveyed much more: not simply come back to work after Fran's illness and death, but come *here* to this new job in Fran's home town. And more: while asking if Bolam thought he might have rushed back too soon, it was clear that McBride was asking himself the same question. Had appointing Bolam to lead this new team been a mistake?

For once, he didn't work late.

After leaving McBride's office, he went down to his own, gathered up his grey trench coat and left, without even checking his computer for messages.

Outside, he paused on the pavement. Traffic rushed past. Gulls screeched from the rooftops.

He could just leave. He could walk away from all this and go back up to the Northeast to live off his savings until he worked out what to do next.

What would it be like not to do this any more? Not to have his head filled with all the what-ifs and the mostly irrelevant detail of the cases he was investigating? What would he do, if he didn't do all this?

He waited for a gap in the traffic and crossed, and then he dipped his head down and walked away from the station, trying to convince himself that this might be possible.

That he could walk away from it all forever.

9

Whitesands High School was on Blacksmith's Lane. From the top you could see past the houses to the bay, the school grounds spreading out to the right. Russell Shaw had made this walk a million times before, or so it seemed to him.

It must be lunchtime because kids in uniform were milling about outside the gates, several quite openly smoking. When Russ had attended this school no one would dare smoke in the open like this, but judging by the occasional adult coming and going the teachers didn't seem to care.

The kids looked smarter than in Russ's day, in blazers, white shirts and ties striped at a slant in the school's colours of black, white and deep maroon, rather than the almost universal polo shirts and jersey sweaters of the past.

One group of young teens was staring at him, pointing. He kept walking. He didn't want to hear what they were saying. Kids could be cruel. But then, so too could adults.

The school itself didn't look much different, apart from a new sports centre where a car park had been. For three years he'd started every school day in a classroom overlooking that car park and – far too often – ended the day there, too, in detention for one misdemeanour or another. He hadn't been the easiest of kids, he supposed, but Mr Sturridge had helped him and his sister Liz, and detentions had been replaced by after-school clubs and the Joint Forces Cadets, and then the Army had sorted him out. Before it had broken him, that is.

He'd paused to stare through the chain-link fence, and now that group of adolescents was pointing again, talking and laughing. He didn't like to think what he must look like, in his filthy clothes, his patchy stubble that was not quite a beard, the bundle of spare clothing tucked under his arm.

He glared at them and they fell silent.

He looked away. If he carried on like this, he'd be getting a reputation – the mad man who stared at people in the town and hung around the school gates. He looked down at himself. He'd only been out one night, but it must be obvious that he'd been sleeping rough. When he was a kid they'd called them tramps, but now it would be *homeless* or *rough sleeper*. It was the same thing though. The scary man who didn't fit. The bogeyman.

He walked to the bottom of Blacksmith's Lane before anyone could challenge him. The road here went straight ahead past the playing fields and holiday camp to the beach, with options heading left through a new housing estate, or right, back towards town.

He chose right, and after a short time houses on his left gave way to St Katherine's church, the graveyard packed tight with headstones and plaques.

The churchyard nearest the road was unkempt but clearly looked after, with paths mown through the grass branching away from the main gravelled path between the lychgate and church entrance. The graves themselves were untended and overgrown, though, most of them dating back to the early twentieth century, at least.

Russ followed the path around the church to the rear, where the newer graves lay. Here the grass was trimmed bowling-green neat, the headstones smaller, fresh flowers in metal holders by the graves.

He walked along the rows, reading the names, recognising none. A woman squatted on her haunches by one grave, plucking dying flowers out of a bunch, trimming the grass with small spring-loaded hand shears like oversized scissors. She looked up at Russ as he passed, her initial hostile expression replaced in an instant by one of sympathy, curiosity.

What had she read in Russ's face?

'Looking for someone, darling?' she said, rocking back on her heels, straightening.

'Shaw,' he told her.

She shook her head, apologising that she didn't know anyone of that name – as if she might reasonably be expected to know the names of all who lay here – then returned to trimming a few grass stems that were a millimetre or two too long.

He found the grave by a high rendered wall separating the yard from a neighbouring garden.

Elizabeth. Dead a few months before her thirtieth birthday, seventeen years ago. His kid sister had been more like a mother to Russ at times. Rock solid. When he'd come out of the Army she'd let him move into her spare room. She'd kept him in food and spending money while he retrained for civilian life through a charity scheme, updating his Medical Corps skills to prepare him for life as a paramedic. She'd always been there for him, even through the worst of it.

Until one day one of Nurse Ward's predecessors had told him the news.

The small headstone didn't say anything more than name and dates. It didn't say who she'd left behind – only Russ – and it didn't say why she had died so tragically young, that she had no longer been rock solid, no longer able to be the strong one for her big brother.

No one had tended this grave and the grass was long, ivy spreading over the stone. When he pulled some of the vegetation away he saw that what he had taken for natural discolouration was, in fact, paint. Years ago someone had vandalised his sister's grave, sprayed it with red paint that had mostly turned a deep brownish hue now. And no one had made more than a cursory effort to clean it up. One corner of the stone was broken away, which must have taken some considerable force.

Whatever had happened here had occurred many years ago, an anger that had faded like the marks it had made, gone to almost nothing. This place had moved on.

Russ pulled at the ivy, doing his best to clear the stone, the letters that spelled out his sister's name.

'Here.'

The woman looming over him, silhouetted in the harsh spring sunlight. Holding the small shears out to him.

He stood, backed away, unable to meet her look, his eyes watering from that harsh sunlight.

Out, through the gate at the back of the churchyard he came to an alleyway. He staggered partway along here, and then he remembered an incident in this alley, a young woman, her face smeared with blood, her eyes wide and staring. He'd helped her, he realised… the young woman. It had been a call.

And the worst thing was that moment, that second or two, when all he had in his head was the image of the terrified, beaten young woman and not knowing why he'd seen her like that, not remembering that it was from when he'd been a paramedic and it was his job to rescue and protect, to save.

He walked on the beach, his head spinning. Hating the images, the memories. Hating the way everything jumbled up so that he struggled to place things and people and events, so that even the *good* things were all mixed up with the bad, and it was impossible even to focus on the nicer memories with Elizabeth because they were tainted by the knowledge of the dark place her association with him had taken her. To be the cause of your own sister's suicide… how could anyone ever deal with something like that?

That was when a rush of panic threatened to swamp him. His bag… It wasn't just a few clothes and personal documents he'd lost with that bag: it was the few precious blister strips of amisulpride, ethosuximide, diazepam and bedranol. His chemical friends, who had calmed the barrage in his head. He'd only had supplies for a week or so, but Nurse Ward had said that once he had somewhere to stay the local mental health team would get him more.

But now…

He climbed the steps back up to the promenade. There were a few people here – a couple with a big black dog, a bent-over old man dragging a walking stick behind him, a lunchtime jogger in skin-tight Lycra.

He came to a café – not the cheap and cheery café as he remembered it from years ago, but now it was more upmarket, with lots of greenery inside and a long bottle-lined bar along one wall.

He paused to peer inside to where a few people sat at tables. Smartly dressed, chatting and laughing and raising wine glasses. A life like that was beyond his imagination. It really was another world.

In one corner, two men sat. One was a compact individual, small of build, dapper in a dark blue three-piece pinstripe suit, his head shaved to near-black stubble that continued down his jaw; when he glanced across to the window, his eyes were the most piercing blue. And the other man…

Russ shrank back into the shadows. He studied the man's features to be sure. So much time had passed. It was more the mannerisms than the face that convinced him, the over-expansive gestures, the toss of the head like a drama student trying too hard to emote, the eyes, always watching, studying.

The man was a part of his past, a lawyer. He'd defended Russ at trial and, years later, he'd visited him at the Rodgers-Stephenson Institute. Pastoral care, he'd said. Something to do with the council and a local group maintaining an interest in his case, and his welfare. But his presence had merely stirred over things best forgotten and simply seeing him here was doing unpleasant things inside Russ's skull. Like something crawling through his thoughts.

He turned away, made himself move.

He needed those meds. Needed something… *anything* that would throw that smothering blanket over the workings of his mind and deaden the world around him.

The old man with the stick was staring now, but Russ didn't care. He just had to get away from here, find his bag.

He half-walked, half-ran along the promenade until, exhausted and gasping painfully for breath, he came to the overgrown embankment where the gun emplacements lay part-concealed, the Martello tower looming beyond.

He retraced his steps as best he could, but it was hard to be sure exactly where he had been, fleeing dogs and voices and harsh lights.

He came to the small clearing where the Kurdish couple had camped out, but their tent was gone, and so were they.

He found the hollow against the base of one emplacement where he thought he had settled, but there was nothing. He followed a rough track through the brambles, but nothing.

Then he went down to the beach, in case he had dropped the bag in his panicked escape rather than merely abandoned it where he had been trying to sleep, but he found nothing.

And now he realised that at some point in his panic to get back here and find his meds he had dropped the bundle of spare clothing.

He had sunk so low, and even then had managed to lose what little he had remaining.

10

Bolam had been in the office since six this morning, going over case notes, trying to work out what they had missed, what might connect it all into a coherent narrative. He would never be able to live with himself if he walked away from all this, and he'd known that to be the case the night before when he had marched purposefully away from the station, McBride's doubting words rattling around inside his head.

Now it was lunchtime and he paused in the doorway of the Crab Pot Bistro.

Gordon Rowe looked no different. The same floppy sandy hair as Fran, the same pale green eyes. The same tendency to over-emphasise everything with the wave of a hand or the toss of a head. All the mannerisms Bolam had loved in Fran, but felt vaguely disturbed to see in another.

Gordon spotted him, made to stand, then stopped himself and sat again.

As Bolam lowered himself into the seat opposite, Gordon raised his wine glass, tipping it slightly so that the dark red contents almost spilled – every move exaggerated – and said, 'I suppose you won't?'

Bolam shook his head. 'I can't stay long,' he said. 'Nothing personal. I just—'

'I know, I know,' Gordon said, dismissing the half-apology with a backwards wave of one hand. 'Raymond has told me all about it.'

'Raymond?' Then Bolam made the connection he should have made far sooner. Cowper and Rowe. Matthew Sturridge's solicitor, Raymond Cowper, was the eponymous partner in Gordon Rowe's law firm.

'I thought you should know,' Gordon said, 'that I asked Raymond to come out of semi-retirement to help with the Matthew Sturridge debacle, because if I'd taken it on, as Matthew requested, I knew it would complicate matters for you.'

And by making sure Bolam knew, Gordon had just recomplicated it all. It was a talent some people had: to draw your attention to something by making sure you knew they were *not* drawing attention to it.

Gordon took a big swallow of his wine, then sat back, licking his lips with a tongue that always seemed too big for his mouth. Bolam reminded himself to stop finding so many ways to dislike his brother-in-law. Apart from anything else, it was far too easy.

'Debacle?' he said, as he reached for the menu.

'Not my place to pass comment,' Gordon said, raising both hands, palms out, in front of himself, as if to push the case away.

Bolam waited.

'But Matthew *Sturridge*? The poor man's been through so much. He must be, what, eighty or so? Talk to anybody who remembers him from the school. He was your caring, pastoral-minded teacher long before that kind of thing became trendy and wrapped up in Leftie ideology. He turned people's lives around.'

'Good people do bad things sometimes.'

Gordon leaned forward, and slowly raised his eyebrows. 'Really? That's the best you can offer up?' Then he leaned back, and gave a short laugh, tossing his head so that the hair flew.

Bolam looked down at the table. He hated to see Fran's mannerisms like that.

'How are you settling in?' Gordon asked. 'How are you coping? We should have done this long before now.'

Bolam hadn't seen him since Fran's funeral, a little over four months ago. Hadn't spoken to him since a brief phone call a couple of weeks before moving here. *Why?* Gordon had wanted to know, and Bolam hadn't been able to explain why he was still making the move. *Because we'd planned to* seemed feeble and, he knew, misleading. In truth, he'd taken a call from a member of DCI McBride's admin team the morning after the funeral, the caller unaware of the circumstances and assuming the move was still on – and Bolam had paused, then said yes, and continued to make arrangements as if nothing had changed. It had taken no thought at all.

But now… Why had he ever thought moving to Fran's home town alone would turn out well?

He realised he hadn't answered, and pretended he'd been studying the menu. 'I'm fine,' he finally said. 'I'm coping fine.'

Gordon's look made it clear that he didn't believe this for a moment.

'You were good together, you and Fran. I always said that.'

Gordon had told Fran it was the biggest mistake possible to commit to a life with a senior detective, because home life would only ever come second to the job. He'd told her that was only a cliché because it was true, and he'd even had the statistics to hand.

Of course, Gordon didn't know Fran had immediately told Bolam her brother had said all this, didn't know they'd laughed about it and had a recurring conversation about to what degree Gordon Rowe was an over-protective older brother, how much a control freak with a finger in the lives of everyone around him, and how much simply a dick.

'Do they do sandwiches?' Bolam asked. He wasn't hungry, and he wanted something he could take away with him if, by any good fortune, he had to leave this lunch early.

His brother-in-law gave a flamboyant wave of the hand to get attention from the waitress, and said, 'The light lunch menu.' He didn't even make eye contact with the girl.

Bolam caught her eye and smiled a thank you, hoping she picked up on the subtext too, although he was sure she'd already reached her own conclusions about Gordon Rowe.

He caught himself. He'd known Gordon for fifteen years, and still hadn't worked out why he got under his skin so easily.

'You okay in the house? I could put some feelers out if you're looking to buy. I'm very well-connected around town.'

Bolam was living in a modest rented terraced house in the old part of town that Gordon had found for them.

'It's lovely, thanks.' Three months, and the place was about as personalised as his office.

'There's the first release of apartments at the Martello tower redevelopment coming up soon,' Gordon told him. 'I could pull some strings.'

'Thanks, but I'm fine.'

Gordon repeated the palms out, pushing away gesture.

They chose food – a minute steak and shoestring fries for Gordon, a club sandwich for Bolam.

'You really should take up our offer, you know,' Gordon said. 'A break would do you the world of good.' Gordon and Maria had a boat on the Norfolk Broads, and at the funeral they'd told Bolam he could use it whenever he needed to escape.

'Thanks,' said Bolam. 'But… new job and all that.'

Their food came, interrupting a growing, and awkward, silence.

Bolam usually knew how to be good with people, but he had no idea what to talk about with Gordon. He didn't want to ask about work, or any of Gordon's numerous activities with the council, the Rotary Club, or any of his other pet causes, because he knew the answers would be long and full of unnecessary detail, and without Fran he really didn't have to try to like the man any more. He asked about the family instead, but as always Gordon skipped over his wife and his son with superficial answers as if they were only a minor part of his life.

'How's Luke doing at school?' Bolam pressed. 'He must be thinking about what comes next? What does he want to do?'

Gordon shrugged. 'He's fifteen,' he said, as if that were answer enough. 'They don't exactly communicate much at that age, do they?'

Now it was Bolam who shrugged. 'Fran and I…' he said. 'All that never quite happened for us.' They'd tried for a time, and later had never acknowledged to each other that failure might have been the best outcome. He supposed it wasn't only fifteen-year-olds who had trouble communicating.

'You should have,' Gordon said, tone-deaf as ever. 'Fran had enough caring for both of you.'

Movement outside one of the big picture windows caught Bolam's eye. A man, hunched over, hurrying away. From the look of him, a rough sleeper. Bolam had been surprised at the scale of the issue in a small town like this, but he supposed because it was a port, with big industrial docks, it was perhaps the kind of place people gravitated towards and then, after a time, found that they had stayed.

Gordon had caught the direction of his look, and gave a toss of the head that Bolam first took to be dismissive.

'We do what we can,' Gordon said. 'To help, you know. But it's a veritable drop in the ocean. Your lot moving them on doesn't help. Like last night.'

Bolam had heard about the operation to move rough sleepers on from the old War Department land last night, but it could hardly be described as 'his lot' moving them on. It had been a private action by landowners and the police involvement had been minimal, and just enough to ensure there was no breach of the peace. But, of course, Bolam couldn't say this out loud, and his brother-in-law knew it.

'Not your fault, of course,' Gordon said. 'We do some work with a local landlords' group, and they want to clear up the area around the Martello tower development. I think someone pulled a few strings to get your boys along to look more threatening. It was an impossible situation for them.'

Immediately Bolam chastised himself for misjudging Gordon yet again.

Just then, Bolam's phone rang. He slipped it from his jacket pocket, shrugged an apology, and answered.

'Boss,' said Billie Grayson. 'You said to call just after one-thirty. Not on the stroke, so I assume you don't want it to look pre-planned. So here I am.'

Bolam shrugged again and covered the phone with a hand. 'Sorry,' he said to Gordon, who immediately raised his hands – no apology required. Then, into the phone, Bolam said, 'Thanks, Billie. I'll be back in soon.'

He rang off. 'My DC,' he said. 'Keeping me on my toes. They can spare me for another twenty minutes, though.' He'd planned to slip away as soon as Billie called, but in a moment of generosity he decided to give his brother-in-law a little more time.

Gordon sliced at his steak, stared at the piece as if to make sure it was dead, then stuffed it into his mouth. Bolam could tell he didn't believe him about the call, and had guessed it was prearranged.

'Look, Gordon,' he said. 'I'm sorry. I should have been in touch. I should have been around to see you and Maria and Luke. I just…'

He felt guilty. Since the funeral he'd discovered that he no longer had to explain anything – just say a few half-formed sentences and let the words trail away. It wasn't a deliberate ploy, but sometimes it just came out like that, and he knew he occasionally took advantage.

Gordon reached across the table and squeezed his forearm, and Bolam used all his willpower not to flinch. He had never been a hugger or toucher.

'It's okay, bro,' Gordon said. He spoke like that sometimes, so down with the kids that even Bolam cringed. 'It's not easy. And it's not going to come any easier any time soon.'

'I talk to her, you know.' He hadn't confessed this to anyone, and didn't understand why he suddenly felt the need to share with Gordon. 'When I'm alone – out walking, or in the house.'

Gordon studied him closely before saying, 'And does it help?'

Bolam shrugged. 'Who knows? It just happens.' He felt stupid saying any of this out loud. Until this moment, he hadn't even admitted to himself that those times when he caught himself muttering as he walked he had not been talking to himself, but rather saying the things he might once have said to Fran.

Gordon tossed his fringe and laughed. 'You only need to worry when she starts talking back. Until then, just do what you need to do. We all had to find ways to cope, you know.'

Bolam nodded. Gordon had lost his sister, after all. They both had to grieve.

Bolam's mobile rang, breaking the moment. He took it out and saw that it was Billie again. He frowned. The first call had been a prearranged escape plan, but they'd not said anything about a follow-up.

'Sorry,' Bolam said again, waving his phone, then pressing Accept. 'Billie?'

'Boss, sorry. This is a real one this time. You need to get back here straight away.'

He was standing already, pushing his chair out with the backs of his knees.

'What is it, Billie?'

'There's another one,' she said. 'Another finger in the post. And, just to complicate things, I think you know the recipient.'

Bolam shrugged an apology at Gordon Rowe, gathered his club sandwich and wrapped it in a paper napkin, then headed out into the bright spring sunshine.

11

'I'm sorry, but we don't take self-referrals.'

The woman sitting across the desk from him was middle-aged, wearing a collarless jacket and a geometrically patterned headscarf. She spoke with an accent – East European, perhaps – and she had kind eyes, betrayed by the standoffish tone of her voice. She must see people like Russ all the time. Must be used to their wiles and their erratic responses, wary of them even though she had chosen this role, wanted to help.

'Self-referral?' he said. He didn't know what she meant.

'Walk-ins. You can't just come in off the street and get a place.'

'I thought that's what you did.' It was a homeless shelter, after all. A hostel for people exactly like Russ, whose only option was to walk in off the street.

That kindness spread from her eyes to the brief smile she gave now. Perhaps she had decided he was not going to be a threat. 'It is, but we can only take clients referred by the council or through social services,' she explained.

'I went to the council yesterday,' Russ said. 'They were the ones who said to come here.'

'Ah, that's better. Do you have any paperwork? A reference number?'

Russ shrugged. 'She just said you'd help.' He felt useless. Out of his depth. And annoyed that he felt like this simply because he had to deal with officialdom.

'Are you in the system?'

How would he know? But he said nothing, stared at his shoes, before tucking his feet under his chair. The office was cramped. The woman must be able to smell him. But then also, she must be used to that.

'Where have you been staying?' she asked. 'Before you came here?'

'I was at the beach last night,' Russ said, wondering how much he should say, how much of what he recalled had even been real. 'By the Martello tower. But—'

'Ah yes,' the woman said. 'There are certain elements in the council who think a problem is solved if it's moved on…'

So he hadn't imagined the raid, then. He supposed he should find that reassuring, even if it did mean the world was against him in yet another way.

'Before then?'

'I…' Again, the struggle with mental calculations in a brain that was off kilter. How much to say? 'I was in the Army,' he told her. 'Five years.'

'You're a veteran? Recently discharged?'

He shook his head. 'Twenty-one years ago. I… I've been in hospital.'

The woman was trying not to let her frustration show now. She clearly didn't see how he could have been in hospital for two decades. 'Which hospital?' she asked, tapping at her keyboard to wake her computer from rest.

'The Rodgers-Stephenson Institute in Cambridge.'

She tapped at her keyboard, then glanced up at him. 'With a D and a P-H?'

He nodded. The Rodgers-Stephenson Institute was a high-security psychiatric hospital.

He didn't try to smile, because he knew that was just as likely to come across as a deranged grimace. He didn't try to meet her look, because that might seem confrontational. Instead, he sank back into his plastic chair, trying to look as unthreatening as possible.

'I'm fine,' he said. 'I'm on medication.' The medication he no longer had. 'I was told to come here and I just need somewhere to sleep tonight and then I'll be gone.'

When he looked up he saw a man filling the doorway to the office, leaning casually against the frame. He had a thick beard, his hair tied back in a ponytail, and an easy, reassuring smile. Did the receptionist have some kind of panic button that had summoned this man, or had he just looked in by chance?

'All okay, Eleni?'

She nodded. 'This gentleman,' she said. 'He needs somewhere for tonight, but I've explained we don't take self-referrals. He's an Army veteran, and he's had—' she smiled awkwardly at Russ, as if apologising for saying this out loud '—psych issues. He's just out of hospital.'

The bearded man was shaking his head already. 'You serve your country, eh?' he said. 'And this is what you get. Listen, Eleni's right: we can't just take people in off the street. You know what it's like out there. We're a tiny charitable trust, run mostly by volunteers, and we're full to capacity every night as it is.'

Russ thought of the rough sleepers around the Martello tower. He should have known there would be no places.

'There's a new scheme, though,' the man said. 'Supported living. Let me take your details and see what we can do. Army veteran with – what? PTSD? I reckon you meet a lot of the criteria. Let's see what we can do for you, eh?'

The man – Stewart – took his details, and didn't press about why Russ had been at the Rodgers-Stephenson. They gave him a warm meal, and he watched a football match on TV in the common room with other residents and volunteers. And then, with a wink and a smile as the room emptied for lights out, Stewart said to Russ, 'Officially we're at capacity, but just for tonight I'm not counting heads, so if an extra person were to grab a blanket and a pillow from the storeroom and hunker down on that sofa, I probably wouldn't notice at all.'

Russ studied the man's features closely, trying to be sure he understood, and still unwilling to accept that finally, for once at least, his luck might just have turned.

He woke on a sofa that sagged in the middle where the frame gave way, and was too short for his lanky form. His neck and shoulders ached from the way he'd had to lie. His lower back, too, from the way he'd had to twist to draw his legs up a little. At some point in the night the blanket had slipped to the floor, and the chill of the air had frozen the kinks and aches into his body.

It was the best night's sleep he'd had in a long time.

He stood, and was stretching just as a woman walked in from what Russ guessed was the kitchen. Her hair was grey and cropped short, she wore big glasses with pink frames, and her denim dungarees were covered with an apron.

She smiled, crossed to the storeroom, then glanced back at Russ. 'Give me a hand?' she said. With a nod she indicated two trestle tables, and Russ hurried across to help her get them out and set them up.

'Breakfast,' she said. 'You hungry?'

He nodded. He didn't know where the next meal would come from after this.

Nobody spoke much at breakfast. Four men and four women hunched over plates of beans on thick, heavily buttered toast; fried eggs with yolks as hard as ice hockey pucks; big mugs of sweet, milky tea.

Russ concentrated mostly on his meal, just occasionally glancing up to check out the shelter's residents. He didn't know if they were all new to this place like him, or if they were here on more of a long-term basis. Ages ranged from about twenty through to an old man with wispy white hair, yellowed eyes and no visible teeth, who might have been anywhere from sixty to ninety.

Russ found that his attention kept returning to that old man. The skin of his scalp was a mosaic of liver spots and other discolourations. The whites of his eyes were stained yellow, and Russ suspected decades of liver abuse taking their toll. He wondered both how a man could end up in such a position at his age, but also how he had survived to *reach* such an age.

This curiosity about the workings of the world around him was unfamiliar, as if a part of Russ's brain was wakening from a long slumber. Back at the Rodgers-Stephenson Institute, perhaps that had been part of the management regime: keep everyone subdued so that they could be more easily managed.

Maybe losing his bag – and his meds – had been a good thing, after all. If his senses and perception sharpened up even a little he might find it easier to make sense of this modern world in which he found himself.

After breakfast, the residents lingered at their tables, eking out the last dregs of that oversweet tea. Russ sensed that they were old hands at this, that they understood that when the meal was over the tables would be put away and they would be sent on their way, out into the cold hostility of another day.

Sure enough, when one of the younger men finally stood, the others followed suit, and still without a word spoken they shuffled through to the sleeping quarters to gather their things.

Russ had nothing, and he had already straightened the sofa, folded his blanket with military precision and placed it with the thin pillow back on its shelf in the storeroom.

The men and women reappeared in coats and hats, a couple of them carrying bags.

Russ made to follow them out, but then Stewart appeared in another doorway. Had he been here all along? Russ hadn't noticed him arriving.

'Russell,' he said, waving Russ across and into the small office. Filing cabinets lined one wall, and a mad array of notes on scraps of paper was pinned to a board on another wall. Stewart perched himself on the edge of the solitary desk rather than sitting behind it, and Russ sat in one of the ubiquitous plastic chairs. He knew the man was trying to be friendly by sitting like this, rather than having the desk as a barrier, but all it meant was that Russ was peering up at him, and the light haloed around the man's head made it feel like an interrogation.

'Sleep okay?' asked Stewart.

Russ nodded. He hadn't spoken a word yet today, and wondered what strange twist of his brain had stopped him from doing so. Again, he was unaccustomed to that sense of curiosity about anything, let alone the workings of his own mind.

'Listen, Russell, I've got some good news. You know that scheme I told you about yesterday? Supported living for people in a number of need categories. Well, I made a few calls after we spoke, and again first thing today. It turns out that you do score lots of points in the various categories, and I spoke to a couple of our steering group members to brainstorm possibilities for you.'

Russ studied the man. He wasn't sure what he was supposed to take from this, what 'scoring lots of points' translated to in the real world. But he didn't want to betray his ignorance by asking.

Stewart smiled. 'This all means that you're a priority housing case for the scheme, Russell. The downside of that is that there's far more need than supply at the moment.'

Finally, Russ spoke. 'So… I qualify for something that's not available?' He still didn't understand why the man seemed so pleased with himself.

Stewart nodded. 'You do, which would, of course, be a bad thing, except I made another call this morning. One of our trustees has access to local properties and takes a special interest in cases like yours, Russell – indeed, on several occasions he's mentioned Army veterans, mental health and fresh starts all in the same breath. So between us we've managed to get our ducks in a row on your behalf, and the short version is that the Trust has been granted the use of an additional bedsit, which we can make available for you right now. You have somewhere to stay, Russell, somewhere you can make a fresh start.'

The bedsit was a few minutes' walk from the shelter, still in the older part of town where narrow streets jostled for space between the North Sea-facing bay and docks sheltered in the estuary. It occupied the upper floor of a three-storey terraced house that had been converted into flats.

Stewart pointed up at a dormer window that protruded from the roof and said, 'That's yours, Russell.'

They paused before the steps, on the narrow strip of paved front garden, only a couple of metres deep. 'Here.' Stewart handed Russ a bunch of two keys, one with a plastic cover labelled 'FRONT DOOR' and the other labelled '14C', which was the number of the bedsit. 'Welcome home.'

Russ took the keys, approached the front door, checked that he'd selected the right key, and slid it home.

The door opened onto a small cubby area. One door labelled '14A' opened off it, with a staircase up to the left. They went up the stairs to a small landing, past 14B, and up the final flight of stairs that simply had the door of 14C at the top. Standing awkwardly on the top step, Russ fumbled the key into the lock, pushed, and stepped into his new accommodation.

It was small, and felt smaller because of the way the roof sloped in from front and back. It was also empty: no furniture, no bed, nothing.

Stewart indicated a door set into the far wall, and said, 'It's even en suite!' Then he added, as if now that he'd spoken he had to continue to fill the silence of the place, 'And don't worry. The place wasn't even going to be made available for a few weeks, so nothing much has been done – that's why it all looks so plain and unfinished. We can get someone in to give it a lick of paint, or even better, we'll supply you with brushes and some paint and you can do it yourself. And we have access to a used furniture warehouse, so we'll kit you out. Really, it's not as bad as it… Russell, are you okay? It's really not as bad as…' He ended with a shrug.

Russ realised his face was wet, and now he shook his head, and said, 'No, it's not that. It's… It's *perfect*.'

12

Bolam had walked to the Crab Pot Bistro, but now he wished he'd driven. He wished also that Billie had told him more over the phone, but then he reminded himself that he was the one who'd hung up in his haste to get back to the station.

He dropped the club sandwich into a bin. Lunch was for people with normal jobs.

A few minutes later, as he paused on the pavement in the town centre, waiting to cross, a slate-grey Ford Focus pulled up and the driver leaned across to open the door.

'Sir? I thought this'd be quicker.'

'Thanks, Aisha.' Bolam lowered himself into the passenger seat and the car was pulling away into the flow of traffic before he'd shut the door. Behind them, a horn sounded.

'Tell me,' Bolam said, clicking his seatbelt home.

'It's almost the same as the first one,' Aisha told him. 'C5 Jiffy bag, handwritten address this time, no postage.'

'And a finger.'

'Slim, Caucasian, looked-after nails. No ring this time. Neatly amputated at the metacarpophalangeal joint again – a complete finger.'

Bolam noted that she was being careful in her description, no assumption that the finger was female. 'And Billie says I know the recipient?' Bolam didn't know many people here, apart from those he encountered in a professional capacity.

Aisha glanced at him.

'Was that Gordon Rowe you met for lunch?' she asked.

It was no secret who Bolam had been meeting: in his online diary he'd put 'Gordon, lunch' with the location set as the Crab Pot Bistro, and the team had access to his appointments. It wouldn't have taken much to work out that 'Gordon' must be Gordon Rowe, his brother-in-law. If it had been a different Gordon, he'd have included a surname, for starters.

'It was,' Bolam confirmed. 'It's his firm that are representing Matthew Sturridge, and Gordon was gently making sure I was aware of that.' And at the same time, no doubt, digging for any more information Bolam might divulge – either openly, or by accident.

'The finger was reported by Gordon Rowe's wife, Maria.'

Bolam stared at his DS. It wasn't often that he was completely thrown like this. *Maria*? And Gordon had said nothing. 'When?'

'The call came through about half an hour ago.'

That made sense, then. Gordon wouldn't even know yet, unless he'd taken a call in the few minutes since Bolam had departed.

'What do we know?'

'Not much more than I've already told you,' Aisha said. 'There should be a couple of uniforms at the Rowes' house, and Raj Khatri and Cath Marshall are en route. The envelope was delivered some time this morning, but not opened until around half an hour ago, after which Dr Rowe reported it immediately. We don't know whose finger it is, or anything more, really.'

'How's Maria?' She was a GP, so had seen more than her fair share of medical traumas, but not in her own house.

'Shocked.'

'And Luke?'

'The son? At school. I called to confirm that.' Just to be sure the finger didn't belong to Luke.

They were on the main road now, heading towards the edge of town.

'Sturridge walked out of the station less than twenty-four hours ago,' Aisha said. 'Maybe he's escalating.'

Bolam bit down on his response. DCI McBride's criticisms still rang in his ears and it would be easy to blame the team for fuelling his rush to conclusions about Sturridge, but he knew the decisions had all been his own.

'I don't suppose we have any idea of Sturridge's movements since we let him go yesterday, do we?'

'There's no official surveillance,' said Aisha.

A request for approval for directed surveillance was on DCI McBride's desk, but was unlikely to be rushed through. The top brass were increasingly cautious in these matters, and there was no urgency as no one was thought to be in immediate danger – and the DCI had made it clear that they needed to tread carefully around Sturridge and his solicitor.

'But…?'

'He left the station with his solicitor and went straight home. A patrol car passed his house a couple of times yesterday evening and lights were on.'

'And today? Do we know his movements this morning, around the time the envelope was being delivered?'

Aisha shook her head.

So Sturridge could have had time to make the delivery… but why? Doing so now would be sure to put him under the spotlight again. Unless, as Aisha had suggested, the old teacher was spiralling out of control. And if that was the case, then they could only hope he'd be more likely to make mistakes.

They drove on in silence for a while. Bolam knew he would have to address his strained relationship with his Detective Sergeant, if only because he didn't quite understand how it had come about.

It was Aisha who spoke first, though. 'I'm sorry,' she said.

He waited for her to go on.

'For being so defensive before,' she finally added. 'I've always struggled with authority.'

'You picked the right career then.'

She glanced sideways at him, then laughed, and the tension eased a little. 'I blunder in,' she said. 'I think out loud, and I know it bugs you.'

She phrased it as an apology, or at least an explanation, but her tone was almost accusatory, as if Bolam was at fault for having a problem with that.

'I've always had to stand out, though,' she said. 'Just to get noticed. To justify my existence.'

It sounded like a well-rehearsed explanation – in her head, at least.

'I've been looking at your record,' Bolam told her, and now he saw a spark in her eyes – wariness, but also anger, which was good. 'High-flyer. Picked out for great things. You were—'

'I told you. Asian, female, gay. I ticked the right boxes.'

'That's not a fair representation, though, is it?' Bolam said. 'I'm not saying the brass weren't rubbing their hands together when they saw how many labels they could hang around your neck, but when it came down to it, you were singled out because you were bloody good. So what changed?'

He was surprised to see now that she was close to tears. He hadn't expected that.

'It knocks it out of you,' she said, after a long silence. 'All that. I was ambitious. Determined to make my mark. But those labels around your neck, they're like lead weights. They always drag you down in the end. I just got… tired.'

'I'm not dismissing any of that,' Bolam told her. 'But even without the labels, the work we do drags you down.' He'd seen enough good people broken by the job. 'If you need help, there's help available, and if there's anything I can do to support you I will. Because I want that old Aisha back, the one I read about in your file. The one who'd been ambitious and leapt at every opportunity, determined to make her mark.'

She tried to speak, but he raised a hand, cutting her off.

'It's okay to be aware of your weaknesses, Aisha. But don't dwell on them and let them swamp everything else, because they can be your greatest strengths too.'

'How do you mean?'

'I'm crap with people,' Bolam said. 'So I've always had to work at it. I learned to study people more closely and read them – not just in the job, but in life. So now it's one of the things I do best.'

'You jump to conclusions, too,' Aisha said. 'Just like you accuse me of doing.'

'Which is why I'm so aware of it in others. And I've learned to judge when to run with a theory and when to take a step back. I always have to remind myself that we're comparing scenarios, not picking a favourite.'

She smiled, which was good.

'You're an excellent officer, Aisha. You work harder than anyone else on the team and you're known as one of the best interviewers in the eastern counties. As I say, I've read your file, I've spoken to people. You don't have anything to prove to me, and you shouldn't feel that you have anything to prove to yourself.'

'But—'

'Just ask yourself, Aisha: Whose opinion do I look for when I walk into the office? Even when I pick apart what you say, you're the one I look for, because you're the one most likely to say something that will lead us in a new direction.' He hadn't realised this until he said it out loud, but it was true.

He paused, just to let that all sink in, then added, 'Was there anything else?'

They completed the rest of the journey in silence.

Bolam had only been to Gordon and Maria's place on the edge of town a handful of times, yet still that familiarity felt disturbingly corrupted by the fact that now he was here in a very different capacity.

The five-bar wooden gate stood open, two patrol cars and a blue Peugeot pulled up in the wide U-shaped drive next to Maria's silver Audi. As they passed between the gateposts, set into a high brick wall, Bolam realised what had been nagging at the back of his mind: the Rowes had an American-style mailbox on a post, just inside the gate. He didn't know if Gordon had any kind of security cameras – although on a property like this it was likely – but would there be coverage of a mailbox situated, as it was, away from the house?

Instead of going straight to the front door, Bolam walked back down the gravel drive and came to stand by the mailbox. He paused and took a deep breath. A robin sang from a thick bush that loomed over the wall. That wall, and the surrounding trees and bushes, limited the view of the road, and if he had not known there were other houses here they could easily not have been there at all. And he'd been right: any security cameras at the house were unlikely to have anything but the most limited view of the mailbox.

Their culprit was either lucky, or a careful planner and assessor of risks. Was someone like Matthew Sturridge really so aware of modern surveillance technologies?

He chided himself. As she'd rightly pointed out, he was as bad as Aisha for making assumptions, rushing to judgement – just because Sturridge was old and had an antiquated manner, it did not mean he was not a sophisticated operator. Indeed, if he was their man, then he'd avoided detection for decades.

The constable standing at the front door was a young woman Bolam recognised from another case he'd worked on. 'Jackie,' he said to her, 'do you fancy a quick stroll along the street to see if there are any cameras or curtain-twitchers? Just a quick look so you can make a note of what you find – we'll interview potential witnesses later.'

She nodded and hurried away, her feet crunching on the gravel. The houses here were big and expensive and Bolam was sure they would be well kitted out with cameras and other security equipment. But also, they were set back from the road and screened by trees and hedges and high walls. Bolam knew they'd be lucky if there was anything that would have picked up the delivery to Gordon and Maria's mailbox this morning.

Cath Marshall was waiting in the doorway. Bolam indicated the white papery Tyvek scene-of-crime overalls she was wearing and said, 'Do I need to…?'

She shook her head. 'Same as the first one,' she told him. 'Jiffy bag on the kitchen table where our witness dropped it, finger lying beside it. All bagged up now, and on its way to the path lab with Raj. I've left my camera in there so you can see the photos.'

Bolam was impressed with their efficiency, although he'd have preferred to see it in situ. 'And the mailbox?' He knew she wouldn't have neglected that as a crime scene.

'No prints. No footmarks in the ground – gotta love all this gravel. Chris swabbed the mailbox for DNA, although I'm not holding my breath.'

'And Dr Rowe?'

'All yours.'

Aisha was already with Maria. They sat at one end of the big kitchen table, mugs of tea before them, another by an empty chair for Bolam.

Maria looked up when Bolam entered the light, airy kitchen-diner, one end of it open to a large conservatory. She smiled, said, 'Hello, stranger. I wondered what it would take to get you over here.'

'Sorry, Maria. You know how things are. I…'

'Whatever,' said Maria. The trailing-off, unfinished sentence thing cut no ice with her. She'd always seen through him, and he was sure she knew what he and Fran had thought of Gordon.

'Are you okay?'

She nodded. He'd always thought she and Gordon made a peculiar couple. Where Gordon was all flamboyant show and front, Maria was strong, straight, efficient. She was a tall, neat woman – not quite twin set and pearls, but the modern equivalent. If Bolam didn't already know that she was a partner in the local GP practice, it would have been easy to assume she was some kind of prim housewife. Now she sat bolt upright in her chair, head tilted slightly to one side – not bothering with small talk, but simply waiting for Bolam to get started.

Instead, he let Aisha ask the questions.

'Dr Rowe, I know you've already told the first responder what happened, but—'

'Of course,' Maria cut in. 'You'll have your own questions.' She took a sip of her tea. 'I was at the surgery until mid-morning, when I returned here for an early lunch before my afternoon appointments. That would have been about ten-thirty and I collected the morning mail when I arrived, so the item must have been delivered after that.'

'When did you check for mail again?'

'About midday – for some reason I looked down the drive and saw the flag up on the box, which it does when there's some post. I went down there a short time later and found the padded envelope.'

'Where did you open it?'

Maria indicated the table where they sat. 'I had the envelope at an angle and the finger just fell out. I caught it. And then I dropped it.'

She glanced across at Bolam, her matter-of-fact demeanour briefly flickering.

'Did you see anybody when you went to get the mail?' Aisha asked.

Maria shook her head.

'A vehicle in the street, perhaps?' Bolam prompted. 'It's a lovely day, isn't it? Blue sky, birds singing. Does that robin always sing from by your gate?'

She closed her eyes. She seemed to understand what he was doing.

'A bird was singing, yes,' she said. 'It was warm, no breeze. The gate was open because I'd left it that way – it's heavy for me and Gordon never listens when I tell him I can't handle it. No… There was nobody. Not even a passing car.'

'What did you do after you opened the package?' Aisha asked.

'I washed my hands. Silly. I kept glancing back over my shoulder while I was at the sink. I couldn't believe what had just happened, but the finger was still there every time I looked.'

'It's a big shock,' Bolam said. This was the kind of thing that would change Maria's life: she would have dreams and flashbacks, she would forever have a different, undermined view of how the world was and the things people could do to each other.

'After that?' Aisha asked.

'I called 999,' Maria said.

Bolam looked around the kitchen. He'd had dinner here a few times with Fran, Gordon and Maria – and Luke, when he'd been old enough to be allowed to join adult company. The place was stark, functional, everything in its place, and most things put away. It didn't feel like a working kitchen.

He picked up Cath's camera and pressed the image preview button. The screen on the back showed the envelope lying on the kitchen table – the address handwritten in childish capitals which Bolam was sure was an attempt to disguise the writing. He used the *Back* button to look through the other images: the reverse of the envelope, the finger in a plastic evidence bag, the finger lying on the table from various angles.

'The colour...?' Bolam asked. The fingertip was stained yellow and blue.

Maria looked away. 'Paint,' she said. 'I think it was paint.'

Bolam continued to study the photographs.

'How neat was it?' he said, interrupting Aisha as she was about to ask something else.

'Neat?' asked Maria.

'The cut. The amputation. You're a doctor – you'd have noticed.'

Maria gave that flicker of a smile again. She was familiar with Bolam's tangential thinking. He noted that she didn't seem as shocked as she might, in these circumstances, and wondered whether that was simply because, in her profession, she had seen far worse, or if it was that mask she wore in company. He would check on her in a day or two, make sure her trauma wasn't being ignored, as Gordon almost certainly would do.

'It was neat. Clean. Someone had taken the trouble to tidy the wound. But it wasn't surgical – the cuts weren't precise enough. A chef's cut rather than a surgeon's. The paint stains seemed incongruous when everything else was so neat.'

Bolam nodded. He'd thought she would do well on such detail. Raj had reached similar conclusions about the neatness of how the first finger had been amputated.

'Was it fresh? The finger?'

She raised an eyebrow. As far as Bolam was aware, she hadn't been told there was another case, but now he could see her mind rushing, realising he knew more than he was letting on, and therefore that there must *be* more to this.

'It looked fresh,' she said. 'It *felt* fresh when I ... caught it. Do you think she's still alive?'

Bolam exchanged a look with Aisha, who this time had been careful not to leap to any conclusions about the sex of the finger's owner.

'We're considering every possibility,' he told Maria.

'Your question implied that you thought there was a possibility that the finger might have been older…' She paused. 'And… the paint…'

Bolam studied her. Her whole demeanour had changed. What had he missed?

Just as he opened his mouth to speak, he heard the front door thudding open against its stopper, and a voice called, 'Maria? Are you through there? What's going on? Why didn't you call me?'

Gordon.

When he paused in the kitchen doorway, the look – briefly – on Gordon's face when he saw Bolam, was thunderous. Bolam understood immediately: their relationship had always been awkward and now Bolam was sitting in his kitchen, in control of a situation that Gordon knew little about.

Then Gordon raised an eyebrow, spread his arms expansively, palms out, and said, 'Letitia called me from the office. She said something had happened, but she didn't know what. I thought…' He paused, peering around the large kitchen, and then the conservatory, as if concerned there had been a burglary.

Finally, almost as an afterthought, he said, 'Are you okay, Maria? Did something happen to you at the surgery?'

'Maria's fine, Gordon,' Bolam said. 'Sit down.'

Gordon remained in the doorway, his eyes flitting between the people at the table.

'You received a delivery to the house,' Bolam went on. 'A padded envelope containing an amputated finger.'

Gordon had a good poker face, as Bolam knew. It was a skill useful in the courtroom, but even more useful in all those long hours in a police interview room, representing the interests of both the innocent and the thoroughly corrupt. A good lawyer like Gordon gave nothing away.

So now he met Bolam's look, raised that irritating eyebrow again, and said, 'A finger. Who was it addressed to?'

'Just the house,' Bolam told him. 'A handwritten address, block capitals.' None of these were details Maria didn't already know, but he wanted to see if Gordon gave any kind of reaction at all, as his brain rushed to reframe his view of his firm's client, Matthew Sturridge.

He gave nothing, though. His green eyes – the same as Fran's, and Bolam had another jolt of painful recognition – flicked to Maria. 'I'm surprised you didn't call me,' he said to her. 'I'd have come.'

'I called the police.'

Bolam studied the two of them. Had things between them always been so… *taut*?

'We would, of course, have called the police,' Gordon said, waving a hand towards Bolam and Aisha. 'But there are implications, Maria. Given that Cowper and Rowe are already dealing with this case.'

A silence now, Gordon and Maria locked in each other's stares. Then, in a measured tone, Maria said, 'And how, exactly, would I have known *that*, Gordon?'

13

Gordon Rowe had sat down opposite Bolam at the kitchen table now, the gap between him and Maria just enough to emphasise the frosty tension between them.

'Can either of you think of any reason why you might have been targeted in this way?' Bolam asked, having milked that tension for as long as he thought he could get away with.

'Well, forgive me, but I'd have thought that rather obvious, wouldn't you?' said Gordon. 'The Sturridge case. Whoever sent one of these... *packages*... to Matthew has decided to have their fun and games with me, now. Obviously, this puts Matthew in the clear: a victim, just like me.'

There was plenty to unpack in that statement, not least of which was the way Gordon Rowe had no hesitation in using even something like this to push his client's interests, but for now Bolam was content to play the silence again, the tension between the couple.

Maria spoke first. 'Matthew Sturridge has received... the same?' she said.

Gordon nodded. 'Raymond has come back to look after Matthew's interests,' he said. 'I didn't want our family connections to complicate matters.'

'Much appreciated, of course,' said Bolam. 'But you're going to have to deal with those complications at some point. You're a partner in a law firm where you specialise in criminal law and I'm the detective inspector in charge of the local Serious Crimes Unit.'

'Of course.' Gordon gave his engaging smile, and did that pushing away gesture. 'But early days, you know?'

'Earlier, Dr Rowe,' Aisha said, her expression suggesting she was having trouble reading the subtext of all these family tensions, 'when Inspector Bolam asked if, in your medical opinion, you thought the amputated finger was fresh. The possibility that it might not be a recent amputation seemed to mean something to you.'

Bolam nodded. He'd been about to bring the interview back to this, and he was pleased Aisha had seen what he'd seen – that change in Maria's manner. The sense that she'd been about to say something just before Gordon burst in.

'Are you aware of anyone who's missing now?' Aisha went on. 'Or, perhaps, in the past?'

In an abrupt shift from the tensions between the couple, Gordon reached out and put his hand over Maria's. 'Joanna,' he said, addressing his words directly to Bolam. He looked deflated, all the usual exaggerated mannerisms dropped.

'Joanna?'

'Maria's half-sister. Joanna went missing more than twenty years ago.'

Bolam took his work phone from a jacket pocket and searched his files for the list Billie had produced, a summary of any possibly related cases over the past thirty years or so – murders and other unexplained deaths, an abduction, missing persons.

'Joanna Clayton?' he said. Maria's previous surname had been Cooper, he thought, but Gordon had referred to Joanna as a half-sister, which would explain the different surnames and why Bolam had failed to make the connection. Joanna Clayton had gone missing twenty-two years ago, and the brief summary note attached to her name in the file said, *18 years old, JD* – which Bolam took to be shorthand for juvenile delinquent – *soft drugs and breach of the peace convictions, considered a runaway.*

How had he not known this?

'Tell me about Joanna,' he said to Maria.

Gordon made to answer, but then saw the sense in letting his wife speak.

'When I was little my parents split up,' she said. 'My mother – and her children – reverted to her maiden name, Cooper. My father remarried, had kids, and endeavoured to put right all the mistakes he'd made in his first marriage. All the clichés. Joanna was spoilt, and spoiled, and all kinds of trouble. She... she wanted to be an artist. She was doing Art A-level.'

'The paint,' Bolam said.

'But... this sounds trivial, but she kept herself clean. The paint on that finger... She wasn't like that.' Yet still, after all this time she had made the connection as soon as she saw the paint and had realised the finger might belong to Joanna.

So Joanna had either been caught unawares, and unable to clean up, or someone had applied the paint afterwards. Making some kind of point? Making sure Maria would make the connection and know the finger belonged to her sister?

'Was your father still local?' asked Aisha.

She nodded.

'So Joanna went to the local high school,' Bolam said.

Immediately Gordon's grip on his wife's hand tightened – he knew where Bolam was leading. Matthew Sturridge was a teacher who had a reputation for reaching out to pupils leading challenging lives.

'So did most of the town,' Gordon said. 'In case you haven't noticed, this is the kind of place people don't escape.'

Bolam noted the choice of phrase. Did Gordon feel trapped by his life here? By his marriage? It was irrelevant to the current discussion, of course, but it showed the man in a different light. He'd always been somewhat two-dimensional in Bolam's experience.

'Yes,' said Maria. 'Matthew taught Joanna, and he did his best to help her when she went off the rails.'

'Off the rails?'

Gordon spread his hands, tipped his head, then folded one hand over Maria's again. 'She was a party girl,' he said. 'Started with Diamond White and weed in the park when she was barely into her teens and headed downhill from there. We did our best.'

'Gordon was a rock,' Maria told them. The frostiness between the couple seemed to have dissipated now. Perhaps Bolam had over-interpreted. 'He was the strong one when it all fell apart. Joanna had run away to stay with friends before she went for good. She came back after a few days the first two times, but the third time it was Gordon who trawled around all her friends' houses until he found her and brought her back. And then the fourth time…'

'Was there anything suspicious about Joanna's disappearance?' asked Aisha.

Although Bolam sometimes questioned Aisha's general approach to cases, she was excellent at keeping an interview on track, gently pressing and deepening and revisiting. Bolam caught her eye, gave a slight nod.

Maria shook her head. 'She didn't take anything with her, but then she didn't the first three times either. She never made contact again, even though Dad still holds out after twenty years. You don't think…?'

Bolam held her look. He was struggling to make any sense of this case, but if there was a pattern, then it was that Matthew Sturridge had been sent the finger of his long-dead wife, and now they had a second recipient who had a long-missing relative. Now was not the time to state this out loud, for a variety of reasons, but he wasn't going to dodge realities either.

'Can you check the DNA so that we know?' Gordon asked.

'We'll confirm identity of the digit from DNA,' Bolam said. 'We'll push that through, but it will still take at least a couple of days. More likely longer.' Which, of course, Gordon knew, but by putting the question he was forcing Bolam to be the one to say it would take time.

'Your sister had a criminal record, didn't she?' Bolam said to Maria. 'Drug possession, breach of the peace.'

Maria's first reaction was anger that he should be raising this now – as if her sister's character had any bearing on her fate – but then she slumped, understanding.

'Fingerprints,' Gordon said.

Joanna Clayton's prints would be held on IDENT1, the national database, and Bolam suspected that even as they spoke Raj Khatri would be running a print from the severed finger through the system.

'How did I not know any of this?' Bolam said. This couple

had been part of his life for fifteen years. Was he the clichéd copper, alert to the subtlest of clues everywhere but in his own life?

'A lot goes unspoken in families,' Gordon said. 'And it was a private matter, from years before you and Fran became a thing.'

In all these years, they'd never really gone beyond polite conversation and formalities. Lunch today with Gordon at the Crab Pot Bistro had been the closest to casual socialising they'd managed.

Fran had known about Joanna – of course she had – but she'd never thought to mention it to Bolam. Or, rather, she must have thought about the subject, and she had made the conscious decision not to tell him. He could believe it of her that she would do that. That she would respect her brother's privacy: if Gordon and Maria chose not to discuss Joanna, then Fran would never be the one to do so.

But the thought that she had kept such a big secret through all the years they'd been together was quite a disturbing one.

'What time did you go out this morning, Mr Rowe?' Aisha, bringing the interview back on track.

Gordon seemed momentarily thrown to be questioned about his movements, then he shrugged, tossed his long fringe back, and said, 'Seven-thirty. I was in the office before eight, and I left late morning to run a couple of errands before lunch with your inspector here. You can confirm with my PA, Letitia.'

'And when you were leaving this morning did you see anyone in the street, or making deliveries?'

'I told you,' interrupted Maria, 'I checked the mail when I came back at 10.30 and I emptied the box. The delivery must have come after that so Gordon would have seen nothing that was relevant.'

'It's okay, darling,' Gordon said, and his patronising tone earned him a sharp look from his wife. 'They're just constructing a timeline, before and after. Filling in the blanks. Witnesses are never a hundred per cent reliable.' Then, to Aisha, he said, 'I don't recall seeing anyone in the street this morning.'

'And Dr Rowe, you told us there was no one. No phone calls? No visitors?'

'Phone calls? Why do you ask that?'

'Someone might have wanted to check if you were in.'

'Well, there was Rob. He called late morning – I'm sure you can check our telephone records to get the precise time. It was the land line.'

Again, Bolam saw an exchange between the couple, a slip in Gordon Rowe's usually good poker face. Why was he suddenly on edge about what his wife was telling them?

'Rob?' Bolam prompted, still studying them closely.

'Yes, a friend of ours. He said he'd called the office but Letitia had told him Gordon was out for lunch. He said he was hoping to see Gordon while he was in town.'

'Robert Walton,' said Gordon. He clearly knew that Bolam would get there in the end and had decided to save time. 'Jayne Sturridge's brother. As Maria says, he's an old friend. My firm handles some of his business interests.'

Robert Walton. *Robbie.*

Bolam gave nothing away. 'I don't suppose you can tell us what kind of business interests Mr Walton has?' he asked. He'd spoken briefly to Robbie Walton early in this case; Walton had been difficult to contact because he was working night shifts, and when Bolam *had* got through Jayne's brother hadn't seemed very interested in events of nearly three decades ago. Bolam chided himself for mirroring that lack of interest, seeing the man as merely a peripheral player, a family member to be informed and treated sensitively. He was guilty of leaping to conclusions about the man, thinking 'night shifts' probably referred to factory work or similar. Not a man to have the kind of business interests that required legal representation, and he hadn't dug any deeper to find that Walton still had ties to the town.

'Mr Walton is an ambulance call centre controller,' Gordon told him. 'But he is also an astute businessman. He owns properties in the town, and our civil law team handles the legal aspects of that business. He's a good man. He does lots with the Rotary Club and other local charities. I know you have to be conscientious and follow everything up, but you'd really be wasting your time with Robbie.'

'Thank you, Gordon,' Bolam said. 'I can assure you that we won't waste our time with him.'

14

The place was perfect, and even its unfinished nature and lack of furnishings suited Russell Shaw: symbolic of life stripped bare, ready to start over.

Stewart left him with the promise that he'd send someone round with a few basics – a kettle, some teabags, a mattress and some bedding. And later, Stewart had assured him, there would be help with form-filling, support services, finances, getting into the health system, and so on. That was a huge relief, in itself: Russ had been trying not to think about the consequences of falling out of the system – remaining in the care of his local mental health team had been a requirement of his release from the Rodgers-Stephenson, and until that was established he was in fear of a knock on the door at any moment…

Russ stood motionless for some time, watching the play of light from the dormer window, the way it picked out motes of dust hanging in the air.

He considered the sequence of events that had brought him here: the train ticket from the hospital, the confusion when he turned up at the town council office, his muddled wanderings around town yesterday before showing up at the shelter where they'd taken pity on him.

And now this. His luck really had taken a turn.

He felt calm, too. No chaotic noise filling his head, and he felt confident that the world around him was as it seemed – no hallucinations, no seeing things that were not there. No absences since yesterday. Atypical absence seizures, the doctors had called them: not a sign of madness, but of erratic electrical activity in his brain. Bad wiring.

He went to the window, which was set back from a deep sill that was actually a window seat. The road below was lined with cars. On the rooftop opposite, a gull with a pale grey back tipped its head back and screeched. If it was nesting there, it was going to be noisy, Russ thought. Already, his mind was looking ahead, accepting the assumption that he would be here for some time.

He didn't think he'd ever planned to come back to his home town and stay – it had more been a case of confronting demons, getting back into the saddle. But then he hadn't really thought ahead. Now, he didn't know what to think.

He supposed he had always assumed that returning to live in this town could not be an option because of what had happened in the past, but now... the place had an air of having forgotten all about him. He thought of Elizabeth's overgrown grave, the angry graffiti a relic from a long-forgotten time. No one recognised him. No one was watching out for him.

This place had moved on, and so maybe there really was a possibility that he could stay here.

Regardless, at least he had a roof over his head for as long as he wanted to be here.

He went out. It was late morning, and although he only had a few coins in his pocket, it might just be enough for a loaf of bread or a tin of beans. He realised he had no idea how much things cost. Before leaving the Rodgers-Stephenson he'd been taken on a few day trips to help him adjust, but they'd passed in a blur, and none of the details of modern life had stuck. The prices he had seen for sandwiches and chocolate bars at the station had taken his breath away. Maybe he *wouldn't* have enough money for a loaf of sliced white, after all.

He walked to where the street – *his* street – joined a larger road. Here he saw a fish and chip shop, a taxi office and a corner shop that seemed to sell a bit of everything.

The cheapest loaf of bread cost more than the total of his loose change. Even a packet of crisps would use up most of his coins.

The kid at the till, who looked about twelve, was staring at him.

For a moment, Russ held the look, felt a swell of noise in his head, and then he turned away. He must be in a sorry state if even that weedy kid thought he could take him on.

Maybe this was a particularly expensive shop. If he found a supermarket they might have offers, or a clearance shelf for produce nearly out of date. Or bins around the back… He knew there was a big store on the edge of town, but also, unless it had all changed in the intervening years, there should be a Co-Op only a short walk from here.

He must have got confused, though, because he didn't find the Co-Op. Instead, where he thought it should be there was a four-storey block of flats that looked as if it had been there for decades.

He turned a full three-sixty on his heels, trying to work out how he had lost his bearings, and that was when he spotted the road opposite the flats, neat little bungalows with gravelled front gardens punctuated by the occasional dwarf conifer or statuette.

Ginnie Lloyd had lived here, with her parents. That was one thing they'd had in common: moving back in with family. In Russ's case, he'd gone to live with his sister while he found his feet again after the Army; in Ginnie's case it was staying with her parents after a divorce.

Sometimes Russ would pick her up here before a shift, or drop her off afterwards. The first time he'd dropped her off there had been an awkward pause while Russ wondered if he *was* merely dropping her off, or if he would go inside for a coffee and messy, awkward sex that would cause problems for as long as they worked together. Then her old man had appeared at the doorway of one of the bungalows, as if he'd been watching out for her. Ginnie had given Russ a quick smile and thanks, and that had been the only time in the two years they knew each other when the possibility of more than just a working relationship had ever reared its head.

Number six. The front garden immaculate, not a weed in sight; the gravel evenly spread, as if someone tended to it every day to put errant stones back in their rightful places. A spotless white Volvo hatchback sat in the drive to the side of the house, the door where Ginnie's father had appeared that first night.

He should leave. He knew that. He shouldn't be standing here, on the opposite pavement. He should never have crossed from the flats and walked up here to look.

Ginnie…

He closed his eyes and saw red. Dark, dark red.

Opened them again. Was that movement in the front room?

He knew now that while this town gave every impression of having forgotten him, some people would never have that luxury. Would never be able to simply move on.

And also, he knew that the clarity he had regained since inadvertently stopping his meds was a mixed blessing, because now the memories came rushing back. That dark red, the splatter across the ambulance's interior; the way Ginnie had been with him that evening – she'd sensed he was struggling, had tried to be *nice* to him, letting him do the driving and listen to the football so he didn't have to deal with people. For all the good that sympathy had done her…

She'd known he was broken, and still she tried to help.

With a monumental effort of will, he turned away from the neat little bungalow and started to walk. Now, he longed for that smothering blanket that muffled the world around him that his meds gave him, deadening everything. The awakening of his brain was a bad thing, the thoughts rushing through his head…

He knew he must never come to Ginnie's old home again.

Because if he did, he had no idea what might happen.

15

Bolam paused in the main office the next morning, his attention caught by the half-raised hand of Billie Grayson. She raised her forefinger when she saw she had his attention, said something into the phone, and then hung up.

'Raj,' she said.

Bolam could see from her expression that it wasn't good news.

'No ID on the Rowe finger,' she told him. 'We'll have to wait on DNA results.'

He opened his mouth to speak, but she cut him off. 'Which I told him you'd want to fast-track,' she said. 'But you know how it is. No immediate threat to life, lack of resources, blah blah blah.'

Raj had already confirmed for them that the finger had been frozen and amputated post-mortem, just as Jayne Sturridge's had, so they knew they were looking at a historical fatality. He'd also confirmed that the staining was from oil paint: cadmium yellow and cerulean blue.

'Why no ID? If it's Joanna Clayton, she had convictions so she should be on record.'

'She was eighteen when she went missing,' Billie told him, 'but she was a minor when she was convicted of breach of the peace. All the other offences listed never went to charge.'

The fingerprints would have been deleted from the system after five years.

At the next desk, DC Wayne Thompson was listening in. Bolam turned to him. 'Tommo. You went to the high school. You knew Matthew Sturridge. Did you know Joanna Clayton?' They would be about the same age – Tommo had just turned forty last month.

'Same year, different classes,' said the DC.

Bolam stared at him. 'And you didn't think to say?' He was still struggling to get a grip on the interwoven web of connections that ran through this town. As Gordon had said, it wasn't the kind of place you leave, and so everyone seemed to know everyone else.

Tommo shrugged. 'Billie finalised the list of old cases,' he said. 'I didn't see Joanna Clayton's name until half an hour ago, and I never knew her that well, anyway.'

'Do you remember her going missing?'

Tommo shook his head. 'Not really. We were in the sixth form, final year. She just stopped turning up. I don't think any of us even really thought of it as disappearing, as such. She just wasn't there. There wasn't a big fuss.'

Bolam was usually good at assessing people, but he didn't know what to make of Tommo. He had a sharp mind, but his attitude was casual. There was a lot of front about him, but it wasn't clear whether that concealed hidden depths, or was a veneer over not very much at all.

'There was an ambulance, wasn't there?' Bolam said, and he was answered by blank looks from Tommo and Billie. 'In the list you came up with. An ambulance.'

'Nineteen years ago,' said Billie. 'It was a big story at the time: a paramedic lost his apples, killed a colleague and a patient in the back of the ambulance, and then just turned up with them at the hospital, cool as a cucumber.'

The description rang bells, even though Bolam had been living at the other end of the country at the time. The case had been all over the news for a day or two. 'And a finger was missing?'

Billie nodded.

'So we have three connections,' Bolam said.

'Three?' asked Tommo.

'The fingers,' said Billie. 'And the location. But the third?'

'Ambulances.' The two officers still looked blank, so Bolam went on. 'Your case in the ambulance, for starters. Maria Rowe is a local GP – although she wasn't twenty-two years ago when her half-sister disappeared… She would have been a med student, but still…' Already, the line of reasoning was unravelling.

'And Jayne Sturridge?' prompted Billie.

'Her brother, Robert Walton,' Bolam said. 'He's a friend of the Rowes, but also he's an ambulance call centre controller with local business interests on the side. When I spoke to him about his sister he seemed evasive, and he phoned Maria Rowe shortly before she found the second package.'

Tommo and Billie nodded, as if the connection should have been obvious, then Tommo said, 'So do you have a theory, then?'

Bolam paused for a second, then said, 'No, I haven't got the faintest idea. But I think we need to find out a little more about Robert Walton.'

The house was an empty shell with no front door and the two ground-floor windows at the front removed. Bolam paused at one of the window openings and peered in.

When his eyes had adjusted, he saw a man with a long-handled roller painting the ceiling, a woman on her knees doing something to a skirting board, and another man standing in a doorway staring out at him.

'Sorry,' Bolam said. 'I was just walking past. I can't help being nosy.'

The man walked across to the empty front doorway, still carrying a can of paint and a brush, which he now proffered to Bolam. 'You can help if you like?' the man said. 'It's all for a good cause.'

Bolam raised his hands and took a step back, then indicated his suit. 'I'm not exactly dressed for it,' he said, and the man laughed. 'A good cause, you say?' Bolam said.

The man emerged, narrowing his eyes in the bright sunlight. He was mid-fifties with salt and pepper hair and thick stubble. 'We give people another chance,' he said. 'The Fresh Start Project. Homes for veterans, the homeless, that kind of thing. We're always looking for volunteers.'

Robert Walton seemed genuine – likeable, even – and Bolam felt momentarily guilty for his earlier suspicions when he'd been looking into the man's activities and had assumed some kind of financial sleight of hand in a scheme where Walton bought run-down properties, used volunteers to transform them and then passed them on to the Fresh Start charity at market value. To be fair, though, Walton had history: two old convictions relating to his fast and loose ways with finance and business practice.

'Go on, have a go,' said Walton, and before he knew it Bolam had the paintbrush in his hand.

He held it between thumb and forefinger, fearful for his suit. 'I…' He wasn't often lost for words. 'I'm not a very practical man,' he finally said, which was an understatement, to say the least. Fran had always been the one with the toolkit and the take-it-on attitude around the house. 'More a problem solver.'

He handed the brush back and Walton took it without a word.

'We've spoken before,' Bolam said. 'On the telephone.'

'I know.'

They remained silent for a few seconds. Bolam had been in little doubt that Walton would have anticipated this encounter – that Gordon or Maria would have forewarned him that his name had come up. People told him his soft northeastern accent was distinctive, and easily recognisable.

'So what can I do for you, Inspector?'

In truth, Bolam didn't know. He'd talked with Tommo and Billie at length about what they'd been able to find out about Robbie Walton. A criminal record for fraud spoke of character, but not psychopathy. Bolam had sat for a long time, staring at the notes onscreen, trying to see something beyond the superficial connections: friend and business acquaintance of the Rowes, brother of Jayne Sturridge, and a long career in the ambulance service.

But there was nothing. And so he'd strolled down here on a sunny spring afternoon, and he'd casually stopped for a chat so he could look the man in the eye and see if it all fell into place.

'You generally like people, don't you, Mr Walton? You try to see the good in them. That's why you do things like this.'

Walton seemed puzzled by Bolam's line of conversation. 'Don't we all?' he said. 'It's a healthy starting point, at least.'

'But you never liked *him*, did you? Matthew Sturridge.' That was something Walton's sister had said: that Robbie had never liked Matthew.

Walton shrugged. 'I haven't spoken to Matthew in years,' he said.

Bolam remained silent, and eventually Walton filled the gap: 'But no, I don't like him. He comes across as Mr Nice, but you can never trust a thing he says. And he's always been controlling. Jayne was much older than me – I was only a kid, but I could still see it.'

Bolam nodded. He'd hoped for more substance, perhaps. Something he could pursue. But all he had was a grammatical nuance: Robbie said he had no contact with Sturridge yet still referred to his character in the present tense.

'Do you remember Ginnie Lloyd?' Bolam asked, as if he was following the same line of inquiry rather than changing tack entirely. 'And Russell Shaw?'

Walton drew back. 'Of course I do,' he said. 'Although not personally. I worked as a call operator at a different centre to them, so I wouldn't have had any direct involvement with them, other than maybe an occasional training event. But what happened had a massive impact on the ambulance service at the time. Lots of people needed counselling, some left the service altogether. We had a big overhaul of our procedures. It was awful. But that was twenty years ago – what's it got to do with anything now?'

Bolam didn't answer. Walton's response was in line with the ambulance service HR records they'd gone through. 'You don't remember them at all?' he finally said.

Walton shook his head. He seemed genuinely puzzled.

'You spoke to Maria Rowe the other day.' He hadn't planned to jump from case to case like this, and wasn't sure if the scattershot approach was a good one or not: Walton was struggling to keep up, but had given him nothing yet, not even a hint of evasiveness.

'I did,' said Walton. 'I called Gordon at the office yesterday, mid-morning, but his assistant said he was out and he wasn't answering his mobile. That's why I called him at home, in case he was there.'

'Mid-morning, you say?'

Walton nodded, which was interesting: Gordon had said he'd left the office late morning, not mid. It might, of course, come down to differing interpretations of 'mid' and 'late', but it did mean that Gordon Rowe's movements were not accounted for around the time the package had been delivered to his home…

16

Bolam sat at his desk. It was late, his office lit only by a desk lamp and the glow from his computer screen. He'd been staring at the case's decision log for the last twenty minutes, working through each decision they'd made, and the notes outlining the reasons for those choices and the possible consequences of the choices being wrong or right. Records like this were essential when it came to building a case for court, but Bolam also found it a useful prompt for his thinking when a case ground to a halt.

What could they have done differently? What might they have missed?

Mentally, he made a list of all they knew – the fingers, the recipients, the rings – but it didn't help.

Aisha Nawaz was still out in the main office, leaning back in her chair and laughing at something Cath Marshall had said. Cath was perched on the edge of Aisha's desk, one leg crossed over the other, leaning in towards Aisha as she spoke.

Bolam stood, went over and paused in his doorway. When she saw him, Cath stood, moved over to a vacant chair and sat.

'Someone's playing games, aren't they?' Bolam said, walking across and taking Cath's place, perched on the corner of the desk. 'All the dramatics. The fingers in the post. The in-person deliveries where they leave no trace and nobody sees them. Even the paint on Joanna's finger to make sure we know it's her. Showing off.'

If Aisha did this he'd be cross with her: constructing a narrative out of what little information they had. He told himself there was a distinction between constructing working hypotheses and making assumptions, but even he didn't believe himself.

'We have two severed fingers, two Jiffy bags, a ring that belongs to nobody… another *missing* ring. The opal ring was put on the finger – that's significant physical contact with both items. Is there any chance there's something forensic we've missed?'

Cath was shaking her head already. She was an experienced crime scene manager. She knew what she was doing. 'Jayne's finger was frozen twenty-nine years ago,' she said. 'And after thawing it started to deteriorate rapidly. Raj is an excellent forensic pathologist, but there are limits. He's not going to miss anything that's still viable, Inspector.'

'We have one known murder victim, Jayne Sturridge,' said Bolam. 'Another unidentified, but suspected to be Joanna Clayton. We have the possibility that the owner of the opal ring might be an additional victim. We have another historical case that bears some similarities – the ambulance murders. And now I have McBride on at me to reallocate resources and hand the investigation over to some chap with an interest in cold cases who's counting down the days to his retirement.'

He hadn't mentioned that last item to anyone yet – McBride had only pressed this on him late that afternoon – but Serious Crimes were already over-stretched after being called in to work with Customs and Excise on a joint operation at the docks, and a flurry of other cases that had been escalated to them.

'What kind of person does this?' Cath asked. 'What kind of *mind*?'

'Someone driven by a deep personal spark-point,' said Bolam. 'Someone who likes to be calling the shots, and to see other people dance to their tune.'

He glanced across, aware that his DS had remained quiet. 'Aisha, what's your take?'

'You say someone's playing games,' she said carefully, as if wary of contradicting him. 'Which, if it gets inside our heads, risks us… personalising it.'

Bolam nodded. 'And…?'

'Well, if we step back and try to be a bit more objective… The obvious question is why send the fingers now?' Aisha said. 'You suggested it was dramatics and showing off, but what if it isn't? What if the fingers aren't a serial killer's trophies, but blackmail tokens, and now, for some reason, the person who's been storing them is making their threats real?'

'You mean Sturridge did kill his wife, but maybe someone knew exactly what he did and has been blackmailing him ever since?'

'And Joanna. The blackmailer knows what happened to her too…'

It was far-fetched, but in the Sturridge case, at least, it kind of made sense. DI Bulmer's notes from the original investigation were poor, but they were clear that the Sturridge home had been searched and no evidence of a crime had been found. Had someone helped Sturridge clear the scene?

But Joanna Clayton? The same rationale would imply that the blackmailer had something on either Maria or Gordon… Now Bolam recalled Maria's account of how good Gordon had been with Joanna, going out to find her and bring her home after her earlier disappearances. Gordon had clearly been closely involved with her.

And when the package had been delivered to his house, Gordon's account of his movements had been inconsistent with what Robbie Walton had said: that unexplained disparity between mid and late morning when he'd been away from the office.

'You should do what McBride said,' Aisha told him. She glanced across at Cath, and he had the sense they'd been discussing this before he came out. 'You're too close to this, Gov. The Rowes are family. If the case is being wound down and reallocated, then maybe it's just the opportunity you need to avoid getting too entangled.'

She didn't add, *and risk blowing the case if it ever gets to court*, but that part was clear.

He sighed. 'Maybe you're right.' Then: 'It's late. I'm heading home with a good takeaway and I suggest you two do likewise.'

'Well, hello, stranger.' Maria Rowe wore a knee-length tweed skirt and a loose white blouse, her hair pinned up asymmetrically. 'If it's Gordon you've come to see, I'm afraid you're out of luck. He's at the Rotary.'

But even as she told Bolam his visit was wasted, Maria backed away from the door and gestured for him to enter.

'And Luke?' he said.

Maria paused, glancing back over her shoulder at him. 'You always got on well with him, didn't you?' she said. 'He's at the skate park. Drinking cheap cider and smoking wacky baccy. Don't look shocked! It's just you and me this evening, darling.'

He should go. She'd been drinking, and there was something unsettling about the way she kept glancing back at him as she led the way through to the kitchen.

But if anyone would give him straight answers, it was Maria.

On the kitchen table there was a bottle and a large glass, half full of dark red wine. Bolam paused by a wooden chair. When Maria reached up to a shelf for another glass, her skirt rode up to mid-thigh. Bolam looked away.

She poured for him, then pushed the glass across the table, both of them still standing.

'I…' she said, then stopped.

Bolam had the distinct impression she had never intended to say anything more than that – that the dangling sentence was designed to say far more than words. She was being very obvious.

The smudged make-up around her eyes suggested she had been crying before he got here. Had she and Gordon argued?

'I was hoping to talk to you about—'

Her finger on his lips, shushing him, was the most delicate of touches, but disturbing. He wasn't a man who handled intimacy well, or easily. Fran had been the exception for him. Maria pressed for a second too long, then let her hand fall, coming to rest on her hip.

He should go. He should never have put himself – or Maria – in this position.

Had she always been this way? Or was it simply a combination of circumstances? The drink, the chance of being alone in the house, the clear tensions between her and Gordon when Bolam had last seen them.

'I wanted to ask you about Joanna.'

She turned away, her whole frame sagging. She sat at the table, and Bolam finally took a chair opposite her.

'You really think it's her?' Maria asked.

'We'll find out soon. But yes, it's likely.'

'Then whoever… did it. They're still out there? And now they're targeting us?'

For once, Bolam was stuck for how to respond to this. On the evidence to date, they had no reason to suspect that this was any more than a macabre reopening of old cases, but they really didn't have a clue where this was heading.

'We don't know,' he said finally. 'But I promise you we're doing everything we can to find out.'

Maria gave a short laugh. 'You don't even sound like you've convinced yourself,' she said.

'You said she was doing A-levels, didn't you?' Bolam said, after a long silence.

Maria nodded. 'Art, English Lit and French,' she said. 'But she didn't really care about anything but her art. She drifted.'

'Tell me.'

'I didn't really know her by then. I was at uni. We'd never lived under the same roof. I just saw her through Dad's eyes, saw what she meant to him, so I did what I could.'

'And Gordon did too.'

'He was a rock. We were early days then and he wanted to impress.' She took a long sip of her wine. Bolam hadn't touched his. 'We actually had a row about it – our first row. I accused him of wanting me to be more like Joanna. More carefree. More easy.' She laughed. 'And look at me now!'

'Did *Gordon* think she was easy?'

Maria's eyes narrowed. 'That's not what I meant,' she said. 'And you know it. He just thought I was a bit uptight back then.'

Bolam was accustomed to painstakingly constructing the stories of people's lives during an investigation, but he found it strange now to be doing so for people he knew – not constructing, but dismantling and *re*constructing. He'd never really thought about Maria and Gordon's relationship or history together. Never seen them as starstruck lovers. But now, to see them twenty years ago, young and in love and yet even then Gordon wanting more… Had he *sought* more with Joanna?

'The day she went missing...'

Maria pursed her lips. All hints of the earlier seductiveness were gone now, and she looked ten years older. 'It wasn't really a day, as such,' she said. 'She simply didn't go home one night. Then another night passed, and my father called me the day after that. It wasn't unusual. I was home from uni so I took my father to the police station to report her missing, and Gordon drove around some of her friends' houses, as he'd done before when she'd stayed away.'

'What did the police do?' He'd seen the reports, and Maria's response confirmed what he'd read between the lines.

'Not much,' she said. 'She was eighteen. She had a history of problems at home, of which the police were aware. They made a few cursory enquiries and advised my father to wait for her to come home with her tail between her legs.'

Bolam shook his head. That was another common element: the police dismissing the disappearance of a woman. A runaway, delinquent teenager; a wife who'd had enough. Easy victims – or well-targeted ones.

'What did Gordon think?'

Again, the pursing of the lips and narrowing of eyes. 'What we all thought,' Maria said. 'That Joanna had run away, that she'd had her head turned by money or drugs or sex. What are you driving at with all this? Why don't you ask *Gordon* what he thought?'

'Do you know where Gordon was on the morning the package was delivered to your home, Maria? There are inconsistencies with the timings.'

She leaned forward. 'You can call a halt to this right now, do you hear me? I know you think Gordon is an arsehole, and he very often is, but he's always been solid when things mattered.'

That was quite a turnaround from the woman who had almost thrown herself at Bolam when he arrived.

Still, he'd hoped for straight answers from Maria, and that's what she'd given him: she seemed genuinely surprised that he should be doubting even the small details of Gordon's story, let alone that he might be casting more serious aspersions.

None of which helped unravel Gordon's involvement in all this:

the inconsistencies in his account, the fact that he was closely involved in events around Joanna Clayton's disappearance, that he was well-acquainted with both Matthew Sturridge and Robbie Walton... Any connection with the ambulance murders was yet to be established, of course, but still...

Maria reached out, put a hand on Bolam's arm, and it was all he could do not to flinch. 'Help us find out what happened to Joanna,' she said. 'And leave Gordon out of it. He's a good man, at heart. He's just a bit crap at it sometimes.'

Bolam made his excuses and left, his wine untouched. He paused once he was past the five-bar gate, his mind still reeling from Maria's behaviour, and the unexpected reassessment of two people he thought he had the measure of. He still couldn't work out if their marriage was on the rocks, or if they had always been this way, and that unsettled him more than he felt it should have.

He woke on Fran's side of the double bed. Sometimes he thought he could feel her shape in the mattress.

Sunlight streamed low through the window. He'd never got around to fitting curtains.

He'd slept for a couple of hours, then lain awake thinking, before dozing again. He was still unable to join the threads. Ambulances, easy victims, trophies – or was Aisha's suggestion of blackmail more credible? But that would mean that Sturridge was a killer, as was someone close to Joanna Clayton – and that somehow someone close to them both was blackmailing them, and now exposing them.

Too many improbabilities stacking up.

'Oh, Fran,' he sighed. 'Why can't I make sense of it all? What am I missing?' He wasn't blind to the irony that when Fran had been alive he'd never felt able to discuss his work with her, but now he could say these things out loud – talking to himself or to the memory of his late wife, he wasn't sure.

He'd mulled over the double-hand amputation case, but always returned to the conclusion that it was a red herring – amputation with body parts never recovered, yes, but clearly a gangland killing. He'd gone over and over the ambulance killings. The brutality seemed out of keeping with the Sturridge and Rowe cases that were their focus, but there was something about the audacity and drama of the staging that kept bringing it back into the reckoning. He would go over the case notes again when he reached the office – there would be time before the Customs and Excise liaison meeting McBride had roped him into. The killings in the back of that ambulance had been so violent that he must ascertain for sure that the amputated digit was missing from the scene itself, and not simply detached. It sounded unlikely, but clumsy wording in an old case file might easily be misinterpreted twenty years later: they needed to be certain that finger was actually unaccounted for.

He showered and dressed. The blue suit. Always the blue suit for work. Although, to be fair, he had half a dozen of them, identical. Police work could get messy sometimes, even at his level. He was aware that the suits were probably over-compensation for his short stature – although he preferred to think of himself as compact rather than short. Dressing well made him feel as if he had a larger presence in a room, and in this line of work you needed as large and imposing a presence as possible. That was something he'd always struggled with, another challenge for him, like his difficulties in understanding people and their motivations. But whereas you can learn to read people and get good at it, you can't learn to be bigger.

He went downstairs and made coffee – long black with an extra shot of espresso. Fran had always joked that his one vice was the coffee machine she had bought him a few years ago.

The mail was early today, a single white envelope. He glanced at it, then looked more closely. The return address was Berg and Associates in Ipswich, and the letter was addressed to Ms F Bolam.

He stared, his heart pounding. He'd tied up all the loose ends after Fran's death – he was sure of that.

It felt wrong to open a letter addressed to Fran, but he slid a finger along the flap, opened it, and pulled out a single sheet of headed A4.

Dear Ms Bolam

With regard to your divorce proceedings, we await your further instructions.

He put the letter down on the stairs, went through to the kitchen, then came back and stared at it again. *Unreasonable behaviour…*

He sat on the stairs. He fumbled his phone out of his inside jacket pocket and called the number for Berg and Associates and they answered straight away, even though it was early.

'Hello? Yes. My name is Iain Bolam. Detective Inspector Iain Bolam.' Instantly he regretted that: he didn't like to throw his title around, and immediately he feared it would only reinforce the 'unreasonable behaviour' label.

'I received a letter from your offices this morning. That is… it was addressed to my wife. My late wife. I've already informed you of her death. Would you please make sure your records are up to date and you send no more correspondence to her?'

They were evasive, as he knew they would be. They would be accustomed to fending off aggrieved parties, and rightly so. But he had sent through a copy of the death certificate, and somewhere he had written confirmation that they had received and registered this.

They assured him that they would investigate, and that there would be no further letters.

He assumed someone had made a mistake, not fully closed her case with them, but still it felt as if someone had plunged a knife into his heart and was now twisting.

Unreasonable behaviour.

She had never said that of him, unless unreasonable behaviour consisted of tunnel vision and a lack of awareness of anyone around him when he was in the thick of a case.

He went back to make another coffee, but found that he couldn't touch the machine Fran had bought him. He paused before his reflection in the window, straightened his jacket, straightened his tie.

He decided to walk this morning, clear his mind. He was still getting a feel for this town, and twenty minutes through the town centre was a part of that process.

The house he was staying in was in the old part of town, on one of a warren of terraced streets – in fact, it was only a short distance from the Sturridge home, and from the house Robbie Walton had been renovating for his homelessness project.

Again, Bolam was struck by how interlinked everything – and everyone – was in this place, and he tried not to feel it as a form of claustrophobia.

Had it been the right thing to come back here after Fran's death?

He could hardly claim it was a reasoned decision, given that it was founded on simply taking the least complicated option when McBride's assistant had called him the day after the funeral.

The town centre was coming to life. A truck was pulled up dangerously across the pavement by the traffic lights, making a delivery to the greengrocers. Commuters meandered towards the town station.

Bolam waited for the green man before crossing, even though there was little traffic.

The walk helped refocus his thoughts, and a short time later he stepped into the Serious Crimes office, and saw that Billie Grayson was already there.

'I had a thought on my way in,' Bolam told her, pausing by her desk.

She raised an eyebrow, waiting for him to go on.

'The finger delivered to the Rowe house,' he said. 'We're assuming it belongs to Joanna Clayton, but what if it doesn't? Might it belong to the paramedic who was killed, Ginnie Lloyd?'

If that was the case, Joanna Clayton was a red herring, and it brought things back to two murders connected to the ambulances, and they had one person of interest named in both cases who still worked for the ambulance service: Robbie Walton.

There was something in Billie's expression. Something she wanted to tell him.

'What is it?' Bolam asked. 'What am I missing?'

'The ambulance killings,' she said. 'Ginnie Lloyd and Ronald Duke. The other paramedic, Russell Shaw, was locked up under a hospital order for manslaughter by diminished responsibility.'

'Yes?'

'Russell Shaw was released from the Rodgers-Stephenson Institute in Cambridge earlier this month,' Billie told him. 'Just around the time all this was starting to kick off...'

17

'We need to trace Russell Shaw.' Bolam was late for the liaison meeting, but that didn't matter now. Billie's news about the ambulance killer changed everything.

'He was released five days ago,' said Aisha from her desk, a telephone receiver wedged between shoulder and jaw. She'd been on hold with the Rodgers-Stephenson Institute for the last ten minutes. 'After that – nothing.'

Bolam shook his head. When someone was released from prison there were clear procedures for parole and maintaining contact – and traceability – once they were in the community. In theory, the same applied for release from a secure hospital, but in Bolam's experience the execution was less strict. It didn't help that many of these institutions were contracted out of the state sector, each with their own procedures, agendas and expectations.

'No credit cards? No mobile phone?' Bolam addressed this to Billie Grayson, who was the team's lead on banking and communications technology.

She shook her head. 'I'm digging now, but without records from the secure hospital, it's hard to know where to start. There's nothing obvious.'

'He's done a runner, hasn't he?' said Aisha.

Bolam said nothing. They didn't know if Shaw had chosen to lie low, had somehow fallen through the gaps, or had simply been living a low-tech, zero-impact existence on the fringes since his release – or even if something had happened to him that would explain his apparent disappearance. Tracing Shaw had become an immediate priority, but it might still be a case of doing so merely to exclude him from their enquiries. They had to be open to all possibilities.

Bolam signalled to Aisha to cut the call, and when she replaced the receiver said, 'I'll try them. Thanks.'

Back at his desk, his office door left open so he felt connected to the team, Bolam keyed a number, but instead of calling the one Aisha had given him for the secure hospital, it was the pathologist, Raj Khatri, who picked up.

'Raj? Bolam here. Do you have a minute for a random query?'

The pathologist laughed, then said, 'Sure, Inspector. What can I do for you?'

'I'm trying to get through to the Rodgers-Stephenson Institute, a secure hospital out near Cambridge. I don't suppose you have any contacts, or insights into how to get past the institutional barriers?'

Raj chuckled again. 'Us doctors, eh?' he said. 'We all know each other...'

'And do you?'

'I choose to socialise with people who dissect corpses, not minds, Inspector.'

'I need to talk to them.'

'And they're putting up the barriers, you say? It's a privately run place, from what little I know – contracts with the NHS and the Prison Service. If they get contact from a serious crimes team, they'll be thinking that either it's for help with an investigation or that you might be onto something they've got wrong.'

'And of course they'd want to help with the former, but their biggest concern is the latter?' He'd suspected as much: Aisha's call to the Rodgers-Stephenson had been like dealing with a suspect hiding behind 'no comment' to avoid self-incrimination. He could imagine the hospital busily lawyering up while his DS was on hold. 'So how do I get round all that, Raj? All I want is some information.'

'They'll follow procedure – just in case your investigations might cause them problems. You'll be wading through paperwork.' Raj paused, then went on. 'Or you could just turn up on their doorstep and try to talk to someone face-to-face. If you're dealing with real people it's easier to persuade them to cooperate, and it's harder for them to hide behind the regulations. When it comes down to it, most people want to help, particularly if you get a chance to explain yourself to them.'

For all that Raj claimed he didn't deal with minds, his insight was pretty damned perceptive. Bolam thanked him and hung up, then called up the route to the Rodgers-Stephenson on Google Maps.

The Rodgers-Stephenson Institute was a modern facility in a science park on the edge of Cambridge. Unless you already knew it was a secure psychiatric facility there would be nothing to indicate that it were so. Even the heavy-duty security fencing and gates seemed standard for this high-tech estate.

Bolam had got DCI McBride's office to call ahead when he was already en route – not with a request, but simply with the information that he was on his way and should be well-received. If they didn't respond to a DS calling them earlier, they might be more amenable to a call from a DCI's office.

On arrival, he was let in through the gates, and they were clearly expecting him.

'Inspector Bolam,' said a tall, suited man who greeted him at the glass doors of the main building. His face was long and narrow, as if it had been stretched at birth and had never popped back into normal proportions. 'Dr Luke Chandler. Pleased to meet you.' He looked anything but. 'You do understand this is most out of the ordinary? There are established protocols for official visits, you know – for good reason. Our work here is of a particularly sensitive, and easily disrupted, nature.'

'If only your ex-patients followed the rules too, eh?' Bolam spoke with a smile, keeping his voice so low the doctor clearly had to strain to hear.

Chandler showed him through to a seating area, something between a meeting room and a waiting room. 'Coffee?'

They used the ritual of coffee preparation to eye each other up. Raj had been right about them being cagey here, wary that Bolam might be pursuing them for something they had, or hadn't, done.

They sat, and Bolam sipped at his espresso. 'It's okay,' he said. 'I'm not looking to cause trouble, and I know there are official channels. For now, all I need is some information about one of your ex-patients.'

'Inspector, I know our patients are of a particular variety here, but still—'

'Patient confidentiality, I know. As I say, we'll be pursuing the official channels. But there's a clear case of public interest here, and the information is required for investigation into a serious crime. You know we'll be granted access when we've jumped through all the hoops, so for now… Russell Shaw.' While he kept his tone neutral, Bolam had been careful to pepper his statement with key phrases that would make it clear to Chandler that he would, ultimately, get whatever he wanted out of the Rodgers-Stephenson.

Chandler kept a straight – and blank – expression on his long face, though. Bolam couldn't work out if he had somehow known in advance why he was here, or was simply very good.

'You released him five days ago,' Bolam prompted.

'Such decisions are not the remit of an individual, Inspector. *I* did not release him. *We* – as in the Institute – did not even release him. It was the carefully considered decision of a mental health tribunal, based on case history and the input of experts, with the ultimate decisions at every stage of the process in the hands of the Ministry of Justice.'

'But he walked out of *here*, right?' Another sip of the coffee and the tiny cup was drained. Bolam was an espresso man, but he wished they came in grown-up sizes. 'So what was wrong with him? Shaw. Do you think he was a psychopath? Would he have killed again nineteen years ago if he hadn't been caught?'

Chandler recoiled at Bolam's deliberately crass line of questions. 'It's okay. I'm not taking notes,' Bolam told him. 'I just want to get a feel for the man.'

'Are you a psychologist, Inspector? No?'

For a moment Bolam thought he was going to leave it at that simple rebuff, then he went on.

'Our patients are rarely so easy to label,' Chandler said, clearly making an effort to talk in general terms rather than directly about

Russell Shaw. 'They suffer complex sets of psychological conditions, some of which are treatable, or at least open to modification and management, while others are more hardwired. There is never a simple label, or a one-size-fits-all approach to treatment and therapy. Our work with our residents takes years, a lifetime.'

'Twelve years for Shaw,' Bolam said. The paramedic had spent seven years at other institutions before being transferred here. 'Do many patients walk out of here, Dr Chandler?'

'It's rare, but it happens. For someone to be released they must pass the most rigorous of assessments.'

'And what happens after they leave?'

'It starts before they leave,' Chandler told him. 'Prior to discharge, patients are moved to a transitional ward, where they have increasing interaction with the outside world, including supervised day release. All of which is closely monitored and assessed. Upon release, the patient would be passed into the care of a community health team for monitoring and support.'

'And all this happened for Russell Shaw?'

For the first time, Chandler looked evasive – just a brief glance away, but enough for an experienced observer like Bolam to spot.

'And…?'

'Sometimes it takes time for these arrangements to be established and there's an extended transitional period.'

'You lost him?'

'We haven't lost him.'

'You just don't know where he is…'

An uncomfortable silence grew. Bolam was frustrated. He'd hoped for more than mere confirmation of what they'd already deduced. Shaw had been released and almost immediately had slipped under the radar. The Rodgers-Stephenson or a community mental health service team should have been monitoring and supporting him, but the fact that Bolam's team had so far been unable to find any trace of this meant something had gone wrong.

Had a crime been committed in how this had come about? Bolam suspected not: if Shaw had been deemed healthy enough to be out in the community, then his terms of release would be couched in language of support rather than legal requirement. He had, technically, walked out of hospital a free man.

'Has he done something?' Chandler asked.

Bolam studied the doctor more closely. 'Do you have reason to ask me that?'

'Only that you've come all this way, and you look rather pissed off that I'm unable to give you more help than I have.'

This was the moment of connection Raj had talked about: the value of being face-to-face with a real human who might actually want to help, rather than being on the end of a telephone line.

The only trouble was, Bolam didn't have a clue what to do with that moment.

'We're going to need access to your records,' Bolam said. 'Patient files, details of any phones Shaw might have, his banking information, the works.'

'We're always happy to cooperate,' said Chandler, retreating into formality. 'But…'

'I know. Protocol. We'll go through the correct channels. But as I told you, we're investigating some serious crimes, Dr Chandler. We *will* gain access to your files. But for now, we just need to find Russell Shaw, if only to exclude him from our investigation and ensure he has support in place. We need to understand him. Is there anything more you can give me?'

Again, that look in the doctor's eyes. He really did want to help.

'You might talk to his caseworker,' he said. 'Informally, of course. But Nurse Ward might be able to help you.'

18

The fresh start was going well for Russ Shaw.

Stewart had helped him sort his benefits, and had given him, and shown him how to use, what he claimed was a simple, basic mobile phone. It all seemed to be falling into place.

The first night, he'd slept on a thin mattress and bedding borrowed from the shelter, but the next day a van had parked outside and Stewart and another man Russ recognised from the shelter helped him take a few things up the narrow stairs to the bedsit. A wooden bed frame, a mattress, a wing-back chair that briefly gave Russ a flashback to that old man's front room from many years before; a table-top hob, a microwave, a couple of pans and some crockery.

After several trips, Russ paused in the middle of the room, peering all around him.

'You okay, Russell?' asked Stewart. 'What is it?'

Russ indicated with both hands the things lying all around. Shrugged. He struggled with words at the best of times.

'It's okay,' Stewart said. 'Don't think of it as charity.' He waved a hand to indicate the bedsit, and said, 'Look at the place. Yesterday it was an empty shell. Unfinished. We've got some paint and brushes in the van so you can decorate. When you're back on your feet and move on to whatever comes next, you'll know you've left this place far better than you found it for whoever comes along after you.'

The words made sense, the argument compelling, but Russ still struggled to believe that this was happening. Did they know him? Did they know what he *was*?

'I…' Russ stopped, then started again. 'I lost my meds. When I was sleeping rough. I…' He pressed a hand to the side of his head. He was struggling today.

'What do you need?'

'I was on amisulpride, ethosuximide, diazepam and bedranol.' It was like a mantra: the chemical friends he'd misplaced.

Stewart sucked air between his teeth. 'Diazepam's easy,' he said. 'I know a few people. Bedranol, too – that's beta blockers, isn't it? Give me a list and I'll see what I can fix up in the short term. And then we'll get you into the medical system and do it properly, eh?'

Stewart had the air of someone who knew all the right people. Right now, Russ didn't care. He just needed help.

'I know what it's like,' Stewart went on. 'I've been there too.'

For a moment Russ was thrown, and he glanced curiously at the pony-tailed man.

'I served in the Army,' Stewart said. 'Royal Anglian. It took me a long time to get over my experiences in Afghanistan and I had a hard time on the outside too. And the police… Make one misstep and they're all over you, aren't they? Manipulating things, turning people against you… I've learned my lesson. Always stay one step ahead of the pigs, that's the way, isn't it? And stay out of trouble, of course. I was helped by a charity to sort myself out, get back on my feet, and now I'm paying it forward.'

Russ waited for him to go on, to say that he'd lost his mind, spent years in a secure psychiatric hospital, was still tormented by mad and terrifying thoughts in his head… but no. They had common ground, but not a complete overlap. The man was simply trying to be nice.

Russ nodded. 'I just never expected all this,' he said, finally, and Stewart clapped him on the arm before saying they'd slacked for long enough and there was more to fetch from the van.

'Thank you so much,' said Judith from the shelter's kitchen doorway.

Russ was becoming quite handy. He'd always been one to roll his sleeves up and try something, rather than hold back, and getting set up in the bedsit had given him the confidence to tackle more. He'd finished up woodwork and painted, he'd put new elastics under the cushion of that old wing-back chair; he'd fixed the kitchen taps that had been fitted incorrectly in the first place by whoever had done up the bedsit, identifying the source of the slow leak and adding isolation valves for each tap.

Now he had started doing maintenance at the shelter – 'paying it forward' as Stewart had put it. Maybe he could find a position as some kind of odd-job man or janitor somewhere. Looking after buildings and not having much to do with people.

He pulled the window closed and it swung smoothly, no longer sticking on what had been a swollen frame.

'You're welcome.'

Judith was still looking at him, and he wondered what subtext he was missing. He'd never been good on body language.

'Cuppa?'

He nodded and she turned away.

Judith had been here the morning after he'd slept over at the shelter. About his age with cropped silver-grey hair and big hooped earrings, and a fondness for wide, garishly printed scarves even indoors.

He never had to say much when he was around Judith, and he liked that.

She brought him a mug of tea, sweet and milky, just how he liked it. 'You *are* the quiet one, aren't you, Russ?'

He shrugged, said nothing, then caught her eye and they both laughed.

'Nothing much to say,' he finally said.

They remained silent for a time, then Judith asked, 'Are you okay in that place of yours?'

He nodded, sipped at his tea.

'Maybe you'd like to show me round some time? Nothing dodgy.'

He shrugged, met her look, then glanced down at his tea. By saying *nothing dodgy* was she simply reassuring him that she wasn't trying to seduce him, or by saying it out loud was she acknowledging that the possibility existed? It was all too complicated.

And, he found, he didn't actually mind that.

He wondered if this little hint of normality meant he was starting to adjust to life outside the Rodgers-Stephenson. That he was starting to find a life that might work for him.

'Yes,' he said, struck by boldness. 'I'd like that. Some time.'

He looked away, looked back and saw how she was studying him closely, and then they both laughed again.

Leaving the shelter that afternoon, he didn't even hesitate. No sudden urge to keep going instead of turning right off the main road, no dark voices telling him it wouldn't do any harm if his route back to his bedsit took him past Ginnie's old home.

Her parents still lived there. He'd seen them the second time he'd passed the house, her father – white-haired and bent over now – coming around that shiny Volvo to help her mother out of the passenger seat. After that, he'd seen them a few more times. When he'd taken the indirect route back from the shelter, or on one of his long walks.

But not today… Perhaps that was another indication that he was adjusting to life outside, letting go of the past. That he didn't feel the need to go there.

When he *had* gone that way, though, it was nothing weird, nothing creepy.

It was a just a *connection*. Like Elizabeth's grave: something that tied him to the past. He wanted to move on, yes, but a part of that process was not denying those connections. It was why he'd come back to this town, after all, rather than making a fresh start somewhere else entirely.

He came to the narrow street where he now lived. As ever, both sides of the road were crammed with cars – these streets had been built long before it became standard for every household to have multiple cars. It had been a nightmare driving an ambulance through streets like this, and it was far worse now than it had been nineteen years ago.

He wondered what to cook tonight. His first benefit payments had come through now, into the bank account Stewart had helped him set up. It was more than enough to get by. Maybe he would go to the chippy tonight. Cod, chips, mushy peas, and a pickled egg and batter scraps like they used to get when he and Elizabeth were kids.

The strip of diazepam Stewart had slipped him this afternoon was bound to help, too, levelling off the ups and downs of the day.

He had his keys ready before he reached the house. Had the one with a plastic cover labelled 'FRONT DOOR' ready to slide into the lock.

He let himself in and breathed the now-familiar air with a hint of damp. He had a foot on the first step before he noticed that there was actually some mail in the wooden pigeonhole marked '14C'. Some glossy flyers, and a pale brown padded envelope.

He gathered them up and headed upstairs. By the time he reached the door to his bedsit and had the key in the lock, he'd already dismissed the flyers as not relevant – an estate agent that had recently sold several properties in the area, a window company that was concerned that owners of older properties with wood-framed sash windows were feeling the cold, and a less glossy flyer for a tree surgeon who didn't appear to have noticed the lack of trees on this cramped street.

He slipped them into the carrier bag hanging from the back of the door where he collected paper and card for recycling.

The padded envelope struck him as strange, not least for the fact that he never received any mail. There were no stamps or frank mark, so it must have been hand-delivered. No address, even, so for a moment Russ wondered if he'd picked it up from the wrong pigeonhole, but no, it had definitely been his – the other two holes had been emptied already, and his was on the far right, so it had been obvious that this was meant for him.

He couldn't work out what was in the envelope, either. It was misshapen, disturbingly three-dimensional.

He left it on the kitchen work surface next to the kettle, which he filled and set to boil. He took the mug from the drainer and dried the rim against his jumper before setting it down and rummaging in the box for a teabag. Water first, then two spoons of granulated sugar, and finally the milk.

He took the tea and the padded envelope and placed them on the small circular table to the right of the wing-back chair.

The envelope was gummed down, and he teased it open carefully, pushed the sides of the envelope in to open the top like a mouth, and tipped a neatly severed finger onto the table beside the mug.

He sat back, barely noticing the envelope falling to the bare floorboards.

His heart hammered. His eyes were wide open, his jaw tight, clamped shut.

He gripped the arms of the chair, his knuckles white, the tendons and blood vessels standing out on the backs of his hands.

The finger was stained a deep red with a coat of dried blood. It had been cut at the proximal interphalangeal joint – he was thinking as a medic, as if that might somehow distance him from what lay on the small table. Because of the dried blood it was hard to tell, but the skin of the finger looked Caucasian, the nail short but neatly shaped. A woman's finger, he guessed, but from a woman who did practical work from the way the nail was trimmed short. And it looked fresh, the blood only recently dried.

He couldn't stop staring.

Finally, he forced himself to breathe again, a short, explosive exhalation followed by a long, deep inhalation.

The cut part of the finger was ragged, and he could see what looked like knife marks on the exposed nub of bone.

The inside of the padded envelope was stained red, indicating that the blood had been fresh when the finger was put inside, and had dried while the package waited in the pigeonhole – the pigeonhole at the foot of the stairs *inside* Russ's building.

He didn't know what to do, let alone why anyone would do such a thing.

Any normal person would call the police. He knew that. He had his phone in his pocket: he could easily get it out, and he knew how to make a call on the device. But what kind of hell would that bring back into his life? A man in his position, just out of a secure psychiatric hospital… A man who a matter of minutes ago had believed he might actually be establishing a life he could handle.

But what would the consequences be if he did nothing?

The finger… He knew it would be possible to determine if it had been severed before or after death, but such a deduction was far beyond his paramedic skills.

What if there was a woman being held somewhere, this finger sent as some kind of macabre warning?

But why would anyone send it to *him*? Since Elizabeth's death he had no one.

Briefly, he flashed back to the exchange with Judith in the shelter's kitchen. The flirting, if that was what it had been. What did they call it these days? A bit of banter.

The finger couldn't possibly belong to her, though. The timings didn't work, because he'd come straight home from the shelter, no deviations, and the envelope had been waiting for him when he got in. Had been there long enough for the blood to dry inside the envelope.

But who would want to warn him of anything? Ginnie's parents? Someone else in the town, with memories long enough to remember?

No. It was just too far-fetched.

But… Somebody knew. He was sure of that. Somebody had tied him to events of that awful night when Ginnie and the old man had died.

What's more, they wanted him to *know* they knew, and they weren't going to let him simply slip back into a quiet, anonymous life.

And that person who wasn't going to let him move on, who would let him know in such a gruesome way… that person had come into this building and put the envelope in his pigeonhole at the foot of the stairs, because if they'd merely posted it through the letterbox no one would have known the unmarked package was meant for Russ.

He didn't know how long he'd been sitting there, staring at the finger, where it had tumbled out onto the small round table, but his tea had a film on the surface now, and looked cold.

His head was racing. His world had been turned upside down. And for the first time in ages he felt on the verge of losing control.

And perhaps *that* was why someone had done this awful thing…

19

Colin Ward walked so fast, Bolam had to break into a trot every few strides to keep up.

'It's my lunchtime power walk,' the nurse explained from a few steps ahead of Bolam on the path that followed the outside of the Institute's high-security fence. 'Only chance to squeeze it in.'

Ward was six-six with square shoulders, shaved head, near-black skin, and a voice even softer than Bolam's. He didn't look as if he needed a midday walk to keep in shape. Bolam suspected that two factors were key to Ward's lunchtime routine: the sheer physical release of walking so fast you're almost running, and the simple fact that the route was outside that oppressing fence, a very visible separation from the pressures within.

'Russell Shaw, you say? Well, he was an odd one, but that kind of goes with the territory at a place like this, doesn't it? What d'you want to know about our Russ?'

'What was wrong with him when he came here?' Because whatever had been wrong with him then was very probably what was *still* wrong with him. Bolam was yet to be convinced that whatever had driven someone to do the awful things Shaw had done could ever be cured enough for them to be trusted in the outside world.

'He killed two people, isn't that enough?'

'What was he diagnosed with? What kept him out of prison and put him in a place like this instead?'

'I'd need to check his file for the specifics. I know Russ was epileptic and psychotic, although not so much by the time I got to work with him. His meds kept it all under control.'

'His grandfather made him do it. The killings.' Bolam had read the police case notes. Delusional visits from an overbearing – and very probably abusive – grandfather.

'No,' Ward corrected. 'His grandfather *did* it. The grandfather who had been dead ten years before the murders took place. I remember that much because Russ mentioned it a few times – along the lines of how could he ever have actually believed that? But it's what he believed when he was arrested.'

'He no longer thought that?'

'He always seemed puzzled,' said Ward. 'Confused that he could have believed anything so clearly wrong. He'd been hallucinating about his grandfather and others close to him long before the night when he finally tipped over the edge. He had PTSD from his time in the Army, but I think its roots went much farther back.'

'His grandfather?'

'Perhaps. Some people are just fragile.'

Fragile seemed a very generous way to describe someone like Russell Shaw.

'Would you say he's cured?' A gap opened up between Bolam and Ward. He couldn't keep this up, but he was determined not to break into a run – he already felt like a small child chasing a grown-up. They'd completed two circuits, now, and the big nurse showed no sign of slowing.

'It's not about the cure, Mr Bolam. It's about finding stability, and reinforcing the barriers that stop most of us from crossing the line.'

That didn't seem very reassuring to Bolam.

'What was your involvement in Shaw's release? Dr Chandler told me you were his caseworker, but he didn't explain what that entailed.'

'I took him on day trips into Cambridge,' Ward said. 'I coached him in life skills. I tried to make sure he knew how the world worked.'

'Tried?'

'Nineteen years is a long time to be out of circulation. Russ struggled with the modern world. He just wanted things to be simple. He never really grasped even some of the basics a lot of the time.'

Nothing Ward had said so far convinced Bolam they were talking about a man fit to be turned out into the world.

'Did he have a phone? A bank account?'

'No phone – he said he didn't need one. I don't think he trusted technology very much. He'd have had a bank account, yes, but you'll need to get the details from Dr Chandler's admin team.'

'Do you know where he went from here?'

Ward stopped and stared at him. 'I assumed *you* knew that. You've just come from there, haven't you? Russ went home to Whitesands. Someone from the local council made arrangements, including a train ticket. They were organising accommodation for him, and establishing a framework for his care in the community.'

That was the first solid thing he'd got from this trip. So Russell Shaw had gone home… He'd get Aisha to talk to the local NHS Trust, find out which mental health team should be responsible for Shaw's care. They'd have Shaw by the time Bolam had finished the drive back from Cambridge.

They started to walk again, Bolam finally trotting to keep up.

'Tell me about Russ. What was he like?'

Nurse Ward gave him that sidelong look, as if it was an odd question. 'Russ? I liked him. You're not supposed to – to like them, or to dislike them, for that matter. It's easy to get drawn in if you establish any kind of emotional connection with the patients, negative or positive. We have to maintain an objective distance.'

'But Russ?'

'You asked what he was like. Well, he was fucked up. Well and truly. But as I say, that kind of goes with the territory in there.' He waved towards the facility on the other side of the fence, and again Bolam was struck by the importance of Ward's lunchtime distancing from the place. 'We get scary fucked up, we get cold and utterly evil fucked up, we get erratically violent fucked up. But Russ Shaw's variety of fucked up was odd. Sad. He was a broken man who didn't understand the world, and didn't understand himself, although he desperately wanted to. He didn't know what had happened to make him the way he was and so he retreated into his shell. It took a lot of hard work to get him to emerge.'

'Could he have fooled you? Could he have fooled the tribunal?' For a seasoned psychiatric nurse who insisted on the importance of objectivity, Ward seemed strangely sympathetic towards Shaw, and Bolam couldn't help wondering if he had been the victim of the kind of charm offensive only the seriously psychologically damaged could pull off.

'Could he have fooled me?' Ward paused, to give his answer some thought. 'Only if he was fooling himself, too.'

And that was Bolam's concern: that Russell Shaw had never let go of that world of illusion and delusion he had built up around himself to shut the world out – delusion that had fed and guided his actions on the night he had killed two people in the back of his ambulance.

'He came back home to Whitesands,' Bolam said as he strode into the Serious Crimes office. It was late afternoon, after the drive back from Cambridge, and only Billie Grayson and Tommo were here.

He didn't expect surprise, because he'd already called ahead to Aisha to get her onto the local NHS Trust. He suspected that's where she was now, out banging heads together to work out how Shaw had slipped through the gaps and where he was now.

'We know,' said Billie. She was tapping at her keyboard as she spoke, and now an image flashed up onto the large wall-screen. A grey canvas shoulder bag, the kind you'd take to the beach to carry your towels and sandwiches and a flask of tea to ward off the North Sea chill. She tapped again, and the image changed to an array of items Bolam assumed must have been in the bag: clothes, a toothbrush, a tatty paperback fantasy novel… and a pale brown Jiffy bag.

'What's this?' Bolam asked. The Jiffy bag looked the same as those that had been delivered to Matthew Sturridge and the Rowes.

'It was found on the embankment between Martello Hill and the prom,' Tommo told him. 'It was handed in a couple of days ago after that action to evict rough sleepers. Then it sat on a shelf somewhere downstairs until one of the uniforms was having a bit of a clear-up and took a closer look – and recognised a name from her morning team briefing.'

'The padded envelope?' Bolam asked.

Billie nodded. 'It contained some documents. A release letter from the Rodgers-Stephenson Institute, an old handwritten letter from an

Elizabeth Shaw, a printed list of medications – some of which were also in an inside pocket in the bag. All in the name of Russell Shaw.'

So he *was* back in town. Had he been sleeping rough, and caught up in that eviction? And, perhaps most worrying of all, did this mean he had been off his meds ever since?

20

Someone *knew.*

They knew who he was, they knew the awful things he had done, and they knew he was back in town. Russell Shaw could think of no other explanation for the severed finger.

He didn't know what to do. He couldn't calm himself enough to even *begin* to think through all this in any kind of logical manner.

This was simply not the kind of thing that ever *happened.*

Every time he closed his eyes now, he relived that terrible evening from many years before. The casual knock on the side of the ambulance as he went round to open up. The heft of the door handle as he pulled on it. The dark glint of blood as light spilled into the interior. The old man lying on the gurney, blood still oozing from the deep gash across his neck. And Ginnie… lying slumped in a corner, her torso a vivid red from all the stab wounds. He remembered lunging towards her, his feet slipping in the gruesome mess, dropping to his knees beside her. He remembered the awful, raw meat feel of her slashed neck as he tried desperately to find a pulse.

He had never been able to fill in the gaps between the pick-up and opening the doors, even as he explored and re-explored events through years of therapy. It seemed any recollection of the terrible things he had done would always be beyond him, but the evidence had been incontrovertible. He'd babbled about someone else being there, someone who had reminded him of his grandfather, but he knew there had been no one.

He'd spent long hours in therapy, exploring how his mind had constructed a narrative that shifted blame. How he'd imprinted on images and figures from his past and somehow hallucinated them. How his brain had reconfigured its interpretation of events because otherwise he would have been unable to handle the knowledge of what he had done.

If someone else had been involved, there would have been physical evidence, not just his mad, garbled say-so. Footprints in the blood. Fingerprints. *Something.*

While those long therapy sessions had failed to clarify his recollections of that night, they *had* allowed him to reconstruct himself – to the extent that after nineteen years of treatment he had been deemed to be no longer a threat to society.

But someone knew he was back. Someone was playing dark, twisted games with him.

Now his head was in turmoil and he no longer had the ability to know what was going on. He couldn't trust his own senses. Couldn't trust the world around him. Couldn't trust even the few memories he had of that awful night.

And he no longer trusted that he truly had rebuilt who he was.

You're not the man you were.

Maybe not, but that didn't mean he had been fixed.

He came round in darkness, shivering.

He lay in long grass, wet with dew.

He sat up. His clothes were soaked through.

He was at the graveyard behind St Katherine's church. Lying beside his sister's grave.

Oh, Elizabeth.

She'd stood by him, but he'd failed her. Lost her.

He didn't know how he'd got here, or how late it was.

He had the keys in his pocket, labelled 'FRONT DOOR' and '14C', but he couldn't bring himself to return, even though he was still shivering violently.

He stood, and started to walk.

It must be late, because the roads were quiet and street lamps in the side streets had been turned off, which Stewart had told him was an energy-saving policy. It was after midnight, then.

He should worry that most of the evening was a blank. He knew that. But for now, at least, he allowed himself the comfort that it *was* a blank. He wished *he* was still a blank. Not living this moment.

He needed his meds. Not just the limited few Stewart had managed to get for him: he needed them all, so that his senses might be smothered by that familiar blanket. But the thought of registering with the local medical system scared him. He couldn't face doctors picking apart the workings of his brain again.

Stewart had offered him other drugs, too. Ones that would numb his senses. He knew that was a slippery slope, but he didn't have many options.

Briefly, he considered heading for the railway line, stepping out in front of a train, if there were any running this late. But in the perverse logic of the moment, such an act would require positive action on his part, and all he could do was put one foot in front of the other, not think any farther ahead than that, and try not to think any farther back.

Walking didn't warm him. His clothes were soaked through from lying in the wet grass and the air was freezing cold. Perhaps it had rained earlier. He didn't know. Couldn't think.

He came to a low-rise block of flats, saw a road opposite, neat rows of bungalows with gravelled front gardens.

He recognised the road, the houses, but didn't know why.

The street was in darkness, but his eyes had adjusted.

He came to a bungalow with a white Volvo hatchback parked in the drive and paused opposite. No lights were on – of course: it was long after midnight.

He was still shivering.

Ginnie had lived here. Immediately, he flashed back to that terrible night, the blood-soaked interior of the ambulance.

Nearby, a ginger cat jumped up onto a low wall and stared at him. After a time, it sauntered away.

Russ crossed the road and came to stand at the foot of the drive of Ginnie's bungalow.

Other than Elizabeth's grave, this was his only connection with the past.

Ginnie had understood him. She'd learned to read his emotional state, knew when to push and when to cut him some slack.

He stepped into the driveway and paused.

When he took another step a security light came on, blinding him. He staggered back, hands to his face, covering his eyes, flashing back even farther, to life in the Army, to explosions in the night and the gut-wrenching crack of gunfire.

When he caught himself, he was standing in the middle of the road, and when he looked up, he saw lights on in the bungalow now.

The door opened, at the side of the house by the car, and a figure stepped out. A white-haired man.

'I…' Russ started, then stopped.

Then he turned and ran.

By the time he reached his own street, his breathing burned in his lungs and throat, and his wet clothes chafed.

He stopped, bent double, coughing and wheezing. Then, before he had time to think, he produced the keys, found the one labelled 'FRONT DOOR', and slid it into the lock.

He stared at the three wooden pigeonholes, but they were empty.

He climbed the two flights of stairs, found the other key, opened his door.

The finger was still there on the small, round coffee table, next to his mug of cold tea.

He went over to the kitchen niche and took a teaspoon from the cutlery drawer, and then he went back to the round table, found the padded envelope where it had fallen to the floor, and used the spoon to scoop the finger back into it.

21

Bolam had visited the Rowe house more times this month than in the past five years or more.

Before, it had been a family obligation to spend time with people he had never either liked or understood. Now, it was work, and equally uncomfortable. He parked in the street and let himself in through the big gate. As his feet crunched on the gravel driveway, he couldn't help reflecting on Aisha's advice that he should distance himself from this case. Indeed, if Gordon were found to be culpable for any part of this bizarre array of offences, the defence team would have a field day with Bolam's closeness to it all.

He supposed that, at heart, that must mean he didn't believe it would come to that, but he had never put any stall by gut feelings and the copper's nose. Just because he couldn't bring himself to believe that Gordon was a wrong'un, that didn't mean he would ever ease up from doggedly pursuing the truth to whatever conclusion that brought.

He paused in what he was sure his brother-in-law would refer to as the portico. Before he could ring the bell, the door was opening. Gordon must have been alerted to his arrival by a security camera or video doorbell. Again, Bolam thought of how that padded envelope had been delivered by someone who had known how to evade such coverage.

'Gordon,' he said. 'I hope I'm not…?'

His brother-in-law tossed his hair, made a dismissive gesture with the wave of a hand, and said, 'No, of course not. You know you're always welcome here.'

Bolam followed him through the kitchen to the conservatory, where Gordon picked up a whisky bottle and waggled it in invitation, and it was Bolam's turn to use a wave of the hand to dismiss the offer. He wasn't technically on duty, but he was not a drinker of spirits.

'Is Maria here?'

Another wide sweep of the hand that was now holding a whisky tumbler. 'Some function or other,' Gordon said, as if he'd forgotten the details rather than had never even bothered to find out.

'It's about Joanna.'

Gordon sat on a rattan sofa, gesturing Bolam into the matching bucket seat opposite. 'So it *is* her?' he said.

Bolam nodded. 'The DNA results came back this afternoon,' he said. 'It's a familial match to samples provided by her father. The finger delivered to your postbox belonged to Joanna Clayton, and she died between twenty and twenty-five years ago.' She went missing twenty-two years ago, so the dates Raj had given them corresponded, and suggested she had died around the time of her disappearance.

Gordon's frame had slumped upon hearing the news.

'Does that mean he's still out there, whoever did this?'

Bolam said nothing.

'Are we in danger? Me? Luke? Maria?'

Bolam noted the apparent order of priority in Gordon's list. 'We really don't know,' he said. 'But there's been nothing so far to suggest escalation. At the moment it just seems to be some kind of psychological torment. But you'd be advised to exercise caution.' He knew how inadequate this sounded, but without any clear sign of threat, a small provincial police force like his was in no position to offer much more.

'Perhaps I will,' Bolam said, indicating the bottle, and Gordon gestured for him to help himself. He poured a small measure, sat back, took a sip. The spirit stung his throat, making his eyes water. There was a reason he didn't drink the stuff.

'Tell me about her. Joanna.' Find out how the victim lived and you have a chance of finding out how they died. But also, Bolam wanted to find out more about Gordon Rowe. To understand him. And the best way to do that was to ask him about someone else, because ask him about himself and he'd relax into well-practised stories that presented the face he wanted the world to see.

'She was young and vivacious,' Gordon said, after a long pause. 'And irritating as all hell. But in the same breath she could charm you with a look or a smile.' Another expansive wave of the hand. 'Oh, nothing like you're thinking. She was seventeen, eighteen. Four years younger than Maria, and barely half my age at the time.'

The age gap between Gordon and Maria had always been the thing no one mentioned. Bolam refrained from pointing out that it was not unheard of for a thirty-something man to be flattered by the attentions of a girl half his age.

'I think she had a thing for me, you know? That's one reason Maria liked to keep her at arm's length. Joanna used to call by the offices in town. She knew I was a soft touch for drinking money. She treated it like a game. A flutter of the lashes, a few flirtatious comments, and she knew she was good for a tenner. I should never have played along with it but, you know…'

Bolam *did* know. Already, he was building a very different picture of Joanna to the one he'd had from Maria. Yes, Joanna had clearly been a handful, but seen through Gordon's eyes the girl was springing to life, whereas Maria's account had been more distanced and judgemental.

'Why were you always the one who brought her home when she strayed, Gordon?'

'I was punching above my weight, wasn't I? Maria was a catch, and I was… older. I always felt I had to over-perform, just to stand a chance of keeping her. I've spent my whole life doing that, and…' He puffed air out between pursed lips, held his hands up, palms out. 'So I put in the hours. I wooed Maria, and part of that wooing involved ingratiating myself with the family, impressing the old man, looking out for the kid sister, even if Maria always pretended she didn't want anything to do with her. So when Joanna got into trouble, I pulled a few strings—'

'The breach of the peace charge? And when she was picked up for possession?'

'I did what I could to make all that go away, yes. She was family, right? We'd all do the same.'

Bolam said nothing. Gordon was family, and right now he was reserving judgement.

He could see why Joanna might have been drawn to Gordon, though: the flashy, show-off lawyer who could make all her troubles go away.

'And when she ran away?'

'Joanna never ran away. She just didn't go home. There's a critical distinction. How many times was it? Three? Four? I drove around, spoke to her friends, worked out who she'd been with and who she'd probably ended up shagging. It wasn't difficult.'

'Was it always the same person that she ended up with?'

Gordon shook his head. 'If you're looking for a suspect from her pool of acquaintances you're going to end up with a long list, my friend.'

'So why Joanna? Why would someone kill her back then, and why would they target you and Maria now?' They were still searching for Russell Shaw, but without luck so far: he appeared simply to have vanished after he came back, leaving only that canvas bag and a few meagre possessions in his wake. And even if they found him... Bolam still hadn't come up with a credible theory that connected Shaw with the deaths of Joanna Clayton or Jayne Sturridge, let alone explained his actions now – if, indeed, he was behind current events.

Gordon remained silent, hiding behind a long sip of whisky and then a pause to hold his glass up to the light as if to confirm that it was now empty. Was that lawyer's brain currently working full-speed, reassessing why Bolam was here and how much he should therefore say?

'You think we're somehow implicated, do you?' he finally said, studying Bolam through narrowed eyes.

Bolam didn't even try to deny it. It was impossible to shake off the fact that he viewed Gordon in terms of suspicion. That he was looking for guilt in every evasion, every half-truth, every inadvertent *truth*.

'Don't we all look back on things and feel responsible?' Bolam said carefully, trying to draw Gordon out. 'You must have regrets, and wish you'd done things differently. It's human nature. Don't you ever feel guilty about that single occasion when you weren't able to keep on punching above your weight and drag Joanna back one more time?'

He thought Gordon was going to hit him. He saw the man's body tensing up, saw the clenching of muscles in the fist and arm. Saw the gradual easing.

'You see darkness in everyone, don't you?' Gordon said, reaching instead for the bottle and pouring himself a refill. Bolam's glass remained untouched after that first, burning swallow.

'Darkness?'

'You think I should feel guilty that I didn't do more. You probably blame Maria, too, for not caring enough. You see some kind of twisted darkness in a gentle old schoolteacher like Matthew Sturridge who has lived his life in grief. You look for that same darkness in a public-spirited man who has only ever devoted his life to the ambulance service and his charitable works – yes, Robbie Walton told me you'd engineered an encounter with him. Can't people simply be good, in your eyes?'

'How often have you come across people who are simply good?' Bolam asked. He was genuinely curious. In his professional life he had rarely, if ever, come across a villain incapable of at least some degree of goodness. Had Gordon ever encountered the other end of the scale, the irredeemably pure? 'You do good works, Gordon, you move in charitable circles… You must have come across genuinely wholesome people?'

'You're looking for black and white,' Gordon said. 'Whereas in reality it's a balancing act, and the best we can do is be more in credit than debit.'

'I think that was my point, Gordon.' But whereas Gordon wanted to sweep aside the bad, it was Bolam's role to root it out and expose it.

He reached for his glass, took a drink, and regretted it. It didn't just burn: the smoky scent as he raised the crystal tumbler made him think of cigarettes.

'What about Russell Shaw?' Bolam had been unable to draw a

direct connection between Shaw and Joanna, but he *had* found other threads… Threads he was now pulling.

Gordon took another long sip, but said nothing.

'You went to school with him, didn't you, Gordon?' He spoke even more softly than usual, a trick he sometimes used in more formal interviews to get past people's guards: because they had to lean in, pay close attention, and somehow that seemed to bypass the usual barriers.

'It's that small town thing,' he continued. 'Everyone here is connected somehow. You grew up here, and you went to the high school – was that where you first encountered Matthew Sturridge, before, years later, he had need of your firm's legal services? You're about the same age as Russell Shaw. Same year group. You would have been in the same clubs, you were both in the Army Cadet Corps, so you'd almost certainly have known him.'

'I can't talk about Shaw.'

Bolam stared, puzzled. Was Gordon simply refusing? Then he realised it had been *can't* rather than *won't*.

'Your firm represented Shaw, didn't it?' It would be in the court records. Someone should have made the connection.

Gordon remained silent.

'Getting him diminished responsibility must be one of your career highs…'

Gordon opened his mouth to speak, but then managed to stop himself.

'Did you stay involved afterwards? Did you have a hand in steering how his hospital order was implemented?' Officially no, of course, but unofficially… Gordon always talked in terms of pulling strings, bringing influence to bear. He had said more times than Bolam cared to recall that a lawyer's success should be measured in all the small victories as well as the big ones.

'Were you involved in his release process?'

Silence, still.

'Do you know where he is now?'

Finally, a response: a brief shake of the head.

Bolam sat back. He hadn't realised he'd even sat forward, hands clenched together, eyes fixed on Gordon.

'It's okay, Iain.'

Bolam looked at Gordon closely, not understanding. He couldn't remember the last time someone had used his first name, either: he was not a man to let people close. Even the people closest to him tended to maintain a distance.

'I know you have to do this,' Gordon said, 'and that sometimes it screws with your relationships with everyone around you. I understand the process, and what is at stake.' He shrugged, waved a hand. 'But that doesn't make it any easier on the people around you, does it? I'm just the same as you. I have to keep home and work distinct, even if that makes Maria think I'm not interested in sharing my life with her. I see cases from a different perspective to you, but I still see it all, and have to deal with it. It doesn't make for an easy life, does it?'

'I spoke to Maria,' Bolam said. 'The other evening, when you were out. About Joanna.'

'And do our stories tally?'

'More or less.' It appeared that Maria hadn't mentioned his visit – perhaps because of the way she had flirted. Bolam found it interesting that Robbie Walton should tell Gordon about his encounter with Bolam, but Gordon's own wife had not. 'Your account was more vivid.'

'There was nothing in it,' Gordon said. 'Joanna was just a kid.'

And you protest too much.

'I've never strayed, you know?' Gordon delivered this statement as if it was some kind of achievement. 'All these years, and I've had my opportunities. But I've remained straight and true.'

'Maria seemed stressed,' Bolam said. 'Are you two okay?' Ordinarily, he would never ask such personal questions of family, but his brain was still in professional mode: he was constructing a picture of their lives, not asking after the marriage of his brother-in-law.

Gordon peered down into the glass cupped in both hands.

'Peaks and troughs,' he said, after a time. 'Maria and myself – the peaks are high. Exhilarating.'

'And the troughs?'

'You saw us the other day. We forget how to communicate. We fight. We've been that way for more than twenty years. This is our normal.'

Bolam said nothing. For all that this felt like some uncomfortably intimate kind of confessional, the line seemed too well-rehearsed. He sensed that things might be worse now than a normal trough in their relationship, but he kept that to himself.

'You and Fran, though,' Gordon said, and Bolam wished he'd remained silent. 'You were always so good together. Something to aspire to – that was mine and Maria's joke.'

'We…'

'I know.'

Bolam had not spoken about this to anyone. He was not one to share. He did not need to use others as sounding boards in order to understand himself. Fran was the only person he had ever felt the need to share with, and he had felt the benefit of that sharing.

'I thought we were like the penguins,' Bolam said.

Gordon peered at him, said nothing.

'Mates for life. I always believed I'd walk across Antarctica for her. Only I never realised how distracted I was by work. How obsessive I get. It makes me a good detective, but not a good person. Not an easy one. And then there was covid…' Fran had been an intensive care nurse, and during the worst of the pandemic she'd stayed in hospital residences for weeks on end. 'All that time, our only communication was a few text messages and an occasional short phone call. I think she realised that that wasn't very different to living *with* me… Not just in practical terms, but in how she felt.' He should stop now. He didn't need to be doing this, and in particular he didn't need to be doing it with Gordon Rowe.

'Fran arranged all this. The move. And – great detective that I am – I didn't see that she wasn't planning the move for both of us. That she talked of "I" and "me" rather than "us". So I applied for the Serious Crimes position here, and was committed before I finally worked it all out. And then she fell ill.'

Fell ill sounded so anodyne. They'd stuck it out through covid and its aftermath, and then cancer had taken her, fast and ruthless.

'She died, and I just sleepwalked into the footsteps she would have taken. Moved into the house she'd arranged to live in without me, back in her home town, which is the kind of place you only ever move to when you're trying to escape everywhere else. And now I'm a fraud, living a dead person's life in a place I never wanted to be.'

He sipped whisky, savouring the pain in his throat.

'It's the forms that irritate me the most,' he said. 'Making this move I've had to complete so many forms that ask for marital status but then there isn't a category that fits, because I can never work out whether it's appropriate to call myself a widower when my dying wife was already in the process of leaving me.' Labels mattered to Bolam – like whether the forensic study of an amputated finger counted as a post-mortem. That gap between separated and widower was a limbo that tortured him daily.

'I know.'

He'd already said that, but now Bolam stared at him.

'I know, man,' Gordon told him. 'I was the one who put Fran in touch with Claudia Berg, the specialist in family law she was using. I was the one who pulled a few strings to secure that house you're now living in, and I knew it was just for her, not for both of you.'

Bolam stared. He didn't know Fran had talked to Gordon about this.

'I had a letter from them this morning,' he said. 'Berg and Associates. Or rather Fran did. They seemed to have overlooked the fact she's dead.'

'What? I—'

'It's okay, I put them right. Just a cock-up.'

'That doesn't make it okay.'

Bolam took another sip of whisky. 'You never said you knew about how things were with me and Fran,' he said.

'Do you think I'm blind, or stupid? Fran was my kid sister. Of course I didn't say anything to you. I was being nice. And then after… after Fran fell ill, it seemed cruel to talk about it. And she always loved you, you know? Never stopped. She just couldn't live with you any more.'

He might as well have punched him earlier. It would have hurt less. Hearing it said out loud like this… It was too much.

He had never cried. Not then, and he wasn't going to now.

He stood. 'I should go. I shouldn't have come here.'

'I know.'

And even now, the part of his brain that never stopped was wondering if those strings Gordon had pulled to secure a house for Fran had involved Robbie Walton, a friend who also happened to have business interests in the local property market.

Outside, there was still some light in the sky, even though it was mid-evening. Bolam crunched across the gravel, let himself out of the big gate, went and sat in his car.

And just as he was about to gun the engine his phone rang.

'Boss?' It was Billie Grayson. 'Can you come in? We've got him. Russell Shaw. We've got him.'

22

He should do something, talk to somebody. He knew that.

But who? He couldn't go to the police. They wouldn't believe a word he said. He was spiralling now, his head full of wildness, but in a police interview room he would crash and burn. It would destroy him.

The Rodgers-Stephenson? Nurse Ward, Doctor Chandler, or one of the other members of staff? Judith or Stewart at the shelter?

No. He couldn't face that. The brief flash of doubt on the faces of people with whom he had built some kind of bond, some kind of trust. Even if they took his story at face value, they would ask questions, would want to know why the finger had been sent to *him*, why someone would want to play such awful games with his head like this.

And then when they understood just who – just *what* – he was, they would go to the police.

He couldn't stop thinking about the owner of the finger. Who was she? What had become of her? Was his own inaction making her predicament even worse, or was it too late for him to influence her fate?

He felt sick with fear and guilt. And utterly powerless. He was a paramedic. All he'd ever wanted to do was help people, and yet now, by doing nothing, he must surely be doing the precise opposite.

Over the next few days, he mostly shut himself away. After ignoring repeated calls from Stewart and Eleni at the shelter, he turned his phone off. As his food ran low, he simply ate less. He didn't wash, or change his clothes, other than that first night when he'd had to get out of his wet things.

Judith had called him once before he switched off his phone, and he had been tempted to answer. He had sat in the old wing-back chair staring at the small screen of his phone, her name and number flashing insistently. He couldn't move. The phone stopped flashing, fell silent. Judith had been a mistake. Letting her in. Welcoming that chink of light of normality.

He should not give in to temptation.

He walked at night, when the town was sleeping and the streets quiet. He had no regular route, he simply walked where his feet took him. It was the one time he could blank things out, the rhythm of his stride almost hypnotic.

A couple of times he found himself in the street outside Ginnie's house, peering at the darkened windows. Her parents must know something. If someone was messing with Russ's head, then they must be doing the same with the old couple too.

He put the finger in its envelope away in a drawer. He couldn't bring himself to look at it again, but even the grotesque bulge of that digit in the padded envelope was more than enough to haunt his thoughts every time he closed his eyes.

He went back to Ginnie's.

Not Ginnie's… her parents' place, the bungalow where she had lived while she was sorting out her life.

The evenings were staying light now. Almost eight o'clock and the sun was only just setting, the western sky glowing with an orange wash. Lights were on in the bungalow, and the front room's net curtains were lit with the flickering light of the TV.

'It's you, isn't it? I don't know how you have the nerve.'

A voice from his left. He turned his head and saw the old man there. White hair, staring blue eyes, a claw hammer hanging from his right hand at his side.

'I just…' He just wanted to know that they were okay. Wanted to see their lives going on. To feel that connection.

The man took a step.

'Thomas!'

The woman, Ginnie's mother, standing in the space between the bungalow's open front door and the white Volvo.

'I've called the police. Thomas, leave it to them.'

The old man lunged with surprising speed.

Russ felt the rush of air as the hammer swung past his face, was only saved by the reflex step backwards he took.

The man toppled forward with his own momentum and Russ caught him, and for what felt like several seconds they staggered in something resembling a macabre dance.

The man twisted, pushed, and they stumbled apart.

He swung the hammer again, and Russ took the impact on a raised forearm, the handle making contact rather than the head, so that it was more a glancing blow than the kind that would have broken bone.

The woman was screaming, and Russ felt an incongruous rush of a sense of injustice, as if the sound she was making implied that *he* was the aggressor and not her husband.

Russ stepped back, and the two stood eyeing each other.

Ginnie's father raised the hammer for another swing just as Russ heard sirens. How did the police get here so quickly? Had a car merely been in the vicinity, or was his sense of time awry? For a moment Russ wondered if he'd suffered another blank, and he looked around himself, fearful of what might have occurred during the absence, but the tableau remained unchanged – the old woman by the car, the old man advancing on him again with the hammer raised.

A dog barked. The door of another bungalow opened and a man called, 'Mr Lloyd? Are you okay?'

A police car screeched to a halt beside Russ, and for an instant the look on Thomas Lloyd's face suggested he was about to have one last swing with the hammer, then strong hands gripped Russ's upper arms, pulling him away, slamming him against the bonnet of the car, pushing him face down against the metal.

'You say you walk past the Lloyds' house on your way home from the shelter.' The interviewing officer, an Asian woman, had a disarming manner, not like a police officer at all.

Russ caught the glance from his solicitor, a young woman in a prim pencil-stripe skirt suit who looked thoroughly bored to be here.

He shouldn't answer. The look was telling him not to incriminate himself. But he'd done nothing wrong!

He nodded. Then, knowing the procedure, he said out loud for the recording, 'I do. Sometimes I take a long route home from helping at the shelter. I don't have anything else to do, and I like to walk. Sometimes I walk at night, too, and I—'

Another glance, and a touch on his upper arm. He was rambling. He should shut up.

'And can you explain why what you admit is a convoluted route takes you to this particular street so often?'

He shrugged, then said, 'It's somewhere I know.'

'And do you ever stop there for any reason?'

He looked away. He hated that they would be reading his body language, his every response and expression. He'd spent the last two decades being observed and analysed. Other people knew him far better than he knew himself.

'You've been seen. Several times. Why are you shaking your head, Russell? Are you denying that you've been hanging around outside the Lloyds' house?'

'No… I just…' He didn't know what he'd been going to say.

'Tell me what this is, Russell.' From a card folder the detective produced a clear plastic evidence bag. 'For the record,' she said, 'I'm showing Mr Shaw a C5 manila padded envelope found in a drawer at his home on an authorised search earlier this evening. Can you tell me what was in this envelope, Russell?'

The envelope was flat, no ghastly bulge. Its contents had been removed.

Another glance from the solicitor.

'No comment,' Russ said.

'Were you planning to deliver this to Mr and Mrs Lloyd? Was that why you were watching their house? Waiting for the right moment?'

'What?' He didn't understand. Why would he want to do that? It made no sense.

Then he realised that now the police had the finger he had nothing more to lose. 'The woman,' he said. 'The woman whose finger it was. Is she okay? Have you found her?'

It was a moment of realisation for him, of truly coming to see the person he had become for perhaps the first time. He didn't care about his own fate – they could do with him whatever they wanted, even if that meant locking him away from the world for the rest of his miserable existence. All he wanted to know was what had become of the poor woman who had lost her finger. He wanted them to tell him that they'd found her. That she was still alive.

The police officer was studying his features closely, letting the silence draw itself out.

'Found her?' the officer finally said. 'She's dead. She died a long time ago, and you know that very well, Russell, because you killed her. You killed her nineteen years ago, in the back of your ambulance. We have good reason to believe that the finger belongs to Virginia Lloyd.'

23

Bolam was in early again.

As the Serious Crimes Unit's specialist interviewer, Aisha had taken first crack at Russ Shaw last night. Bolam had watched over the video feed as his DS carefully teased out the man's version of recent events. After coming back to town after his release from the Rodgers-Stephenson Institute with no real plan for what to do next, Shaw had slept rough for a night or two. Then he'd hooked up with a local homeless charity – the Fresh Start project Robbie Walton was involved with, no less – where he'd been given accommodation and some casual work. He walked the streets for hours on end, as if trying to find again a world he'd lost, and those walks always seemed to bring him back to two anchor points from his previous existence: his sister's grave at St Katherine's, and the bungalow Ginnie Lloyd had shared with her parents.

His account was rambling and confused, and he came across as a thoroughly broken specimen of humanity, out of his depth in the modern world and barely able to function. Which, of course, did not mean that within those limitations he had not been orchestrating some perverse campaign of psychological terror against families who had lost loved ones. He was a man who knew this town well; he had connections with the Rowes and the Sturridges, so might easily know of their losses – and even have been responsible.

Aisha had been winging it when she told Shaw that the finger in his possession had belonged to Virginia Lloyd, but she had phrased it carefully: *we have good reason to believe…* They had no fingerprints on record for Lloyd, and it would be days before any DNA results came back, but the circumstantial evidence made the identification a reasonable assumption at this stage. Raj had said the finger matched physical descriptions of Ginnie, and a clumsy amputation at the proximal interphalangeal joint – rather than the metacarpophalangeal joints of the other two victims – corresponded with case notes from the time. It was a leap, but a reasonable one for the purposes of the interview, and unlikely to cause serious problems if the defence raised it at any trial.

What was particularly gruesome in this instance was that the finger was in poor condition, showing not only signs of deterioration but also a coating of dried blood. Was there some kind of meaning attached to the condition of the fingers? Jayne Sturridge's, immaculate and neat, Joanna Clayton's daubed in the oil paints she had used in her art, and now Virginia Lloyd's, as gruesomely bloody as the interior of that ambulance had been, twenty years before.

Shaw had no explanation for why he was in possession of the severed finger of Ginnie Lloyd, although his account that it had been hand-delivered to his home tallied with the stories of Matthew Sturridge and Maria Rowe. But that correspondence of accounts could easily be explained if he already knew exactly how the Sturridge and Rowe fingers had been delivered… The preservation of these digits for a period of almost two decades while Shaw had been locked away in a secure hospital would take some fathoming out, though, and right now, the morning after Shaw's arrest, Bolam had put Tommo and one of the support staff onto tracking down any lock-up or other facility where Shaw might have kept his trophies on ice during that time.

But…

This morning, Bolam followed Aisha back into the interview room where Shaw waited with a young solicitor from the on-call list. After they'd gone through the formalities of introducing themselves for the recording, Bolam sat back and gave himself a few seconds to study the paramedic up close for the first time. He was tall and skinny, but he sat hunched over, as if trying to shrink into his seat. He wore a grey tracksuit provided by the custody team, his clothes away in Cath Marshall's custody for forensic scrutiny.

'Tell me about that night in the ambulance,' Bolam said. He'd already prepared the interview strategy with Aisha, although she had made it clear that she was unhappy with his approach. She'd pointed out that events of that night nineteen years ago had been established in court: what they needed to do today was fill in the gaps to find out how those events had led to what was happening now. But Bolam wanted to hear for himself.

'Unless you can clarify why that's relevant to the current investigation,' interjected the solicitor, 'then I suggest we move on to matters that *are* relevant.'

Bolam smiled at her. He'd assumed she would say something to this effect, but when it came down to it, this was *his* interview, and if he decided it was relevant then it was, indeed, relevant. 'Russell?' he said softly.

'We went to the docks,' Shaw told them. 'False alarm. Then we got a call to West Street to attend an elderly gentleman with heart problems. Mr Duke. We assessed him, moved him into the ambulance, and transported him to hospital.'

'Except that's not all that happened, is it, Russ?' asked Aisha. 'At some point in that sequence of events you went into the back of your ambulance and killed your patient, and your colleague, Virginia Lloyd.'

Shaw looked down at the desk between them.

'In your initial statement you said there was someone else there, with the patient,' said Bolam. 'Waiting with him at the house.'

Now Shaw shook his head. 'I wasn't well,' he said. 'I'm not that man now. I didn't know what was happening to me. In my head.'

'You lied,' said Aisha.

'I didn't know what was real.'

His assertion was almost too insistent, as if he didn't dare let slip the version of events he had clung to for the past nineteen years.

'You were listening to the football, weren't you, Russ?' Bolam said. Aisha gave him a sharp look, clearly frustrated that he appeared to be derailing their agreed strategy. 'The England game.'

Shaw nodded. 'I had a radio for the commentary. I shouldn't have, but it helped my head and Ginnie didn't mind.'

'Helped?' prompted Aisha.

'My head had been getting bad. My nerves. It hadn't been like that since I was in the Army. Ginnie knew I was having an episode that shift. She'd noticed things were getting worse, and she'd told me I needed to see a doctor. She was so kind to me when I didn't really deserve it. She told me to do the driving so I could listen to the game, but she was being nice. She was dealing with the people because my head… So much noise in my head. So many voices.' He ran out of words, pressing both hands to his temples.

'You hear voices now, Russell?' Bolam asked. 'Whose voices do you hear?'

'My grandfather. Liz. Nurse Ward. *Everyone*. I can't cope.'

'Tell us what you mean by that,' Aisha said.

He shook his head. 'I couldn't handle things sometimes. I still can't. It's too much.'

'Even with your medication?'

'I came off my meds for a while after I left the Institute… I'd have to register with a GP for more, and—'

'You knew we'd find you if you got back into the system,' Aisha finished for him. 'And that's the last thing you'd want, isn't it?'

'They should never have played Lampard and Gerrard in the same team, should they?' said Bolam. That prompted another sharp look from Aisha. 'I always said one or the other, but not both. The two of them with Beckham – just too airy-fairy, wasn't it? No backbone to the team. Do you think Gerrard was overrated?'

Now they were all staring at him. Russ Shaw clearly didn't know how to answer, probably suspecting a trap. Finally, he said, 'Lampard didn't play in that one. Calf strain.'

'My bad. I just assumed. Can you remember who scored first?'

'Wayne Rooney.'

'Now *there* was a player. You missed it, though, didn't you? The goal.'

Shaw nodded, a brief flash of frustration flitting across his features. 'We were inside,' he said. 'Nothing much happened in the game until we reached that house, then Rooney scored while we were inside assessing Mr Duke's condition. We got back out and England had scored and I'd missed it by seconds.'

'When did you get back to the hospital?'

'Stroke of half-time. The whistle had just blown when I went round and… found them.'

'Found them?' asked Aisha. 'Do you mean when you went round and did what you did?'

'Yes. Yes, that's what I mean. I… I suffer gaps. Absences. It's all muddled in my head.'

'Did you suffer any absences that night?' Bolam asked.

Shaw wouldn't meet his look.

'Do you remember the journey back to the hospital?'

'I… It was a long time ago,' said Shaw.

'But it's a night you've relived hundreds of times, isn't it, Russ?' pressed Bolam. 'Did you suffer an absence on that journey back to the hospital?'

'I was listening to the match,' said Shaw. 'Trying to… but the voices.'

'Whose voices? Your grandfather?'

Shaw looked sharply away again, confirming Bolam's suspicion: that he'd heard his grandfather's voice that night. In his original statements, Shaw had blamed his grandfather.

'He was shouting at me. He told me to stop the ambulance.'

'Stop?' asked Aisha. 'Where did you stop?'

'Just before the hospital entrance.'

Bolam and Aisha exchanged a look. As far as the DI knew, Shaw had never said this before.

'Was that when you did it?' asked Aisha. 'Did you go into the back of the ambulance when you stopped outside the entrance?'

Shaw stared down at the interview table between them now and said nothing.

It didn't make sense to Bolam. If Shaw had committed the double killing at that point, he'd have had to get back into the driver's seat to drive on into the hospital. There would have been blood all over the seat and steering wheel.

'Tell me about your grandfather,' Bolam said. 'What did he say to you?'

'He wasn't there. I told you that. It was a delusion, a psychotic episode.'

'When you were a child. What was he like? Were you close?'

Shaw recoiled, visibly shrinking back into his seat. 'He… he was a hard man to impress.'

That seemed an odd way to describe your grandfather. 'He was a soldier, wasn't he?' Bolam said. 'He fought in the Second World War. Was that why you joined up? To impress him?'

'I wasn't a soldier like him,' Shaw said. 'I wasn't much more than a stretcher bearer.'

Russell Shaw was a highly skilled paramedic, with commendations for bravery. 'Is that how your grandfather saw you?'

Shaw said nothing.

'If it wasn't your grandfather in the ambulance, who was it?' Again, he was aware of Aisha looking at him. They weren't supposed to be investigating Shaw's original crimes.

'There was nobody.' Shaw seemed calmer, that brief period when Bolam's line of questioning had appeared to disorient him, over now.

'What were you doing with that finger in your possession?' Aisha asked, bringing the interview back to where she clearly thought it should be. 'How did you acquire it?'

Shaw looked from Aisha to Bolam and back. 'I don't know,' he said. 'It's all… I don't know.'

They said nothing for the length of two corridors and one flight of stairs. Bolam sensed that Aisha was still cross with him, and he didn't want to deal with that right now. He wanted to think.

He paused at the top of the stairs, and said to Aisha, 'You go on. I'll be a minute.'

He gazed out of the narrow window. Beyond the rooftops he could see the North Sea, that distinctive blue-brown shade it took when the clouds were grey.

When he walked into the Serious Crimes office, Aisha was standing with Billie and Tommo by the coffee machine. 'He was denying everything,' she was saying to them. 'He—'

'He wasn't denying anything,' Bolam said, crossing the room to join them, thumbing the button to pour an espresso into a mug that was far too big, and none too clean. 'He just didn't seem to know. He doesn't seem to understand much, does he, for someone who might be responsible for the sort of elaborate crimes we're investigating? The world just happens around him.'

'I know the feeling,' said Tommo with a grunt.

'Whoever decided to turn him out onto the streets?' Aisha was not finished yet. 'I thought there were strict criteria? Does he really come across as a man who has been made better by his time in hospital?'

Bolam sipped at the coffee. 'So what's your take, Aisha?'

Before she could answer, Billie Grayson said, 'The timings don't work, do they? The first finger was delivered to Matthew Sturridge before Shaw came back.'

Not that he wanted to fuel Aisha, but Bolam said, 'He was on phased release in the lead up to full discharge. Supervised days out at first, but then unsupervised.'

'He could have planned all this from hospital,' Aisha said. 'Then started his activities while he was out on day release. It fits.'

'But why?' Billie asked.

'He's not all there,' said Aisha, tapping the side of her head. 'It only has to make sense to him. It's as if he's putting on a show for us, demonstrating how clever he is. Maybe he's spent his nineteen years inside writing the script.'

'That's a very convincing narrative,' Bolam said.

The three said nothing, waiting for him to continue, but he remained silent. Finally, Aisha said, 'But you don't believe it.'

'It's not about belief,' Bolam said. 'It's just… It's the football that bothers me.'

'It bothered me, too,' Aisha said. 'What *was* all that Gerrard and Rooney stuff about?'

'I remember the game. I watched it on TV.'

'I didn't know you were a fan, Gov,' said Tommo.

'I'm not. Fran was the sports fan.' He fell silent. He didn't bring personal stuff into work. He hadn't meant to say…

The three were watching him, waiting. 'It was a dull game – even more so than usual. Two teams scared to take a risk. It had nil-nil written all over it.' That's what Fran had said, and then she'd had to explain what she meant. It had been early days for them then –

amusement and excitement and novelty in every conversation, no matter how mundane. Days when even a dull football match lingered in the memories, not for the match itself but for the realisation that quiet shared evenings like that meant a relationship might be moving onto something *more*.

'There had been no goals by the time Shaw's ambulance reached the patient's house on West Street,' Bolam went on. 'And Shaw and Ginnie Lloyd had time to assess the patient and get him into the ambulance before setting off for hospital. By that time England had just scored, and half-time was approaching. The goal came in the thirty-ninth minute and they reached the hospital on the stroke of half-time.'

'Thirty-ninth minute?' said Tommo. 'You've got a good memory.'

'No, I don't,' said Bolam. 'But the internet's a wonderful thing. Anyway… Six minutes, plus maybe two or three for stoppage time. How does that allow long enough for Shaw to get to the hospital, go around and into the back of his ambulance, and commit double murder? I've checked the timings of the route from West Street to the hospital. It doesn't add up.'

'Why believe Shaw about that timeline, when the psychologists have cast doubt over his other memories – or claims – of that evening?' asked Tommo.

'It's the football,' Bolam said. 'What's the famous quote? Football's not a matter of life or death, it's more important than that. People remember the details. Shaw remembered that Frank Lampard hadn't been playing that night. He remembered who scored the opening goal. He may be unsure about everything else, but he remembers those details. Just as he remembers missing the goal, and getting to the hospital just as the half-time whistle blew. There must be logs at the ambulance call centre: they'll confirm the timings of the call to Shaw's ambulance, and his arrival at the hospital.' CCTV would have been handy, but coverage was patchy nineteen years ago on the route the ambulance would have taken through the old part of town.

'He was found guilty nineteen years ago,' Tommo said. 'That's not our case.'

'But if they were wrong back then,' Bolam said. 'If someone else was responsible, and now Ginnie Lloyd's finger shows up in the middle of *our* case, then it's all the same investigation…'

'There's the state of the finger, too,' Aisha said. 'And the fingerprints.' Bolam looked at her, waited for her to go on.

'The finger sent to Matthew Sturridge appeared fresh,' she said. Her tone and slow, considered delivery suggested she was in the process of rethinking everything. 'It appeared to be in good condition. It took examination in the pathology lab to confirm that it was actually a frozen finger that had been thawed out. The same for the finger delivered to the Rowes.'

'But the finger in Shaw's possession was different…' Bolam completed for her. Not only was that finger covered in dried blood, it was in poor condition, showing distinct signs of deterioration. It had been thawed out several days before they'd found it at Shaw's flat. 'But what do you mean about the fingerprints? What's odd about them?' He thought Aisha meant the prints belonging to the amputated fingers.

'There were no finger marks on the first two envelopes other than those of the recipients. No forensics at all. The fingers and envelopes – and letterboxes – had been handled carefully, by someone who was forensically aware.'

Now he understood. 'But the envelope in Shaw's possession was covered with them, wasn't it?' he said. They'd assumed Shaw had been planning to deliver that envelope to Ginnie Lloyd's parents, in which case they'd expect him to do so in a forensically clean manner – but his prints were all over the envelope.

As Aisha had worked out, it didn't fit the pattern.

'So,' concluded Bolam, 'we have two cases where everything was clean and precise, and a third where the finger appears to have been in Shaw's possession for several days, with no attempt to maintain forensic discipline. We're looking for someone with the opportunity, mindset and ability to carry out a clever and elaborate sequence of crimes, and use them to create some kind of, I don't know, a *game* that teases anyone trying to make sense of them. And in our custody we have a broken individual who appears to possess none of these attributes…'

'It's almost as if he's telling the truth, isn't it, Gov?' said Tommo.

24

'Thanks for agreeing to talk,' Bolam said.

Seeing Doctor Chandler from the Rodgers-Stephenson in a video-call window on his computer screen had the uncanny effect of making the man's elongated features look as if some kind of special effects filter had been applied, a normal face distorted as if seen in a carnival mirror.

Since Bolam's visit to Cambridge, the Institute had been more forthcoming with their cooperation, while still remaining cautious over their obligations towards patient confidentiality.

'Russell Shaw,' Chandler said. 'What can I tell you?'

Bolam had already explained that Shaw was in custody, connected with a major inquiry.

'You've been at the Rodgers-Stephenson for a long time, Doctor,' Bolam said. He'd done his research: Chandler had been on the psych team when Shaw had transferred there twelve years previously. 'You were involved in Shaw's initial assessments when he arrived. You probably know his case better than I do.'

Chandler didn't deny it.

'When he was arrested, he said there had been another person present in the ambulance. Someone who reminded him of his late grandfather.'

'That was demonstrated to be a false claim.'

'A lie?'

'He believed it.'

'That there was someone there?'

'That his *grandfather* was there,' Chandler said. 'Which we know was impossible because his grandfather was dead. Shaw was delusional. He also saw his sister here at the Institute. Putting aside the high levels of security that would have prevented her from just walking in here without any of us being aware, she had been dead six years, too, by then. He used to talk to Virginia Lloyd, also. Were you aware of that? The most lucid conversations he had for a long, long time were those with an empty chair opposite him where he insisted Ms Lloyd was sitting.'

Bolam knew none of this. He tried not to think about the times he caught himself talking to his own dead wife. That was different – just another way of talking to himself. Russell Shaw heard voices; his conversations with the dead were two-way.

'I'm struggling with the timeline,' Bolam said. 'On the evening of the murders.'

'Manslaughter by diminished responsibility was the verdict, Inspector, not murder.'

'Indeed. That evening they had eight or nine minutes to get the patient to the hospital. Shaw was driving. So by the version of events accepted in court, he either stopped en route, committed a violent double murder, then somehow got back into the ambulance and drove on to the hospital, without leaving the driving area covered in forensic traces. Or he committed the killings once he reached the hospital. We believe now that he did stop briefly en route, but—'

'My understanding was that he parked at the hospital and did it there,' countered Chandler. 'That makes for the most convincing narrative, forensically speaking.'

'But England had just scored,' said Bolam.

Chandler stared.

'He was listening to the football. England scored six minutes before half-time, and the ambulance reached the hospital when the teams were leaving the field, and that corresponds with witness accounts of when hospital staff reached the ambulance. The journey would take most of that time. I'm struggling to understand how he managed to fit it all in. But if there had been someone else in the back…' They could have done the deed en route, perhaps slipping out when he stopped briefly before reaching the hospital, or at the hospital, before Shaw realised what had happened.

'Has anyone considered that Shaw might actually have been telling the truth?' Bolam concluded.

'What, that there was a mystery man in the back of the ambulance after all?'

'Not necessarily,' said Bolam. 'But everything about the man I have in that interview room says he's someone who is desperately trying to understand. He's trying to tell the truth because how else will he find an explanation? So his account of that night – before the prosecution messed with it by convincing him he had a screw loose – was his best attempt at the truth, within his screwed-up understanding and perception. Does that make any sense at all, Doctor Chandler?'

The doctor was shaking his head. 'Forgive me for saying, Inspector, but *you* sound delusional now, and your rather melodramatic account does not help. Wasn't there a forensic case against Shaw, too?'

'It was a mess,' Bolam said. 'Shaw was covered in the blood of both victims, but his statement said he had checked for signs of life on both, and was trying to staunch the flow of blood from Ginnie Lloyd's neck. The forensics only prove he was there and had contact with the victims, which no one ever denied.'

'There was no indication that anyone *else* had been there, though.'

The case notes were a jumble. It had taken Bolam's team long enough to be sure simply that Ginnie Lloyd's severed finger had been unaccounted for. From what he could determine, the interior of the ambulance had been chaotic. Blood everywhere, and by the time of the forensic examination the scene had been contaminated not only by Shaw, but by at least five members of hospital staff who had wrestled the paramedic out of there and pinned him to the ground to wait for the police, and then gone back into the ambulance to also check for signs of life.

'Doctor Chandler, would you answer just one question for me? If we accept that Russell Shaw's therapy was designed in order to correct the delusions that shaped how he recalled events of that evening, if there were elements of those recollections that were *not* delusional, would the therapy have "corrected" those towards the accepted version of events too?'

Chandler started to speak, then stopped. Then, 'It's more complicated than your presentation, Inspector.'

'But…?'

Chandler shook his head, and said nothing.

The call was interrupted by a figure appearing in Bolam's open doorway. DCI McBride.

Bolam nodded, turned back to Chandler, thanked him, and made excuses. Then he stood. 'Sir?'

McBride came in, pushed the door closed behind him. 'I've just had a call from Souter,' he said. He sat, and indicated for Bolam to do likewise. 'He wasn't impressed.'

Andy Souter was one of the local Customs and Excise officers.

'I called and apologised,' Bolam said. 'It was urgent.'

'The liaison meeting had been calendared for weeks.'

'We'd just received intel that a multiple murderer had been released back into our community,' Bolam said. 'That tied in with our investigations into two historical missing persons cases, which we've subsequently confirmed were murders.'

'I know, I know. But at your rank you have to be able to juggle and prioritise, Bolam. You know this. The meeting with Andy Souter may seem like just another distracting layer of bureaucracy, but in a town like this these things form a key part of our operations. Most of our serious crimes are related to the port, and jurisdictional boundaries between Customs and Police are often fuzzy. We need to keep the likes of Souter on board.'

'I'll talk to him,' Bolam said. 'I'll take care of it.'

'You used the H word. Historical.'

As soon as he'd said it, Bolam had known it was a mistake.

'Serious Crimes is not a cold case unit.'

'We have two murders that are historical, yes, sir.' Bolam didn't think now was the time to voice his concerns about a third case, the Virginia Lloyd and Ronald Duke double murder. 'But the reason they've come to our attention is a sequence of recent events.'

'The fingers in the post, I know. Raymond Cowper spoke to me about that, and now he's pressing the Chief Super.'

'Ah, Cowper,' said Bolam. 'He's made sure I know he has connections in this town.'

'And, of course, that should have no sway over your work, I know.' McBride raised his eyebrows, fixing Bolam with his gaze. 'But we both know people like Cowper *do* have influence, and as a senior criminal lawyer of long standing who has had a high profile in this town for decades, he's going to be a part of your professional life for some time to come. All I'm saying is, that we need to remember that.'

'I know, and I do.' And this was exactly the point Cowper had been trying to make when he'd cornered Bolam after the Sturridge interview.

'But still,' continued McBride, 'this is, by your own admission, fundamentally a historical case, or cases, and there's a complex psychological layer to it. I think we might need to call in specialist help from the National Crime Agency and divert your team's resources back to more recent events. This may seem unfair, but right now you're giving every impression that this role is too much for you to handle. You need to focus on areas where you're likely to get results.'

Bolam understood the politics, and all the other pressures, but he just wanted to see this through.

'Give us a little more time, sir,' he said. 'We have a witness in custody, and some solid leads. I think we're making progress.' And he realised he'd just described Russell Shaw as a witness, rather than a suspect.

McBride paused to study him carefully, then shrugged, nodded. 'I'm watching closely, Bolam, as are others.' He stood to leave, then paused in the doorway, turned, and said, 'And call Andy Souter. Use some of that northern charm.'

The Customs House dated back to the seventeenth century, a grand building on a slight hill overlooking the docks. Andy Souter's office was small, but high-ceilinged, with a tall leaded window that commanded a view of two-legged cranes and rows of containers stacked four or five high, and the wide sweep of the estuary beyond.

The man himself was balding, with thick ginger sideburns as if to compensate. He could easily play a character in a period drama. He sat back in his office chair, twisted to one side so his legs could cross. 'So Phil McBride sent you along with your tail between your legs, did he?' he said with a laugh. 'Don't worry. No one on my side is pissed off. Your boss just likes to do things properly, that's all.'

Bolam smiled in return. He felt he had McBride's measure, and he didn't mind having a superior who cared about procedures. At least you knew what to expect.

'I really didn't mean to miss my first liaison meeting since starting here,' Bolam said. 'I do appreciate their strategic importance, and I do need to get up to speed on our joint activities.'

'Well, that's settled,' Souter said. 'We'll carry on with the quarterly meetings and we all agree it's a good thing. But more important is little chats like this, in my book. We get to know each other, and build a bit of trust and respect, so that when my team has something on the horizon that might be more your territory we'll pick up the phone. And likewise.'

Bolam wasn't sure if that was a rebuke or not. The way Souter had emphasised the need to build trust…

'Noted,' he said. 'And agreed. Now what do I need to know about?'

Souter paused to study Bolam more closely, then gave that short laugh again. 'I think we're going to get on,' he said.

They talked for close to an hour, by the end of which Bolam knew far more about people trafficking networks and drug smuggling than he'd learned in the previous three months here. The port wasn't a major player in either of these areas, but Souter's team had several low-key monitoring operations on the go. Bolam recognised some of the names of people involved from intel reports, which was reminder enough that McBride had been right to be cross with him: a significant proportion of serious crimes in a town like this were always likely to revolve around the activities of the port.

As they were winding up, Bolam said, 'How long have you worked here, Andy?'

'Too long.' Souter laughed, and tipped his head back to indicate thinking. 'Twenty-two years in June,' he said. 'Does it show?'

'Do you remember a punishment killing, about twenty years ago?' Bolam asked. 'Victim's name was Linda Rawlings. Particularly brutal. A machete slash that came close to decapitating the victim. Both hands removed, presumably to delay identification of the victim.' Fingerprints were so much faster for ID than dental records or DNA, particularly back then.

Souter was nodding. 'I was a junior customs officer,' he said. 'We were up against a Russian gang that was trying to muscle in on the port. Heroin from Afghanistan was their main stock in trade. I remember we all assumed at first that the killing was part of that, but the victim was a woman from London, no obvious connection. Why do you ask?'

'Oh, it's probably nothing. It came up in relation to a current investigation.' Up until now, Bolam had come across nothing to indicate that the hand-amputation case was *not* gang-related, so Souter's version was interesting, to say the least.

'I do remember the lawyer, though,' Souter went on. 'Flash git. Even though that killing was a red herring as far as we were concerned, it brought an ongoing investigation to a head because we thought the gangs were escalating. There was a joint operation between Customs and Police to raid a warehouse, but somehow word got out and the lawyer was all over us. By the time we actually got in, the place had been cleared.'

'A lawyer, you say?'

Souter nodded. 'He's still around. A real show-boater, likes to pull the strings and orchestrate everything so he can stand up and be the big I Am.'

'What's his name?'

'Rowe,' Souter told him. 'Gordon Rowe. He's probably got more crooks off than prison porn.'

Late afternoon, and Bolam, Aisha and Billie gathered in the main office to review progress.

Russell Shaw had been released a couple of hours earlier. 'We have to regard Shaw as a victim,' Bolam said. 'And a potential witness. He might know something he simply doesn't have the mental ability to either understand or communicate.'

Aisha rolled her eyes. Then she did a double take, realising Bolam had seen. 'Sorry,' she said. 'I just… I can see that the evidence doesn't necessarily stack up against him, and he might not be our man. But twenty years ago he killed two innocent victims with extreme violence. Somehow all he got was a cushy hospital number, and now we're supposed to forget all that and treat him with kid gloves.'

'It's the criminal justice system,' Bolam said. 'We see verdicts and sentences we disagree with all the time. But in the eyes of society he's served his time, and within the scope of this case, Shaw is no longer a person of interest, so we have to treat him the same way we treat Sturridge and the Rowes.'

As soon as he said it, he realised this was not the best point of reference. They'd already interrogated Sturridge as a suspect, and as for the Rowes… He recalled what Andy Souter had said about Gordon Rowe…

'Throughout this,' Bolam said, 'we've all had the feeling we're being played. That someone is orchestrating events and watching them unfold. Milking the drama of delivering long-preserved trophies to the families of victims. Even Shaw's release from hospital – that business about a benefactor sponsoring his return to the community. It just seems *controlled*. Manipulated.'

He paused. 'I think there's another name we need to consider,' he said, and with those words he was committed. 'I had a very interesting discussion with Andy Souter in Customs and Excise today. He indicated that the double-hand amputation case from twenty years ago might not be as straightforward as we'd assumed – he didn't seem convinced it was a gang thing. And he said a lawyer had been involved. One who was overly dramatic and orchestrated things… That lawyer's name keeps cropping up: he went to school with Russell Shaw and represented him at trial. He knows Matthew Sturridge well – he was taught by him, has handled his affairs, and is also a close friend of Jayne Sturridge's brother. And he was very close to Joanna Clayton, perhaps intimately so.'

'Gordon Rowe,' Billie Grayson finished for him. They all knew Gordon was Bolam's brother-in-law, and that complicated things hugely.

'He knows all three cases inside out,' Aisha said. 'And whoever is behind all this always seems to be one step ahead. It does make far more sense than thinking someone with so weak a grasp on the world as Russell Shaw might be responsible.'

Bolam couldn't help but admire the way she was willing to accept a stronger argument and immediately review her own interpretation of a case, so swiftly.

'And…' Billie hesitated. 'Well, it's nothing specific, but Tommo mentioned that every time he sees Gordon Rowe, he feels as if he's being interrogated. Lots of apparently casual, bloke-to-bloke "Tell me how it's going" stuff.'

Tommo was acting as Family Liaison Officer for the Rowes. The description of Gordon's behaviour rang true to Bolam.

'He knows not to tell him anything that hasn't previously been agreed,' she hurried to add. 'But…'

'Gordon does the same to me,' Bolam said. 'Always digging.'

'How old is he?' asked Aisha. 'Wouldn't he be too young?'

'Mid-fifties,' Bolam told her. He'd already done the maths: Gordon was fifteen years older than Maria – and his kid sister, Fran. 'Same age as Russell Shaw. Our first case, the murder of Jayne Sturridge, took place twenty-nine years ago. Rowe would have been in his mid-twenties at the time – at university in Norwich, studying for his Master of Law degree, but that's only an hour or two away, and he'd have been back here in the holidays and probably some weekends. Twenty-two years ago, he was a senior solicitor, in the practice that became Cowper and Rowe. He had just started dating Maria, and was, shall we say, closely involved with Joanna Clayton prior to her disappearance – and, we now know, murder. Nineteen years ago, he had been made partner at Cowper and Rowe, and he represented his old schoolfriend, Russell Shaw, before they handed over to a barrister at trial.'

'But…' interrupted Aisha. 'He'd have been, what, mid-thirties at that point? If we're really putting any credence by Shaw's initial account, he said there was a man who looked like his grandfather in the ambulance. That can't have been Rowe. And even if it was, Shaw would have recognised him.'

'As far as we can determine,' Bolam said, 'Shaw *was* delusional. He has a history of hallucinating, particularly involving people close to him. By his own admission he was having what he termed an "episode" that evening and he was hearing his grandfather's voice in his head. The grandfather appears to have been a bully, and perhaps worse: maybe the only credible thing we can take from Shaw's account is that if there was a third party involved, they might have played on his vulnerability in much the way his grandfather did, and perhaps somehow intimidated him into silence. Perhaps that's all he meant at the time, when he said the person was like his grandfather – like the voice he already had in his head – and everything else has come from subsequent conflation and reinterpretation of those recollections.'

No one said anything, until finally Bolam added, 'I know. It's tenuous, but we have to include Gordon Rowe in our list of persons of interest in this case.' And maybe McBride had been right: they needed specialists if they were to have any chance of understanding someone like Russell Shaw.

Bolam didn't have much in the way of belongings. Apart from his coffee machine, he had very few gadgets or tools. He read books but rarely kept them. In the living room of the small terraced house he rented he had a single shelf of CDs – Robert Johnson, Fats Waller, Billie Holiday – but most of his music was downloaded or streamed, New Orleans jazz by the likes of Meschiya Lake and Tuba Skinny, or other quirky Americana.

In his old home in the Northeast, his old life with Fran, he had indulged himself in house plants – mostly ferns and orchids – but like much from that former existence, he had not brought it with him when he had moved down here.

The house was mostly empty, save for a few pieces of basic furniture, and the few items of crockery and clothing he needed to get by.

There was not much to disturb.

But tonight, when he had finally walked back across the old town from the station and let himself in through the front door that opened directly onto the living room, the place was different.

He noticed a scent first of all, a hint of mint, a whiff of cigarette. Not enough that someone had actually smoked in here, but enough to notice, because in the three months Bolam had been here not a single smoker had entered this house.

He had already turned on the living room light when he noticed the scent, so if there was any intruder they would be aware of his arrival, even if they had not heard the scrape of key and thump of front door.

He paused, still.

The place was silent. The CDs were lined up on the shelf in the alcove by the fire, the shelves above them empty. The armchair sat precisely in the hollows worn into the old carpet where it always sat, the coffee table just a fraction too far out of reach before it. The TV sat on a deep built-in shelf in the other alcove.

Bolam paused at the foot of the stairs and listened, then passed through to the kitchen-diner, and the bathroom beyond. The back door was locked, and bolted from the inside.

He paused again in the kitchen. Cigarette, mint, a sweet spiciness from last night's takeaway from the Golden Wall.

His bedroom was upstairs at the front. The double bed, a small chest of drawers, a wardrobe.

The back bedroom was empty. No furniture, nothing.

He went back down. Paused in the kitchen, and then the living room.

He could smell nothing now.

He should never have moved to this house. It was Fran's. She'd arranged it all. Three months and he still felt as if he were camping out in someone else's space.

That letter from Fran's solicitor only served to remind him of that. Messing with his head. He knew it had disturbed him far more than he had let himself believe.

He took his jacket off, sniffed it. Tommo smoked, and Cath and Aisha puffed all varieties of nasty-smelling vapes together in the smoking area to the rear of the station.

Here, back at home, he was tired, imagining things. He needed to sleep, and start afresh in the morning. He needed to not let things get under his skin.

25

Russ Shaw was losing it again.

He knew that. He recognised the signs. He'd spent the last nineteen years learning to understand himself, after all.

Only... What if that understanding had been constructed on false foundations? Just another delusion?

He saw people. Talked to them, even though they weren't there. He knew that.

Elizabeth. Ginnie. And when things became dark, Grandpa.

'I'm sorry, Liz.'

Russ sat before the small headstone, at the foot of the high wall that bounded the St Katherine's graveyard. Elizabeth would never leave this place now. She was six feet down, though. He wasn't actually talking to her.

'I wish I really believed you'd forgiven me, Liz.'

But she'd died. Killed herself because it was all too much. And he knew she'd never really stopped blaming him.

'You okay, love?'

He turned, and for a heart-lurching moment it was her. Elizabeth. Looming over him, that too-kind smile on her face, because she always *tried* so hard.

Then her face blurred, smeared like a thumb dragged through condensation on a window, and it was the woman he'd seen here several times before, always tending an immaculate grave.

'I...' He gave up on words, just nodded. Turned away from her, scared by even that momentary lapse, that fragment of his sister come to life on another's face.

Nothing good ever happened when his head was like this.

Thankfully, he heard footsteps receding along the gravel path as the woman walked away.

He didn't deserve *nice*. Had never deserved Elizabeth trying so hard to love him and to forget.

Nineteen years ago, he'd seen his dead grandfather. Mocking him. Belittling him. And then, only later, he'd come to understand that sometimes what he saw wasn't actually what *was*.

And now... That police officer with her persistent drip-drip-drip of questions, and her boss, the detective inspector, with his disarming chat about football when it was clear he was only using it to pry deeper. That had got under Russ's skin. Into his head.

He didn't know what he believed any more.

Nineteen years' work undone.

'It's okay, Russ. It's not your fault.'

That was Elizabeth's voice. He peered all around, but there was nobody there.

He forced himself to his feet, staggering with headrush.

He looked around again, but she was not there.

It's not your fault.

It was dark, late in the evening. His clothes were damp again, from the night air and a spell of drizzle earlier.

He left the graveyard by the back lane that led down to the seafront.

He hadn't heard Elizabeth's voice again, which was good.

He needed to get back on his meds. The stuff Stewart had got for him wasn't right and he still wasn't registered with a local doctor. He needed help.

The tide was out, a fringe of white sand separated from the bay by a wide expanse of dark grey mud. He walked along the promenade with only a couple of dog-walkers for passing company, which suited him.

He should go back to the flat. But whereas before it had been a place of refuge and new beginnings, now the place was tainted by events. By the delivery of Ginnie Lloyd's severed finger. By the police: he knew they'd been all over it. Everything there would have been touched by them, moved, examined.

It had become a different flat now.

He continued to walk until every muscle in his body ached and he feared he would collapse in the street. Finally, he made his way back to the old town, to the street, the house. He fumbled in his pocket for the keys marked 'FRONT DOOR' and '14C'. Inside, his eyes went straight to the row of three pigeonholes, but they were empty.

He climbed the stairs until he stood before the front door of his flat. Unlocked it, went inside.

The place looked no different. He had so few possessions that any search would have been brief, displacing little, he supposed. He went to the fridge, expecting for some reason that the milk would have gone bad by now, but he'd only been in custody for one night and the milk was fresh. He emptied the kettle and refilled it, then flicked it on to boil. He found his cup, and a teabag from the box.

He should eat something, but he wasn't hungry.

He should change out of his damp clothes.

His phone buzzed with a message from Stewart. He didn't open it.

He didn't want to deal with people right now, real or not.

The next morning, he woke in clothes that still felt moist, and had the musty smell of damp.

He peered around the room. He didn't feel safe here. He felt exposed. Whoever had delivered that padded envelope last week had entered the building to do so, placing the package directly in his pigeonhole.

He found a packet of instant noodles. Chicken curry flavour. Breakfast.

He ate the noodles from a bowl, sitting in the flat's one armchair, knees drawn up to his chest. Facing the door.

He couldn't go out. His head was swirling. He didn't want to see people because when he saw faces and his head was like this, sometimes the features blurred into something else, like that woman at the graveyard yesterday.

Instead, he spoke to Elizabeth.

He knew she wasn't there, but it helped. He told her his head was a mess again. He told her about the woman at the grave, how for a second or two he'd seen Elizabeth's features on her face and he'd been happy, and then the worst feeling in the world was when he'd realised he was imagining it all. He told her about the police. He told her that even though they'd been careful to treat him with respect – respect he knew he didn't deserve – it had still been clear that they thought he was the lowest of the low, and they were merely waiting for him to incriminate himself.

He told her he was experiencing absences again. Probably because he'd stopped his meds. He said he was scared because he didn't know what that meant, what he might do and then not recall. The doctors had told him that when he lost touch with the world like that it was a straightforward absence: he simply froze, blanked out, and he didn't actually *do* anything. But he had never believed them, because what if, sometimes at least, he did not freeze? What if he did things?

Elizabeth didn't say much, of course. She wasn't there. But it helped to talk.

Late morning, he heard a gentle tap-tap-tap at his door. Russ was still in the armchair, knees drawn up, arms wrapped around his shins. He said nothing, did nothing.

The tap at the door came again.

'Russ? Are you in there? It's Stewart. I just wanted to make sure you're okay.'

A tall man with a thick beard and a ponytail. That was how he pictured Stewart. From the charity, the shelter. Stewart had helped him with lots of things.

Russ went to the door and stood with his forehead pressing against the cool wood.

'I'm okay,' he said. 'I'm fine.'

'That's good, Russ. Can I come in?'

Russ stepped back, thumbed the catch on the door and pulled it open.

Tall man, full beard, ponytail, walking into the bedsit.

'Russ? Are you okay?'

Russ let him in, then shut the door and returned to his chair. Stewart leaned back against the kitchen worktop, arms folded.

'I heard what happened,' Stewart said. 'That must have been shit. Once the pigs get you in their sights they don't let go, do they? The bastards wouldn't like it if it was them, eh? I was worried about you, mate. I just wanted to check in on you, you know?'

What had he heard had happened? That Russ had been in custody? That he'd been hanging around the home of Ginnie Lloyd?

That he was… *what he was*?

'I'm fine,' Russ finally responded.

'Do you need anything? Food? Milk? A pint?'

Alcohol was the last thing Russ wanted. Anything that might make him lose control…

'The police spoke to me,' Stewart said. 'At the shelter. They were asking about you, but they wouldn't say why. Data protection.' He laughed at that. 'So I googled you.'

Russ didn't understand. He knew it was something online, but he didn't do all that stuff.

'Everyone deserves a fresh start, though, don't they?' Stewart told him. 'I've taken advice from people at Fresh Start who know how the system works. We all want to help you. Support you. Why don't you come back to the shelter with me now? Judith's there, and we have a list of jobs that need doing around the place. And there's always work to do with Robbie at the renovations. Come on, it'll do you good to get out and do something.'

Russ shook his head. No more people. No more faces.

'You should go,' he said. 'I need…' He put his hands to the sides of his head and pressed.

'Come back to the shelter with me, Russ.'

'No.' He was rocking in his seat, he realised.

Stewart watched him for a time, then pushed himself away from the kitchen bench. He opened the fridge and nodded, and then a couple of the cupboards. 'Feed yourself, Russ. And stay in touch, you hear? I'll be checking in on you again.'

He clearly meant it as an indication of support, but to Russ it sounded like a threat.

Stewart let himself out of the flat, leaving Russ alone again.

Russ forced himself to stop rocking, but still sat with his legs drawn up, as if to shield himself from the world.

'I just wanted to make sure you're okay.'

Russ had come outside, into an afternoon that was so bright he had to squint against the harsh sunlight. A small, neat man walked at his side.

Those same words... He remembered earlier when Stewart had come softly tapping on his door. How had he got in, and up the stairs? The shelter must have a key. The flat belonged to the charity that ran the shelter.

I just wanted to make sure you're okay.

He hunched forward, tried to walk faster. Heading for the promenade, the sea. He always felt better there: it was as if the world was only closing in on one side of him, rather than all around.

The man at his side speeded up too.

It wasn't Stewart, even though he had used the same words. He was shorter, his dark hair shaved to a stubble the same length as that on his jaw. He wore a dark navy suit, complete with waistcoat and tie. It was the detective inspector. Bolam.

When Russ had emerged from number 14 the DI had been there, across the street, as if he'd been watching the place, although he insisted he'd just arrived as Russ was leaving. He'd come to see him. To make sure he was okay.

Russ didn't believe him, though. He didn't believe anyone now. Trusting people was always a mistake. And anyway, the police didn't just drop in to make sure people like him were okay.

'I think you want to help us,' Bolam said at his side. 'I think you want to understand.'

Russ peered at him. The man's voice was so soft it was almost as if it was inside his head. He didn't like the sensation.

'You should leave me alone,' Russ said. 'You shouldn't be doing this without a solicitor. Once you get someone in your sights, you don't let go, do you?' He knew he was repeating Stewart's words from earlier.

The man stopped. Nodded. 'You're right about the solicitor part, at least. And if I was treating you as a person of interest in any way then that's exactly how I'd be approaching things. But I genuinely only wanted to make sure you're okay. I know life is hard for you. And I know all this hasn't made things any *less* hard.'

Russ had to really concentrate to hear his words, his soft voice over the sea breeze and traffic.

'But as I say,' the man went on. 'I think you want to do the right thing. So if there's anything you know that you haven't mentioned, you can tell me. You might not even realise something is relevant. Just talk to me. It might make you feel better.'

Russ peered at him again, struck by the thought that he might be about as real as the Elizabeth he'd been talking to in his flat. He talked to *her* too, and it made him feel better. Was he finally losing touch with reality?

'I've spoken to the community mental health supervisor at the local hospital,' Bolam said. 'They can get you back on your meds. They'll spend time with you, helping you to adjust.'

He was real. He was too irritatingly intrusive not to be.

They crossed East Bay Drive and came to stand above the promenade. The North Sea was the colour of London clay, grey-brown with a sheen of blue running through. Out on the horizon, a huge container ship shimmered in the haze.

'Tell me about Mr Sturridge.'

Russ had his wits about him enough to see what the man was doing: the subtle use of *Mr* Sturridge, rather than calling him Matthew, taking Russ back to his youth, seeing the man as his school teacher.

'He helped kids like you, didn't he?' Bolam continued. 'Kids who were having a hard time at home.'

'I liked him,' Russ said. They were walking down towards the promenade now. The breeze was cold. 'He cared about us. He organised projects. Art groups outside school. Charity stuff with his friends. Army Cadets.' It had given Russ something to focus on when he'd been a bit of a delinquent. A direction. A way out.

'Did he help Elizabeth too?'

Russ stared. He didn't want to talk about Liz. Not with strangers. He started to walk faster, and the short detective had to scurry to keep up.

'We had some of your belongings at the station. I brought them for you.'

For the first time, Russ noticed that the detective was carrying a bag – the canvas shoulder bag Russ had lost at the beach.

'I know about your grandfather,' Bolam continued. 'I read the letter. I'm sorry, but it's my job to do intrusive things like that. I know it's personal.'

Russ stopped to sling the bag's strap over his shoulder, then turned and put his hands on the cold solidity of the concrete sea-barrier that separated the prom from the drop to the beach.

Elizabeth had written to him just before she'd killed herself.

'It's clear your grandfather loomed large in your life,' the man went on, relentless. 'He bullied you, didn't he? He belittled everything you did, so you never felt you could live up to the man he was. I thought he did worse to you, too, but I was wrong, wasn't I? It wasn't you he singled out – it was Elizabeth.'

Bolam put a hand on his arm, and somehow that simple gesture meant a huge amount, because it was clear that the DI was a man who kept himself separate from people and didn't find it easy to reach out.

'You can't blame yourself, Russell,' he said. 'Believe me: I've seen enough of this. The victims always bear the guilt, and you most certainly are a victim.'

Liz had been unable to bear it. She'd done so for most of her life, and she'd leaned on Russ, who was the only person who understood. He'd never been able to protect her from their grandfather, though. In the end he'd run away to the Army. And then when he did what he did and was locked away, she had no one.

He'd failed her, and he knew she had never been able to understand or forgive.

And finally it had become too much to bear, even though their grandfather was long dead by the time Russ was locked away.

She'd said all this in the letter he'd carried with him for years, until he'd lost it along with his bag during that raid on the homeless sleepers at the Martello tower development.

That was the last letter she'd written.

Back at the flat, another dark evening, the wind whipping up into a gale outside.

Somehow he'd extricated himself from the detective inspector's attentions this afternoon and had continued to walk. He'd followed the promenade for as far as it went, before it petered out into a mud track along the top of the sea wall to the north of town. He'd cut inland from there, come round by the school and back onto the high street.

Walking, and talking to no one, with no one talking to him – imagined or real.

He was angry now that he'd had time to process the encounter.

Angry that Bolam had read the letter, that he'd made feeble excuses about it being his job to pry. If Russ was no longer a 'person of interest', whatever that meant, then what business did the DI have nosing into his personal affairs?

He didn't believe that Bolam had his interests at heart, that he just wanted to make sure he was okay. He'd only found Russ so he could dig and twist deeper. That was all they ever did, people like him. Just like Stewart said.

Before they parted, Bolam had given him a business card with a telephone number and an email address. 'Call me,' he'd said. 'Any time you want to talk. Just call.'

Russ boiled the kettle and poured the water over another packet of instant noodles.

They were all as bad as each other. Bolam. Stewart. Everyone he ever encountered. They never had his best interests at heart, and why should they? Always manipulating, using him.

The letter hurt, though. It was Elizabeth's. They could do what they liked to Russ, and he would deserve it, but not Liz.

He gave the noodles a stir with a fork. They still stuck together, needed another minute or so.

He heard a sound, then told himself to think nothing of it. The street was narrow, the houses tightly packed. He was always hearing noises. Traffic. People walking past, laughing and shouting, or talking too loud into their mobile phones. People in the flat below – a young couple, perhaps also beneficiaries of the Fresh Start charity, although he'd never asked, not even spoken to them, and probably never would.

Glass shattered.

The dormer window, set into the slope of the roof, facing the street. Its lower pane of glass was smashed, shards all over the floor. What looked like a tightly wadded ball of paper lay on the carpet.

Russ looked more closely. Not a ball of paper, but a fist-sized stone, wrapped in paper that peeled partly away to reveal the stone within.

Someone must have found the rock in one of the gardens, or brought it all the way from the beach. Someone who was strong and accurate enough to throw it through his window from the street.

He squatted, pulled at the paper, then let it fall to the floor. It looked like part of a newspaper page, but printed on A4 paper – something from the internet, he assumed. The news story's headline screamed AMBULANCE DOUBLE MURDER, and next to the story was a head and shoulders photograph of Russell Shaw.

There was a second sheet of paper, with just a photograph printed on it. A fuzzy picture of Russell Shaw looking down at something in his hand – standing at the doorway of this very building, his new home, looking for the right key to let himself in.

Someone knew who he was, and *where* he was, and they were coming for him now. Coming to get him.

Russ was standing with his back to the wall farthest from the broken window.

He waited, but there was nothing more. No Molotov cocktail. No piss-filled bottle. No angry mob smashing down his door.

He thought of the finger in the envelope. Ginnie's finger.

This was different. No subtlety or cleverness in this assault: it was open, public.

Word was spreading.

Someone knew he was here. Knew who he was. *What* he was.

The police knew. And Stewart had been talking about him at the shelter – 'taking advice', he'd said. Ginnie Lloyd's family knew – he remembered the swing of the hammer as her father had lunged at him that night. The old man wouldn't have been physically capable of throwing that stone through the window, but he could have put someone up to it: tracking Russ down and making him feel unwelcome.

And, in a way, this little thing, this rock hurled through his window, was more disturbing than that envelope had been, because it was a reawakening of his initial fears on returning to his home town. That people knew. That the mob was lying in wait.

And perhaps that was exactly what whoever was behind this campaign of twisted terror wanted.

He picked up the sheets of paper and put them in his recycling bag. Then he found a dustpan and brush and cleaned up the glass, before going over to the frame to break away the few remaining shards.

Outside, the street was empty, but that didn't matter. Now that they knew he was here, he would never be safe.

26

Bolam sat at his desk, working through paperwork from other investigations while he waited for Aisha Nawaz to return from a call-out.

The encounter with Russell Shaw hadn't gone well. Bolam had tried to keep it casual, an informal offer of a shoulder to lean on coupled with the suggestion that Shaw might help himself if he felt he was assisting the investigation.

He'd only wanted to help the man, but he feared Shaw was too damaged for any kind of approach to work – particularly from a police officer. He was suspicious of everything, feared the world around him, and was, it became clear from that encounter, seriously mentally and emotionally unstable.

Bolam hoped the community mental health care team would be able to help. He was still ambivalent about what had happened in that ambulance nineteen years ago, but the one thing he was convinced of now was that if Russell Shaw did not get help then no one would benefit.

He'd pulled a copy of Elizabeth Shaw's letter from evidence yesterday afternoon. It was his own mistake: he'd assumed someone would have actually read it, rather than merely filing it as physical evidence found in Russell Shaw's abandoned bag, but when he had asked about it no one seemed to know.

Elizabeth's letter was a suicide note, although no one would have realised that was what it was until after she'd taken her life.

The letter was handwritten, and brief, and one sentence stuck out. *I wish I hadn't told you, I wish you hadn't had to live with what grandpa was like because nobody should have to live with that.*

Bolam had assumed Russell Shaw was the victim of abuse at his grandfather's hands – either physical or sexual, or both – but it had been his sister who was the principal victim. The Shaw kids had grown up without a father in their lives, and with a mother who was constantly in and out of care with psychological and addiction issues. Their grandfather had been the dominant presence in their lives, and it was a situation he had exploited for years, from what Bolam could determine. He imagined Russ being bullied by the old man, being told no one would ever believe him and he would split up the family if he ever said anything. He imagined years of that, until finally Russ, at least, had broken away and the family had torn itself apart regardless.

He didn't have to imagine it, though, because he'd dealt with enough similar examples during his career to recognise the pattern.

Bolam had asked Shaw about Matthew Sturridge to try to draw out any connections between the cases. The response about Sturridge working with local charitable groups had been interesting, as that did seem to be a common element across the investigation. Had someone in the charity sector used their special access as a kind of vetting process to identify victims who would be easy to manipulate, like Sturridge's vulnerable kids? Shaw had been manipulated, it was clear; and Joanna Clayton had been singled out as a teenaged girl who might not be missed. Had Elizabeth Shaw also been targeted and manipulated in this way, or was she simply one of Russell's points of vulnerability?

He glanced at the wall clock, Aisha still not back. He knew she disapproved of his approach to Shaw. In her eyes it was simple: Shaw was a convicted killer and he could never move on from that. For Bolam, though, it was not so much a case of Shaw moving on. Whatever the truth of what had happened nineteen years ago, Shaw was clearly a vulnerable person and they'd hauled him into custody and kept him overnight, putting him under intense pressure. Maybe there was none of the old-school brutality that there had been back when DI Bulmer had questioned Matthew Sturridge about the disappearance of Jayne, but were they really much better?

When Bolam was twenty, partway through a degree in biological sciences that he never completed, he had witnessed a fight outside a pub in the Bigg Market in central Newcastle. Nothing to do with him, he hadn't even been out drinking, but it had all kicked off as he walked past. He'd always been fascinated by the way interactions between people could simply flare up like this – a look, a misjudged or even mis*heard* comment. One moment people were having a good time, and the next… *this*.

People had been rushing and jostling all around him while two lads of Bolam's age kicked and stamped another who lay in a foetal ball in the street. The noise had been disorienting, as if all of a sudden Bolam had been transported into another reality, and then there were sirens and more shouting, and flashing blue lights merging with the glaring neon all around.

On his knees, trying to stop the injured lad from getting up and risking making his injuries worse, Bolam felt hands on his arms, and suddenly he was propelled back and dumped, sprawling on the pavement.

More men shouting in his face – police officers – swearing at him. The sudden pain of a blow to his ribs: a police baton, striking him full-force in the side, cracking a rib. Another blow, and he was struggling to double over, coughing, while the coppers pinned him down.

The rest was a blur. He remembered being hauled painfully to his feet and bundled into the back of a van, the hard bite of handcuffs, and the awkward way they pulled his arms back, putting extra strain on those broken ribs. He felt every bump on the road on the short drive to Forth Banks police station.

'What were you doing there?' Questioned by a tired-looking officer with dead eyes.

'I was in the process of trying to save a young man's life. How about you?' Even at the age of twenty, Bolam spoke like an old man, and his soft tone seemed to wind the officer up, but that didn't stop him. 'Did you get them?' Bolam went on. 'The ones who actually beat that lad up?'

They kept him until morning, the night punctuated by the repeated groans and shouting of drunken occupants of the neighbouring cells.

The young Bolam might have taken so many things from that night. A justified resentment at his wrongful treatment. A lifelong hatred of the police. A noble desire to right the wrongs of a system that had treated him that way when all he'd tried to do was help and the only thing he'd been guilty of was being cocky when questioned.

But the one thing that stayed with him, and changed the course of his life, was an intense feeling of curiosity summed up by the look in that officer's eyes. He *wanted* Bolam to have been guilty, simply because it would justify the instant dislike and hostility he had felt towards him.

Why would someone in such a position of trust and authority be so keen for an easy answer when surely he should be looking for the *truth*?

And now Bolam acknowledged to himself that this lay at the root of his current unease with how he had been operating since coming to Whitesands. For the first time in his career, he had started to give in to the temptation of *easy*. First with Sturridge, and then with Shaw, and every time someone in his position made that mistake, it was a mistake with lasting and profound impact.

What they needed now was to find a way to keep pushing forward towards the truth, rather than opting for the easy explanation.

And right now, Bolam felt that they were no further forward than when he had opened that first padded envelope in Matthew Sturridge's kitchen and seen the finger inside.

'We're scaling back the investigation,' Bolam said, as Aisha Nawaz closed his office door behind her. She sat, saying nothing.

Finally, she nodded. She understood. The cases would remain open, of course, but resources were needed elsewhere, and there appeared to be no imminent risk to the public.

'We have to prioritise our resources,' Bolam said. In the end, it was always about the money and, as DCI McBride had emphasised earlier, it wasn't as if they were short of open cases on their books right now. Missing persons from a couple of decades ago did not tick enough of the boxes to justify the level of resources Bolam had allocated up to now.

McBride had said he was going to take advice from cold case

specialists in the National Crime Agency on how to proceed, but that would be a slow process. He'd also mentioned the Chief Superintendent several times as if to emphasise the importance of tackling investigations where they might actually deliver some results. Some day McBride would come to realise that that was not an argument likely to sway Bolam.

The underlying message had been clear though: after three months in the role, Bolam still had to prove himself, and his rush to bring in the frail – and well-connected – Matthew Sturridge for questioning had done him no favours.

'Maybe it's a good thing,' Aisha said, hesitantly. 'With your brother-in-law becoming the focus of the investigation, maybe you're too close. McBride should give it to someone else.'

'You're right, of course,' said Bolam, even as he mustered the arguments to prove her wrong. 'But in a town this size, maybe things are a bit different. Everyone is connected. You can't recuse yourself from every investigation involving people you know. And Gordon Rowe is only one of several persons of interest. Yes, we have to tread carefully, but we still have to *tread*.'

They remained silent for a time.

'We're carrying on,' Bolam said, finally. 'But we're just going to have to do so with far more limited resources. We're going to have to be creative. Are you up for that?'

Aisha shrugged. 'So what now?' she asked.

He'd expected a bit more fight from her. He'd been hoping that this news – and the challenge – would fire her up, but instead she seemed resigned.

'Come on, Aisha,' he said, on the verge of losing patience with her altogether. 'We can't just let this go, can we?'

'But you said DCI McBride—'

'Where's that old Aisha? The one I read about in your HR file? The one who shines through whenever I ask people about why you were appointed to this team? The one we spoke about that day when you drove me to the Rowe house. Where is she?'

Aisha wouldn't meet his look, and for a moment he feared he'd pushed too far.

'She got tired,' she said, finally. 'She got tired of never living up to expectations.'

'Whose?' Bolam asked softly. Then, when she didn't respond, he went on. 'Because when I look at your file I see nothing that indicates you failed at anything.'

'It got too much for me,' she said. 'I had a breakdown.'

'I know.'

She met his look, at last. A spark of defiance, annoyance. 'It was hard,' she said. 'I went from golden girl to someone who'd lost all sense of proportion. I couldn't make judgement calls. I couldn't make decisions – I was too scared to commit to anything, and I never really understood why. I didn't know myself any more. I lost track, and I've never quite found my way back.'

All that sounded painfully familiar to Bolam: questioning your own judgement, losing your way, and all under the scrutiny of your superiors…

'Maybe you need to find a new normal,' Bolam said. 'Maybe you need to find a new set of expectations. A new Aisha.'

'Mark two,' she said, forcing an awkward smile.

'Indeed.' Then he added, 'I could certainly do with it, now the investigation is being scaled back.'

'So…' said Aisha. 'The Sturridge-Rowe case?'

'I've spoken to Billie and Tommo,' Bolam said. 'They're throwing everything at other cases that have come in now. So that just leaves you and me, and we're going to be spread thin. So tell me, Aisha, what should we do now?'

'The same as we have been.'

Her answer was quick, and confident, and Bolam was surprised by it. He'd hoped his little pep talk might have inspired some radical thinking, a spark of inspiration. He raised an eyebrow and waited for her to explain.

'We've taken the approach we have because it was the best approach,' she said. 'Solid policework, tracking down witnesses, trying our best to get our heads around decades-old cases, excluding possibilities.'

'Textbook stuff.'

'It's textbook because it works. Sometimes boring is good. So we carry on with the dull plod work, looking for cases, connections, inconsistencies. Eventually something gives. A mistake is spotted, an insight gained.'

She was right, he realised. He'd hoped to fire her up, and that maybe her tendency to leap to conclusions might produce a new approach, but instead she'd simply confirmed what he'd known all along: the only way to make a breakthrough in a case like this was by good, solid policework.

Mid-evening and it was still light outside, although the Serious Crimes office was always gloomy by now as the sun had moved around to the west, away from the windows. Bolam sat at his desk, the small side office lit by the glow from his computer screen; out in the main office, a desk lamp lit Aisha Nawaz's workspace, and at the far end Tommo stood by the coffee machine, waiting for his umpteenth cup of the day.

Aisha caught Bolam's eye and raised a hand, beckoning him over. She had something.

He went out, pulled a chair across from another desk and sat.

'I think there might have been one in Norfolk,' Aisha told him. 'Eleven years ago.'

'Tell me.'

Tommo came across and joined them as Aisha pulled up an image of a young woman onto her screen. Big eyes with dark shadows beneath, black hair pulled tightly back, mid-brown skin.

'Marcia Fredericks,' Aisha told them. 'Twenty-seven years old when she went missing. She was volunteering with a homeless charity, having spent several years on the streets herself since her late teens. When she went missing it was assumed she'd returned to her old life, or simply made herself scarce, perhaps when something, or someone, from her past caught up with her.'

'So there are parallels,' Bolam said. 'A homeless charity, like the one that's housed Russell Shaw here. A victim who presumably wouldn't be missed – if she'd been homeless for a long period she probably had no family ties. An absence that could easily be explained by assumptions made about how she lived her life. There always seems to be an easy explanation that encourages lazy – or hard-pressed – investigators to look no deeper; just as Jayne Sturridge's disappearance was assumed to be a domestic, and Joanne Clayton was assumed to be a runaway.'

He knew the ambulance killings didn't fit that theory, but any pattern they found only ever seemed to apply to most, but not all, of their cases… Their perpetrator clearly liked to mix things up.

'Marcia's body was found washed up on the beach at Caister-on-Sea, just north of Great Yarmouth,' Aisha said. 'She'd been missing for six weeks. Her left little finger had been severed at the metacarpophalangeal joint, although the pathology report says the wound was untidy, making it impossible to be certain if this was carried out before the body was dumped in the sea, or if it was the result of some kind of post-mortem trauma suffered in the sea.'

'Norfolk?' Tommo said. 'Then that's another connection, isn't it?' When no one responded, he went on, 'Robbie Walton, Jayne Sturridge's brother. We know he's down here a lot because this is his home town and he has properties and charity connections here, but he's based in Norfolk, isn't he?'

'Aisha,' said Bolam. 'How's your schedule for tomorrow?'

'Nothing I can't shuffle.'

'How do you fancy a trip up to Great Yarmouth to talk to our counterparts in the Norfolk Constabulary and see what you can turn up?'

As he'd been reminded on his trip to the Rodgers-Stephenson in Cambridge, meeting people face-to-face could be far more effective than a mere telephone call, particularly when working on a case as complex as this. He'd have gone himself, but he wanted to do a bit of digging closer to home.

In particular, while the Robbie Walton connection was interesting, there was another player who kept drifting centre stage: Gordon Rowe.

Gordon seemed to be connected to everyone – to the Sturridges, to Russell Shaw, to the double-hand amputation, and of course there appeared to be a lot more to his relationship with Joanna Clayton than had yet been said out loud. There was also the point that

Gordon was actively involved in charitable works, including several homeless charities.

But now there was one more connection. Robbie Walton wasn't the only person of interest with a Norfolk address. Gordon and Maria Rowe had a boat on the Broads, and holidayed there regularly…

Bolam got home late.

As had become his routine, he paused just inside the front room and checked to see that everything appeared normal. Nothing had been moved. No strange scent on the air. Then he went through to the back, and then upstairs to check his bedroom and the empty back room.

He worried that he was close to some kind of breakdown. Getting paranoid. Talking to himself – or Fran. Aisha's description of her own mental health issues had brought this home to him, too. Was he losing his grip?

He slept fitfully, his head full of possibilities. He knew the time had come for him to convince his DCI to escalate this inquiry again, but he was wary of doing so. His rush to bring Sturridge in for questioning had been misjudged and premature, and they'd similarly got nowhere with Shaw. McBride had made it clear that his confidence in his new DI was not exactly high.

But if Marcia Fredericks was, indeed, another victim, it was becoming hard to overlook the likelihood that they had uncovered a serial killer who had operated in this area for decades. Why was it escalating now, and how long before the next killing?

He woke early, showered and then dressed, and then went down to the kitchen to fire up the coffee machine for his usual long black with an extra shot of espresso.

With his coffee, he went through to the front room, and that was when he noticed an A4 manila envelope on the doormat, below the letterbox.

Junk mail, he assumed, although it was early for a delivery and the envelope only bore a printed address, no branding.

And no stamp, although he barely registered this as he pulled a corner open and ran a finger along to tear an opening at one end.

Photographs spilled out onto his lap, and for a moment their details didn't register. Who would send him photographs? Fuzzy, pixelated images, as if they'd been printed from social media or poor phone images.

A picture of a small group of people, and still he didn't quite make the connection, because the one person he would have identified instantly had her face scratched out.

He recognised the blouse, though, a tunic top that was tight across the shoulders and then pleated so it hung loose, because Fran had always insisted she'd passed the age where she could get away with anything more tight-fitting. The woman to her left was a colleague from the Royal Victoria Infirmary; the man to her right someone Bolam vaguely recognised but couldn't name.

The next photo was of Fran with three other colleagues, again with her features scratched out.

The next: Fran featureless next to a surprised-looking, grinning Gordon.

The final photograph was of a wedding group from about ten years ago, and Bolam gazed upon his own awkward smile, always reluctant to be captured in photos. And, by his side, in the heart of the group: Fran in a low-cut floral dress, her face scratched out beneath a wide-brimmed hat.

Bolam didn't allow himself to react like a normal person would do. He sat for a few seconds, gathering himself, and working out a plan. He didn't have gloves within reach, so carefully, he eased himself forward until the photographs and envelope tipped, slid down his lap and fell to the carpet.

He stood, stepped over the items, and went through to the kitchen where, in a drawer, he had a supply of latex gloves and some evidence bags.

Finally, he returned to the front room and placed the envelope and each photograph into a separate bag, so that they could all still be examined through the plastic, even with the bags sealed.

He went through to the back room and spread the bagged photographs out before him on a work surface. He didn't know yet what he would do with them, but treating them as evidence and protecting them like this and preventing any further contamination was the sensible thing to have done.

He didn't know what they might be evidence *of*, though…

Mysterious, threatening items in the post drew obvious parallels with the current case, of course, but this felt different. Defaced photographs rather than anything more physical and macabre. And he knew beyond any morsel of doubt that there was nothing suspicious about Fran's death, so this was no grim taunting to open up an overlooked murder case.

Indeed, the more he thought this through, the more he became convinced that this was something entirely different, something directly personal tied to his – and Fran's – former existence in the Northeast.

Fran had always been guarded about aspects of her life, for no good reason that Bolam could determine other than that it was her nature: she had simply never felt the need to spell out every detail of her existence if she did not have reason to do so. Bolam didn't know much about Fran's childhood with Gordon. He'd known nothing about Joanna Clayton, the long-time missing half-sister of Gordon's wife. And he'd had no idea Fran had taken things so far with that divorce solicitor…

Were there other aspects of her life she had never thought to mention? Past lovers or rivals? Animosities she had moved on from, but which might still burn deep for others? Deep enough to trigger hate mail like this, designed to make Bolam do exactly what he was doing now, rethinking and reconstructing the past of the woman he had loved.

He didn't know.

He stacked the evidence bags, placed them in the drawer where he kept the gloves. Went back to the front room and drank coffee that had gone cold.

He would mull it over, let it process in the back of his mind before deciding what, if anything, to do.

And in the meantime he had to get his head back into a work place, because he had a visit lined up that could make or break this entire investigation.

27

Raymond Cowper lived in a former farmhouse just north of town. It was a solid red-brick building with arched windows, set back from the road down a long gravel drive. The garden was immaculate, laid out symmetrically to either side of the drive, subdivided by neatly clipped, knee-high box hedges.

Bolam pulled up before the house and gathered himself, stepping out of the car and straightening his tie and jacket. Depending on how things went, he knew this interview could have serious consequences both for his career and for the few, shaky connections he retained with Fran's family, because Cowper was a man of significant influence in both areas.

Cowper waited for him at the open front door, standing in the shade of the house, and resting with both hands on the head of a gnarly old walking stick. He wore a tweed jacket and tie, and something about him reminded Bolam of a slightly younger version of Matthew Sturridge: the same fastidious air of formality and propriety, a sense of being out of his own time.

'Mr Cowper,' Bolam said, approaching and then stopping before the house. 'Thank you for agreeing to see me.'

Cowper nodded. 'Of course,' he said. 'I know enough of your investigation to want to do whatever I can to help.'

Bolam suspected it was more a case of wanting to keep abreast of things and protect his own interests, but he said nothing.

'Tea?'

Cowper turned and led the way through to a sitting room and indicated a chair. 'Let me boil the kettle,' he said, and left Bolam to seat himself.

The room was spotless, the furniture a polished dark wood that hinted at age. Photographs hung from the walls and stood in frames on a long, dark sideboard. Historical prints of the town: the docks, the narrow streets, the seafront. Old school photos, and group pictures from functions. One of Cowper and Gordon Rowe standing either side of the Duke of Cambridge.

Cowper came back a short time later, walking with the stick so that he had to hold a tray bearing teapot and cups with one hand.

Bolam jumped to his feet and took the tray. 'I'm sorry,' he said. 'I should have…'

'Oh, don't worry yourself, Inspector,' said Cowper. He raised the stick, then tapped it against his leg. 'Old sporting injury. Don't worry: it doesn't hamper me too much. I still get around a lot, but even so, Gordon always teases me about it, says it's what keeps me sharp, because if the body's not willing then all you have left is the brain, eh?'

Bolam could imagine his brother-in-law being crass enough to say something like that. 'That's why I'm here, actually,' he said. 'I wanted to talk to you about Gordon.'

That was clearly not something Cowper had anticipated, although he tried to maintain an expressionless face. 'Gordon?' he said. 'Why would you want to talk to me about him?'

'Tell me about him,' Bolam said. 'Is he a good lawyer?'

'Gordon has an excellent reputation and standing in his field,' Cowper said, as he lowered himself into a chair opposite where Bolam had been sitting. 'Do sit down, won't you?' Bolam sat too, and Cowper continued. 'He is the youngest partner we've had at Cowper and Rowe, and he has been the driving force behind our consolidation and expansion over the past three decades. He also has considerable standing in our community, and has been responsible for a large number of charitable initiatives.'

Bolam hadn't asked for the kind of reference you might give someone applying for a job, but Cowper's response was pretty much what he'd expected.

'He's a bit flash, though, isn't he?' Bolam said. 'A bit of a show-off.'

Cowper paused, again as if thrown by Bolam's line of questioning. Then he laughed. 'You take an interesting approach, Inspector. The Chief Superintendent told me you were something of a square peg, you know.'

'Would you say Gordon's a grandstander?'

Cowper nodded. 'Of course he is. We all are, in our profession. We're performers, whether it's in court or in your interview room.' He leaned forward to pour tea. 'But yes, you're right. Gordon is theatrical. He does like to put on a show for the galleries. But why are you so concerned with his adversarial style?'

Russell Shaw had referred to this: he'd said Gordon Rowe ran interviews and trials as carefully orchestrated set pieces. Was that the mind of someone who delivered trophies to his victims in padded envelopes? Who carefully managed the revelations of decades-old crimes in a theatrical manner designed to show off just how clever and successful he had been?

He still couldn't quite believe he was entertaining such thoughts about his brother-in-law. He'd never liked the man, but that was because he was boorish and a bore, not because there had ever been any suspicion that something more serious was amiss in his personality.

But if his speculations had any foundation in truth, Gordon had been doing this for decades... How had Bolam not suspected at least *something*?

'Gordon's name has cropped up in several branches of our inquiry,' Bolam said carefully.

'He's a criminal lawyer,' Cowper said, as if explaining to an imbecile. 'It's what we do, you know. Cowper and Rowe have probably been involved in one way or another in at least half the major investigations in this town in the last thirty years. Your brother-in-law is a good man, Inspector. You'd do well to keep him on your side.'

'Do you remember Joanna Clayton?' Bolam said. 'Maria Rowe's half-sister. She disappeared twenty-two years ago.'

'I remember the case,' Cowper said. 'And of course I remember the impact it had on poor Gordon and Maria. But you imply I should recall more than that.'

Bolam nodded. 'Joanna used to hang around Gordon,' he said. 'She used to come to the Cowper and Rowe offices to get money off him.'

Cowper looked blank. 'That's not something I recall,' he said. 'But I'm sure it was all above board. A lot of people visit our offices.'

'Were they having an affair? Gordon and Joanna? It's not as if it would have been so bad: Gordon had only just started seeing Maria at the time. They weren't married, or even engaged.'

'She was half his age,' Cowper said. 'A minor.'

He'd said he didn't recall whether Joanna had hung around the law firm's offices, but he clearly remembered *some* of the detail. 'Were they, though? Having an affair.'

Cowper paused. He knew interview technique inside out, but clearly wasn't accustomed to being on the receiving end. 'I have no way of answering your question in any way that would be helpful,' he said finally. 'It was more than two decades ago, and even though I have no recollection of there having been such a relationship, I clearly was not with Gordon twenty-four hours a day, so I would be unable to give a categorical answer. I consider it highly unlikely, though. I think I would have been aware, and if I was, then I would certainly *remember*.'

Bolam sipped at his tea out of politeness, and as punctuation to their exchange, giving Cowper a few seconds to run over his response in his head and wonder if he'd said too much, or not enough.

'Has Gordon ever let you down?'

Again, Cowper paused. He seemed to have realised why Bolam was here, and must now be considering every answer carefully. 'You don't get to where Gordon is in life if you have a habit of letting people down,' he said. He raised his cup to his lips, keeping Bolam fixed with his gaze the whole time. 'As soon as all this started,' he said, 'I told Gordon and Maria that I would put myself at their disposal. I have absolute faith in Gordon, and I care deeply about him and Maria.'

Then, when Bolam thought he had finished, Cowper added, 'And believe me, Inspector. If there ever *was* any evidence of wrongdoing on Gordon's part then my firm would act swiftly and without prejudice, because nothing will be allowed to undermine the firm's high moral standing and reputation. But until such time as there *is* any such evidence, I will fight fiercely to protect a colleague – and friends – as close and inspirational as Gordon and Maria Rowe. Is that clear enough for you?'

Bolam imagined that Cowper, in his prime, would have been a force to reckon with in any court in the land, and even in this prim and proper sitting room he retained the ability to intimidate almost anyone.

Bolam smiled. 'I would expect no less,' he said. 'And I'm very glad my brother-in-law has you at his side, Mr Cowper.' Although that assertion that the firm would always come first was cold: Cowper would support Rowe one hundred per cent, but not beyond a certain point. Did that undercurrent of ruthlessness mean there was at least a hint of doubt in the old man's mind about his partner, or was Bolam over-interpreting?

Cowper leaned forward to put his cup back on the tray, on the low table between them. 'Gordon is under considerable pressure at the moment,' he said.

Bolam studied his sagging features closely. The lawyer was choosing his words carefully – he wanted to say something, but not to do so indelicately.

'He is?' Bolam prompted. Gordon always liked to give the impression of being under pressure – he liked the spotlight. But Cowper knew him well, and clearly saw more.

'Gordon and Maria,' Cowper explained. 'There are… tensions. And the boy, Luke, shows signs of becoming something of a delinquent – following the same path as the aunt he never knew.'

Luke was fifteen. At that age Joanna Clayton had been going off the rails, becoming too much to handle for those around her. Bolam remembered Maria telling him Luke was off with his friends, smoking 'wacky baccy', as if she was deliberately trying to shock – or to show off what a liberal parent she was.

'I know Luke's a handful,' said Bolam, 'but…?'

Cowper rolled his eyes. 'He makes a poor choice of friends,' he said. 'Or that's the excuse, and it's a lot more palatable than confronting the possibility that the trouble is of his own instigation.'

'Trouble?'

'At school, of course,' Cowper told him. 'But he's had a couple of run-ins with the police too. Minor matters, easily dealt with.'

Cowper fell silent then, but Bolam could imagine what he had meant by 'easily dealt with'. Favours called in, friendships relied upon – Cowper had made it clear more than once that he was on friendly terms with the Chief Superintendent.

'Gordon didn't step back from representing Matthew Sturridge out of deference to your relationship, you know.'

'No?' That was the line Gordon had taken: that he'd not wanted to complicate matters by representing someone Bolam was investigating.

'Gordon was struggling with the pressures,' Cowper said. 'I'm not closely involved these days, but I could see the strain, and I stepped into the breach.'

Bolam had known there were stresses in the Rowe family dynamic, but he hadn't realised quite how bad things had become. For it to affect Gordon's professional activities, things must be bad.

And a part of his mind couldn't help filling in the gaps... Throughout this investigation, a recurring question had been *Why now*? Why were decades-old crimes being stirred up, and clues being ostentatiously dropped into their laps? Might the break-up of a marriage somehow be the trigger?

He thought, then, of the photographs he had received, Fran's face scratched out. A personal attack on Bolam and his family, but also personal to Gordon. Might Fran's death have contributed to all Gordon's stresses coming to a head in recent months?

'I don't like doing this,' Bolam said. 'Digging into the lives of my own family.' Now he thought of how Gordon had done his best to juggle things when Bolam's marriage had been breaking down, how he had helped Fran get the advice she needed, but still did his best by Bolam. That had been an unexpected revelation, to say the least. 'I know that Gordon is a decent man at his core, and he's had my back in difficult times.'

'If you didn't ask the difficult questions you'd be in the wrong job,' Cowper concluded for him. 'I know it's not easy, but you have to separate yourself from all of that. Step back from the personal element.'

That's exactly what Bolam told himself, but he knew there were dangers in putting up that kind of distance. Everyone in the job knew about the tension between giving it one hundred per cent and living a normal life.

They fell silent again. Bolam wondered how he'd allowed this exchange to get so personal. He didn't speak like this even with friends, but there was something about Cowper that made it easy to talk – a useful skill for a lawyer, he supposed. Some lawyers liked to maintain a distance, knowing only what they needed to know, but others needed to understand exactly how their clients ticked, and Cowper was clearly one of the latter.

'But if you do manage that separation,' Cowper went on, after a time, 'then you must always remind yourself that you are dealing with real people, real lives. The choices you make in your work can have a significant impact on those you encounter. Have you ever lost someone, Inspector?'

It was like a knife, plunged deep and then twisting.

'Your wife, of course,' Cowper went on. 'Then never let yourself forget: every one of the people you are pressurising has lost someone too. Matthew Sturridge. Gordon and Maria Rowe. Each of those deaths has changed lives, then and forever after. I see that in my work, because I deal with those consequences, whereas you have the luxury of being able to move on and maintain that professional distance. That's why you suffer the shock you do now, when it comes closer to home. Never forget, Inspector. Never let go of that humanity, for without it you are just as bad as the people you pursue.'

28

Bolam had gone to interview Raymond Cowper looking for information, and a different perspective on the personality of Gordon Rowe.

He hadn't expected insight into the workings of his own mind.

Cowper had been right though, and perceptive. Doing what Bolam did, you had to maintain a distance, not get involved. You had to remain objective. As soon as you lost that, you started to make mistakes.

But while Cowper's reminder that you must also make the effort to stay in touch with your humanity was perceptive, it was not something Bolam could afford to indulge at the moment. He had to pursue answers wherever that took him, putting aside the consequences.

Right now, he stood at the school gates as a flow of adolescents surged past, the school day over.

Luke Rowe was the focus of a group of five teenagers. He was the tallest, speaking fast and emphasising every phrase with an expansive gesture – hands waving or pointing, head tossed back to flick the long sandy fringe away from his eyes, which rolled expressively or narrowed as he pulled a face. He looked like a fifteen-year-old version of his father, and he'd probably punch anyone who ever said that out loud.

Luke spotted Bolam when he'd almost walked past, and stopped, staring, eyebrows arched.

'Uncle Iain,' he said, gesturing for his friends to continue without him. 'Mum said you were knocking around.'

'I'm sorry,' Bolam said. 'I should have called in to see you. I…'

The sentence trailing off thing didn't work with Luke. The boy just laughed and said, 'Can't stand to spend more than a minute in Dad's company. I know.'

That was something Luke got from his mother: he saw right through his uncle. Bolam had always liked the boy.

They walked together, heading slowly up the hill, even though Bolam had parked nearby. Sometimes walking made it easier to talk.

'How's life been?' Bolam asked.

Luke shrugged, tossed his head. 'All good,' he said, and left it at that.

'School?'

'Okay.'

Bolam was glad that most of the people he dealt with were not adolescents. Put him in an interview room with a fifteen-year-old and he'd never get an answer to anything that consisted of more than two syllables.

'And what are your views on world peace?'

'Cool.' Luke laughed. He knew exactly what he was doing.

'What are you going to do?'

Luke stopped and stared. He didn't have even a single syllable answer to that one.

'When you reach the end of school and have to make choices about what you're going to do with your life,' Bolam said. 'When you realise you should have worked harder because that would have given you more options, but now all you can do is try to make the best of a bad lot, and you're faced with the relentless grind of years passing until you retire.'

'You should have been a careers adviser,' Luke said.

'You can't wait for this to all be over, can you? To be done with school, and having to do what your parents say. To have money and choices. But I'll let you in on a secret, Luke. No matter how insecure and out of your depth you feel now, you'll feel just the same in thirty years' time. We're always that kid. We always have impostor syndrome.'

Bolam didn't know where that had come from. He'd only wanted to get under Luke's skin, see if he could get another angle on Gordon

Rowe. But now he realised he was scared for the boy, and for the possibility that Luke's world might be on the edge of being ripped apart.

Luke took a moment to absorb the rush of words, then he looked across at Bolam again, and said, 'You're telling me it really doesn't get any better than this?' And then he laughed again.

'Shit happens, Luke. And good things, too. You just have to learn to survive one and appreciate the other.'

They walked in silence for a little longer, turning at the top of the street to head towards Luke's home.

'I liked Auntie Fran,' Luke said, finally. 'I'm sorry she…'

Bolam nodded. He was sorry she… too. 'Thanks, Luke,' he said.

Do you think your father is a psychopath who keeps trophies of his victims so he can torture their loved ones years later?

Do you think your father is such a good actor that he's managed to hide his dark side from everyone for pretty much all his adult life?

Do you think your mother is maybe the only person up to now who has suspected that something is fundamentally wrong with her husband's personality?

He'd planned to be more subtle than that, of course, but now he found he couldn't even approach these topics indirectly. If, and when, things did blow up in his life, Luke would remember this conversation, and he would mark Bolam against it. For the first time in his career, Bolam wasn't willing to take that kind of hit.

'You'll be okay,' he said, instead. 'You'll find your path through it all, just like the rest of us.'

'That's encouraging,' Luke said. He met Bolam's look briefly, then glanced away.

Bolam remembered something he hadn't thought about for some time. On those rare occasions when a family visit to Gordon and Maria had been unavoidable, he and Luke had shared moments like this – private jokes, conspiratorial looks when the boy's parents weren't looking. Fran had noticed, and she'd always given them the kind of disapproving looks that could only ever be intended to encourage.

A car pulled up in the street beside them. A silver Audi. Maria Rowe.

The window nearest the pavement slid down, and Maria leaned across. 'Luke?' she said.

The boy glanced from his mother to Bolam and back again. He had the look of a child who knew he was in trouble and didn't have the faintest idea why. He didn't make a move to get in, and Bolam could imagine him desperately trying to work out if that made things better or worse.

'Raymond called me,' Maria said, addressing Bolam now.

Bolam nodded. When Cowper had told him earlier that he had put himself at the disposal of the Rowes that had not been a sharing of confidences but rather a shot across the bows.

He looked around and saw Luke's retreating back. The boy was heading along an alleyway between the houses, his head tucked low, as if trying to make himself smaller.

When Bolam looked back, he saw Maria open her mouth to call after her vanishing son, then stop herself, clearly not wanting to appear needy. She met Bolam's look. 'Really?' she said. 'You're interrogating children now?'

Bolam said nothing.

'Can't you see how ridiculous you're being?' Maria continued. 'Why have you suddenly got a bee in your bonnet about Gordon? Raymond told me you were digging the dirt. Well, you're wasting your time. I really thought you were better than this.'

'I'm just asking the same questions I would about anyone else,' Bolam said. 'Most of my work is about exclusion.'

Excluding persons of interest until there was only one left…

'Gordon is a good man,' Maria said. 'You've known him for years. You know that.'

Maria had known him for even longer, though, and in that instant Bolam saw the cracks. The uncertainties.

And he knew that those doubts about the man she had once loved might finally be what ended their marriage, whether the doubts turned out to have any substance or not.

It was gone seven by the time Aisha Nawaz returned to the Serious Crimes office, and Bolam was wondering if she had simply gone straight home and he'd have to wait until the morning for her to report back.

Bolam came out to stand in the doorway to his office, and the instant he met Aisha's look, he knew her trip had been worth the effort.

'She's one of ours,' Aisha said. 'Swap the names and she could be another Jayne Sturridge, eighteen years on.'

She sat at her desk, and Bolam moved across and pulled a chair up, then Tommo came across to join them, repeating the gathering from the previous evening.

'Marcia Fredericks lived with her long-term boyfriend in Great Yarmouth. On the face of it, they were a respectable couple. She was a careworker in the charity sector and he was a teacher. Nothing exciting ever happened to them and they never *did* anything exciting.'

'On the face of it?'

'Neighbours said they rowed a lot. Said he was over-protective to the point of controlling.'

'And she was vulnerable,' Bolam said, remembering the case notes. 'A former addict. The kind of woman who might easily end up involved with a controlling personality like the boyfriend.'

'None of which is criminal,' Tommo reminded them. 'Up to a point, at least.'

'When she went missing, the boyfriend reported it, but the local force did little beyond giving *him* a hard time.'

'Just as the locals here did Sturridge,' Bolam said.

'Then it all went quiet. I spoke to the boyfriend today. He said he went back to the station every day for a month, but nobody was interested in a former homeless addict's disappearance.'

'Him behaving like that probably just reinforced the assumption she'd done a runner,' said Tommo.

'So she was an easy target,' said Bolam, 'and there was the obvious assumption that it was just domestic and she'd walked out, and if there is any suspicion, then the boyfriend is a good suspect.' He could see why Aisha had said it was just like the Sturridge case.

'She washed up on the beach at Caister six weeks later, minus the little finger of her left hand.'

'It always is,' said Bolam. Aisha and Tommo stared at him. 'Little finger, left hand,' he explained. 'That has to be significant. Cause of death?'

'Strangulation by ligature,' Aisha said. 'Something narrow, no fibres left, so maybe an electric cable or a coated washing line. There was no significant forensic evidence on the body after six weeks in salt water.'

Bolam wondered whether their killer worked from behind, or preferred to look into the eyes of his victims. Linda Rawlings, the double amputee, had been killed with a single machete slash across the throat, and the ambulance victims had been stabbed, which suggested that either their perpetrator adapted to circumstances, or that not all the cases were related after all.

'Has the boyfriend received a finger in the post?' Bolam asked.

Aisha shook her head. 'No report, and when I spoke to him he didn't mention anything like that.'

'Did you ask him?'

'Not explicitly, no. But I asked if he'd had anything unusual in the mail, or delivered to him by any other means. And I asked if he'd had any other unusual approaches, either from people he knew or from strangers. The poor guy is utterly freaked out now: all my questions about Marcia, and now not only is he wondering why we're asking again, but he has to have put two and two together and have realised some weird shit might be about to fall on him any time soon. I asked a contact in the Norfolk Constabulary to keep an eye on him, and to watch for any related reports.'

'That's good. Thanks, Aisha.' Bolam sat back, trying to assess where this left them. Another probable case, in a location related to two of their persons of interest: Gordon Rowe and Robbie Walton. A victim involved in the kind of charity work favoured by Walton.

Bolam stood. 'I think we should call it a day. Regroup tomorrow and review our strategy.'

'I took a call today,' Tommo said.

Bolam turned to him. He wasn't even supposed to be working on this case at the moment, but he'd been putting in extra for the last couple of days.

'Stewart Doherty,' Tommo went on. 'From the Fresh Start shelter.'

Bolam raised his eyebrows in question.

'We spoke to him earlier in the investigation,' Tommo said. 'When Russell Shaw was taken into custody we interviewed everyone at the shelter. Doherty helps run the place. Ex-Army. Long-haired hippie-type now. All round do-gooder, with a particular dislike of the police.'

Bolam suppressed a smile. Stewart Doherty sounded like just the kind of person to get under Tommo's skin. 'What did he want?' he asked.

'He said he's concerned about Russell Shaw,' said Tommo.

'Concerned?' said Bolam. 'That he might harm himself?' He remembered his encounter with the man after his release from custody: a man close to the edge.

'Possibly,' said Tommo, 'but he seemed to be implying he was more concerned about the people *around* Shaw, and what might happen if Shaw "flipped again", as he put it.'

'You think we should put eyes on Shaw?'

'No, that's not what I'm saying,' said Tommo. 'Doherty seemed just a little *too* keen that we should do exactly that. I know we're interested in Robbie Walton and Gordon Rowe, and maybe still even Matthew Sturridge. But I'd say that if we're looking for someone involved in homeless charities, close to the case, and maybe even inserting themselves *into* the case – and someone who is trying to manipulate the progress of the investigation – then maybe we should look at Stewart Doherty too.'

29

Bolam stayed late, digging into the background of their latest person of interest.

Stewart Doherty had served in Afghanistan and the Balkans during his time in the Army. He'd also spent time at what members of the forces called the 'Glasshouse' – the Military Corrective Training Centre at Colchester – having been found guilty by military court of assault on two young female recruits. From what Bolam could determine, the assaults seemed like classic cases of hazing – intense psychological and physical bullying of new recruits, particularly any who showed vulnerabilities – but as both assaults concerned young women, they were of particular interest in the current context.

According to the official report Bolam had tracked down, Doherty had served twelve months in the Glasshouse and used the time to turn his life around. He took IT and business administration courses, and became a mentor to fellow inmates, skills he used in later life when he joined the charity sector to work with the homeless and dispossessed – a role he'd never have been given if his criminal record had been in the civilian sector and not military.

Despite his apparent reform, Doherty's record was suggestive: bullying and assaulting young women made sense in a progression of offences centred around controlling – and ultimately murdering – vulnerable female victims. Bolam knew it was likely that, regardless of whether Doherty was their man, he had very probably committed other offences against similarly vulnerable women, and may well have escalated.

Upon completing his sentence twelve years ago, Doherty had left the Army and gone to live with his brother in Norwich… Which meant that they now had three persons of interest who also had connections with Norfolk around the time of the Marcia Fredericks murder.

It seemed that, rather than excluding possible suspects from the investigation, they were steadily *adding* them.

Doherty was local and would have been in his mid-teens when Jayne Sturridge was killed, which was interesting as it meant he could easily have been one of Matthew Sturridge's pupils at that time. Perhaps it was Sturridge who had steered him towards life in the Army – Russell Shaw had said Sturridge was involved with the Army Cadets, very likely using them to bring order to the chaotic lives of unsettled teens.

The timings of Doherty's tours of duty overseas did not exclude him from Joanna Clayton's killing either. And now he appeared to be trying to manipulate the police investigation by steering it back in the direction of Russell Shaw.

In Stewart Doherty, it appeared that they had a suspect who ticked most of their boxes. Just as importantly, there was no obvious reason to discount him at this stage.

Bolam's personal mobile, lying on the desk by his computer monitor, buzzed with an unfamiliar number.

'Bolam?' he said, answering the call.

'It's Luke.' Hence the unfamiliar number: teenagers went through phones like used socks.

'Luke. What's up?' Bolam hoped he hadn't made life hard for the boy by approaching him after school this afternoon.

'It's Dad. Mum and Dad. They've been fighting ever since Dad got back from work this evening. Mum said something about Mr Cowper talking to you, and it just went downhill from there.'

Bolam recalled that flicker of an expression on Maria's face earlier, the momentary faltering that had betrayed the doubts she seemed to feel about Gordon. Doubts like that always reached the surface in the end.

'Listen, Luke. There's nothing you can do. It's hard, but your parents need to work things out between them. Like I told you earlier, shit happens. You just have to see it through, and do what you can to pick up the pieces afterwards, okay?'

'Oh, it's gone beyond that,' Luke said. 'Dad stormed out, and now Mum's in the kitchen, crying her way through her second bottle of Merlot.'

Perhaps that was best. He held back from suggesting Maria should get the locks changed.

'Do you know where your father might have gone?'

'I don't.'

'I'll come round,' Bolam said. 'I'll make sure your mother's okay and we'll see if we can work out where your father's gone, and make sure he's okay too.'

His desk phone rang then, and he said, 'Listen, that's my other phone. I have to take it. But I won't be long, okay?'

But he was.

He rang off, answered the desk phone, and was told that Matthew Sturridge had committed suicide.

Sturridge had even done the washing up. That was perhaps the most poignant thing about a scene so domestic it was heartbreaking.

Bolam had told Cath Marshall to treat Matthew Sturridge's house as a crime scene, which of course it was, and to subject it to detailed forensic examination – beyond what might normally be done for an apparently straightforward suicide. They had to be absolutely sure there had been no third party involved in Sturridge's death.

Bolam wore a white Tyvek coverall over his pinstripe suit, and protective bootees over his shoes, but even so he didn't enter the living room where Sturridge had been found. From the doorway he'd seen Raj Khatri leaning over the body, still where it had been found in a wing-back chair. Sturridge sat upright in that seat, a hand on either arm of the chair. He wore a tweed jacket, a matching waistcoat, a striped tie that might have been a school or college tie. The death had been called in by a neighbour who had seen him like this through the net curtains.

Elsewhere in the room, a technician dusted the windowsill for prints, and another was on her knees, peering beneath a sofa.

In the kitchen, everything was neat and organised. Sturridge had eaten this evening, and then he'd washed the dishes in the sink, where now a plastic washing-up bowl stood propped up to drain. A plate, a knife and a fork stood in the drying rack, along with a single saucepan and a wooden spoon.

'Raj will confirm, of course,' said Cath, 'but there was a pill box with two empty blister packs, and an empty glass on the table in the front room. Blood pressure pills. They slow the heart: take enough of them in one go and they slow it to a halt. It's about as peaceful a way to go as possible. Perhaps a few moments' panic when reality strikes and you simply don't have the strength to move, but then by their nature the pills calm you down, so the panic would be brief.'

'He always struck me as painstakingly methodical,' Bolam said.

'To the end.'

'Indeed.'

'There was a letter.'

The note was in an evidence bag on the kitchen table. Bolam read it through the plastic.

My dearest Jayne,

I can only apologise. I let you down when you were here and I let you down when you had gone. As a husband I was inadequate; and so when you were gone from my life I did not feel as bad as I should have done, for the simple reason that I believed you had made the rational choice to forge a better life without me. For twenty-nine years I bore the guilt that I should have felt more. I did not know, of course, that you did not take yourself from me, but rather were taken. In the short time that I have been aware of this I fear I have borne a full twenty-nine years' worth of grief. That is too much burden for any mere mortal; and it is too much for me. I would like to be able to believe that you are out there somewhere, and I will join you in a life after this, but I fear that instead I join you in the void.

My love, I am sorry that I could never be more for you than I was.

Matthew.

'We failed him, didn't we?' Cath said, standing at Bolam's shoulder and reading again the note she must have read several times already.

'Twenty-nine years of his life shaped by the loss of his wife – first the guilt of hoping she'd chosen a better life without him, and then the sledgehammer of realising she'd been murdered – and even at the end he never knew what had happened to her.'

Bolam said nothing. Cath's was the sensible interpretation, supported by the content of Sturridge's suicide letter. They had failed him once, twenty-nine years ago, by failing to recognise the true nature of his wife's disappearance, and they had failed him again by neither offering him an explanation for her murder nor providing the support he needed. But Bolam felt this new development deeply, for they had not only failed him, but Bolam's rush to haul Sturridge in for questioning must surely have contributed to the man's state of mind leading up to this point.

Bolam, of all people, knew what it was like to be falsely accused. Even now, he could close his eyes and feel that relentless weight of certainty he'd felt as a twenty-year-old, unjustly locked up and knowing there was nothing he could do. Until recently, that night in a police cell had been the worst, and longest, night of his life.

On the rare occasions Bolam talked about that experience, he told people that it was what led him to joining the police: not simply the injustice, but the deep need to understand how it was possible to get it so wrong, and lock up an innocent person.

Maybe he finally had his answer.

Not a complicated psychological explanation where good people can be blinded by prejudice, or one where bad people secure positions of authority in organisations that do good, but simple, clumsy incompetence.

He'd been wrong about Matthew Sturridge – badly wrong – and he hadn't anticipated where that might lead.

Bolam parked across the gateway and took a deep breath, before getting out and walking up the gravel drive. When he rang the doorbell it was Luke who answered.

'I'm sorry, it's late, I know,' said Bolam. 'I couldn't get here straight away. That shit: it keeps on happening. Is your mother still…?'

Luke nodded and stepped back from the door. Bolam could see

along the hallway that Maria Rowe was still at the kitchen table, a steaming cup before her now, rather than the Merlot.

She saw him in the same instant. 'He's not here,' she called to him. 'Your work is done.'

Bolam glanced across at Luke, but the boy was already retreating up the stairs with that same head-down posture as before, trying not to be noticed.

'Maria,' Bolam said. 'Are you okay?' He wasn't going to get drawn into a blame game.

She rolled her eyes, then reached for the cup and drank.

Bolam sat opposite her. 'What happened?'

'You can't stop digging, can you? Is that why you're here? Looking for anything you can use against him?'

'I just want to help.'

'No wonder Fran was in the process of leaving you.' She stopped herself, putting a hand melodramatically to her mouth. She was far more drunk than she had first appeared. 'I'm sorry. I didn't mean...'

Bolam remained silent. He didn't blame Fran for wanting to end their marriage either. He was not an easy man to be with.

'I told Gordon you were digging,' Maria said, as if guilt at her faux pas was making her speak. 'I said you'd visited Raymond, and you'd been quizzing me and Luke. He was angry. He wanted to know why, and I said wasn't it obvious? That he was involved in all this crap and you were just merrily doing your job. He said it was all nonsense.'

'That was it?'

'I hesitated too long before agreeing,' Maria told him. 'That's all it took. He wanted a hundred per cent and I could only give ninety-nine.'

Bolam could understand that, because even that tiny sliver, that one per cent, indicated a willingness to at least entertain the possibility that Gordon Rowe had murdered her half-sister.

'Where is he, Maria?'

'I don't know. He didn't take anything, so he might be back. I don't think he will though. Not tonight.'

'I'll talk to him. I'll try to make him see sense.'

'You're going to fix our marriage? How kind. But don't flatter yourself: we were well and truly screwed before this. Papering over the cracks for as long as I can remember. But if you think you can wave a magic wand, be my guest. I'd have him back in a flash, even now.'

He remained silent for a few seconds. Then… 'There never is a magic wand, is there?'

She reached out and squeezed his hand. 'No,' she said. 'There never is.'

He left her sitting there, left the house and crunched his way along the drive.

He thought of Fran, and he wished he had understood back then that there was never going to be a magic fix for the things that were wrong, that it could only be down to the things they did themselves.

30

Russell Shaw stood in the darkness by the window, looking in. He didn't know how he'd ended up here.

He couldn't remember much from today at all. The absences were frequent now, both a blessed release from the world but also a reopening of his darkest fears: periods when he did not know where he was, or what he might be doing. And now he was here…

He should leave.

He leaned closer to the glass.

The living room was lit only by the flickering glow from a large TV screen – or computer monitor, he wasn't sure: they all had big, flat screens these days. The screen showed tangled limbs. Pale flesh. A young woman, wide-eyed, mouth sagging open, her head held tipped back by a man's fist buried deep in her dark hair.

On the sofa, a man leaned back, hands behind his head. He seemed unable to sit still, kept shifting in his seat, his movements disturbing, sinuous. He put one hand down to the front of his jeans and started to rub himself.

Russ looked away.

When he'd first met him, Stewart had seemed so supportive, so genial. Seeing him like this jarred.

Russ knew he shouldn't be watching. Shouldn't be here.

He didn't know what he was intending to do. He'd just got it into his head that Stewart was being too intrusive. Coming to his flat like that. Letting himself into the building.

He didn't trust Stewart any more. It had been a mistake to let him get close.

When Russ looked again, Stewart was leaning forward, lighting a cigarette. Breathing deep and then puffing out blue smoke in a big cloud. On the screen, the woman was naked, reaching towards the camera, beckoning.

Russ felt sick.

He looked away again. He pressed one hand against the cold, gritty surface of the brick wall, trying to force his breathing to calm.

When he looked up, Stewart was standing before him, studying him closely. Had he blanked again?

'What are you doing here, Russ? How did you know where I live?'

He'd followed him, obviously. It wasn't hard.

'Why can't you all leave me alone?' Russ said. 'Just… Leave me alone.'

'You're the one who came here.'

Russ shook his head, not in denial but as if to shake loose what was within. 'You're in my life,' he said. 'In my head. It's too much.'

'I don't know what you mean, Russ.' Stewart still had his cigarette, and now he took a long draw on it. 'You want to come in? Have a beer, a joint, watch some porn?'

Russ shook his head again. It felt as if Stewart was playing with him, taunting him. 'Someone threw a stone through my window.'

'Really?'

Something about the way he said that made Russ wonder if it had been Stewart who threw the stone. Winding him up. Stirring.

'And the police…' said Russ. 'They won't leave me alone.'

'I know. They forget they're here to serve *us*, protect *us*. Not pick on people like you, Russ. Like I say, once they've got you in their sights that's it, isn't it? And that short one always preening himself in the three-piece suit, the inspector. He's the worst of the lot. He needs teaching a thing or two.'

There was an intensity to Stewart's words that disturbed Russ.

'I know who you are,' Stewart went on. 'I know what you did. What was that like? Can you remember? How did it feel?'

Russ took a step backwards. He didn't want Stewart in his head like this. More winding up. More stirring.

'The police are all over you, aren't they, Russ? And it's not about what you did in that ambulance, is it? You served your time for that. So what else have you done? There must be something.'

Russ took another step back.

'Is it your sister?'

Russ stared. He didn't understand.

'I know she's dead. Did you do that too? Is that what they're after?'

His head was spinning. He'd been in hospital. He hadn't… He couldn't…

'Did you kill Elizabeth?'

Russ lunged forward, hands out. He felt contact, felt flesh tearing under his clawing nails, his fingers dragging across Stewart's face and getting tangled in his beard. For a moment they staggered, then they collided with the wall. Then he felt hands on his arms, using his momentum to turn him, slam him even harder against the bricks. The air rushed from his lungs, his head struck hard, and he felt his legs buckling. Another blow in his back – a punch or a knee to the kidneys – sent sharp bolts of pain shooting through his body, and he collapsed.

He fell on his side, and immediately felt another painful thud as Stewart's boot caught him in the belly.

He drew his knees up, coughing, tasting blood in his mouth.

He waited for the next blow to come but it didn't, and in that instant he felt a perverse sense that he had been robbed, that he deserved this and he wanted it to carry on until his body could take no more.

Russ sat with his back to the wall, his knees drawn up.

To his side, Stewart sat in the same position.

'You okay?' Stewart asked.

Russ said nothing. His body hurt. His mouth still tasted of blood.

Stewart had another cigarette on the go, and he offered it to Russ, who shook his head.

'I might as well have,' Russ said, finally. Then, in response to Stewart's look, he went on. 'Killed her. Elizabeth. I was in hospital when she died. I wasn't there when she needed me. I brought her world down around her.' A world she'd barely ever been able to hold together, even when he *had* been there. 'I might as well have.'

'They were all over the shelter, you know,' Stewart told him. 'The police. Snooping. Asking about you. They don't care what impact that kind of thing has. Everyone was scared. Talking about you. We had to have a special meeting.'

'Meeting? What do you mean?'

'Putting concerns to rest. That's what Robbie called it. He said we should stand by the name of our charity: Fresh Start. That you'd done your time and deserved the same fresh start we all had.'

Robbie Walton. He was one of these figures who lurked in the background at the charity, a name mentioned often, but someone who only occasionally ever showed his face at a renovation project or a steering group meeting.

'He knew about you already, you know, before you came back. Robbie did. That's what he said. He knew you were coming back but he never said anything because you deserved a fresh start.'

Russ closed his eyes and tried to visualise him, this man who had told them that Russ should be allowed to move on with his life.

He pictured Walton as a thin man, dark hair flecked with grey. And something in his empty eyes that made Russ think of his grandfather.

31

Bolam left the house early, but instead of going to the station he drove on north, following the main road inland from Whitesands.

The municipal cemetery was off a roundabout about a mile out of town. The tall iron gates were still closed this early but there was a parking area outside, and he was able to let himself in through a small gate to one side that was always left unlocked.

It was the first time he'd come here since Fran's funeral, four and a half months before – a dismal grey day just before Christmas, the open cemetery chilled by a North Sea wind straight from the Arctic.

He paused, just inside the gate. In contrast to the day of the funeral, it was a bright spring morning and birds were singing. Tulips and a few late daffodils swayed in the slight breeze.

He'd told himself he didn't need to come here. He knew what he'd lost – that awareness would never leave him – but now he realised that a part of him felt a fraud for even being here. A fake widower.

'Oh, Fran,' he sighed. He still couldn't quite work out how they'd reached this point.

Her ashes had been buried in a tiny plot partway along one of the long, grassy rows. Brass plaques were set into the turf; Fran's simply bore her name and dates, no message, no meaningful epitaph, no mention of the loved ones she left behind.

He kneeled, the knees of his suit trousers instantly wet through from the morning dew. 'I'm sorry, Fran,' he said. For nothing in particular, but also for everything.

He sat on a bench nearby, closed his eyes. The birds were still singing.

Again, he considered the possibility of simply walking away from all of this: the job, the people, the place. He knew it had been a mistake coming to this town and simply trying to carry on as if nothing had happened; and he knew that had led to more mistakes. Largest of all of these was Matthew Sturridge. He'd blundered in, blinded by the possibility of getting a quick result. Not only had he risked derailing the investigation, but he knew his actions had played a part in the old teacher's choice to end it all.

His was not the kind of job where you could ever get away with failing to give one hundred per cent.

And now that he understood the scale of his failures, he found himself questioning every new choice he made, which would surely lead to more errors. Fran would tell him that was the biggest mistake of all: to lose confidence in his own judgement and dodge the major decisions. He should trust his own experience.

He opened his eyes. He was still the only one here, which was a relief because he had the horrible feeling he had been voicing his thoughts aloud again: talking to Fran, or talking to himself, the distinction really didn't matter.

He ground the heels of his hands into his eyes. 'Be strong,' he said. 'Don't let yourself be beaten.'

He stood.

He needed to find a way to move on – with the investigation, but also with his life. He'd allowed himself to hide in this semi-limbo state for too long, but now he needed to take control again.

Fran had left him, but he couldn't work out how to leave *her*.

He turned, and started to walk away, which was a start, at least.

The third delivery to Bolam's house came that morning while he was at the cemetery, and this time there could be no mistaking that it was both personal, and part of the broader case of murder, intimidation and cruel manipulation.

The solicitor's letter addressed to Fran had been the first, and with hindsight Bolam could see clearly that it had been an initial blow, a cruel stab at his most vulnerable point. Opening the old wound of his unresolved relationship with a woman who was in the process of leaving him even as she was dying. Something – or someone – had triggered that letter deliberately to target him, he was sure now.

The photographs had elevated things to a more overt basis. The photographs themselves could have been downloaded from any of Fran's old social media accounts – or those of her friends and contacts – but the act of printing and defacing them had been personal, and cruel, and directed at Bolam. But still he had thought it might be unrelated, perhaps tied instead to unresolved issues in Fran's life in the Northeast.

But this morning…

The package was waiting on the doormat when he got home from the cemetery to have another coffee and change into dry clothes for work. It was the same as before, an A4 manila envelope, the address printed in generic font, no stamp or frank.

He didn't touch it. He stepped over the envelope lying on his doormat and went through to fetch gloves and evidence bags before picking up the envelope, placing it on the kitchen worktop and easing the flap open.

It looked like the same photographs as before, and he tried to remove them one by one to place in individual plastic bags but he couldn't because they were stuck together with blood.

He stopped himself from reacting, partly because it was his responsibility to remain rational and logical and partly because he knew this could only have been designed to get under his skin and he was not going to concede victory so easily.

One by one, he peeled the photographs apart and placed them in evidence bags. As he had suspected from the first glance, the pictures were the same as before, Fran's face scratched out on each one. They were daubed with blood that had dried in streaks and patches, and now he saw that wherever Fran's hands appeared in the pictures, the fingers, too, had been scratched away.

Fingers, blood, the use of the dead to torment and break their surviving loved ones. Not only some perverted serial killer, but someone who revelled in the psychological and emotional torment of others… in breaking them so thoroughly that some, like Russell Shaw and Matthew Sturridge, might never recover.

Bolam would not break, though.

He had seen worse and survived, even if it had not been directed at him.

Only this morning he had, again, been on the verge of walking away from all this, but this personal assault hardened his resolve.

He would get through this.

Compartmentalise it.

And use it against whoever was responsible.

He peeled off the gloves and bagged them, too, in case they might have picked up any trace contact evidence from handling this morning's delivery.

Then he reached into his inner jacket pocket, found his work phone, and thumbed a contact.

'Cath? Are you at the station today? I have something on the Sturridge-Rowe investigation. New evidence that requires every forensic test we can throw at it.'

Bolam lost most of the day to meetings and admin. A strategy group chaired by McBride. An HR meeting in the afternoon, followed by a review of notes for a case of Billie Grayson's that was coming to trial soon.

He'd handed his bagged evidence to Cath as soon as he arrived at the station: today's delivery, plus the earlier photographs, and the solicitor's letter, even though the latter was unlikely to have been handled by anyone of significance. 'These were sent to my home address,' he said. 'I've noted the details. I didn't think they were connected to our investigation until the third package arrived today.'

Cath had looked through the bags and nodded, saying simply, 'I've got this. I'll fast-track everything.' No judgement. No suggestion that he should have acted sooner, rather than dismissing the significance of this personal targeting.

By the end of the day he felt worn down, not just because his mind had been circling around what was happening, but because he'd been trying to push that aside and not be frustrated that he was being sidelined by mundanity. He'd never come into the job to end up as a middle manager, though, and often wondered why the system seemed designed to take people away from the real work as soon as they had acquired experience and demonstrated their skill at the job. He often wished he was still a DC.

Mid-afternoon, he had called Cath, but she had little to report. 'I promise I'll call you as soon as we have anything,' she told him.

He left the office no more than an hour after he was supposed to, one of the few times he had done so since starting this job. A short time later, he parked on East Bay Drive and took a moment to gaze out over the North Sea. It had been a lovely spring day, and the sky was still a deep blue. Families were down on the beach and gathered around the multicoloured beach huts. It was a different world.

Bolam could not imagine living a life where you were unaware of the grim reality of what surrounded you – although he sometimes wished he could. The neighbours on the cusp of violent break-up. The paedophile in halfway-house lodgings across the road. The dealer down the street. The disturbing number of perfectly ordinary people with psychopathic and other dangerous personality disorders who somehow managed to lead mundane lives, but never perceived the world as one might assume.

He'd read studies that argued that up to thirty per cent of the population showed at least some psychopathic traits. Most came across as merely quirky or eccentric; some channelled these traits into single-minded pursuit of success in their fields. So in some ways psychopathy could be seen as merely part of humankind's rich diversity.

Only a small proportion of that thirty per cent ever crossed the line into violent crime, their condition blinding them to the true impact of their actions.

Bolam was convinced that they were pursuing one such person. A cold manipulator of people, immune to normal emotional response. Someone who saw the world, and the people in it, in a very different way to how Bolam did. As the classic description put it, a person who could hear the words, but not the music.

Was Gordon Rowe such a person? He was intensely driven and successful. In his personal life you could easily make a case for emotional blindness, and monstrous ego, and he regularly manipulated the people around him to achieve his own ends. And the way Bolam had been singled out for attention suggested a significant personal element motivating the current escalation. Gordon Rowe ticked a lot of the boxes. But just because he might fall into the thirty per cent, it did not mean he was their man.

Gordon was staying in a first-floor flat in one of the Victorian villas that lined one side of East Bay Drive, just north of the town centre. Bolam had called the offices of Cowper and Rowe earlier and spoken to Gordon's assistant, Letitia. She'd been reluctant to share details at first, but Bolam had charmed her, told her he was Gordon's brother-in-law on a mission for Maria to try to get them to patch things over. Letitia turned out to be something of a romantic at heart, and a poor respecter either of her boss's privacy or data protection law: Bolam could have been anyone.

The villa had been subdivided into four flats. Bolam pressed the buzzer for Flat B.

'Yes?'

'It's me, Gordon. Can we talk?' The doorbell had a camera, so Gordon would already have seen who it was.

The door buzzed, and he stepped into a wide lobby with a sweeping staircase ascending from one side. He climbed the stairs and the door to Gordon's flat was open before he'd reached the top.

For a moment they glowered at each other, then the moment passed, Gordon stepped back, and Bolam entered the flat.

He'd anticipated something far more basic than this, a real descent from height; a bachelor pad bedsit with the bare minimum of furniture, and old takeaway packaging strewn across the floor. Instead, he smelled onions and garlic cooking in the kitchen, and the place was spacious, light, stylish. It had a worrying air of the long-term, as if Gordon planned to stay.

'Nice,' said Bolam, moving across to the tall sash window giving a view across East Bay Drive to the North Sea.

Gordon shrugged. 'None of this is mine,' he said. 'I have a few things in the bedroom, but that's all. This is just a place Raymond made available to me. It's usually an Airbnb.'

That made sense. Even now Cowper was protecting his partner. He wondered how much the old lawyer had known or suspected over the years and even helped cover up, perhaps to protect the good name of his beloved firm.

Bolam still found it bizarre to be thinking along these lines, to be standing in a room with a man he had known for years, wondering just how much he had overlooked.

Gordon was staring at him, a strange expression on his face. For once, he was not animated, no quick-fire changing of expressions, no tossing of the hair or expansive gesturing with hand and arm.

'Why are you doing this?' he said, simply.

'You feature in some way in every branch of the investigation,' said Bolam, considering his choice of words carefully, before deciding that Gordon knew almost as much as anyone about their investigation. 'Matthew Sturridge – you were closely connected with him and with his brother-in-law Robbie Walton. Russell Shaw – so many involvements over the years. Joanna Clayton – I'll leave that one there. Linda Rawlings – I know you threw yourself into the middle of that one, delaying a search at a critical juncture. There's nothing that excludes you from at least being a person of interest. I'd be failing in my job if I didn't treat you like anyone else.' He had deliberately omitted the Marcia Fredericks case from his list: Gordon had no reason to know they were looking at that one, as yet. He had considered pressing him on the packages sent to Bolam, too, but had decided against that: he would share nothing that was not either known to third parties or a legal requirement.

'I heard about Matthew.'

Bolam looked away.

'I specialise in criminal law,' said Gordon, his compassion for Sturridge apparently short-lived. 'Of *course* I'm involved in high-profile cases in the town. It's like throwing suspicion on you because *you're* involved. It goes with the territory.' Then he stopped, tossing his hair back with a flick of the head – the old Gordon emerging. 'Linda Rawlings, you say? Why are you dragging that old case into all this? Am I missing something?'

'There are correspondences,' Bolam said, still treading carefully.

'Amputation?' Gordon said. 'Is that all you have? Come on, man, you're clutching at straws with that one. Linda Rawlings was a gofer for a gang from the East End. They'd operated out of the port here for years, but – what was it, twenty years ago? – they were up against the Bratva, Russian mobsters moving in on people- and drug-trafficking in all the UK ports at the time. Linda Rawlings was a punishment killing, and a warning to anyone who might cross their path.'

It made sense. Bolam had never been comfortable including Linda Rawlings in their investigation, even when it looked increasingly tempting.

'And you know all this *how*, exactly, Gordon?' According to Andy Souter, Gordon had been responsible for delaying the joint Customs and Police raid that might have caught the culprits, or at least uncovered evidence of what was going on. By the time they'd untangled themselves from Gordon's red tape, everything had been cleaned away.

Gordon waved his hands, as if brushing the question away. 'Come on,' he said. 'Like I say, Rawlings was a warning to anyone who might dare to get involved. Cowper and Rowe have never touched anything gang-related again. You seem to be accusing me of lots of things, but I don't think you've ever accused me of bravery…'

Bolam followed his brother-in-law through an archway to the flat's small kitchen. Gordon expertly tossed a frying pan to redistribute the frying onions, then broke two eggs and whisked them in a jug.

'Omelette?' he asked, reaching for more eggs without waiting for an answer.

Bolam watched as he poured the eggs over the onions, then dropped slivers of Gruyère into the mix.

'Talking to Luke was stooping low,' Gordon said. 'I'd have hoped for better from you. You should leave him out of it.'

'I did leave him out of it,' Bolam responded. 'I didn't ask him about you. I intended to, but I couldn't. We just caught up on things. You should talk to him. He sees what's going on.' And as soon as he said that he knew that he *should* have remained objective and quizzed Luke about his father, for exactly that reason.

'Do you realise how this tears people's lives apart?' Gordon asked. 'Interrogating Maria and Raymond. And look at me now...' He waved both hands to indicate the flat – hardly the descent into ruin that he probably intended to convey, but still a reminder of a marriage that was perhaps broken beyond repair. 'I'm not saying Maria and I didn't already have our difficulties, but, Jesus, the crap you throw at people! And my professional standing, the practice – mud sticks, you know.'

'Cowper gave as good as he got,' Bolam said, sidestepping his guilt over Maria. 'He has your back. And you've hardly ended up in the street – this place is nice.' Gordon Rowe's flat probably cost three times as much as the entire house Bolam was currently renting.

'It's empty.'

Gordon flipped the pan again and the omelette folded itself neatly in half. Bolam had no idea he had such skills. Maria had always prepared the meals on the rare occasions he and Fran had visited – either salads or stolid, beige food, depending on her mood.

Gordon sat in a big armchair in the main living area, Bolam at one end of a sofa. They balanced plates on knees and ate the omelette with forks.

'Do you cook?'

Bolam shook his head. Fran hadn't either. They'd lived mostly on ready meals, takeaways and eating out.

'I think all this was a mistake,' Bolam said after a time. He wasn't referring to calling on Gordon this evening – he meant coming to this town, going with the flow of a new job he'd already accepted, even after he'd lost everything.

Gordon nodded, seemed to understand. 'Did you have a better offer elsewhere, though?' he said.

Bolam shook his head. When Fran died, all he had left was the job. He was an only child, his parents dead ten and twelve years; his friends were Fran's friends, and the people he worked with were never close, and had a regular turnover. Acquaintances rather than friends. Bizarrely, Gordon was now the closest thing he had to a friend outside work.

'So where do you go from here?' Gordon asked.

He meant with the case, on the assumption that he, himself, would be excluded from the investigation at some point. Bolam was intrigued that even though he still did not like the man, he and Gordon seemed to have developed a verbal shorthand between them.

'It's a process of exclusion,' he said. It always was. 'And laborious policework.'

'Joanna was obsessed with me,' Gordon said. 'She had it in her head that I reciprocated her feelings, but I never did. Perhaps it was because I was the one who dug her out of her scrapes. Maybe she read that as actually caring.'

Bolam found it quite staggering how in one short speech Gordon could start by convincing him that he was innocent – simply by opening up, unprompted, and speaking with apparent honesty – and then incriminate himself again. *Maybe she read that as actually caring* – the cold, stark statement of a man blind to emotional nuance, and implying his own manipulative nature: a reminder that he'd only ever helped Joanna in order to impress Maria.

'What happened to her, Gordon?'

Gordon shook his head. 'I really don't know. All I remember is the relief that she hadn't come to the office that day to pester me for money, being tempered by the later realisation that her absence was only because she'd made one of her dramatic exits again.'

'So how do I exclude you from the inquiry?' Bolam asked.

Gordon threw his arms wide, almost sending his plate flying to the floor. 'You want solid evidence going back twenty years?' he said. 'Well all I can say is your illustrious predecessors didn't spend long on me back then. They seemed satisfied with my innocence.'

'They didn't spend long on anyone,' Bolam said. 'They seemed far too content to mark Joanna down as a teenaged runaway and move on to more deserving cases. But now it's a murder investigation.'

Gordon looked down, either chastised or at least going through the motions that he should feel that way.

They finished their meal in silence, and then Gordon stood and took the plates back to the kitchenette. He came back with a bottle of Talisker and two glasses. Bolam couldn't help feeling that Gordon was well aware of his dislike of spirits and this was some form of punishment.

After depositing the bottle and glasses on the low, glass-topped coffee table, Gordon moved across to the window and peered out.

'He's here again,' he said. 'Your man, the ambulance driver.'

'Russell Shaw,' Bolam said. 'You went to school with him. You've represented him. You know his name.' He stood and joined Gordon at the window. Shaw stood across East Bay Drive, leaning on the railings and gazing out across the bay.

'He's watching me,' Gordon said.

Bolam peered at him. He seemed to believe it. He looked back, and Shaw was still gazing out to sea. 'He walks along the seafront all the time,' Bolam said, recalling the time he'd walked with him, trying to make sure he was okay after his night in custody. 'He likes to be by the sea. It's not all about you.'

Gordon shook his head. 'I've been working from the flat all afternoon,' he said. 'I brought a laptop back with me from the office. A bit of peace and quiet, you know? Every time I look out of the window, he's there. He's not just walking and taking the sea air.'

As if to demonstrate his point, at that moment Shaw turned and stood leaning back against the railings, arms folded, staring directly up at Gordon's building.

'Why would he be watching you, Gordon?'

Gordon shrugged, spreading his hands wide. 'He's a damaged man, from what Raymond told me,' he said. 'I think he latches on to anyone who figures large in his life. I handled his case twenty-odd years ago. I should have represented him upon his most recent arrest too, but I didn't return the call. Perhaps he feels I've let him down. I don't know. I'm guessing. All I know is that every time I look out of the window he's there. You can't blame me for being concerned, can you, considering his past? In fact, believe it or not, I was on the verge of calling you for a spot of advice when you showed up at the door.'

Bolam waited for a gap in the traffic and then crossed East Bay Drive. Russell Shaw watched him approach, but made no attempt to leave. Two uniformed officers loitered further along the road – Bolam had waited for them to respond to his call and arrive at the scene before initiating this encounter.

'Russell,' he said. 'What's all this about then?'

He knew he had to choose his words carefully if he was to stand a chance of getting anything out of Shaw, and also because Gordon had followed him from the building and was now lurking within earshot, just across the road.

He wondered what it might be that Russell Shaw knew about Gordon that had prompted him to stake out the flat like this, and what he might have intended to do. Shaw had recent history of similar behaviour with Virginia Lloyd's family. Was he simply stalking his victims, or did he suspect Gordon Rowe of something?

Shaw shifted from foot to foot where he stood, arms hugging himself tightly now rather than merely folded across his chest. His upper body was rocking back and forth, and Bolam wondered if he'd finally reached some kind of breaking point.

Close up, Bolam saw bruising around Shaw's left eye, and he wondered if they were already too late for something. What had Shaw done?

'Why are you here, Russell?' Bolam asked, letting his voice drop so that Shaw had to focus on his words. 'Why are you watching Gordon Rowe?'

Shaw looked puzzled, then. Shook his head. 'Mr Rowe?' he said, glancing across the street to where Gordon stood. 'I'm not… not watching him. I saw him with you. A week… two weeks ago. I don't know. At the café by the beach. Through the window. I recognised him. He was my solicitor, years ago. He kept telling me what to say. And he's visited me at the Rodgers-Stephenson Institute, making sure everything is okay.'

Bolam looked across at Gordon. 'Telling you what to say? When you were first arrested, you mean?'

'He said I was mad. Said I should go for diminished responsibility.'

For a moment Bolam had thought Shaw was telling him that Gordon had manipulated him, but no, it sounded no more than run-of-the-mill legal advice. He remembered that day at the beach-side bistro: lunch with Gordon disrupted by a call from the office, and a homeless man briefly peering in through the window at them – had that really been Shaw?

'I never liked that. Never liked him. He got into my head. When I saw you with him, it was just… bad memories. It made me feel bad.'

'You like to watch people, don't you, Russell? Not *like*, perhaps, but you do it, it's how you try to make sense of your world, isn't it?'

Shaw wouldn't meet his look.

'Have you been watching me, too, Russell? Was that how you happened to see me and Gordon at that café?'

It was Gordon who had pointed out that Shaw seemed to latch onto anyone who loomed large in his life. Virginia Lloyd and now her parents, Gordon Rowe… Was it Shaw who had been to Bolam's house, that smell of cigarettes and mint? Sending him photographs in an attempt to get under his skin?

'Have you, Russell?'

Shaw gave him a short, defiant look, before turning away again. 'No,' he said. 'I don't know what you mean. Why would I watch you?'

'You just said you were watching us at the café by the beach.'

'No! Not watching. I was just… Just there, at the beach, and I looked in the window because it had all changed from how I remembered, and you were there. I wasn't following anyone.'

Bolam could see him retreating into himself.

'How did you get the bruises, Russell?' Bolam gestured at his own eye. 'Have you done something we should know about?'

Shaw shook his head. 'It's nothing,' he said.

'It doesn't look like nothing. Have you been watching other people too?'

'No!'

For a moment Bolam thought he'd lost him, tipped him over the edge, but then he calmed again.

'It was Stewart,' Shaw said. 'It was my fault. I deserved it.'

He must mean Stewart Doherty, the shelter administrator who had drawn himself to the investigation's attention by trying to steer them towards Shaw. The ex-Army man who'd served time in military prison for assault.

'Why did Stewart Doherty hit you, Russell?'

Shaw shrugged, looked down at the ground, and then back up. 'I know he's spoken to you. He hates the police but he'll talk to you if it might get me in trouble.'

'You confronted him?'

'We talked,' Russell said. 'He told me to come here.'

'Why would Stewart Doherty tell you to watch Gordon Rowe?' Bolam felt that this interview was starting to slip out of his grasp.

'No, not Mr Rowe,' Russell told him. 'I was looking for Robbie Walton.'

'Why Robbie? You're going to have to spell it out for me, Russell. Why were you looking for Robbie Walton, and why did you think you'd find him here?'

Shaw waved a hand towards the building where Gordon was staying. Gordon had crossed the road now, and was standing nearby.

'He stays there. That's what Stewart told me. He stays there when he's in town.'

Bolam glanced across at his brother-in-law now.

Gordon nodded. 'It's true,' he said. 'Cowper and Rowe's property division manages the place. Robbie has an arrangement to stay in one of the flats whenever he's in town.'

'But why, Russell? Why are you looking for Robbie?'

'He… They talk about me at the charity,' Russell said. 'Robbie and the others. They gave me my flat. And Stewart told me…'

'What did he tell you, Russell?'

'He said they already knew about me, before I walked into the shelter. He said Robbie had told him I'd be coming in, and that I should be treated the same as everyone else.'

'How did they know that, Russell?'

'They'd been in touch with the hospital. With Nurse Ward and Dr Chandler. They'd helped make arrangements for me, paid for my train ticket, told the shelter to be looking out for me. Robbie had told them. And… and his *eyes*. The way he looks at you.'

Bolam took a moment to absorb all this. Then he said, 'And what were you going to do to Robbie Walton when he showed up here, Russell?'

Shaw shrugged again. 'I don't know,' he said. 'I didn't think. I just… I just wanted to know why he hates me so much.'

32

Bolam had convinced Russell Shaw to leave Robbie Walton alone. 'Just go back to your flat, Russell,' Bolam had told him. 'Get something to eat. Find a football match to watch on the TV. Try to put all this out of your head, even for a couple of hours, and *breathe*. Take each day as it comes, okay? And you still have my card? It has my mobile number. Call me if you need help, even if you just want to talk.'

He was worried for him, though: someone was clearly having fun tormenting him. He made a mental note to contact the mental health support team when he got back to the office, make sure they recognised the urgency of getting support in place for Shaw.

The investigation had a new focus now. Not Russell Shaw or Stewart Doherty, or – for now, at least – Gordon Rowe, even though Bolam was intrigued that Shaw had confirmed that Gordon had followed his progress at the Rodgers-Stephenson Institute.

'We need to talk to Robbie Walton,' Bolam told his team. 'Even if it's only to finally exclude him.' It was barely eight in the morning, but already in the main Serious Crimes office he had an audience of Billie Grayson, Aisha Nawaz, Tommo and Cath Marshall. They all had a multitude of other cases to juggle, but nobody wanted to let this one go.

He stood before them, hands behind his back. Over his shoulder, on the big screen, Billie had projected a couple of photographs of Walton. One was recent, the man with whom Bolam had engineered an encounter at one of the Fresh Start charity's renovation projects: salt and pepper hair, thick stubble, a pint glass in one hand and a fat cigar in the other. The second was an older photograph, recognisably the same man as a teenager, looking awkward as he stood with his older sister's arm around him – Jayne Sturridge.

Bolam wasn't entirely convinced the pictures added anything.

'Fifty-four years old. He's been named by Russell Shaw as having prior knowledge of Shaw's release from secure hospital, and also of having involvement in that release, and we've confirmed that the Fresh Start charity, of which Walton is a board member, did liaise with the Ministry of Justice review panel about ensuring that Shaw would have support upon his release into the community. It also looks as if that release was sabotaged, perhaps with the intent of stressing Shaw to breaking point: he was dumped into the community with inadequate preparation and minimal information, and he was told to go to the town council offices to ask for accommodation. They knew nothing about him and had nothing to offer, so he ended up temporarily homeless and sleeping rough.'

Bolam had been up late into the night, and again from the early hours this morning, piecing together the background information. 'We're looking for someone who appears to have been stage-managing the opening up of long-forgotten cases: manipulating the victims' families' grief decades after disappearances – and, as we now know, murders. It's hard to escape the observation that the manipulation of Shaw fits into this pattern, and there's another example that's come to light, which we'll come back to in a minute. Robert Walton is the brother of Jayne Sturridge, the first of our victims. We don't, as yet, have any direct connection between him and Joanna Clayton, our second victim, although he *is* acquainted with Gordon Rowe, Joanna's brother-in-law. He is, however, closely involved with the ambulance service, which is a possible tie with the Russell Shaw case—'

'Are we including the ambulance killings in all this, then?' asked Aisha. 'Shaw was found guilty of those by unanimous verdict and the MO was quite different.'

Bolam knew Aisha was reluctant to reopen a closed case like that – they all were. The repercussions of a major miscarriage of justice would be huge. 'Shaw received his co-worker's finger in the mail,' he said. 'Or at least he was in possession of it. I think the common factor between these cases isn't the victimology, or even the method of killing: it's the psychological manipulation and staging, and that's what's happening with Shaw. Whether Russell Shaw was guilty or not, our perpetrator has brought at least Virginia Lloyd's murder into the scope of this investigation, whatever the explanation may be.

'And then eleven years ago, we have Marcia Fredericks, in Norfolk,' Bolam concluded. 'The timing excludes Russell Shaw from suspicion, as he was incarcerated in a secure hospital at the time. Marcia was involved in the homeless charity sector, as is Robbie Walton, so their paths might easily have crossed, and it's possible that our perpetrator has been using charities and other voluntary groups to identify vulnerable victims who might not be missed.'

'What about Linda Rawlings, the double amputee?' asked Billie.

'The link was always tentative, at best,' Bolam said. 'The double-hand amputation rather than a single finger, for starters, and not even a suggestion of the crime being stirred up again years later to torment those close to the victim. Gordon Rowe was involved in that case at the time as a solicitor throwing red tape in the way of the investigation. Informally, he's intimated that it was a turf thing, in a conflict between rival people- and drug-trafficking gangs. I'm not sure we'll manage to get a formal statement from him to that effect, but his testimony was compelling.'

'What I want to know,' said Aisha, 'is where are the bodies? Excluding the ambulance killings, we only have Marcia Fredericks. Where is Jayne Sturridge? Joanna Clayton? What if that opal ring on Jayne's finger is from another victim?'

It was a question they'd talked about before, but never with a satisfactory answer.

'Destroyed, or buried somewhere that hasn't been disturbed in the intervening years?' Bolam said.

'So why was Marcia dumped in the sea?' asked Aisha. 'The currents were always going to wash her up somewhere.'

'Perhaps she was killed too far away from the killer's preferred disposal site,' Billie said.

They were getting nowhere.

'You said there was something new,' prompted Tommo.

Bolam nodded. 'Cath,' he said. 'Those two forensics reports you said had come in. The first – Virginia Lloyd's. What did Raj find?'

'Mostly as we'd already worked out,' Cath said. 'The finger was less well-preserved than the first two, explained by it having been thawed out several days before we seized it. A clumsier amputation, which could be explained by time constraints in the back of the ambulance. And severed at the interphalangeal joint rather than the metacarpophalangeal joints of the first two.'

'And the blood?'

'This is where it gets interesting. The blood is bovine, not human.'

'So not a result of the amputation, or the bloodbath in the back of the ambulance, but applied later, for decoration?'

'If you can call it that,' said Cath. 'Done for effect.'

'To intimidate and disturb,' Bolam said. 'To take Russell Shaw back to the night of the killings, perhaps.'

He paused, then clicked the *Forward* button on the remote. The big screen showed a set of photos – the second set delivered to Bolam, Fran's face and fingers gouged out, the images smeared red with blood.

He heard a gasp, but didn't look around the room. Until now, Cath was the only one who knew about this personal aspect of the case.

'I've had three deliveries to my house, at least two of which I'm now convinced are part of a campaign to disturb and intimidate me. They've escalated, which is why it was only with the third delivery that I was convinced they were relevant to the investigation and brought them to Cath for forensic examination.'

'Who's in the pictures?' asked Billie. She was staring at the picture to the right of the screen – the one that also included Bolam.

'My late wife, Fran, is in each one. She's the individual with features scratched out. This appears to be a crude attempt to use her death to taunt me.'

'And… the blood?' said Billie.

'Cath?' said Bolam.

She nodded. 'As with Virginia Lloyd's finger,' she said, 'the blood is bovine, which would appear to confirm the link between the finger sent to Shaw and the items sent to you. This is all connected.'

'Cow blood…' said Tommo. 'Where do you get cow blood? Might that help us?'

Cath was shaking her head. 'Not really,' she said. 'It confirms a connection between the two deliveries, but beyond that it doesn't really tell us much. It's most likely that bovine blood was used simply because it was easy to source. A little blood smears a long, long way. You'd get enough from a juicy steak to achieve this kind of effect.'

'Was there anything else?' asked Bolam.

Again, Cath shook her head. 'Forensically clean,' she said. 'As with everything else. No prints, no skin cells, no fibres or hairs. We've swabbed for DNA and it'll be a few days before we get results, but I think we can guess the outcome, unless our perpetrator has made a mistake.'

'Further confirmation that this is all part of the same series of events,' said Bolam.

'There's one other thing,' said Cath. 'The campaign against you has clearly escalated, from something that's not even obviously connected to what can only be seen as a direct psychological assault in an effort to derail the investigation. Should we be concerned about what might come next? Should *you* be?'

Bolam had had the same thoughts. 'We need to be watchful, yes. We *all* do, because if this is an attempt to derail the investigation then any of us might be targeted next. But I'm not going to be beaten so easily.'

Cath held his look, her eyebrows raised. Finally, she said, 'Your call.'

'So let's recap,' said Bolam. 'We're looking at multiple murder, with all the traits of a psychopathic serial killer: meticulous and clever planning, focus on detail, a whole lot of ego on display, and the collection of trophies. But beyond that, something has triggered our killer to escalate in the last few weeks, using those trophies as part of a campaign of psychological torment targeted against the victims' loved ones. A key part of this campaign is the manipulation element: finding vulnerable targets and using their weak spots to break them and turn them against those around them.

'And this is where we have the personal element: using these methods to disrupt the investigation. Now he's casting wider, finding deaths he cannot possibly have been a part of in order to target individuals. Our target is clearly close enough to the investigation to have at least a rough idea of what we're doing, and to have singled me out as either a threat, or someone to taunt. Close enough to have found what they think is *my* vulnerability, in order to use it against me. But I don't get upset and emotional. I don't get rattled, or let villains get under my skin. I distance myself from all that.' From everything…

And he realised, as he spoke, that this was true. He'd made mistakes on this investigation, it was true, and he *had* allowed his personal issues to intrude, but for the first time since coming to this town he felt in control again. He was going to get to the bottom of all this – he just needed to focus.

'What can we learn from this?' he said. 'How can we use it?'

'We were talking about Robbie Walton,' said Aisha, doing exactly what she did when interviewing a witness, bringing things back on track.

'Do we really think he's capable of all this?' asked Tommo. 'He's been guilty of a few dodgy practices over the years, but I've seen his record: he doesn't exactly seem the sharpest pin in the box.'

'What do we know?' asked Bolam, turning back to Aisha.

'He spends his time between Norfolk and here,' she said, 'which also happen to be the two loci of the crimes we know about. Should we look at his other movements? Family connections in other parts of the country? Holiday homes? Regular travel patterns? Even Canada, where his sister lives, in case he's ever spent time there? If there are other similar disappearances anywhere he frequents, then…'

Bolam nodded. 'Can you take that on, Aisha? We need to look closely at all aspects of his life. Where he spends his time. Who he mixes with. Can you look at his social media again, Billie?

'Tommo, have a look at everything we have on Joanna Clayton's circle of acquaintances. A fresh pair of eyes.' Previously it had been Bolam and Billie who had looked most closely at Joanna. 'See if Walton might have been even a fringe figure in her life around the time she disappeared. We know she used to go missing for nights on end, and that she mixed with an older crowd. We need names, statements.'

'I will,' said Tommo. 'But, Gov. Shouldn't we just step back for a minute, here?'

'How do you mean?'

'I get that there are reasons to be looking at Walton, but as I say, he doesn't seem a good fit, and as I understand it, the main reason we're interested in him is that Russell Shaw told us that Stewart Doherty told *him*...'

'I know,' Bolam acknowledged. 'A thoroughly unreliable witness on the brink of breakdown telling us about information given to him by another person of interest who has already shown a tendency to interfere and try to steer our investigation... It's a rickety sequence of claims, at best. But that doesn't get away from the point that the information appears credible enough for us to at least examine it. We have to look closely at anyone who ticks even a few of our boxes.'

'Exactly, so—'

'And that's also why my next action on this case will be to go and speak to Stewart Doherty in person.'

33

'You didn't just ask me to come along to the briefing to talk about the forensics, did you? You implied there was something else…'

Cath Marshall had caught Bolam's eye as he headed back to his office. Now he waved her through ahead of him and indicated the chair by his desk. When they'd seated themselves, she said, 'Is it something to do with Gordon Rowe? I know that's bound to be tricky territory for you. Family and all. I'm surprised McBride hasn't pulled you off this one.'

'He's not been pressing for updates since putting this investigation on the back-burner, and I haven't told him that Gordon is of any significant interest. I don't really think he is, but I'm keeping an open mind and if he starts to look more likely again I'll reassess.'

Cath said nothing, which was comment enough. He was pretty sure she'd already been discussing this with Aisha, who had already made it clear that she was concerned about his closeness to the Rowes.

'Tell me about the Sturridges,' Bolam said. She was right that he'd invited her to the briefing to do more than talk through the forensics; he also wanted another perspective on this strange jumble of cases from a specialist who, more than anyone, focused only on the detail.

She looked at him, tipping back a fraction in her chair. Then she barked her gruff laugh and said, 'You asked me that once before. You said, "Tell me who Matthew Sturridge is."'

'And?'

'You wanted more than just the facts.'

He nodded. As crime scene manager, Cath focused on the tiniest details, but what interested Bolam was forcing her to step back from the minutiae and look afresh at the broader canvas.

'Matthew Sturridge we know,' she said. 'An odd cove. Very prim and proper and precise to the point of obsessively so, but apparently a man with a heart of gold. He spent his life helping other people live to the full in ways he was unable.'

'And Jayne?'

'A scattergun,' Cath told him. 'A free spirit. Haphazard and wayward. Passionate.'

'You got all this from the Sturridge house?'

She nodded. 'Matthew was the organiser, the one who liked to be in control. Jayne was more *laissez-faire*. He still had a lot of her things in the house: clothes, sketchbooks; her taste in music was very different to his – she liked all sorts, from 1970s prog rock to Abba and the cheesiest of disco music, whereas he only listened to classical.'

'And you know this because...?'

'He kept her records and cassette tapes filed away with her other possessions; his music was on CD, filed alphabetically by composer on shelves in the living room. Why are you asking all this?'

'There's something, somewhere that ties all this together,' Bolam said. 'A connection we've overlooked. A trigger point that lies somewhere in the history of our main players – that's where this all started. The fingers kept as trophies, the swapping of rings. The desire to open up old wounds after all this time and exploit all these people's grief – *my* grief.' He paused, looked down, surprising himself by the sudden rush of emotions simply from applying that word – *grief* – to his own frame of mind, an indulgence he'd refused himself all this time because he knew he did not deserve it. 'The results so far are a suicide, the breakdown of a marriage, the mental collapse of another of our victims. Who knows where this will all end up? There must be an explanation buried away decades in the past.'

'And, as far as we know, the Sturridges were the first victims,' finished Cath. 'So that's where we're likely to find the trigger point.'

'Is there anything we've missed?' Bolam asked. 'Or not completed?' McBride had been keen to shift resources to other, more contemporary, cases from the outset, and Bolam was now running this investigation on fumes alone.

'Matthew Sturridge kept everything,' Cath said. 'He had bank statements going back decades, utility bills, magazines even. Everything.'

'Anything personal?'

'We carried out all the forensic examinations that were deemed appropriate within the resources available,' Cath said carefully. 'But Sturridge had so much *stuff*... We were only partway through cataloguing all the paperwork when Callaghan's kicked off.'

She was referring to a fire at an industrial unit at the docks a few days ago. Close to a million pounds' worth of damage, and suspected arson. Cath had been working long hours coordinating the forensic effort on that one, along with all the other duties that came with her role.

'Any chance you could...?'

She rolled her eyes, highlighting those long, blonde lashes. Then, turning serious, she said, 'As I say, we've carried out all the forensics, so Sturridge's items are either in storage or were returned to his home. That's Billie's area – she's exhibits officer. Can you get her to have a look at what's been catalogued, and see if there's anything that might help build up a picture of the Sturridges' lives?'

'You're right, Cath. I'll have a word with Billie.' His DC wasn't going to be happy with that – she and Tommo were already taking on extra to free up Bolam and Aisha to continue working on this investigation. Sometimes Bolam wondered just how much faster cases might be closed if they had more resources to throw at them, but he knew that in the real world it was always a question of juggling those resources they actually had. Right now, though, those resources were stretched about as thinly as they could possibly be stretched.

As Cath got up to leave, Bolam said, 'You and Aisha.' Cath sat back in her chair, as if she'd been expecting this.

'Inspector?'

'You're close to her, aren't you?'

Cath sighed, looked away, then, more defiantly, met his look again. 'We've been discreet,' she said.

They had, but Bolam had seen the looks, the body language, the after-hours chats at Aisha's desk.

'I know there are rules,' Cath went on. 'Relationships in the workplace and all that. And yes, Aisha and I have become… friends… but I don't know if we've reached the point where we need to inform HR yet.'

'It's not the rules that concern me,' Bolam told her. 'It's just… Tread carefully with Aisha, okay? She comes across as tough and capable of fighting her corner, but she can be fragile too.'

Cath was about to say something, but stopped. He could see in her face that she was making the mental shift from resenting his interference to understanding where he was coming from.

'I'll do that,' she finally said. 'Believe me, the last thing I want to do is hurt her.'

The Fresh Start shelter was in the older part of town near the docks. A couple of streets from Bolam's house, and also from Matthew Sturridge's house, and the flat where Russell Shaw was staying. There was no mystery to this – just the tight-packed geography of an old seaport – but again it reminded Bolam of how everything in this town felt claustrophobic and intertwined.

Inside, the main room held a long trestle table being dismantled by two skinny, bearded men who eyed Bolam and Aisha suspiciously when they entered and then paused in the doorway to look around. Doors opened off this area into a large storeroom where the furniture was being moved to, and what looked like offices and a kitchen. Swing doors in the corner partly concealed a stairwell, and Bolam assumed the residents' accommodation was on the floor above them.

'We're looking for Stewart Doherty,' Bolam said, waving his ID in the men's general direction. They looked away, as if they might simply ignore him.

Instead of Doherty, a woman with tightly cropped grey hair and big glasses emerged from the kitchen. 'Stewart?' she said. 'He hasn't shown up yet. He's usually here by now.'

Immediately Bolam was alert. He remembered Russell Shaw's bruised eye, and his fumbled excuse that he'd had a run-in with

Doherty. Replaying that conversation in his head now, Bolam realised that although Shaw had said the two had fought, and Doherty had told him about Robbie Walton, the actual sequence of those events was open to interpretation.

Had something happened to Stewart Doherty?

'Do you have his number?' Bolam said to Aisha, but already she had her mobile up to her ear.

She nodded, waited, then said, 'Voicemail.'

'Has something happened?' the woman with the big glasses asked.

'You are?' Bolam asked.

'Judith Pearson. I help out here most days.'

'Do you know where Mr Doherty might be?' Bolam asked. 'We have his home address, but is there anywhere else?'

She shook her head. 'I've known Stewart for five years,' she told him. 'But I wouldn't say I actually *know* him. He's friendly with Russell Shaw. Perhaps Russ would be able to assist?'

She must have read something in the look Bolam and Aisha exchanged, because she went on. 'Are they all right? Is Russell okay?'

'What can you tell us about Russell Shaw, Judith?' Aisha asked, trying to soften the question with a smile.

Judith looked away. 'He always seems so gentle,' she said, and there was real warmth in her tone. 'Despite what…'

Bolam and Aisha waited for her to go on.

'Well,' Judith said. 'We all know his history, don't we? I just… It's hard to…'

'Don't lose your faith in him,' Bolam said, and Aisha looked at him strangely. Every time he thought of Russell Shaw now, he was struck by just how many lives had been torn apart by all this, dating back decades.

'Is Russell okay?'

'He was fine when I spoke with him yesterday,' Bolam told her. 'We just need to find Stewart Doherty now. We think he may be able to help us.'

Judith's shoulders visibly slumped. She was clearly concerned for – and perhaps *about* – Russell Shaw.

'Tell us about Stewart and Russell,' Bolam said. 'You say they're friends?'

'Perhaps not *friends*,' Judith told them. 'But Stewart took Russ under his wing when he came here. They have a lot in common. The Army, and the struggle to make a fresh start in civilian life. They're a similar age, too. I think Stewart saw something of himself in Russ when he came through that door.'

Then she said something that, again, made Bolam's senses snap to alert.

'He was watching over him, too. He told me that.'

'Watching over him?' asked Aisha, with that encouraging smile again. 'How do you mean?'

'We had a meeting here, when word got out about… Russell's history. Putting minds to rest, Robbie told us.'

Robbie Walton, always cropping up…

'Stewart stood up for Russell. He said he'd been helping him re-establish himself. And he said he'd been watching over him, just in case… I didn't like the way he said that. You said Russell's okay?'

'What did the others say about that at this meeting? Who else was there?'

'Well, there were me, Stewart and Eleni Kapino, our office manager. Robbie Walton and one or two others. I'm sorry – it's a bit of a blur…We spent a lot of time talking about procedures. We have to be so careful to do things properly, you know, but I'm afraid I zoned out a bit. I was still absorbing what Robbie had told us about Russell…'

'Can you remember anything at all about what was said at the meeting?'

'Well, as I say,' said Judith, 'there was a lot about procedures, and our legal responsibilities, and managing potential risks for Fresh Start, but at one point Robbie did get a bit intense… He's close with Stewart, too, and he seemed far too keen that someone should be watching Russell, and ready to step in if they had to. It felt like he was deliberately winding Stewart up.'

So much for charity, Bolam thought: it seemed that at least two members of Fresh Start would rather be vigilantes…

Or rather, that Stewart Doherty was working himself up into vigilante mode and Robbie Walton was standing on the fringe, egging him on.

Orchestrating…

Outside, Bolam was immediately in contact with the station, despatching a patrol car to Russell Shaw's address, and another to Stewart Doherty's on the north side of town. Bolam had the horrible feeling that they'd suddenly found themselves in the middle of another major incident unfolding: tensions being cranked, animosities and misfounded suspicions being fuelled.

Without further word, they returned to Aisha's car and navigated the narrow streets of the old part of town to Russell Shaw's flat.

They arrived before the patrol car.

Out in the street, Bolam peered up at the dormer window of Shaw's flat. One pane of glass was missing, the gap covered over with brown corrugated card that flapped in the breeze.

'Russell?' Bolam called up, as Aisha went to the door and pressed on the buzzer.

No response. 'Try the others,' Bolam said, but she already was.

A short time later, the front door opened, and an elderly man peered out.

'Sorry,' said Aisha, flashing her ID at the man. 'Police. We need to gain access.'

The man stepped back and Bolam led the way up the narrow stairs, just as a blue-lighting patrol car pulled up in the street.

Bolam ascended two flights of stairs and came to stand before a door that opened directly off the top step. He hammered a fist on the door, and shouted, 'Russell? It's Inspector Bolam. Are you in there?'

Nothing, again. He glanced at Aisha on the step below, and the two uniformed constables coming to a halt partway up.

Then he leaned back, took a breath, and swung forward. His shoulder thumped against the door, and he felt a bolt of pain through his upper body and something giving in the flimsy wood of the door.

A big crack had appeared in the door panel – his assessment that it was only a lightweight interior door had been right.

'Sir?'

One of the constables was a couple of steps from the top now, but even so he was at Bolam's eye-level.

Bolam nodded and pressed back as the constable braced against the wall, raised a big boot and slammed it against the door.

They'd have a small battering ram – an Enforcer – in the car, but on a door like this a heavy boot was just as effective, and faster. The thin wood gave and the door swung open, leaving long slivers of wood still attached to the lock on the doorframe.

Bolam went inside.

Russell Shaw was there, in the room's single armchair, his knees drawn up and his arms wrapped around his shins. Rocking back and forth, back and forth.

'It's okay, Russell,' said Bolam, approaching cautiously. 'We had to force entry in order to make sure you were okay. We're here to help you. We're here to protect you, okay?'

Again, there was no response. He wondered how long Shaw had been sitting like this, and he wondered if it would ever be possible for this broken ruin of a man to recover.

They sat for a time in Aisha's car, gathering breath and thoughts. It had been a long day.

Just as he was about to suggest making a move, Bolam's phone went. It was Tommo, with negative news. Bolam rang off, turned to Aisha, and said, 'No luck with Stewart Doherty. His flat was empty and no one has seen him. Patrols are looking for him now. I'm sure they'll round him up soon.'

'He's a soldier. They're trained to lie low.'

Doherty *had* been seen out and about earlier today, though, so whatever the nature of his altercation with Russell Shaw, the outcome had not been serious. They'd left Shaw sitting in his flat with a PC, waiting for the paramedics to arrive and assess his needs.

After another pause, Aisha gunned the engine and pulled out. A few minutes later they were outside Bolam's house. The place was in darkness, and it struck him for perhaps the first time that he hadn't even hung curtains in the windows. Maybe it was time to stop feeling sorry for himself and make a bit of an effort. This town was his life, now.

He went up to the front door, before turning to nod to Aisha as she left.

As he stepped inside, he glanced down. Now it had become a default thing to check the front doormat, under the letterbox – when he came down in the morning, when he came home at night – but there had been no new delivery, no new attempt to mess with his head.

He thought of Fran, and couldn't help seeing those defaced images, and he knew that even that was a small victory for whoever was behind all this, a defilement not only of a few photographs, but of the attached memories.

He looked up, his hand paused on its way to the light switch.

No new delivery, but that scent: cigarettes and mint, faint but unmistakable, and he knew he hadn't brought it in on his suit.

A figure stood in the dark doorway through to the kitchen-diner, tall, and filling the space.

Bolam flipped the light switch, and was momentarily blinded, but he knew the other man had been lurking in the darkness for longer, and so would be more blinded than he was.

'Stewart,' Bolam said. He recognised the big, bearded man from photos.

He'd shut the front door and would have to step aside to swing it open again, but he might still have time before Stewart could advance across the room.

They appeared to have reached a stalemate already: Bolam by the front door, Stewart in the heart of the house, unsure what to do.

'Tired of just sending photos?' Bolam said. He wanted to provoke Stewart's first move, so he could work out whether the man was a direct threat or had merely been caught up to no good.

'Photos?' Stewart said. He seemed genuinely puzzled.

'The ones you've been sending me.'

'I don't know anything about photos.'

'Then why are you here?'

Doherty took a step into the room, but still it was unclear whether this was a threat or simply giving himself options.

'You lot,' said Doherty. 'Always picking on the little guy, like Russ and me. I was just looking. Keeping one step ahead, because I know what you're like.'

Bolam resisted the temptation to point out the irony of a man who was well over six feet tall accusing the diminutive detective of picking on the little guy. He also resisted the temptation to point out that it was Doherty, himself, who had tried to steer the investigation in Shaw's direction: he was trying to have it both ways.

Instead, he took advantage of the interaction to shuffle a step sideways, so that it would be easier to swing the front door open into the room.

'You're concerned about police harassment, and this is your solution?' Bolam said, still trying to get his opponent's measure. 'Did you feel harassed when you were arrested for assaulting those girls when you were in the Army, is that still bugging you?'

Doherty's body tensed: Bolam had clearly found a sensitive spot.

'Who is it, Stewart? Who's behind all this? Who's stirring up your rage?'

Because one thing was clear: Doherty might be a violent fool of a man who thought he could stay one step ahead of the authorities by breaking in and snooping, but he was neither clever nor devious enough to be the mastermind behind all that had been going on.

'Who's feeding you all these paranoid delusions, Stewart?'

And that was when Bolam realised he'd got this seriously wrong.

Stewart Doherty wasn't just here to snoop.

He'd been holding one arm slightly behind himself and now as he swung it forward Bolam could see that he was holding a knife.

'Stewart, this isn't what you want. Believe me. It—'

Doherty lunged across the small living room, only three steps and suddenly the knife was high above Bolam and swinging down.

Bolam stumbled back against the front door, arms raised, as if that might protect him.

The knife missed, and Doherty staggered, but Bolam could do nothing: he couldn't physically overpower such a big man alone, and in order to open the door and flee he would have to step into the space occupied by Doherty.

Instead, he opened his mouth to speak, desperately trying to find words that might get through even as Doherty raised his arm again and lunged.

The knife came down, Bolam's hand went up, and he grabbed it, felt the blade cut into his hand like a knife sinking into cheese, slowly meeting resistance, embedding itself as metal came up against bone.

All he felt was an instant bolt of pain going up his arm, then the feeling froze, lost in shock.

They stood there as if time had stopped, arms raised, each gripping the knife.

Doherty stared into Bolam's eyes.

Bolam wouldn't let go, even as Doherty tried to pull away. He felt metal dragging through flesh, felt the hot wetness of blood over his hand and down his arm.

Doherty stumbled back, caught a foot on the room's one chair and sprawled back against the far wall.

Bolam still had the knife, the blade still embedded in the palm of his right hand.

Then he fumbled for the door, pulled at it, and staggered out into the street.

34

He spent the night in hospital before discharging himself. Twelve stitches across the palm of his right hand, and the doctor told him that while he'd been lucky to have avoided significant damage to any of the major tendons and nerves, he might never regain full use of his hand again.

He was under strict instructions to go home and rest, and above all to avoid any strenuous activity, but he didn't even try, because he knew he could not step back now.

Instead, he sat in DCI McBride's office, eager to get on with things.

'I've spoken to Charlie Bowes,' the DCI told him. Bowes was the consultant who had seen Bolam in A&E last night. So much for doctor-patient confidentiality. 'You should be at home, or even better, still in hospital. But instead…' McBride gestured with a wave to indicate Bolam sitting there, hunched awkwardly in his seat, his right hand bound in bandages and his arm angled upwards across his chest in a tight sling.

'It's only my hand,' Bolam said. 'I can still use my head.'

McBride just raised an eyebrow, as if the very presence of Bolam in his office contradicted that claim.

'Robbie Walton,' Bolam said. 'We believe he's heading here from Norfolk. Patrols have been alerted to look for him, but not to approach him. There's an address on East Bay Drive that Cowper and Rowe have made available to him, and I have officers waiting there, ready to make the arrest.'

McBride sat back, fingers steepled before his face, nodding. 'And after that?'

'We're in the process of securing warrants to search two of Walton's properties in Norfolk, and DS Nawaz has prepared the interview plan,' Bolam said. Their killer had hidden the bodies somewhere, and a property developer like Walton had more opportunity to do so than most. 'We'll explore his connections with Marcia Fredericks and Joanna Clayton, in particular, but we plan to start with establishing his version of his, and the Fresh Start charity's, involvement in the release and community support of Russell Shaw, and from there proceed to explore what discussions were held at the charity about that, and in particular what encouragements were given to Stewart Doherty.'

'And what about Doherty?'

'Aisha's in with him now.'

Stewart Doherty was in custody, arrested on the seafront after Bolam had staggered out into the street and caught the attention of a passing cab driver, who had then called for help. Aisha was about to start the first interview with Doherty any minute – and Bolam was itching to get down there and observe.

'Do you really think it's him? Behind all this? Walton?'

'I don't know, sir,' said Bolam. 'But Walton ticks a lot of the boxes. We need to start bringing people like him in and asking the hard questions, even if it's only to give him a chance to exclude himself.'

'Okay, Bolam. Go ahead. But keep me informed.'

'I'll do that. Every step of the way.'

Stewart Doherty sat upright in his chair, Aisha Nawaz across the small table from him, a uniformed PC at the door. Doherty had declined the offer of legal support and confirmed that he understood his rights when being interviewed under caution. He stared straight ahead, blinking only rarely. Bolam, watching the video feed from a neighbouring office, wouldn't have been surprised if his response to every question was a recitation of name, rank and number.

Doherty had lacerations down one cheek and into his beard, and rather than start with the attack on Bolam last night, Aisha started with these.

'You have scratches on your face, Stewart,' she said. 'Can you tell me how you came about these?'

Doherty said nothing.

'Did Russell Shaw inflict these wounds, or was it someone else?'

Again, silence.

'Tell me about the knives, Stewart.'

Nothing.

'Is it normal for a person to have hunting knives, a machete, and two clasp knives stored in their flat? Not to mention the knuckle dusters and nunchuks we found.'

'Self-defence is not a crime,' Doherty finally said. 'I have military training. I know how to look after myself.'

'Military experience that culminated in twelve months in the Glasshouse, isn't that right?'

Even on the video feed, and through thick beard, the clenching of Doherty's jaw was clearly visible.

'You took a knife with you when you broke into Inspector Bolam's home last night, didn't you?'

Doherty remained silent.

'Was that for what you call self-defence, or did you go there with the intention of attacking Inspector Bolam? Just as you attacked the Military Police officer who arrested you back when you were in the Army…' They'd only turned that up minutes before going into this interview: when Doherty had been arrested for hazing young women in his Army days, he'd also seriously assaulted the arresting officer. The records released by the military authorities implied that it was seen at the time as more a case of resisting arrest and for various reasons he'd only been charged with the hazing offences, but that arresting officer had been hospitalised for two weeks.

'I was defending myself,' he said. 'You can't trust… you lot.'

'Why did you go to Inspector Bolam's home, Stewart? What were you looking for?'

'Evidence,' Doherty said. 'Corroboration.'

'Of what?'

'I know you're going after Russ. I wanted to know what he's done. I've heard things about him, but I wanted to know for sure. And I know Bolam is the one who's been doing all the digging.'

'We know you fought with Russell Shaw recently. Was it about the stone that was thrown through his window? Was that you, Stewart? Were you trying to provoke something?'

'Some people say he should be encouraged to leave town,' said Doherty. 'You can't blame them.'

Not quite a confession, but close, and pretty much as they thought. Bolam had seen the printouts that had been wrapped around the stone put through Shaw's window, a clear attempt at intimidation. The talk circulating around Shaw was turning everyone around him against him.

'Were you planning another confrontation with Russell Shaw? Were you going to encourage him to leave?'

'I didn't plan anything,' Doherty muttered, finally breaking and staring down at the surface of the table. 'I just wanted to protect people.'

'From what, Stewart? From Russell?'

He looked up at Aisha, eyes narrowed. 'Is that what he told you? Has he complained about me? You have to watch him. I know he's devious. He manipulates people.'

'How does he do that?'

The twitch of the jaw again, and a return to silence.

'Did you work that out for yourself from spending time with Russell, or did someone tell you that? You said you'd heard things about Inspector Bolam. Did someone tell you about Russell Shaw too?'

What Doherty didn't know was that, when it came to it, they weren't really interested in him – beyond the obvious, last night's assault and the stash of dangerous weapons in his flat, for which he was now facing a hefty prison sentence. What they really wanted to know was how actively Robbie Walton had been drip-feeding him juicy titbits about Shaw and Bolam, goading him from the sidelines.

Because, increasingly, it looked as if the Doherty-Shaw dynamic was another flashpoint being orchestrated from the shadows, the players being coaxed towards extreme violence. A flashpoint which had come to a head last night…

Now, though, Doherty had retreated into silence.

'Tell me about your friends at Fresh Start,' Aisha tried. 'What do they think of Russell? Do they want to help him, or are they scared of him, like you?'

That jaw twitch was Doherty's one tell, but still he said nothing.

'How about Robbie Walton? Did he think you should be letting Russell forget his past?'

She was trying to provoke him – he was never likely to respond well to being pushed around by a woman, let alone one in authority over him. But while her questions were clearly getting under his skin, she wasn't making much progress.

'Tell me about the meeting you had at the shelter,' Aisha said. 'Stories were circulating about Russell, weren't they? So a meeting was called to air concerns and reassure people. Am I putting the right spin on it, Stewart?'

'We were unanimous in support of Russ's right to a fresh start,' Doherty said. 'The clue's in the name of the charity.'

'It's a worthy cause,' said Aisha. 'I've donated in the past. And yet there were concerns about Russell, weren't there?'

'He was in a trusted role before,' Doherty said. 'A paramedic.'

'People should have felt safe with him.'

Doherty nodded. 'But he flipped,' he said. 'Robbie kept reminding us of that, kept saying we couldn't risk him doing that again, that the public shouldn't be put at risk.'

Now they were getting somewhere: incitement on Walton's part. Then Doherty went on. 'And Mr Cowper said that, too. Kept banging on about protecting the charity's reputation if anything happened. Protecting the public, too – from people like Russ, and from you lot, from Bolam, pushing us all around, attacking all our work. Said we couldn't run the risk if Russ ever looked like losing his shit again. He didn't put it like that, but…'

Bolam stared. Until now, no one had mentioned that Raymond Cowper had attended the Fresh Start meeting. It made sense that he would involve himself, though: he was known to be a supporter of local causes, and he might simply be protecting the charity's – and Robbie Walton's – interests, just as he had done for Gordon, and always did for the law firm. Sometimes Bolam wished he had a guardian like Cowper.

But there was something odd about the way Cowper's name kept cropping up. Just like Gordon Rowe, he always seemed to be involved in one way or another, but whereas Bolam had been prepared to think the worst of his own brother-in-law, somehow Cowper had always been far more convincing as the upright professional, only ever involved in an official capacity. And now Doherty was implicating the lawyer not only in the victimisation of Russell Shaw, but in stirring up the animosity that had led to the assault on Bolam. Had Cowper known of Doherty's assault on the military arresting officer, and hoped to lay the foundations for something similar by winding Doherty up into a righteous frenzy?

'Was that how you saw your role in all this, Stewart?' asked Aisha, bringing the interview back on track. 'Doing as Robbie Walton told you and watching Russell? Ready to intervene if he looked like "flipping" and damaging the charity – because your life is built around Fresh Start, isn't it? You couldn't risk that.'

It was exactly the right thing, sticking to their agreed strategy, focusing on Doherty's activities in an attempt to draw out the involvement of Robbie Walton. But…

Bolam left the small office where he'd been watching the feed. Out in the corridor he paused, hit by a sudden wave of pain from his hand. He took a deep breath, and then entered the interview room.

Aisha looked up, thrown off her stride by his unexpected intervention. Bolam pulled up another chair and sat, introducing himself for the benefit of the recording.

Doherty stared at him, his eyes flitting between Bolam's face and his right arm, strapped across his chest.

'Does the charity often take legal advice at these meetings?' Bolam asked, doing his best to blank out Aisha's angry stare and hostile body language at his side.

Silence. Doherty had been thrown by his sudden appearance too – not just the shock of seeing him so soon after the attack, but also because he seemed to have realised that something had just happened but couldn't work out what.

'If the charity were taking financial advice, then I would understand,' Bolam went on. 'Or specialist advice on things like charitable status and housing law. That makes sense to me. But Mr Cowper is a specialist in criminal law. Why would he be involved in a run-of-the-mill meeting like the one you just described, Stewart?'

Doherty rolled his eyes at that. 'Run of the mill?' he said. 'It was murder. That's what Russ was locked away for. I think that comes under criminal law, doesn't it?'

'So it was unusual for Mr Cowper to be involved, was it?' Bolam asked. 'It was only because of Russell Shaw that he attended?'

'He's on the board, isn't he?' said Doherty. 'He's always supported Fresh Start. He gives advice, he raises funds, he connects us with supporters.'

'And he took the opportunity to raise concerns about the impact the police investigation – *my* investigation – might have on the work of your charity? Did he specifically tell you that I might be a threat to your work? Someone to be stopped?'

Doherty shrugged.

'Does Mr Cowper provide property for the charity to use?' Bolam asked, still talking softly, but he sensed that both Aisha and Doherty had picked up on a new intensity to the questioning. 'Buildings to renovate. Flats you use to rehouse residents of the shelter?'

Doherty looked down at the table again. Perhaps now he was wishing he'd taken up the offer of legal support, someone who could keep pace with these questions a bit better than he was now managing. 'Mr Cowper's a good man,' he said. 'He's always had my back.'

Of course! Bolam should have made that leap without Doherty's assistance. 'Did he help you when you left the Army?' he asked. How long had Cowper been grooming Doherty? 'After your time in the military correction facility?'

Doherty remained silent, but his eyes had glazed over. He knew he was in the middle of something he was not equipped to understand.

'Did he help you sort yourself out after all that?' Bolam pressed.

'He… took an interest,' Doherty said. 'He persuaded me I could make a difference – that's why I stayed at Fresh Start, giving back to other people who need help.'

'People like Russell Shaw?' Bolam said. 'A veteran like yourself. You understand those kind of pressures, don't you? The struggles you face in the outside world that are unique to people in your position. Particularly if you're trying to make up for the past. Did he encourage that, Stewart? Did Raymond Cowper encourage you to take a special interest in Russell Shaw's rehabilitation?'

'He helped me find my confidence again,' said Doherty, talking in more general terms rather than answering directly. 'He convinced me I could actually do something significant with my life.'

'Like tackle Russell Shaw if he "flips"?'

Aisha was still fuming. 'We had a plan,' she had said, the moment they had emerged from the interview room. 'You shouldn't even be here.'

Bolam indicated the vacant office where he'd been observing the video feed, and followed her inside.

'I'm sorry that I intervened like that,' he said. 'But plans require flexibility.'

She opened her mouth to respond, then stopped herself. Bolam guessed she'd finally worked out how he operated and knew he would explain.

'Doherty's a puppet,' he said. 'One of many. And while that's no excuse for what he may have done, we're really interested in who's pulling the strings, aren't we?'

'Robbie Walton.'

'Or Raymond Cowper,' Bolam said. 'A man who's been involved in this town for years. Someone who through his good works has access to groups like Fresh Start that help the vulnerable – using them to identify easy targets. Someone who has cultivated friends like Matthew Sturridge and Robbie Walton who had similar access to the vulnerable. Someone who's spent his life controlling people, and who is so smoothly convincing that manipulating everyone around him is second nature to him, and I count myself among those, because I've never regarded Raymond Cowper as anything more than a frustratingly good legal opponent.'

'Are you saying we roll back our plans to bring Robbie Walton in?'

'I'm saying we broaden our scope a little, and maybe reassess. Walton still has a lot to tell us, so we do need to bring him in, but perhaps you could review the interview strategy with all this in mind?'

He walked back through the station building. The custody and interview suite was in a 1950s extension to the rear, and the transition from institutional straight lines to the nineteenth-century part of the building, with its narrow corridors, high ceilings and sheer sense of age, was always stark.

It seemed like madness to be switching focus to a well-respected man like Raymond Cowper, but the offences under investigation dated back decades – Cowper hadn't always been a frail old man. He walked with a stick, though, something he blamed on a sporting injury. Bolam wondered how long ago that had happened. Perhaps that was a subconscious reason why he'd never considered Cowper a suspect until now: an assumption that sporting injuries tended to happen to younger people, and if Cowper had been incapacitated in this way for much of his adult life then surely the physical demands of murder and disposal of bodies would be too much?

Perhaps, more than anything, he felt exposed: that he might so readily have been convinced – and charmed – by Cowper when he should have been looking more closely.

Billie Grayson had taken over one of the side offices off the Serious Crimes open-plan area as a temporary working space. She was supposed to be on leave today, but she'd come in to carry out the review of Matthew Sturridge's possessions. Before Bolam had reached his own office, she was standing in the doorway, gesturing.

'Do you never check your messages?' she called across to him.

Bolam reached awkwardly into his jacket pocket with his wrong hand for his phone. He'd switched it to silent when he'd gone to see DCI McBride, and then down to observe the Stewart Doherty interview.

He shrugged, then said, 'What is it, Billie? What have I missed?'

She beckoned him over. 'Come and have a look,' she told him. 'I think you'll want to see this.'

35

Billie Grayson had printouts spread across both the desk and the floor of the small office she had taken over for the day. Copies of handwritten documents and typed letters.

She saw Bolam's look and said, 'This is only a fraction of it. Sturridge kept everything. It would take us weeks to read through it all.'

'But…?'

'A lot of it's safe to ignore, or at least relegate for later examination. Bank statements, utility bills, receipts, circulars even.'

'What have you found?'

'Jayne Sturridge didn't keep a journal,' Billie said. 'But there was a time when she tried. Maybe she was trying to find ways to deal with things, maybe it was something she was encouraged to do by a therapist.'

'The things we can't talk about out loud,' Bolam said, briefly distracted by the intense ache in his hand. 'Sometimes it's easier to write them down.'

He took a deep breath and sat in the office's spare chair, dizzy.

'You okay, boss?'

He nodded. It was just pain. 'What did Jayne write about?' Billie hesitated. Bolam had never seen her like this. Hesitant, struggling to hold his look. 'What is it, Billie?'

She reached for something on the desk – a transparent evidence bag. Paused again, then handed it to Bolam.

He took it in his good hand. The bag contained a hospital ID tag. Adults would wear them on the wrist, but this one was far smaller than the one Bolam had worn last night when he was getting his hand seen to. This one was a baby's ankle tag. The name written on the tag was Alicia Jayne Sturridge.

'Their baby was born?' Bolam asked. Every mention of the baby had been in terms of 'losing the baby', and it had always been talked of as a miscarriage, which was awful enough in its own right. There had been nothing to suggest the Sturridges' baby had come to term, though.

'Alicia survived for two weeks after birth,' Billie said. She gestured at the papers spread over the desk. 'Matthew Sturridge kept all the hospital letters. Alicia was born with an underdeveloped heart that simply wasn't able to cope with the demands of the outside world.'

Then she handed Bolam a copy of a handwritten page. It began partway through a sentence, clearly part of a longer document – a journal entry, Bolam assumed.

but Matthew is such a good man and I simply can't bear it. He tries so hard it's like a weight round my neck dragging me down. Every time I look into his eyes it's like a knife in my heart, it's too much. He should hate me but he only knows how to love me.

Bolam glanced up at his DC.

'It goes on like that for pages,' Billie said. 'Poor woman, she was heartbroken and consumed by guilt and her husband didn't seem to have a clue how to respond.'

'Guilt that she'd lost Alicia?'

'Maybe more,' she said. 'I think she blamed the hospital. She seemed to be pursuing a legal case against them – relentlessly, to the point of obsession.'

Now, Billie handed Bolam another printout, this time a copy of a letter on Cowper and Rowe headed paper. Bolam read it quickly.

'A cease and desist?' he said.

'They had been acting on her behalf, but in this letter they say her case against the hospital is futile. All procedures were followed correctly in Alicia's care. The hospital has nothing to answer for.'

'So why not just say there's no case? Why write to Jayne in heavy legalese warning her to cease all communications with her solicitors?'

'From what I can see—' Billie waved at the array of documents papering every surface of the office '—Jayne Sturridge became obsessive. She kept visiting the solicitors, demanding their attention. She had to be warned to stay away.'

'But there's one odd thing, isn't there?' Bolam asked. Billie stared at him. She'd spent all morning trawling through this stuff on what should have been her day off, and he sensed she was going to be mightily irritated that he could just swan in and spot what she had missed.

He held up the letter, pointing at the signature.

'Why is this letter signed by Raymond Cowper?' he asked. 'We're talking about a civil case against a hospital, but Cowper was the senior partner specialising in *criminal* law.'

The pattern was disturbingly familiar: a woman repeatedly visiting the offices of Cowper and Rowe. A woman who subsequently disappeared, and was found many years later to have been murdered. Seven years later, Joanna Clayton had done the same thing, in pursuit of Gordon Rowe: had that episode been orchestrated somehow, a repeat performance?

But whereas the reasons for Joanna visiting the office were clear – her flirty relationship with Gordon, and using that relationship to get money from him – why had *Jayne* become so obsessive about visiting the offices, to the extent that she was instructed not to do so?

'They were lovers, weren't they?' Bolam said. He thought of the way Cowper had faltered the first time they had talked about Jayne, after the interview at the station with Sturridge – a flash of discomfort that Bolam had taken for merely the awkwardness of discussing a friend's marriage. 'Jayne Sturridge and Raymond Cowper. Right under Matthew Sturridge's nose.'

'And baby Alicia,' said Billie. 'Was Cowper the father?'

Bolam nodded. Jayne Sturridge had worn a silver ring on her little finger – the finger kept after her death as a trophy – to remember her lost baby. Now, he saw that the ring also bore special significance for the baby's father, and that ring had been removed from the finger before it was delivered to Matthew Sturridge, and was still missing.

He recalled the wording of Matthew Sturridge's suicide letter, even after all these years chastising himself for being an inadequate husband.

'Matthew knew they were lovers,' he said. 'If not at the time, then later, when he read all these letters of Jayne's that he'd kept.' Because he would have read everything she had left, just as he regularly looked through that well-thumbed photo album he'd shown Bolam. 'That's why he thought Jayne had left him: he'd known she thought their marriage was over. He even *hoped* she had gone on to find a better life without him: that was the guilt he carried for all these years.'

Matthew must have known that Cowper had been Jayne's lover, and yet he had still complied with Cowper representing him when he'd been questioned recently by police. Had that been an exquisite torture he'd felt he deserved?

'Do you think Matthew suspected that Raymond Cowper killed Jayne?' Bolam said, finally saying out loud what had been forming in his mind.

'We believe he's at his home,' said Bolam, sitting in the same chair in DCI McBride's office. 'I've sent a patrol car to do a drive past and see what they can see. I'll head there immediately with another patrol car to make the arrest.'

'Haven't we already had this conversation today?' said McBride, leaning back in his chair. 'But about someone else?'

'It fits,' Bolam told him.

'Raymond Cowper will run rings around us if we let him,' McBride said. 'We need to tread very carefully indeed. Hold back, Bolam. Wait until we have everything in place. You'll only get one chance at him. And *delegate*. You're not fit, man.'

Bolam hated that McBride was right. All they had done so far was join the dots, but not only was their case against Cowper circumstantial, it was mostly decades old. They had neither witnesses nor forensics to tie Cowper to the recent intimidation of victims' families, and nothing to tie him to the actual murders all those years ago. Bolam suspected that the only real hope of finding solid evidence was a search of Cowper's home and any other properties he had, but they could not do that without making a very public move against the man. And to do that, they would need more than just Bolam's suspicions.

'It has to be him,' said Bolam.

'Then build your case.'

Back in his office, Bolam took some time to update the case's decision log in meticulous detail, even though it was a struggle to type one-handed. McBride had been right: get the slightest element wrong and a lawyer like Cowper would be all over it. Every judgement call, every choice, must be carefully documented and justified.

Including the most painful choice of all: to make no move against Cowper until they were absolutely sure they had built up an undeniable case against him.

'Gordon? What is it? I'm up to my—'

'How are you, Iain? I heard about what happened.'

'I'm fine. And busy.'

'Raymond dropped by the flat this afternoon. I thought you should know.'

That cut through Bolam's resistance. He almost hadn't answered when he saw Gordon's name on the screen of his phone. He needed to focus. He needed some stroke of insight that might guide him in how to make progress with this case.

He put the call on speaker and sat back in his chair.

'What did he want?' Bolam said. *And why did you think I should know?*

There was something odd in Gordon's tone, an element of uncertainty. Gordon was usually so sure of everything.

'He wanted to know how I was coping,' Gordon said. 'He asked about Maria and Luke, and he said he wanted to make sure I wasn't just living on takeaways. He asked me how I liked the flat and I joked that it sounded as if he was leading up to saying he was going to start charging me rent. We laughed.'

'And…?' Bolam was tired, and increasingly aware of the throbbing ache in his hand as the painkillers wore off again. He still couldn't work out if this was just an idle call, or if that hint that Gordon actually had something to convey had been genuine.

'We talked about you. I brought Raymond up to speed on your investigation. No, don't object, it's not worth it: I know you carefully selected everything you told me with an awareness that I might discuss it with others. Don't get all high and mighty with me.'

'Why talk about the case, Gordon?'

'Well, I just thought it was business as usual,' Gordon told him. 'We're the best criminal law practice for miles around. Hell, we're the *only* criminal law practice for miles around. Chances are, if you're anywhere near as good at your job as I've been led to believe, we'll be landing a new client pretty soon, and a major one at that. Of *course* we talked about your investigation.'

'So why are you telling me now?'

'Raymond got weird about it. I've not seen him like that before. He asked which cases you were looking at, and if there might be any more.'

'Did he mention any that you didn't know about?'

Go on. If Cowper had asked about the Marcia Fredericks investigation, or the packages delivered to Bolam, they had him: nobody outside Bolam's team and colleagues in Norfolk knew they were looking at the former, and even fewer knew about the packages. Or there might be other cases they didn't even know about yet. Just one slip…

'No, we just discussed the ones you mentioned: Joanna, Jayne Sturridge, Russell Shaw. But that's the weird thing: I'm sure Raymond actually came to talk about those cases – asking how I was coping with the bachelor life was just pretext.'

'Why would he do that?'

'I think he's covering for someone,' Gordon said. It was a huge step for him to raise these concerns about his long-time business partner and mentor with Bolam. He must have been edging towards this position for some time.

'Who?' Bolam pressed.

'I don't know,' Gordon said. 'I think he was fishing to see where you'd reached. I've been wracking my brain, and I've checked through our client files, but for the life of me I can't think who it might be. I'm aware that you're interested in Robbie Walton, but we all know that'll come to nothing. That's not who Raymond is protecting. I just can't think who it might be.'

Bolam could, and he guessed that – whether he would consciously allow himself to accept it or not – Gordon Rowe also had a suspicion about who Raymond Cowper might be covering for, and it wasn't a client at all.

Aisha drove, leading the way. A patrol car tucked in behind them as they swung out onto the Main Road.

Bolam's heart was thumping. He knew this was all or nothing. One mistake and Cowper would be all over it, but they were committed now.

He turned to Aisha. 'You think we're right?' he asked her. It was true what he'd told her before: she was the one person whose judgement he really valued, and whose opinion he sought.

'I think we're right, yes,' she said. 'I just wish we had something solid to back us up.'

Bolam nodded. 'We just need to make a detour,' he said. 'The Golden Wall.'

'The Chinese? You want a takeaway *now*?'

36

Russ Shaw had known watching the seafront flat was wrong. Standing by the railing on East Bay Drive that separated pavement from greensward, and then the promenade. Then walking in one direction or the other before stopping, turning, *returning*.

Watching.

He'd worked out fairly quickly that Robbie Walton wasn't staying there, but rather that brash lawyer, but still he'd persisted.

When the police came, his first impulse had been to run, but his second was to stay there, do whatever they wanted of him, and maybe they'd take him away from all this again.

Even that had not happened, though, and instead, once he'd been left alone again, he'd tried to follow DI Bolam's advice. Tried to walk away and stop puzzling over why Robbie Walton hated him so much.

He'd gone back to his flat, with the empty window now only partly covered with cardboard that had become damp and torn. He'd eaten instant noodles from a bowl, read a free newspaper from cover to cover, adverts and all. He'd wanted to go out for an evening walk, get away from the place, but he'd been frightened of where he might end up and what he might do, so he stayed in.

The next day, the police had come. He'd thought that was it, they were finally going to end all this and take him away. He didn't know why. He didn't care. He just wanted it to stop.

They smashed the door in, and Russ tried to shrink back into his chair, expecting them to seize him, drag him away.

But instead, Bolam had spoken to him. *Apologised* for forcing entry. Said they were only concerned for his safety.

After Bolam left, a young PC waited with him until an ambulance came to take him to hospital. Bolam had arranged for the mental health community support team to assess him and work out what help he needed. The PC was kind, with brown eyes like Ginnie's and an accent from somewhere in the Midlands.

Russ focused on her dark brown hair because he couldn't look into those eyes for long and he had to focus on something. Anything. Just to stop himself from thinking about the ambulance waiting for him in the street. He needed help, he knew, but…

He followed them outside, the PC and two paramedics, a man and a woman. The uniforms were different these days, and the ambulance more modern, more high-tech.

Russ couldn't do it.

He couldn't bring himself to climb into an ambulance again. Too many awful memories.

He ran.

They shouted after him, but didn't seem to know what to do. He wasn't under arrest. They couldn't force him.

The PC didn't move. She seemed content to have handed over responsibility to the paramedics, one of whom followed at a brisk walk – Russ wasn't exactly in any condition to do more than jog for a short distance. The other paramedic cursed, then climbed into the ambulance and followed.

Russ came to the end of the road and turned, came to the junction with East Bay Drive and crossed, regardless of traffic. A horn blew, but he didn't care.

When he came to the gap in the railing where a path cut down through the greensward he took it. The ambulance couldn't follow him here, and when he looked back he saw that the other paramedic had stopped at the top too.

He came to the concrete wall and looked down at the beach. The tide was out and grey mud glistened, almost the same shade as the sea. Birds scurried across the beach like tiny clockwork toys.

He followed the promenade south to the point where the hook-shaped peninsula curved back in towards the mouth of the estuary, and the docks.

He tried not to think of what he would do next. He couldn't go back to that flat. The place was all wrapped up in the bad things that kept happening to him. Tied to Stewart, who alternated between saviour and paranoid bully. The flat was tied, too, to the delivery of that amputated finger that they said belonged to Ginnie, although he still struggled to understand how that could be possible. To stones through the window, and the police breaking in the door. He could never feel safe there again.

He didn't know what that left for him.

He stared out to sea. Considered climbing down to the beach, and keeping on walking until the tide swept him away.

He didn't have the guts for that, though, despite thinking about it often. People said it was the coward's way out, but he did not even have the courage to kill himself.

He turned, headed north again.

Eventually, he came to the place where DI Bolam had confronted him yesterday. A row of Victorian villas lined the road to his left, watching over the bay like sentinels. One of them was where the lawyers had a flat, the place Stewart had told him Robbie Walton sometimes stayed when he was in town.

He saw movement in one of the windows. Why did Mr Rowe march around the place like that? He seemed unable to stay still. Russ remembered him from years ago, all the grand gestures, the way he'd walk across a room, adopt a pose, then give a big wave of the arm and resume pacing, talking all the time.

Russ dipped his head down and started to walk again. This time he headed north, past the café where he'd seen Bolam with that lawyer, however long ago. On, past the old War Department land, and the Martello tower, to another promontory. To the north of this, the land swept inwards again, and Russ could see a holiday camp: ranks of static caravans and small, box-like chalets.

Perhaps he would find somewhere among the caravans where he might sleep tonight. The chalets could not be hard to break into. For now, though, he just ducked his head down and kept walking.

Russ spent the night camped out in a gap between two beach huts. It was cold and damp, and he barely slept at all, but he couldn't face going back to the flat. When dawn broke, he started to walk again, north to the edge of town, then back south to the mouth of the estuary.

Eventually, though, he couldn't help himself. He was drawn back to the lawyers' flat. He had nothing else.

He was smart this time. He didn't stand by the railing in full view. Instead, he waited by the bus shelter a short distance along the road, only moving away whenever a bus came, so it wouldn't stop just for him. He was nothing if not a considerate stalker.

He saw the lawyer again, occasionally. Still pacing. A couple of times pausing by a window, talking into a phone and gesturing wildly with his free hand, as if the person at the other end could see him.

Maybe Robbie Walton would show up. And maybe Russ would have the guts to confront him.

When it rained, he was glad of the cover of the bus shelter, but the shower was brief, and soon spring sunshine took over again.

An old man paused before the door to the building where the lawyers' flat was.

At first, Russ paid no more than passing attention, but then…

He knew the man. He'd seen him once before, many years ago.

Russ swallowed. He felt hot, then cold. Now he wanted to be back in his own flat, in the familiarity of that old chair, knees drawn up to his chin, arms wrapped around his legs, rocking back and forth.

The man looked exactly the same, as if he'd never aged, or as if he had always been this old. The only difference was, he walked with a stick now.

Russ drew away, hid behind the bus shelter again. Pressed his head against the cold Perspex that encased a cosmetics poster.

A bus came, but this time he didn't move away. The bus stopped, the driver leaned across, peered at him, and when Russ didn't move, the bus pulled away again.

He turned and took a couple of steps across the pavement so he could lean on the railings, but now the sea had lost its power to calm him.

He moved to the end of the bus shelter and peered across at the building. Nothing. No gesturing lawyer, no faces at the windows.

He tried to convince himself he had imagined the old man, but it was no good. He knew he had suffered hallucinations in the past, that he had often struggled to separate fantasy from reality, but never anything as mundanely real as this. An old man, walking up to a building and letting himself in.

At that moment, the same old man reappeared, emerging from the building and softly shutting the door behind him. He straightened, as if taking a deep breath of the sea air, and then walked slowly down the path to the pavement. There was something strangely compelling about the way he did this, and the way he paused every so often – perhaps out of breath, but also giving that impression again of taking the air.

There was something about all this that drew Russ, made him cross the road at a safe distance, and follow.

Russ was good at following people; it was something he had done several times since leaving the Rodgers-Stephenson. And anyway, the old man was slow, walking with a limp and leaning heavily on his stick, and still pausing at regular intervals to straighten, breathe deeply, look all around, and then continue on his way.

The man lived in a big red-brick house on the edge of town. It had taken them close to an hour to walk, and Russ wondered why the man did not drive or take a taxi. Perhaps when you reach that age, you revel in every opportunity to use what strength you have left. Perhaps he simply liked to walk. Russ did, too, after all; walking allowed you to blend in, go unnoticed, and also to stay in tune with the world around you.

The house was set back from the road along a gravel drive. Flower beds to either side were neatly tended, roses and other bare-branched shrubs and lots of exposed soil, all subdivided by rows of neatly clipped, knee-high shrubs.

A farm track ran between a field and the garden boundary, mostly shielded from the house by trees. The garden to the rear of the house, away from public display, was less well-tended; a kitchen garden gone to nettles and other weeds, and beyond that, what might once have been an orchard, although now the trees were tangled and twisted and merged together in a thicket of brambles.

The kitchen door was unlocked. Russ let himself in.

The kitchen alone was bigger than his flat. Chunky wooden cupboards with marble worktops; a free-standing island unit with sink and gas hob. Russ crossed the large room and paused in a doorway.

He didn't know what he was doing here, what he was planning to do. He couldn't even remember crossing the kitchen garden from the lane. He'd been on autopilot.

He should go.

He was scared of what he might do if he stayed.

'Come through, Shaw. Stop mucking about.' A voice from deep in the house. A familiar voice – one that came to him in his nightmares. The voice he had heard one night nineteen years before: a calm and efficient tone, with no time to suffer fools like Russell Shaw. The other man at the house they'd attended the night Russ's life was torn apart.

He walked along a hallway lined with photographs and books, came to an open door to a living room. The furniture in the room was of a dark and shiny wood, and more photos stood on a long sideboard and hung from the walls.

The old man sat in a high-backed armchair, hands clasping the knob of his walking stick that now stood upright between his legs. His eyes were intense, so that when you met his look you could never be the first to look away. But now Russ realised that it wasn't the eyes that made him think of his grandfather, it was the timbre of voice: chiding and bullying even when the tones were calm.

'You took your time, Shaw.'

He'd known he was being followed. Russ had thought he was being so clever, keeping his distance, ducking out of sight every time the man paused, straightened, breathed the spring air deep, but he had known.

The man laughed harshly. 'Oh, for God's sake, Shaw. Have you come here to do something or not?'

He didn't know how to answer that because he did not know why he was here.

'What do you want? Revenge? Well, *do* it, man.'

'I just want to know… *why*?' Russ said, only himself understanding as he said the words. Why did people hate him? Why were they doing this to him? Why was the world like this?

The man laughed again. 'I didn't think you'd have it in you to actually *do* anything,' he said. 'You never had the balls.'

It was the kind of thing his grandfather used to say to him. *Come on, Russell. Be a man! Or don't you have the guts?*

'You were there,' Russ said. 'In the ambulance that night.' The heart patient's friend, or companion, or whatever he was. 'And then you were gone.'

'I wish I'd stayed to see your face,' the man said. 'Such a dramatic staging in the back of that ambulance! But sadly… I couldn't stay to watch.' He paused then, his gaze distant, as if remembering, revisualising. 'She was a bleeder, your Ginnie. Not so much him. Old man. Weak circulation, especially after I'd dosed him up so you'd think he was on the brink.'

Ronald Duke's symptoms had never been clear-cut. His heart was erratic, enough for them to take him in, but it had not been clear what was wrong. And they'd had no reason to suspect his condition had been instigated by another.

'They weren't the first, you know. Ginnie and Duke. Not my first rodeo, as they say!'

Russ stared. He'd never really thought beyond that awful night – thought that there could be any broader picture. 'There were others?'

The old man gave a short laugh, his lips shiny and wet. 'Others like your Ginnie, yes,' he said. 'But not Duke. He was just…'

'Just what?'

'He was a paedo,' the man said. 'Just like your grandfather. Ronald Duke was a paedophile. I was representing him. Nobody missed him, you know. But he saw something… something in me. He worked me out and he thought he had a hold over me, but I couldn't have that. He was just in the way and he had to go. Your Ginnie was more interesting, though. And you, of course.'

Russ wanted to react, to do something, but his feet were rooted to the spot. 'Why?' he simply repeated, once again.

'Why you? Just look at you. So damned *weak*. So malleable. People are so easy to control, when you work out how. Everyone has a weak spot. Everyone can be manipulated. And you all deserve it! Don't ask why of me. Ask why you are what you are. So pathetic. I knew you when you were a boy, you know. Your grandfather, he always needed help. Someone who could extricate him from the messes he got himself into, and I'm good. I'm very, very good.'

The man paused to moisten his lips with the tip of his tongue. 'I kept an eye on you. You and little Lizzie.'

Russ tensed, but still didn't move. He wanted to understand.

'I encouraged Sturridge to get you into the Army Cadet Force. Toughen you up. I thought you might have the balls to tackle your grandfather, but no. I thought I'd lost you when you joined the Army, but you came back, and you hooked up with Virginia Lloyd, another of life's drifters.'

The man leaned back in his chair, and paused again, as if he'd run out of words – or was savouring his memories.

'That night... Oh, how everything fell right into place! All it would have taken was for one element to be wrong – Virginia driving instead of you, another ambulance altogether showing up, *anything* – and I wouldn't have been able to do it that night. I'd have had to just accompany Ronald Duke to the hospital and wait for a better convergence of circumstances. But no. All I had to do was apply the right pressure and Ginnie told you to drive, and everything fell into place. Choreographed. It was truly beautiful.'

'You told me to stop, didn't you? Just outside the hospital. So you could get out.' It came back to him now, hearing that voice that sounded so like his grandfather's... that tone.

The old man nodded, an incongruously gentle smile on his face. 'That was the biggest risk I ever took,' he said. 'But it went like clockwork. I waited until we reached a street where I knew there was no CCTV coverage, and made you stop the ambulance. I'd tucked my big coat out of the way when I settled in the ambulance, and then I just put it back on afterwards to cover my bloody clothes, and then

I walked away along a dark route home. I had a plan B, of course. If I hadn't been able to slip away before we reached the hospital I would just have tussled with you when you came into the back of the ambulance: we'd both have been covered in the evidence and it would be the word of a respected lawyer and community stalwart against that of someone who was quite clearly psychotic.'

Russ stared. He couldn't even begin to understand how someone could see the world in such a way, and talk so calmly of such horrific things.

'I got you wrong, though, didn't I? As soon as you got back out of the Rodgers-Stephenson, I thought you'd flip. Sooner or later. But no matter how hard you're pushed, you just yield a little more, don't you? You don't break. You don't act. Even Robbie can't get through to you.'

Robbie Walton. 'Why?' That was the only word Russ could manage.

'Why Robbie? He's been mine for years. A prod, a poke, a nudge. Ever since Jayne, he's been on the edge. He's never forgiven the world for all that has happened to his family – and that makes him so easy to wind up and steer. He reacts to everything, wears his heart on his sleeve. That's something I just don't get: naked emotion. So vulnerable. I thought he might make you flip if I poured on enough fuel. I thought he'd either go into overdrive or wind up everyone around him. A fight with your friend Stewart, a rock through your window from one of Robbie's boys when I'd convinced him you needed to be encouraged to leave… as soon as people learned who you were they turned on you, didn't they? No one wants you here. They're all terrified of you, but they don't know you like I do.'

The man was a shell. A human canvas stretched over… *nothing.* Russ was finally beginning to understand, and what he saw terrified him. There *was* no reason for all that had happened. Nothing beyond one monster of a man, shaped in human form but with neither heart nor soul nor anything that truly made him human.

'Can't you see what you *are*?' pleaded Russ.

'What I am? I'm so much more than you'll ever be, that's what I am. I had a child, you know. A baby. That changes a person, they say, but I don't know. She was born with an underdeveloped heart. I think she got that from me...'

Russ tried to see any trace of emotion on the man's face, or hear it in his words, but there was nothing.

'Look at me, Russell. A helpless old man who's ruined your life and taunts you about it and still you're unable to act. Because even now you think you see value in all human life.'

Finally, Russ was able to move. He took a step backwards, prompting another harsh laugh from the old shell of a man.

'Go on, Shaw. Do what you do best. Run.'

Tears spilled, rolling down Russ's cheeks.

'Did you cry then, too? When your grandfather was still alive?'

In that moment, Russ understood himself, too. He was, just as the old man said, weak. He wouldn't stand up for himself. He wouldn't react. He just wanted a quiet life without people who hated him in it.

He turned, stumbled, and then half-walked, half-ran back along that dark hallway to the big kitchen.

He paused at the island unit, his breath ragged, his heart raging.

That was when he noticed something he had missed before: by the sink, a whisky bottle, something with a complicated Scottish name, and beside that a cut-crystal glass and four emptied blister packs with pills lined up beside them.

And now he understood what was so compelling about the way the old man had walked from the seafront house, the way he kept pausing to breathe deep and look up at the blue spring sky: an appreciation of the world, and a sense that this would be the last time he would experience that.

37

Bolam had left a message with DCI McBride's office, informing him that he was abandoning their agreed cautious strategy with regard to Raymond Cowper. The lawyer's visit to Gordon Rowe changed everything: where before – for close to thirty years – Cowper had been cautious, now he was digging clumsily, risking breaking cover just to find out where the investigation had reached.

Bolam didn't know why the balance had shifted, but he knew it must mean that Cowper was prepared to accelerate whatever he was up to, regardless of risk.

But Aisha had been right. They needed something solid, and that was why they'd detoured via the Chinese takeaway just round the corner from Bolam's house.

'CCTV,' Bolam had said to Molly, the owner. 'How long do you keep your CCTV footage?'

Long enough, as it turned out. When Bolam had brought Cath the packages delivered to his house for forensic examination he hadn't gone as far as ordering CCTV checks for the area around his house too. With McBride breathing down their necks they'd had to focus their resources. But now…

The footage was fuzzy, a jumpy, pixelated view of the forecourt and pavement in front of the Golden Wall. But there… There could be no mistaking: an old man, leaning over his walking stick as he passed slowly by. Raymond Cowper on his way to deliver the third package to Bolam's house. When Bolam had visited the old solicitor at his house, he had said he still got around despite his frailty: did he do so on foot? Did he walk everywhere? Nobody notices a frail old man with a stick.

So now Bolam found himself reaching across with his left hand to ring the bell at Cowper's grand old red-brick house on the edge of town once again. This time, though, he had Aisha Nawaz at his side, two uniformed officers behind him, and another two patrol cars approaching up the long, gravelled drive.

A voice called from within the house. 'The door's open, Inspector.'

Even now, Cowper wanted to be calling the shots: let the police come all the way to him, rather than emerging to meet them halfway. Bolam pushed the door and stepped inside. Frankly, he didn't care about these games and power plays; they meant nothing in the end.

Cowper was in the living room again, sitting in an armchair, an empty crystal glass on a small table beside him. As Bolam appeared in the doorway, the old man raised his walking stick and waggled it. 'Forgive me, Inspector,' he said. 'I've already taken one long walk today, and the old joints…'

Bolam and Aisha entered the room, the constables hanging back in the hallway.

'I'm surprised to see you, Inspector.'

Bolam looked closely at the old man. All pretence had been dropped now. Bolam flapped his right elbow an inch or two from his body, indicating the strapped-up arm. 'I think Stewart was scared at the sight of blood,' he said.

'Forgive me, Inspector. Doherty is on such a hair-trigger, what with his burning sense of injustice and his resentment of anyone who might call him to account. He just wants to lash out at the world. I didn't think he'd actually *attack* you. But who knows what might happen when you get three individuals like Stewart, Robbie and Russ weltering in a violent brew of paranoia and hatred of the authorities, eh?'

All stirred up by Cowper…

'All I did was tell Stewart you were onto him. I didn't even have to fill in any of the gaps. That boy is *so* paranoid.'

Bolam looked around, realising now that this was not a live-in room, but rather one kept pristine for special occasions, special guests. He went across to the long sideboard and picked up a framed photograph of Cowper with Gordon Rowe at what looked like an awards ceremony, or perhaps a charity function.

'No stick?' Bolam said. In the photograph it was hard to put an age to Cowper – who always seemed to look like an old man – but Gordon was clearly in his fifties, so the photo must be from within the last few years. So when had Cowper acquired his 'sporting injury'? Bolam put the photo down again in a different place and noted Cowper's reaction to the disruption of his carefully arranged display.

'A white lie,' Cowper told him, with a smile. 'Not a sporting injury. Cancer. It came back again at the turn of the year. It's in the bones now.'

The trigger, Bolam realised. The answer to their long-standing question of why all this was happening now: because Cowper had run out of options, and time.

Bolam picked up another of the pictures. He realised now that they had been rearranged since his last visit. Before, they had shown landmarks throughout Cowper's career and significant encounters, but now…

The photo that had snagged Bolam's attention showed Cowper with Jayne Sturridge, arms around waists, cheeks pressed close as they smiled for the camera; Matthew Sturridge loitered awkwardly to one side, a gap between him and his wife.

Another picture showed Cowper at the Fresh Start shelter, shaking hands with Robbie Walton in front of a big ribbon that was about to be cut.

The next picture Bolam picked up to examine more closely showed Cowper at a school event from perhaps twenty years ago, judging by the clothes and hairstyles. Cowper surrounded by adolescents… and among them, unmistakably: Joanna Clayton.

He didn't recognise the haggard-faced man shaking hands with Cowper in the next photograph, but there was something about the set of the mouth, the eyes…

'Harry Shaw,' Cowper said. 'Russell's grandfather. An utter charmer. If you ever want to see pure evil incarnate, I'd suggest you start there – if he were still alive, of course.'

Bolam put the photograph of Harry Shaw face-down on the sideboard. 'Russell Shaw,' he said. 'You've played him his entire life, haven't you?'

'He was here,' Cowper said. 'Not long ago. I think he's finally flipped for good.' He seemed far too proud of that, as if it was the culmination of his efforts and he deserved some kind of recognition for his achievement.

'You've never let him out of your grip, have you?' Bolam went on. 'You controlled his trial. You let Gordon Rowe handle that, even though you were the senior partner and he a newcomer. You did that because Russell might recognise you, didn't you? You used your contacts to influence his placement in the hospital system, and his subsequent treatment. Did you facilitate his move to the Rodgers-Stephenson, where, presumably, you had more contacts, more influence?'

Cowper shrugged. He was enjoying this, and Bolam hated playing to that, but he wanted to grasp the extent of the man's scheming.

'I have contacts on the hospital board, yes,' Cowper said. 'I've been an informal adviser there for years, and occasionally Gordon or I pay them a visit on a consultancy basis – they always need good criminal law advice at a hospital like the Rodgers-Stephenson.'

'Then you used Fresh Start and the town council as intermediaries to facilitate Russell's release and return to the community – albeit ensuring that he was given the wrong instructions for finding accommodation so that his return would be traumatic right from the outset. And the raid on the homeless sleepers at the Martello development – instigated by a mysterious group of concerned property-owners. Orchestrating it all.'

'Orchestrating,' Cowper said. 'That sounds so Machiavellian, don't you think? I like to stand back, wherever possible, and watch over things. I am the sole custodian of the story of my life, and now I'm merely fine-tuning the presentation of my legacy to the world.'

'Custodian. Whatever. You set Russell up to fail, to break. Arrangements that fell through. Steering Stewart Doherty so that his "help" was, in fact, the opposite. Delaying Russell's contact with the community mental health team – and his medications – stirring him up, unsettling an already disturbed mind. Where is he now? Where's Russell? You said he was here.'

Cowper shrugged. He had clearly lost interest in Russell Shaw. 'He ran away,' he said. 'He always does. One of life's disappointments.'

'Even now, you're orchestrating all this, aren't you?' Bolam said. 'Pulling our strings, right to the end. Why?'

'I want to see what happens,' Cowper told him.

Cowper had known all along that at some point he would be exposed, and after that, he would remain central to their unpicking of his history and crimes, a drama to beat all dramas in his final weeks or months.

'I had a choice,' Cowper went on. 'Spend my dying days disposing of all thc evidence in an effort to avoid being exposed when my estate is processed after my death – and in an age of forensic exactitude, we all know how difficult that would be: there is always evidence *somewhere*. Or I could put on one final display and see how the cards fall, setting individuals against each other, and against their own guilt. We're all capable of awful things, Inspector. I'm no different to the rest of you, really.'

'The evidence,' Bolam said. 'Where are they? The bodies.'

Cowper smiled. 'Suffice to say, for now, that I kept them close.' Cowper paused then, staring off into the distance.

'I want to be remembered,' he said, finally. 'You don't have children, do you, Inspector? You know what it's like. No one to pass it all on to. No one to keep the memories alive. How does it feel to know that one day soon you will be completely forgotten?'

'You're not a man to take the quiet option, are you?' Bolam said. 'It would be like preparing for a show that never happened.' So he had made sure that he would finally be noticed. Showing off his handiwork and mastery to the world.

Cowper was visibly preening himself now, taking satisfaction in the unravelling.

'It was Jayne, wasn't it?' Bolam said. 'The start of it all. She loved you but you never worked out how to love her back, and that broke something in you.' He didn't have to care about the *why* of it all: that didn't matter to Bolam's role in this; all he was concerned about was building the case. But…

Cowper was shaking his head. 'No,' he said. 'That's the thing. I *did*. Love her. She's the only person I've ever loved, but I didn't recognise that that's what it was.'

'It scared you.'

A shrug. 'It was a foreign feeling, and it consumed me for a time. But it wasn't me. It wasn't who I *was*. So I drove her away, and then I realised my mistake and I tried to win her back, and… I think it was my intensity that scared her. There was an instant, a look in her eyes. Some kind of realisation of what she had got herself into. She fought me off and I…'

'And you killed her in the one moment of real passion in your entire life,' finished Bolam. 'And since then you've never felt anything like it again, except for when you kill.'

Cowper didn't contradict him.

He'd come close to loving, but had never allowed himself to fall.

Now, Bolam looked into the old man's eyes and recalled the phrase: he could hear the words, but not the music.

'Jayne loved me,' Cowper said. 'She was desperate. She pursued me everywhere, and poor Matthew was powerless to intervene – never man enough to give her what she wanted.'

'You couldn't really, though, could you?' said Bolam. 'Love her. Not properly, even when you tried. You didn't know how.'

Jayne Sturridge had been head over heels in love with Cowper and he'd been unable to trust those feelings within himself. She'd lost the baby, and that had underlined the deficit in himself even more starkly.

Raising his stick, Cowper pointed to the door. 'Through there,' he said.

There was another room across the hall. Bolam went through, leaving Aisha standing in the doorway, watching over Cowper. The room was the same size as the first, and filled with similar dark furniture, and dark panelling halfway up the walls.

More framed photographs stood on a long sideboard, just as in the other room, only this time the photographs were different, more explicit.

A woman's body, sprawling supine on rough ground. Eyes wide and staring, and lifeless. One hand resting in a pool of blood on the abdomen, one of her fingers removed.

Another woman – Marcia Fredericks, Bolam was sure – lying in a similar pose, a bloodied hand drawn up to rest above her heart.

Among these: more photographs, grainy from where they had been enlarged and cropped, so that the school group on display in the other room now showed only Joanna Clayton, glancing shyly at the camera, an awkward grin on her face. Or Jayne and Cowper, with Matthew Sturridge cropped out.

'Gov?' Aisha had entered the room, leaving the constables to supervise Cowper. She had a framed photograph in her hand, the picture of Bolam and Fran at that wedding, Fran's face and hands gouged out.

Bolam swallowed, looked away.

This was an exhibition, he realised. A visual CV of Cowper's crimes. He might be too physically weak to continue his life's work – other than by taunting and provoking others to violence – but he could still mount one final display of his handiwork. Using his own terminology, he wanted to be the custodian of his own legacy, and he wanted to be sure they would overlook nothing.

But in that case, many of the photographs disturbed Bolam: the dead woman he had not recognised, Cowper with other women who did not appear to have featured in the investigation to date. More victims?

How many had there been?

'It's in the middle drawer.'

Cowper had joined them, and now stood unsteadily in the doorway beside Aisha. He looked as if he might collapse at any moment.

Bolam opened the drawer. Inside was a single velvet cushion, and nestled on top of that was a small jewellery box. Bolam didn't touch it, leaving it for Cath Marshall and her scene-of-crime team.

'Jayne's ring,' Bolam said.

'She wore it to remember Alicia,' Cowper said, pausing to allow Aisha to guide him to a chair. 'I never understood Jayne's attachment to such things, but I knew they were important. I gave her that ring in an attempt to understand, and for a brief instant I thought that I *did*, and that she understood me, too. But that window closed. She wore the ring as a symbol, a shield, and ultimately it was a shield she used to fend me off, a reminder of all her mistakes. She shut me out and focused only on her vendetta against the hospital. She thought I could help, but I just wanted that… that glimmer. The thing I'd felt, so briefly.'

'But why the fingers?'

'It was never about the fingers,' Cowper said. 'I'm not some kind of monster. It was the ring. Our child's ring. It wouldn't come off… but I couldn't just dispose of it. It mattered so much to Jayne, don't you see? I had to keep it, by whatever means.'

He spoke as if there was an undeniable logic to it all, but it was a logic that only showed itself to Cowper. Unable to dispose of the ring with his lover's body, somehow that had manifested into something he had to do whenever he killed, trying to replicate the high he had felt when he killed Jayne.

'And the opal ring? Why put that on her finger?'

Cowper shrugged. The opal ring didn't matter to him. 'She had an unsightly tan line on her finger,' he said. 'It was ugly, so I covered it.'

'And the paint on Joanna's finger and the blood on Virginia's and on the third package you delivered to me?'

'It took you far too long to identify Jayne's finger,' Cowper said. 'I wanted to make it easier. Some oil paint for the girl, a bit of blood as a visual reminder of the scene in the ambulance. You clearly needed help.'

'That was your mistake, though, wasn't it? Not just being caught on CCTV—'

Cowper looked genuinely surprised at that, and Bolam could imagine his mind racing to work out where he had been filmed.

'—but the material you sent me.'

'The photographs?' Again, Cowper seemed puzzled. Until now he seemed to believe he was still in control of proceedings, but now he appeared to be starting to understand that he had lost this particular game.

'No, not the photos,' Bolam told him. 'The first one. The letter.'

'The *letter*?'

'A letter from my late wife's solicitor,' Bolam said. 'There aren't many people who would have the contacts and influence to initiate something like that: an off-the-record call on behalf of an acquaintance, a bypassing of protocols and confidentialities to make sure a "friend's" divorce proceedings were on track. That's the kind of thing a fellow solicitor could do, but once we'd excluded Gordon Rowe from our investigation, who did that leave?'

Bolam turned away. Finally, he allowed himself to meet Aisha's look. All this time, she'd been twitchy, disapproving, but he'd been unable to ease up.

'Sir,' she said.

He nodded.

'We should be doing all this under caution,' she hissed at him. 'At the station.'

Doing it all by the book, just as he'd agreed with DCI McBride. He knew she was right.

Cowper laughed, breaking the moment. 'That won't be necessary,' he said. 'We won't have time for all that. All that we've just discussed – don't worry: that will stand as the statement of a dying man.'

Bolam stared. Testimony of a dying person had legal standing that superseded the need for formal interview under caution, if circumstances meant that was all that was possible.

'How?' Bolam asked. Cowper had been so calm through all this, indulging them – and he looked so frail now. He'd known he was not going to leave his house alive.

'Pills,' Cowper told them. 'Before you came.'

'The same pills Matthew Sturridge took?' asked Bolam.

'Of course. Do you think poor Matthew had the imagination to come up with that himself?'

'But I thought you wanted to observe,' Bolam said. 'Watch your final staged event unfold, and the world finally come to recognise your achievements?'

'Oh, Inspector Bolam, I rather think that's already happening, don't you? But for now, I think I'm ready to take my leave of the pain…'

'I know, I know,' Bolam said to Aisha as they stood in front of Cowper's house, watching two uniformed officers leading the old man away in handcuffs. 'I did it all wrong. We should just have taken him to the station and got all that in a formal interview. But do you think he'd have played along with that? He wanted the theatre. He wanted to be in control of the telling. What was the phrase he used? He said he was the custodian of his own legacy, controlling the unveiling of his masterwork. At least this way we have an understanding of the scale of this, of what he's done, and who he really is.'

He expected her to pile in, and she'd have been right to do so. They had established procedures – and safeguards – for good reason, and Bolam had stopped counting the number of protocols he had just broken.

'You knew it had to be like this, didn't you?' she said, instead. 'You'd worked out that he'd prepared for his own exit.'

'At some stage, perhaps,' he said. 'There was something about him. He'd set the stage. He was going to talk under his own conditions or not at all. But…'

Cowper was in the back of a patrol car now, peering out at them. He looked confused. Puzzled.

He should be dying by now, but clearly was not.

One of the PCs found Russell Shaw on a wooden bench in the sprawling back garden. He sat with his knees drawn up, surrounded by twisted apple trees swamped in a bed of nettles and brambles. Some of the trees were breaking into blossom.

Bolam approached him and sat, a space between them.

'All this,' Russell said, gesturing at the overgrown orchard. 'I like it. Much more than the front garden.'

Bolam said nothing, although the wildness here disturbed him. He was a man of straight lines and smart suits and order – except when it came to letting an interview with a suspect run away from him, as he had this afternoon with Raymond Cowper.

'I suspect all this will be in ruins before long,' Bolam said. 'Once the searches get under way.' This was clearly the area that Cowper had not allowed his gardener to go near, and there had to be reason for that.

'What did you do, Russell?'

Shaw met Bolam's look briefly, then turned away again.

'I followed him,' he said. 'From your friend's place on East Bay Drive. I followed him here, and I went in to the house and confronted him. It's the closest I've ever come to doing something brave, something heroic. But I couldn't. I failed again.'

'I've seen your military record, Russell. You don't have to prove yourself to anybody. I've read an account of a young medic who sat in a military ambulance under shell fire. Forty miles along a road notorious for ambush and IEDs, literally holding a young soldier's body together.'

Bolam thought of Stewart Doherty's vigilante-inspired vision of heroism and knew he'd take a quiet, unassuming hero like Russell Shaw every day of the week.

'You did something, didn't you, Russell? In there, in the house. Tell me what you did.'

Shaw looked down, then shrugged.

'He laughed at me,' he said. 'I couldn't take it. Someone like him, someone so *empty*, just laughing at me, and I couldn't work out how to respond. So I ran away. I didn't understand why he was so calm about it all, the way he was trying to wind me up. All the things he's been doing. You don't do that if you're worried about the consequences, do you? Then I got to the kitchen and had to stop to catch my breath, and that's where I saw what he was planning to do. He had pills, and whisky to wash them down. I know *I* ran away, but he was planning to do the same. They were blood pressure pills: if he took that many in one go his heart would slow right down until it killed him. Peacefully. Painlessly.'

'You're a medic. You know these things.'

'Suicide's no good for anybody, even him, so I swapped the pills. It was easy: he'd already popped the pills out of their blister strips, so I just replaced them. He has a cupboard full of medicines. Painkillers, antibiotics, lots of different things for a bad stomach.'

'What did you give him?'

'Don't worry. Nothing bad. The pills that looked most like the ones he'd laid out won't do anything worse than leave him constipated for a week. You've got him now. I saw. But I was going to call you.' He reached into a pocket and produced the card Bolam had given him. 'He has to be stopped. You have to do that.'

Bolam sat back, and watched the bees on the apple blossom. He suspected that Russell Shaw had already done most of the work in stopping Raymond Cowper, but he would be happy to add the finishing touches, so that the old lawyer spent what time he had left locked away from the world he had never managed to understand.

Coda

Russell Shaw left the flat. Not a significant event for most, perhaps, but for Russ it was a landmark, because he'd gone from never wanting to go back there to never wanting to leave.

But the sun was bright, the sky blue, and for the first time in a week he felt the pull of the sea.

Outside, he paused, straightened, breathed deep. Briefly – disturbingly – he was reminded of Raymond Cowper's last walk through the town, the way he had kept pausing, savouring the air and the sunshine because he knew it was the last time he would do so. Of course, Cowper did this because he planned to end his life, but instead he was now locked away, awaiting trial.

Russ walked. Up to the end of the street, and then along the next street to where it met East Bay Drive. He crossed the road, and the bay spread out before him, reflecting blue from the colour of the sky instead of its default grey-brown.

He was going to the hospital this afternoon. Just to talk. All he wanted was to understand. To get to know himself again. To convince himself he was not the person he had thought.

But now…

He paused, straightened, breathed deep.

Judith had called, and he had answered, finally. She told him they were having a special meeting at the shelter and they wanted him to be there. She'd assured him that Robbie Walton would not be involved, and of course Stewart was on remand for his attack on DI Bolam: this meeting would be just the volunteers.

After all that had happened, the Fresh Start charity was being dismantled, but some of the volunteers, led by Judith, wanted to keep the shelter going, and they wanted Russ to be part of that.

Judith wanted him to be involved, and that had been enough to get him out of the flat, to come out into the sun and breathe deep, and he couldn't really ask for much more than that from the world.

Bolam met Gordon for lunch at the flat overlooking the bay. The ownership of the place was in limbo, and Gordon had boasted over the phone that he'd entangled it in so much red tape he could stay there for as long as he liked. Bolam didn't find that hard to believe.

Gordon opened the door and stepped back with a wave of the arm. 'Come in, come in.'

The place smelled of frying garlic and onions.

'How are you doing?' Bolam said, pushing the door shut behind him with his left hand, the right still cradled in a sling.

Gordon rolled his eyes, and said, 'Oh, you know.'

His long-term business partner was being held on too many charges to list, including the murder of Gordon's sister-in-law, he was still separated from his wife, and barely on speaking terms with his teenaged son, and the best he could manage was *Oh, you know.*

'What's the tally?' Gordon asked now.

'Nine,' Bolam told him, which gave nothing away that wouldn't pretty soon be all over the news. At Cowper's house they'd found three more frozen fingers, one of them confirmed as belonging to Marcia Fredericks and two unidentified. Buried in the overgrown orchard they'd located four bodies: Jayne Sturridge, Joanna Clayton, and two that did not match any of the frozen fingers and remained unidentified.

'That's a lot.'

'We're going back almost thirty years,' Bolam said. 'It's been a lot of work just to get this far.' And it was going to be an awful lot more, for a lot of people, to sort out all the details and prepare the case. Cowper would almost certainly be dead before any of this came to trial.

'Omelette?' Gordon asked.

Bolam nodded. 'Omelette would be lovely,' he said. 'Again.'

Omelette had turned out to be the only thing Gordon knew how to cook.

Later, they sat with plates on their knees.

'Fran was right, you know,' Gordon said. 'She always said you were bloody good at what you do.' Then after a second or two, he added, 'Just crap at all the rest.'

Which, Bolam supposed, was something, at least.

About the Author

Photo credit courtesy of Nick Guthrie

Nick Guthrie's work has been published in a number of leading magazines and anthologies, including *Alfred Hitchcock's Mystery Magazine* and *Ellery Queen's Mystery Magazine*. Under other writing names, he is the author of more than twenty books, and his work has been shortlisted for various awards and optioned for the movies. You can find out more about Nick and his work at nickguthrie.co.uk – where you can also sign up for his newsletter.